2-89

SCIENCE
FICTION

COLE, BURT
THE QUICK.
c1989

89
90
91/11
93
94/1
95/11
98/1
96/1
09/1

BVA90
0
ORC90
11

DEMCO

2-89

THE
QUICK

Books by Burt Cole

SUBI: THE VOLCANO
THE LONGEST WAY ROUND
OLIMPIA
THE FUNCO FILE
THE BOOK OF ROOK
SAHARA SURVIVAL
THE BLUE CLIMATE
BLOOD KNOT

THE QUICK

Burt Cole

WILLIAM MORROW AND COMPANY, INC.
New York

2-89 BT 1500

Library of Congress Cataloging-in-Publication Data

Cole, Burt, 1930-
  The quick.

  I. Title.
PS3553.045Q5 1989   813'.54   88-8470
ISBN 0-688-08478-8

Printed in the United States of America

First Edition

1 2 3 4 5 6 7 8 9 10

BOOK DESIGN BY NICOLA MAZZELLA

THE
QUICK

CHAPTER ONE

Tahu-Tahu

Anai

Three hours out of Jalang in the Sulu archipelago, Anai M'Nap leaned over the side of his lipa to feel the sea, to touch the tide. He closed his eyes.

"We will be there. But it will be night."

He and his wife and their children had set the lines with foot-long hooks, baited with stingrays, and now they were trolling, the patchwork sail puffing its chest to the sun. Old Itomi slept, the children played naked on their mats, Araissa was making a supper of rice and mullet, and all around was the empty horizon.

The other boats, of Anai's tribe and kinsmen, were there, everywhere; he could feel them in the water, though they were far away.

Scattered across thousands of square miles of emerald-green sea from Zamboanga to Borneo to the Celebes, were all the landless Bajau people, in their little wooden boats, called lipas.

Lipas are the same small outrigger fishing boats/nipa-thatched houseboats Magellan saw, the Bajaus the same aboriginal sea nomads "who dwell always on their vessels, and have no homes on shore."

Since 1521 the Spanish had come and gone, the Americans and Japanese too, and at times in between, Chinese pirates, In-

7

donesian pirates, and Malay pirates; lately it was Moslem smugglers of arms to Mindanao and motorized pirates who preyed on them, and government gunboats that pursued them both, while the little wooden lipas hid and fled from them all.

Fisherfolk in dangerous waters, keeping to their nomad ways, asking only to be let alone, the Bajaus are gentle little animists who talk to spirits of wind and water, read the sky, foresee storms, and give place-names to familiar spots on the trackless sea as landsmen name mountains and valleys.

Anai could put his hand in the water, shut his eyes and know his exact whereabouts and the distance to his destination, a certain rendezvous in the Sulu Sea.

Araissa watched him with nervous worry.

"Do not make us late. I am afraid of Tcham Ahn."

"There is time to fish," Anai said.

The fin came near, circling the boat, cutting the water with a silken hiss.

Anai sang:

"O Kalitan, come, come, come to Anai! Come and eat, take the hook, bite the barb! Come you killer, murderer of little ones! Anai is waiting, you are beautiful! Come to me, you must be mine!"

For hours he had leaned over the side, shaking a pole in the water, empty coconut shells tied to the pole, to summon the shark, to tempt it, and now it was here.

It had come far and straight, its fin so long out of water that its tip was dry in the sun, and now it circled the boat. Anai sang his anting-anting, a charm to catch sharks, and now it struck.

It bit the bait, gulped and swallowed. It fought, it flailed, jerking the boat, powerful, long as a man. Anai yanked the line, slackened, yanked and slackened, hauling in till Kalitan came close, revolving in the water, spinning in a trough of froth; then Anai spun the line around a cleat and Araissa sprang to him with the dart, the harpoon.

Anai seized it and froze, waiting. The shark stood on its tail, yawning in the sun. He thrust.

Anai sang in shouts and grunts and sharp cries, wrestling the wildly thrashing short shaft, blinded by salty spray:

"O king of killers, do me battle—feel my hooks and barbs, feel my strength—fight me and die! Surrender, surrender, O prince of the sea, for I am Anai of Jalang, and your life is mine!"

When the shark lay wallowing alongside, Araissa tied a rope around its tail and all heaved, the shark coming aboard, not dead yet but dying, pumping blood; and Anai spiked the great jaws open, hacked off the grinning head, and gave it back to the sea.

There was already a catch of rainbow-colored fish and three little leaden tuna from that day, and now there was the shark. It was a good day for fishing. The body of the shark could be sold for meat in Tawitawi or anywhere, even at the moorage in Jalang, and the fins could be dried and sold to the Chinese traders of Bongao, who used them to make powders when they did not eat them. Only the head was returned to the sea, to give food and strength to other sharks, for future battles.

Then it was night; the lipa lay light and still on the water; mild wavelets patted its sides; the tip of the mast described a slow figure eight against the starry sky.

Old Itomi was asleep, or lying awake with her memories; it was not possible to tell which. The children were asleep. Araissa lay on the mats with them, under the thatch, watching her husband, who sat in the starlight by the tiller. Sometimes they whispered to each other.

"I am afraid of Tcham Ahn," Araissa said.

She had never met or seen him.

Anai said: "Tcham Ahn said do this. I do what Tcham Ahn said."

Anai knew him only by reputation.

The headman at Jalang moorage had told him that Tcham Ahn required a boat of the Bajau people to meet him at a specific spot on a certain night. It had happened before and no harm had come to anyone, and this time Anai's boat had been chosen, and that was all Anai knew and all he wished to know.

Tcham Ahn was the chief of one of the bands of pirates who prowled the sea, preying mostly on those who smuggled guns from Borneo to the insurgents fighting the government on Mindanao. Tcham Ahn did not rob the Bajaus, as some of the pirates did, taking their fish and women and sometimes killing them. On the other hand, he was known to be a Milikan, the word meaning Occidental, and it could not be known what Occidentals would do.

"Ummalani, who went to Dawitan, saw him wearing a string of the ears of his enemies," Araissa said.

Pat, pat, went the wavelets.

The first faraway sound came very late in the night. Anai sniffed and tasted the wind that brought it to him. In the darkness under the thatch he could see Araissa's eyes like faint phosphorescence.

"Pamboat," he said.

Pamboats are the lipas of the pirates, newer, bigger, better built, with reinforced outriggers for boarding parties to clamber across with their swords and guns. Some pamboats are equipped with machine guns or other military weapons, and the pamboat of Tcham Ahn was said to be the most heavily armed of all. Pamboats have powerful gasoline motors instead of sails, although sometimes sails are hoisted to fool victims or government gunboats. A pamboat with a sail might look like a lipa, but on board is no peaceful, unarmed Bajau family. On board is death.

The crews of the pirate pamboats are the half-caste cutthroats of a thousand ports from Java to Macao, and they take no captives and leave no witnesses.

Araissa crept to him across the deck and they sat side by side, listening to the distant puttering of the pamboat; they sat with drawn-up legs, hands crossed on their knees, chins resting on their hands.

"What if it is not Tcham Ahn?"

"What if it is other pirates?"

"What will we do?"

"What *will* we do?"

Then the first sound stopped; the motor stopped, the pamboat still at some distance, losing way, drifting to a halt, sagging low and dark in the water. Anai closed his eyes and saw it, like lifeless floating wreckage. Then came the second sound.

It came from far away to the south, a heavier, deeper sound, throbbing in the water, not heard in the air. It was the motor of a kumpit, a power launch, fifty feet or bigger, like those used for interisland transport of cargo or passengers; and now Anai was grinning, now he understood.

He shifted his buttocks, his knees quivering. He wriggled all over, grinning. "See! See!"

In the huge, hollow darkness the sound came nearer, the kumpit came on, but there was nothing to see.

"Where?" Araissa stared blindly.

He held his hand on her neck, aiming her head; there, where a dust of stars met the horizon: what might have been a smudge, like floating wreckage.

"Watch!" whispered Anai.

By now the second sound was as near and loud as the first had been, the kumpit a vague gray ghost becoming visible, rushing onward without running lights. In another moment the smuggler would cross the pirate's bow.

"Look!"

Low in the water, a little light, like a glowworm, and then a whizzing, trickling trail of sparks rising from the pamboat, gaining speed, straight into the sky—soundlessly exploding in fire at the top of its flight—and then banging, reverberating; a star shell.

The night sky shook with concussion. It streamed down green-white light in petals like a bursting flower. Smiling and open-mouthed, hugging their knees, Anai and Araissa gazed up, breathing wonder. The report woke the children, and they came to see.

"Pretty?"

There was the smuggler, a launch twice the pirate's size, churning in a puddle of vivid light, flare light reflecting in the glass of its pilothouse, crates and boxes on deck, men in turbans casting elongated shadows as the light sank down.

There was the pamboat, motor roaring, gathering speed, aiming dead on; and another flare soared up, popped and banged, and the children clapped their hands.

They watched as the pirates built a bridge of light. It grew from the pamboat to the kumpit, a bridge of streaks and smears of tracer ammunition in a flat arc over the water, hammering wood and glass. They saw the bridge established and the messenger go across; rocket-red roaring messenger that struck the pilothouse, blew it apart, and scattered its bits and pieces everywhere.

A ball of flame went up, darkening into smoke; tracer flashed, the bridge shimmered; green-white flare light glowed and sank, and the kumpit burned, all against the backcloth of the velvet night.

It was the climax of the attack, in many colors of fire. Anai and his wife held hands raptly; the children were dumb with ecstasy.

The kumpit slowed, drifting a little broadside, sloshing to a stop. Turbaned men shouted and shook their arms in the air, and the machine gun stopped, the bridge collapsing into itself. The pamboat drew alongside and throttled down; the last flare fell into the sea; lanterns on poles were lit; the pirates went aboard and began putting out the fire.

Anai breathed deep with awe and satisfaction and turned to his family.

"That was beautiful."

Old Itomi crept from the shelter, peering angrily.

"I want to see too!"

Sudden gray-green dawn. A thin trail of smoke was rising from the jumble where the pilothouse had stood; a pirate was dipping buckets of seawater to put out the last sparks. Two others were guarding the captives, seven men in bright turbans, their elbows wired together behind their backs. The rest of the pirates were busy transferring the cargo of the kumpit to the pamboat. This much Anai saw from a hundred yards' distance.

A man on the pamboat was observing Anai through binoculars, making no move or sign. Anai waved and smiled, trembling.

"Here am I. Anai is here. Just as Tcham Ahn ordered."

He felt foolish, whispering to a man who could hardly have heard a shout, but he was afraid.

Someone was sitting in the dimness under the thatch of the pamboat, someone wearing black shiny boots. Boots were a rarity; everyone else was barefoot. Now and then one of the pirates would approach and lean under the thatch to speak to black boots. Nothing else of the man was to be seen.

The transferring of the cargo was finished. All of the crates and boxes were now on the pamboat. No one was left on board the kumpit except the men wearing turbans. Anai knew who they were. They were Tausugs and Samals, men of the islands, brother tribes to the Bajaus, but converts to Islam. They smuggled arms to fight their rulers, and sometimes the pirates attacked them, and sometimes the gunboats caught them and they died. Anai nodded sadly. This comes of living on shore and having rulers.

Black Boots came from under the thatch. From a distance he looked tall and thin. He was dressed in green with many belts and wore a big green hat. A white man in green. White and green are mystical colors to the Bajaus, like the white and green flags on the burial islands of Bunabunaan and Bilatan Poon. Anai knew this must be Tcham Ahn.

Tcham Ahn tiptoed nimbly across the outrigger and sprang on board the kumpit, carrying a package. He disappeared below. He was down inside a long time. He appeared again and crossed back to the pamboat, empty-handed. Cries followed him, the captives screeching at him; Anai could not distinguish the words.

The motor was puttering slowly, the pamboat backing away, swinging around, low in the water, heavy with crates and boxes. Then the motor raced, the stern wallowed and the bow rose sluggishly, pushing forward in a long sweeping curve.

"He is coming now," Anai said.

Araissa had seen; she knelt in the shelter, one arm wrapped around each child; they felt her fear and were big-eyed and still. Old Itomi did not understand or did not care, huddled by the firepot, chewing betel, wagging her jaw and saying: "G'lap, g'lap, g'lap."

The man with the binoculars was observing Anai from the bow of the pamboat as it came on; he grew larger and larger as he came closer and closer. Morning sun flashed on glass.

"Anai is here. Anai is waiting. As Tcham Ahn said."

Anai was quivering as a fish quivers suspended in the water in the instant before it flashes away with a flick of its tail.

The man put down the binoculars and picked up a carbine as the pamboat slowed, gliding; he held the carbine ready across his chest, looking the lipa up and down for signs of danger. He was naked except for a sarong, a pistol belt, and a rag around his head. He shouted something and two more pirates came forward to join him; he said something and they pointed their shotguns at Anai.

Anai fell on his knees and put his face in his hands.

He felt the lurch and crunch as the pamboat's heavy outrigger overran his own flimsy bamboo struts. Then he heard the thump and stagger of bare feet jumping on board, and the carbine touched the back of his neck. A voice said:

"You had better be the one old Malajirin sent."

Anai understood only the name of the headman at Jalang moorage.

"Malajirin! Yes! Yes! Anai is here! Malajirin!"

The man with the carbine was a big black man with red, filed teeth.

The lipa rocked as more men swarmed on board. Kneeling, Anai looked up, his hands folded over his mouth, watching. They searched everywhere, toppling and turning everything, ripping apart the thatch, finding only a few knives—Anai's fishing knife, Araissa's pot knives—one by one throwing these into the sea, along with the two harpoons.

"You understand," Red Teeth said.

He was grinning pleasantly, making motions: Anai was to get up, be easy, feel tranquil.

"Cacique. Big chief. You understand. Precautions."

He hung his carbine over his shoulder by its strap, stood with his fists on his hips, gazing around the lipa.

"All well!" he shouted.

The pirates stopped where they stood, grounded their rifles and slouched carelessly over the muzzles, scratching and grinning sleepily as black boots thumped on deck and Tcham Ahn came aboard.

He was a tall, thin Occidental with his arms full and a pencil held crosswise in his mouth. He lighted near Anai and Anai cowered.

Tcham Ahn chuckled and spoke around the pencil: "You must have scared the living shit out of him."

"Yes, tuan," Red Teeth said.

Tcham Ahn's right arm embraced a canvas seabag packed fat as a pig; his left carried a knapsack fitted with straps and buckles; he dropped both and one of the pirates seized them and stowed them away under the ruined thatch.

Tcham Ahn shrugged first one longarm and then another off his back: an automatic shotgun with a short barrel, and a bolt-action rifle with a telescopic sight. With the pencil in his mouth he spoke indistinctly:

"You worry too much. Old Malajirin is a friend of mine. He would not send an unreliable member."

"Yes, tuan."

"There was no need for bullying."

"Yes, tuan."

Tcham Ahn took his longarms under the thatch personally, to see to them, and came out again. Disburdened, shaking his shoulders, he grew even taller before Anai's upraised eyes.

"Salaam, little brother," Tcham Ahn said. "Peace." And winked at the kids.

The green clothing was a many-pocketed, one-piece garment, belted both at the waist and across the chest. Revolvers hung in Tcham Ahn's armpits, and knives on his hips. A white silk scarf of some length was wrapped around his neck. When he removed the pencil from his mouth to shove the green slouch hat back with it, his short-shorn hair was nearly white from the sun. Also, Anai had not seen blue eyes before.

The eyes were extremely pale blue eyes, almost white like the hair. The eyes frightened Anai more than the guns or the knives.

Tcham Ahn pointed the pencil at Red Teeth and said in the language Anai did not understand: "Don't worry about little brother. He'll get me to Jalang moorage all right. Just you worry about meeting me there in ten days. You'll be in more danger than I am. They're looking for pirates, not Bajaus."

"Yes, tuan."

"I want to get back to business. Checklist."

"Yes, tuan."

"All the prize cargo we can float has been transferred and is lashed down. All casualties have been gutted and sunk. All prisoners are on board their boat, and the engine has been disabled and the fuel line diverted to the hold. Shame. Too bad it had to be a diesel; we could have used the gas. Miscellaneous valuables and booty shared out, crew away. Charge set and timed. What else?"

He took a small notebook from his pocket and added quickly in it.

"Here is the sum you are to receive from Chien S'al. Not one cent less; do not argue, do not bargain. If he doesn't want it, the rebels will. Pay the men and take your share, and bring my share to Jalang in ten days. That's all. Now, then: What are your duties during the voyage?"

"Avoid the gunboats at all cost," Red Teeth said.

"Do you need instructions to do that?"

"Hoist the sail if they see us. Jettison the cargo if they pursue us. We are only poor fishermen."

"I mean during the passage, fool."

"Ah," Red Teeth said. "The guns."

"The recoilless rifle must be completely disassembled, cleaned, and oiled. The machine gun must be completely disassembled, cleaned, oiled. Individual firearms must be disassembled, cleaned, oiled, as always after every firing. Followed by daily field-stripping, cleaning, oiling. You know why this must be done. What happens if this is not done?"

"The sea eats them," Red Teeth said, grinning.

"Salt-sea air, iodine, and IMR ball-powder residue doth corrupt and corrode," Tcham Ahn said. "Now that's settled, what is it we are waiting around here now for?"

"Wah-*room!*" Red Teeth said.

"Dead men tell no tales," Tcham Ahn said.

They strolled down the deck. Back aboard the pamboat the rest of the pirates were waiting too, staring intently at the kumpit as it lay rocking slightly on the mild swell, about a hundred yards away. Tcham Ahn consulted a complicated wristwatch.

"It's already about four minutes overdue."

Red Teeth was gazing in fascination at the indeterminate number of men in bright turbans still remaining on the kumpit's deck. They were small in the distance. One went as he watched, leaping awkwardly with elbows wired together.

"Some always jump to the sharks," Red Teeth said wonderingly. "Some wait for the fire."

"Each man's fear is his own," Tcham Ahn said.

The kumpit bucked in the water. A piece of its side blew out with a sodden noise that traveled slowly across the distance. With a flash the diesel fuel in the hold ignited, burning with a dark red flame and greasy clouds of smoke that hid everything.

Red Teeth said: "I remember the charge that did not explode at all and you had to go back on board."

"I was always lousy with detonators," Tcham Ahn said.

They punched each other in the chest.

"Jalang."

"Jalang."

Red Teeth scampered quickly across the outrigger; the pirates yelled and waved; the pamboat motor coughed and puttered.

Tcham Ahn stepped to where Anai still knelt on deck, hands clapped over his mouth again.

"Come on, get up, little brother. Anchors aweigh."

Anai's hands descended to disclose a loose, quivering grin; he was terrified. The eyes were the color of the venom of certain sea snakes, the most deadly in the world.

"You can tell the wife and family there is nothing to fear from me. It's no fun killing spitouts."

Anai understood only the word *luwa'an*, an island term for the landless Bajaus.

"Cacique! Big chief!"

"That's right. Let's get going. Don't you speak Pilipino?"

"Pilipino? Pilipino. *Pilipino!* No."

"Well, never mind. Jalang. Do you understand that? Jalang. And chop-chop about it."

"Yes, tuan!" Anai said. He ran to set the sail.

But Tcham Ahn was staring away at the burning kumpit which was now a low settling heap, like a black and red bonfire on the emerald sea.

"It's no fun killing anybody anymore, when you think about it," he said moodily. "Where's the challenge? Where's the sport?"

Jalang

Dark green twilight rain fell heavily on the island of Jalang, wetting no one there. No one lived on the island.

Jalang was tiny, a chip in the sea, one of hundreds like it. Just big enough to have a name, too small for anything else, except an acre or two of coco palms, a long-abandoned copra plantation, and a few ramshackle fish-buyers' sheds by the lagoon.

There were no houses at all. In the shallows off the beach stood some huts on stilts, but even these were vacant. The Bajaus lived on their boats.

The moorage was twice again as big as the island; scattered across a wide area of tranquil lagoon between island and reef were from sixty to seventy houseboats, a floating village. Tomorrow it might be a village of a hundred boats or ten, or none, depending on the weather, the events of the night, or the nomad mood in the morning. But tonight it was raining, the lipas moored, blinds closed, mats let down, rush thatches dripping, the smoke of cook pots drifting low, the surface of the lagoon dappling and popping.

The lipa of Anai M'Nap was moored close to shore, close to the row of stilt houses. From a high doorway in one of the houses, yellow old eyes looked out and watched. Anai and his family were not there; they had been living with kinsmen for a week. Anai's damaged outrigger had been replaced with a new one during this time; the thatch pulled apart by the pirates had been repaired with new nipa rushes and was keeping most of the rain out of the shelter where the Milikan sat alone in the dark.

A woman came down to the shore; she might have emerged from one of the fish-buyers' sheds; she wore an ankle-length shirt that looked purple in the gloom. She crossed the beach, barefoot and bareheaded in the rain, and walked out into the lagoon. The water rose to her knees and then to her middle, the lagoon no deeper anywhere. She waded leaning forward but without apparent urgency or effort, trailing her arms and hands in the water.

She reached Anai M'Nap's boat and touched it; she put her cheek to it. With a quick fishlike movement she squirmed aboard, legs flourishing once in the air. Bits of seaweed clung to her calves and ankles.

At the entrance to the shelter she squatted down, running rain and seawater in a puddle. After a moment she raised one arm, holding open the cloth, letting herself be seen from inside. When nothing happened, she rose to a low crouch and stepped in, dropping the cloth behind her, and squatted down again.

She squatted with both feet flat, her upper arms on her knees, her knuckles almost touching the deck, her head hanging down. She did not look; she could not have seen anything; there was no light in the shelter. The air was hot and thick and smelled of whiskey.

The rain rushed on the thatch, leaking through in places. After a moment a match was struck, a hand lighting a small lantern; a naked man sitting on a pile of mats yawned soundlessly and scratched his ribs, smiling at her.

"They have sent me a mermaid."

The words meant nothing, but in the voice was a throaty chuckle she knew well enough.

"They have sent me a ripe oyster from the sea to receive my pearls."

Her hair was soaked flat around her face and down her back, and another puddle was forming between her feet where she squatted. Without rising she picked the stuck shirt loose from her belly and breasts and tugged it over her head; it made a squeak like silk; her elbows caught and she writhed with her arms upraised; black hair fell forward as the shirt came free, and she flung it back with a wet slap, confronting him with an expressionless Mongol stare. She saw that in the few instants it had taken her to undress he had grown ready for her.

The throaty chuckle became a languid murmur.

"Once more into the breach, dear friend. You will have to pump the handle, though; I just can't move," he said, beckoning. He lay down on his back.

She came in her low crouch and straddled his legs, squatting down again, trying to fit him into herself, but it was no good. He was lying with his head back, and after a time he raised up and began to laugh.

"They have sent me a clam!"

Then he saw that she was afraid.

He saw that she was frozen and rigid and dry with fear of him.

Her eyes were quite blind with it, and she was deaf and speechless: *Now he will kill me.*

Instead he slapped her dismissingly on both buttocks, so hard that water flew; his laughter was kindly. She sat down backward, her knees over his legs. He got up, limping at half mast, groping under the mats, looking for something, finding first his silk scarf and draping it over her shoulders lightly, then a bottle, then a towel. Meanwhile she sat with legs out straight, like a child.

"*Ya aziz*," he said, smiling. "Did you think does were fair game?"

He drank from the bottle, to show her, and put it in her hands, and then he was behind her with the towel, patting and rubbing, drying her hair. Combing it out with his fingers and fluffing the ends. The slow murmur was coaxing now, encouraging her.

"That's it, drink up. Come fill the cup, and in the fire of spring your winter garment of infibulation fling."

It did not matter what he said. Murmuring soft and close, first in one ear, then in the other as he toweled and fluffed.

". . . And if the wine you drink, the lip you press, end in what all begins and ends in: Yes! Ta-dum, ta-dum, ta-dum, ta-dee. Brought to you courtesy of the Yohimbine of Omar Shaman."

Murmuring in her damp cloud of hair, body pressed to her back, legs one on either side of her, arms beneath her arms as he dried her throat, her breasts, her belly, her sex; letting fall the towel.

"Drink! For you know not whence you came nor why. Drink! For you know not why you go nor where."

Until it became possible, without violence or pain. Urging her gently forward onto all fours, mounting easily with soothing words meaningless to her.

"All the jolly chase is here, with hawk and horse and hunting spear, hounds in their couples yelling . . ."

Afterward she sang to him *tenes-tenes*, Bajau love ballads, in sweet and whining words meaningless to him in his turn.

He sat by her smilingly, but was staring into the darkest corner of the shelter as though something were happening there.

She found the white scarf and held it out to him, then drew it back, touching it to her breast, nodding yes? And he said: "Keep it."

At the rear of the shelter palm fronds and sticks were piled, ready to light in an earthen firepot, and a pot of cassava and fish stood by.

"Cook," he said, pointing to his open mouth with thumb

and two fingers, but he was watching the corner where the shelter was darkest.

Looking forward over her back, hands gripping her hips, face lifted and strained in his moment of throe, he had seen something. Yellow old eyes.

"Tuba," he said. She had begun to light the fire; she went and got the bottle of fermented coconut milk where it hung by a string from one of the thatch posts.

He held the bottle out toward the darkest corner and said in a loud, sudden voice:

"*Ya Malajirin.* Come and drink."

And added in still another language unknown to her:

"*Nomimashó!*"

The headman came shuffling from the darkness into the lantern light, on bowed legs and crippled feet; wearing fatigue greens cut short at elbows and shanks, a white rag knotted around his head; one hand gripping his sword of office, a U.S. saber with tassels.

He did a namaste with gnarled fingers, toothlessly grinning his own welcome, and climbed onto the mats, sitting down cross-legged. He reached for the bottle and held it high with both hands.

"*Kampai!*"

His voice was a thin, sandy wheeze.

Tcham Ahn said: "You crazy old coot—you're lucky I didn't shoot you."

Malajirin drank long and then waved the bottle worriedly. "I came to tell you something. You have to start dying tomorrow."

"What does that mean?"

"I don't know, but it starts tomorrow."

"What does?"

"I don't know, but it starts tomorrow."

"When am I going to die?"

"I don't know, but it starts tomorrow."

"How do you know?"

"Don't ask me. That's all there is."

He shook his head wonderingly; he seemed genuinely puzzled; he took another drink and handed the bottle back.

"I just came to tell you."

Old Malajirin in his youth had fought against the Japanese on Luzon; they said he killed thousands with the garrote before being betrayed by the Hukbalahap; then he was put in a Japanese prison camp, where he died, returning after the war full of the wisdom of survival. There were many stories about his powers. Some things were hard to explain.

For instance, he was dry. He had come on board the lipa only a few minutes before, and yet the lagoon had not wetted him, nor had the rain, and even the thatch did not seem to leak over his head.

Old Malajirin said: "Where is it you have to go tomorrow?"

He seemed sincerely disturbed and anxious to work it out.

"You old bastard. You know we've got a foray laid on."

The woman had put the pot of cassava and fish over the fire and was stirring it; she dipped out a spoonful and brought it to the Milikan to taste.

"Num, num!"

"Tomorrow is the first day you start to die in a far place," old Malajirin said, watching the two exchange warm glances over the dripping spoon. "I just came to tell you. I have to go now."

"Far place, that's funny. What do you call this place? If I tried getting any farther away, I'd be headed home."

"Don't go home," Malajirin's voice said; it seemed to come from the darkest corner of the shelter. He was not sitting with crossed legs on the pile of mats anymore. He was not in the corner either. He must have been on deck or on his way ashore.

Tcham Ahn rubbed his face with both hands.

"*Shimpai-nai.* Don't worry about it."

It was better not to look. It was better not to see that Malajirin was no longer aboard and that there was no dugout or other boat and no one wading ashore across the lagoon.

Red Teeth said: "What, then, he was a spy?"

An Iban Dyak from North Borneo, Red Teeth had been a jungle policeman in Selangor State during joint operations with British forces against the Malayan People's Liberation Army. Certain independent operations of his own had earned him a pounds-sterling price on his head, but not before his modern military experience had taught him that prophetic information comes most often from informers, not sorcerers.

"No. He's just an old man with his feet burned off by the Japanese. Leave him alone. I don't want to hear that he has been killed."

"Yes, tuan."

They sat together on the pirate pamboat moored amongst Bajau houseboats in the lagoon. The sides of the thatch were rolled up and early sun slanted in. At Tcham Ahn's feet were his two longarms, the shotgun and sniper rifle, both cleaned and minutely inspected.

"Maybe he just clear-viewed that I've been pissed off lately, and invented something. Maybe the old bastard was picking up on my own extrasensory vibrations, if you know what I mean."

"Yes, tuan."

"Sure you do. In any case, he's mistaken about me dying. How could I? I was never born. I'm all there ever was or will be, if you follow me."

"Yes, tuan."

"Sure you do. Let's get back to business. Checklist."

He was leafing through his notebook. He wore the green garment, the slouch hat, a pair of dark glasses, and another of the scarves.

"Tell me about the trip."

"Yes, tuan. Chien S'al paid the sum, in gold coins. He has stores of caliber-fifty ammunition to sell. I did not buy because you did not say to buy anything. The crew was paid and got drunk in Dawitan. Your share is here—I put it in your seabag—gold. Do not drop it overboard. It is heavy."

They watched the pirate crewmen come and go both on the pamboat and on neighboring houseboats, most with supplies and equipment, a few with bottles of *tuba* or Bajau girls.

"You cleaned the guns."

"On my honor we cleaned the guns. We cleaned the guns."

"How many rounds are left for the recoilless rifle?"

"Seven. Soon we will need more."

"Although it might be interesting at that," Tcham Ahn said musingly. "What if we did run out? It might be more of a challenge. Without the reckless, it might be more of an equal combat. Remember the noble Duke Hsiang of Sung, in the *Art of War*, who chivalrously gave over the advantage to his enemy?"

"You are a sportsman," Red Teeth said. "I have heard that the smugglers are arming with Bofors guns."

"I have heard that rumor for three years," Tcham Ahn said.

Around them the life of Jalang moorage went on. Children were swimming and playing in the water; women waded back and forth, visiting from boat to boat; on one of the lipas a cockfight was in progress; some men had drawn their dugouts onto the beach and upturned them, to scorch the bottoms clean of salt and seaweed.

Pirates were loading the pamboat with rice, fish, meat, bananas, papayas. The cook, a little Annamese, came aboard in triumph: he was carrying a pot of *adobo*, spiced pork and chicken cooked in oil and vinegar, stolen still steaming from the fire on some Bajau houseboat. Tcham Ahn and Red Teeth ate some and passed it on.

"Let's hear the plan."

"Yes, tuan. Sajavit Roxas of the Bataan underground has paid Chien S'al ten thousand dollars for seven crates of hand grenades. They come across tonight with other supplies for the HMB. The launch is the *Indigente*, and we can catch it as it passes out through the Tunkalang Strait. I have put a man on Bongao Island who will light a fire when it comes."

"What if they go around the long way?"

"They must go through the strait because there are gunboats at Simunul, and also, they will not go past Rop Island."

"What is Rop Island?"

"Island of Devils." Red Teeth grinned, as though to say: pagans!

Tcham Ahn raised the rifle to his shoulder, slowly traversing, scanning the moorage through the telescopic sight. Notches were cut in the wood of the stock. He said:

"All we have to do is wait just outside the strait."

"Yes, tuan. They must pass us within a mile."

"See what I mean?"

"Yes, tuan."

"No, you don't. It's too easy."

"Yes, tuan."

Tcham Ahn suddenly fired his rifle at nothing. In the quiet morning the angry crack/boom shook the air like a cannon shot and the whole population of Jalang moorage stopped still in its tracks. He yelled:

"It is like shooting cripples in the water! It is like jacking summer deer with a spotlight! It is like killing doped-up catamounts on a fucking game ranch!"

Tcham Ahn laid the rifle carefully on the mats, bolt handle up, and sat with his chin in his hands.

"It's too easy anymore. Where's the fight in it? I have been here too long. Just because it was the only game in town. Something has to happen. It's time for a change. When is the next war? Where *is* this far place?"

Red Teeth shook his head admiringly. He knew English when he heard it, since Malaya.

"Cheery up, old bloody."

"Maybe that's what Malajirin sensed. He sensed I was getting ready to try something new, to push my *barraka*, you know what I mean?"

"Yes, tuan."

"Sure you do, you ape. You know all that French Foreign Legion lingo. *Barraka* is crazy, wild luck, to see how far you can push it. When you've got it, you can do anything!"

Red Teeth gazed at him, grinning agreeably.

"Do what, tuan?"

"Don't ask me. That's all there is."

Rop

The Tunkalang Strait lies between the big island of Sanga Sanga and the little island of Bongao.

On Bongao on a hill overlooking the eastern exit, a pinpoint of fire flickered in the dark night.

Twenty minutes later came the sound of a motor, hollow and noisy in the narrow strait, flat and faded when it reached the open sea.

From a dark, low-lying clutter on the water, like floating wreckage, a flare went up, exploding six hundred feet in the air.

The thin cloud cover, drifting at an only slightly higher altitude, reflected the glare, increasing the total luminosity.

In the baleful light the pirate pamboat was already driving forward, machine gun hammering.

Tracers arced out, hosing, finding the target, as the muzzle of the recoilless cranked left, lining up.

"Hold your fire! Don't shoot!"

Tcham Ahn leaped across the deck to the recoilless rifle, colliding with the gunner and knocking him sprawling.

Tcham Ahn yelled: "Christ! You'll sink it!"

The machine gun stopped. Everyone stared.

Instead of a clumsy interisland cargo launch, the quarry was a trim little sport fisherman. Barely forty feet overall, with a hardtop pilothouse and a flying bridge with Plexiglas windshield. It had everything but a tuna tower and Murray fighting chairs in the open cockpit. In any other waters it might have been a weekend charter, complete with bluefin fishermen and aloha shirts.

"Would you look at that? They're trying to flimflam us!"

Red Teeth was staring through binoculars, trying to see the name. "It cannot be the wrong boat."

"It isn't," Tcham Ahn said. "We're supposed to be fooled. All they need is beer and bikini girls."

The flare sank down, illuminating the side.

"Indigente," Red Teeth said, reading the bow.

As if in confirmation, a spurt of shots came from the fisherman: submachine gun fire, nine-millimeter slugs falling far short and harmlessly dispersed.

"They must be crazy," Tcham Ahn said.

Indigente was turning, swinging away, in full retreat. Although not back into the strait, the way she had come, but heading south, along the Bongao coastline, going around the long way. Or else dead straight past the tip of Bongao and out into the open sea.

Red Teeth yelled excitedly: "Shoot! Shoot!"

"One shot from the recoilless and we can fish for those grenades off the bottom," Tcham Ahn said. "That is, if all seven crates don't go sky high first."

"They will outrun us!"

"They could. Sometimes those things have twin diesels. But I don't think so," Tcham Ahn said. "Look at her wallow—she's half sunk already. That's what happens with a load like that. She can't make anything near her top speed. They were counting on fooling us."

Then the flare hit the water and the dark closed down. A concerted growl of anger came from the pirate crew.

"Shut them up," Tcham Ahn said. "Have I ever lost a prize yet? Let me think this out."

Frustration was in Red Teeth's voice: "They are going away!"

"Follow," Tcham Ahn said. "Full speed ahead. In an hour it will be morning, then we'll see. Maybe they can outrun us, and maybe they can't. Luck of the chase. Let me think it out. Can we follow by sound?"

"Or by the wake," Red Teeth said, pointing to the phosphorescence on the water.

"Then do it. That's all we *can* do until daylight. Whatever happens, don't lose them. But don't *catch* them either. I'll think of something. By God," he said, "we may get some fun out of this yet."

In the first dim light of dawn Red Teeth ducked under the thatch to call him from his study of a chart of the waters off Bongao.

"Come and see, tuan."

There was excited jabbering amongst the pirates on deck. During the last hour of dark the gap between the two boats had closed slightly; the pamboat was slightly faster than the little fisherman with its overload.

Red Teeth exulted. "Now we catch up and board!"

"Sure we do, you fool," Tcham Ahn said. "We pull alongside at eight knots and just step across the outrigger. *If* we had a few more hours to finish catching up. And *if* they didn't have a machine gun on board."

In the growing light he studied the boat dead ahead, beating its way south, steered from the flying bridge by one of the bright turbans. Two more turbans were in the cockpit looking back. These three seemed to be the entire crew. The range was about 150 yards.

"Now we shoot them with the machine gun!" Red Teeth said.

"Sure we do, you fool," Tcham Ahn said. "Then we make the boat stop by chopping her down to the waterline with fifty-caliber bullets. If we can manage to hit the engine under the cabin floor. If we don't put one into those grenades first."

Red Teeth stared ahead in gloomy comprehension. "Wa-room!" he said.

"Exactly," Tcham Ahn said. "The machine gun is out. Like the recoilless. Like boarding. Luckily, there's no need. They have already made their mistake. Now let's see how we will play it to our advantage. Do you know what their mistake was?"

"Yes, tuan."

"Sure you do. They failed to lighten ship the moment they saw us."

Red Teeth was gazing ahead. In the sky the thin cloud cover drifted away and the morning sun blazed up in the east. Red Teeth suddenly banged his fists together, his eyes bulging.

"Lighten ship! Lighten ship! Jettison the grenades! Twin diesels! Twenty knots! Father of bleeders! They will outrun us!"

"No. They had their chance," Tcham Ahn said.

He was laughing now; he knew what to do and how to do it—how to capture the prize and meet the challenge too. He ran quickly to the thatch, returned dragging several sleeping mats; went again for more; went again and brought the sniper rifle and a cleaning rod and a dry patch. It was a question of time, a question of moments before the morning sun shed illumination on the turbans as it had on Red Teeth.

Tcham Ahn knelt on the piled-up mats, hurriedly wiping the oil out of the bore of the rifle with the rod and the patch.

"Throttle back. Slow down. Hold our position exactly. Don't catch up with them any more or we'll be in range of that chopper."

He had no idea why the smugglers had not dumped their impossible cargo in the night and been long gone by morning. Or at least enough of it to boost their speed. Possibly because the grenades were of great value to their revolution, possibly because they had cost ten thousand dollars, or even possibly because the smugglers had not realized the danger until first light showed them the pirate pamboat close behind. In any case it was too late now.

He loaded five 180-grain lead-tipped expanding rounds into the rifle and propped himself on his elbows in the prone position on the mats, disengaging the safety as he did so.

The telescopic sight picked up the churning wake first, then rose to scan the boat, from the open cockpit where the two turbans stood to the flying bridge where the third manned the auxiliary helm. The crosshairs swung and swooped and swayed sickeningly, magnifying seven times the motion of both boats.

He screwed the magnification down to 2X and the image steadied a little. The crosshairs centered temptingly on the helmsman's back, hovered on his head. It would be a brilliant shot, a shot worthy of a rifleman, when the moment came.

He adjusted his elbows and the crosshairs sank down, centered on the hatchway just under the hardtop of the pilothouse.

"Just in case they get any bright ideas."

The report was not loud on the open deck with the pamboat motor roaring. The bullet passed between the two turbans in the cockpit and smashed into the overhead just above the hatchway. The turbans ducked out of sight; the helmsman high up on the flying bridge seemed to shrink small, headless and hunched. But the single shot was all, enough.

"Just to make the impasse even on both sides," Tcham Ahn said.

Red Teeth squatted down by the mats. "I do not understand, tuan."

"Interdiction," Tcham Ahn said, his cheek flat to the stock. "There is no access from the foredeck. The only way they can dump the grenades is to bring them up from below through that hatchway, across the cockpit and over the stern. And the first one who tries it is a dead man. That was the message I just sent them. But it's only half the plan."

"Good," Red Teeth said. "Because if they cannot lighten ship to run away, and we cannot increase speed to catch them, where is the purpose?"

"The purpose is to play this ridiculous impasse to our advantage."

"Good," Red Teeth said, "because the men want to throw you overboard and shoot the recoilless."

"To know your enemy is to whip him in a thousand battles,"

Tcham Ahn said, quoting Mao. "I am saving our little edge in RPM for last, and following at this exact pace because we are going to capture both *Indigente* and her cargo without destroying either. Now do you see the plan?"

Red Teeth grinned baffledly. "Yes, tuan."

"We know that our enemy sees that we are not gaining on him but that he is not getting away either. And we know that he sees that he has but one course left open to him, to save all that can be saved now: his life. Due south on the open sea. Have you studied the chart? Have you looked ahead?"

"Yes, tuan."

"He must run for Simunul."

"Simunul!"

"Simunul."

"But there are government gunboats at Simunul!"

"Better gunboats than us," Tcham Ahn said. "He will hope we abandon the chase in time for him to escape both, but even so, better government jailors than bloodthirsty brigands. Better prison than death at the bottom of the sea. Know thine enemy as thyself."

Red Teeth's head wobbled. "They will get away, then!"

"You have not looked ahead," Tcham Ahn said. "How far is it to Simunul?"

"A few hours, more or less."

"And what lies between? Look ahead."

"Look ahead?"

"Look ahead."

Red Teeth looked ahead, over the bows of *Indigente* to the low island like a tan sandbar in the sun.

"Rop," he said with an odd intonation.

"That's where I shoot the helmsman," Tcham Ahn said.

"Which way will they pass?"

"I do not know the island, tuan."

"I think they will go around to the west. They will shave the shoreline to hold as straight a course as possible, and to the east are rocks. The chart does not show much, but there may be a channel to the west."

Rop Island was coming up fast.

Rop Island is forbidden. That is, it is a sacred place of the Bajau people. Not many of their neighbors pay much attention to the lowly sea nomads, the spitouts; their burial islands, Bunabunaan and Bilatan Poon, are often casually violated. But in the case of Rop, the prohibition is generally observed. One never knows.

Rop Island is an island of devils. Here, successfully exorcised evil spirits are exiled, imprisoned in queer anthropomorphic shapes, undead.

"Now!" Tcham Ahn said. "They've turned. Put on full speed and move west, pull outside them. I want us alongside when we get there. I want them squeezed between us and the shoreline."

He glanced quickly up from the telescopic sight to be sure Red Teeth had understood; his eyes had become washed, a pale sky blue.

Still 150 yards ahead, the desperately plodding *Indigente* had altered course to bypass the island, the pirate behind it immediately turning too, swinging a little wider, opening its throttle all the way, beginning to gain.

Tcham Ahn lay on the piled-up mats, sighting. Red Teeth squatted uneasily beside him, relaying the orders.

Behind them the pirate crew gathered sullenly on the deck, muttering together: *"Dakma."*

Evil demons.

The island came closer. First its tan expanse appeared to be barren and flat, then tumbled with boulders and rocks and patched with thickets of stunted bamboo. Closer still and it was seen to be populated.

Hundreds of figures stood upright amongst the rocks and thickets, unseeingly staring out to sea. Each one was alone, apart, and still, dressed in tattered green and white rags. They were scattered over the whole island of Rop—a population of stick bodies with animal skulls, fish jaws, or dirty, unidentifiable bundles for heads.

Some stood near the shore; one or two stood in the very water. From a distance now of only a dozen yards they were seen to be hung with talismans and charms.

The pirates gathered in a huddle on deck, muttering: "*Tahu-tahu.*"

In their state of fierce, nervous concentration, the thundering crack of the shot echoing back from the rocks startled them out of their wits.

High up on the flying bridge of *Indigente*, the helmsman hunched forward with the impact and then spread his arms out wide and fell flat on his back, his head hanging over the edge upside down.

"Shoot! Shoot!" Tcham Ahn bellowed, emptying his rifle. "Shoot into the pilothouse! Keep the other two away from that wheel!"

Indigente was squeezed between the pamboat and the shoreline.

Far from trying to reach the helm in the pilothouse, the two turbans in the after cockpit were ducking up and down behind the coaming, firing ineffectively with the submachine gun and a pistol.

"Crowd them in! Ram the bow! Beach the son of a bitch!"

Tcham Ahn's face was as white as his hair, and the pale eyes glittered with triumph.

Side by side at eight knots the two boats ran pitching and sloshing with little more than wild spray and the flying outrigger between them.

"God damn it, we're pulling ahead!"

Tcham Ahn ran full tilt the length of the deck to the stern and collided with the steersman, knocking him sprawling; he leaped for the tiller and threw his whole weight against it.

The pamboat slid yawing toward *Indigente*, cutting into her path and heeling over so steeply that the port outrigger rose vibrating from the water.

The outrigger struck *Indigente*'s bow a single splintering blow and buckled, but it was enough.

Both helms spinning freely, *Indigente* drifted toward shore, dragged her keel on the bottom, staggered, lost way, and grounded with a lurch.

"Backwater! Backwater! Backwater!"

Tcham Ahn was swinging the heavy tiller hard across the deck as the pamboat motor howled in reverse.

At the same moment the two turbans went over the side of the stranded *Indigente*, floundering in the shallows with guns raised high like amphibious assault troops splashing for cover in a hell of small-arms fire.

Tcham Ahn inspected the prize. His face had not lost its cold pallor and his eyes were still washed empty. His body moved strangely in a hard, compressed way with minimum motion, tightly controlled, like a fighting crouch.

Red Teeth knew him in this state and spoke conciliatively: "They escaped, tuan."

"Because your men failed to pursue them."

Tcham Ahn had also noticed the unnecessarily complicated maneuvers the men had put the pamboat through to board *Indigente* directly without stepping on shore or even wading in the waters of Rop.

"Superstition."

He was staring out over the landscape of rocks and boulders and bamboo thickets, populated by mock men clothed in green and white tattered rags: the *tahu-tahu*, each one inhabited by an exorcised demon.

The island was at least two miles wide and three long. The turbans were far gone out of sight, hidden. In the silence the seawind flapped the tatters and tinkled the little metal charms of the *tahu-tahu*.

"It is not a good place, tuan."

"No, but it's where the game is afoot," he said absently in English, words Red Teeth did not understand.

One of the pirates yelled down from the flying bridge: "Yoi!"

The body of the helmsman rolled over the edge, shoved by a foot; it flailed in the air and fell heavily into the cockpit. The pirate shouted: "This one lives."

Red Teeth squatted down, looking at the blood pumping from the fist-sized hole in the helmsman's breast. At the source of the flow a rapid rhythmic pulsing was discernible.

Tcham Ahn drew a revolver from his armpit; he opened a pouch on his belt and took out a light-loaded wadcutter, less likely to pass through and damage the deck; he substituted it for the magnum in one chamber.

He bent over and fired the wadcutter into the helmsman's head, just behind the ear. There was no particular reaction, no shuddering or urinating; the man had been far gone.

"Field dress him," Tcham Ahn said.

The pirates gazed down at the corpse. Catlike, Tcham Ahn always insisted on neatly covering up the evidence, leaving no mess behind.

"Get a couple of good rocks from on shore."

No one moved; Red Teeth and the other pirates in the cockpit looked at each other and at Rop Island. Tcham Ahn glanced around, saw two big boxes of sinkers amongst *Indigente's* tackle. Leaden line weights weighing almost a pound apiece; they would do.

With a knife from his belt Tcham Ahn slit the corpse open, downward from the bullet exit in its chest—where a protrusion of shattered bone looked like crooked teeth—to its pelvis.

With Red Teeth's help he hauled the body upright and leaned it over the side. The heavy mass of the intestines slithered out and hung down into the water; the knife searched in the cavity and sliced away the adhesions.

The body was laid out on the deck again and the lead weights poured from the boxes into the cavity. Red Teeth brought a length of rope and wrapped it several times around from chest to hips to hold the incision closed. Four pirates picked up the body.

"Wait a minute," Tcham Ahn said, looking into the monkeylike small dead face. He gazed up at the flying bridge and said in a rough voice:

"He was a good man and a worthy adversary. He stood up there under fire and steered straight and never left his post. Okay."

The corpse fell into the water and sank immediately.

"Checklist," Tcham Ahn said. "Casualty gutted and sunk. Let's get to the rest of it."

He wiped his red right hand on the leg of his coverall.

Red Teeth came back from where he leaned, looking down. "Yes, tuan."

"Cargo secured. You might as well have the crew start transferring it right away. Inventory. Take careful inventory because there's more than grenades below. Other useful equipment as well. When that's done, get four pounds of Tovex and a detonator and leave it in the pilothouse. Don't drop it. Two enemy are still at large. I'll place the explosive and time it when I get back."

Red Teeth gazed at him with grave speculation.

"You are going after them, then."

"I owe two clean kills. If I don't get back, that makes you big cacique. Until then I don't want you here. Get that boat off the rocks—she should float when you unload her—but anchor her right where she is. Leave her there for bait, then get out of here. Sail away over the horizon, good-bye and farewell. Just come back about twilight, is all, and watch for my signal from the beach."

Red Teeth looked at him with keen comprehension. "You are going after them alone, then."

"That's the whole idea."

"Good, because we do not want to go ashore there."

"Good. A man hunts better alone."

Of the two turbans on the island of Rop, one was a fanatic and the other was a soldier. In the white light of noon the fanatic was sweating with anger, and the soldier with fear.

They were lying hidden amongst big rocks at the approximate center of the island, its highest point. The slight elevation was sufficient to give them a view of the entire island and the empty sea all around.

They lay back to back, watching in all directions. The soldier had the submachine gun, and the fanatic an automatic pistol.

"Give me the submachine gun and I will go!" said the fanatic, hissing with rage.

"No," the soldier said. "It's a trap."

"There is no one there!"

"Then you don't need the submachine gun," the soldier said, clutching it to him.

He believed that somewhere between them and the boat was an ambush. Probably close to the boat, if not on board it— otherwise why would the pirates have left it floating there so invitingly? The pirates had unloaded it and left; he had watched them out of sight. But he believed that there was an ambush nonetheless. He said:

"I would do the same thing. It is good military tactics, withdraw from the objective and ambush the counterattack. Besides, pirates do not leave boats. They take them or they sink them. The boat is undamaged. They did not even disable it or drain the fuel. I believe this is the pirate band of Tcham Ahn. They do not leave boats to escape in, or survivors to escape."

The fanatic believed that the pirates had taken the cargo and gone. The hand grenades were worth ten thousand dollars anywhere, and pirates took risks for money, not to sink boats or ambush survivors—why would they risk a shore party or linger in these waters with gunboats no farther away than Simunul? He believed they were gone, and believed also in his cause.

"My responsibility is to the cause of the people's war," he hissed bitterly. "They have robbed the people. But they have defeated us in a battle, not in the war. The boat is undamaged and has fuel. It has no cargo now and can cruise at eighteen knots. We can follow them, we can outspeed them and keep out of range and avoid them this time, and follow them to their hiding place and come back and bring the anger of the people down on them and butcher them to bits in the cause of freedom. But every minute we waste arguing here, they are getting away!"

The soldier had better sense. "Tcham Ahn can get away as far from me as he likes."

"It is not Tcham Ahn! Tcham Ahn is known to have a cannon!"

"Maybe he did not choose to shoot it."

"Where is the shore party, then?"

"Maybe they are hiding."

"No one can hide for long in the sun on this bare rock without making a move or giving a sign!"

"We have."

"*I am going down to the boat!*"

"I am not."

The fanatic suddenly sat up, twisting his hips, jabbing the muzzle of the automatic pistol into the soldier's ear.

"I am taking the submachine gun! Give it to me!"

The soldier threw it at him. "Take it! Take it! Here it is!

Go down to the boat! Go fall in the ambush! If they don't get
me too, I will give you a hero's burial!"

"There is no one there!"

"There is no one there, there is no one there! How do you
want me to bury you, facing east toward Mecca, or north toward
Moscow?"

"Ha, ha!" the fanatic said. "You are going first. You are
walking ahead of me to test your theory. How do you like that?
And when we return to Sarawak, I am going to have you executed
for cowardice and treason. Get on your feet!"

Just at that moment his eye was caught by movement on the
far south shore of the island. Both men looked. It was a flight
of birds. They were boobies, a kind of gannet seen on all the
islands. They flew into the air as though startled, then settled
back, hidden from sight in the rocks.

"Nothing. Get moving," the fanatic said.

But the soldier was holding up one hand; he was gazing
south.

"Wait a minute. Listen to me. You are right, I agree with
you now. We will go to the boat. But not because you threaten
me. I am not cowardly, but there are tactics. I am a soldier."

"Then behave like one."

"I am. I use skilled judgment. There *is* a shore party, but
it is possible that it is searching for us on the southern side of
the island. Don't you see? It is the birds. I use my skilled
judgment to improve our chances, that is tactics. If I am right,
we have a chance to reach the boat now. But it would be a
better chance if I had my gun."

"You will have a gun, but I will have the submachine gun,
and I am right behind you."

"You are like all revolutionaries. They always want a submachine gun. You always wanted mine."

"No, I don't trust a coward," the fanatic said. "Every minute
you waste talking so much, we are losing our best chance."

He made the soldier stand up and face away, toward the
shore where the boat lay anchored, and then he gave him the
automatic pistol, with instructions to aim it always ahead.

"You go first."

They descended from the slight elevation; there was a for-mation of rock ledges like wide stairs, then a slide; below the slide a group of motionless standing figures, their rags whispering, their metal charms clinking in the light wind: the *tahu-tahu.*

"They say there is a *dakma* locked up in each one," the soldier said.

"There is a *dakma* behind you with a submachine gun," said the fanatic, who was a historical materialist. "No more talking. Listen hard for any sound, and shoot at any movement."

It was nearly a mile to the shore. Every few yards they passed another figure; sometimes there were groups of them standing together in bare patches where there were no rocks; sometimes there were single *tahu-tahu* perched up on rocks like lookouts. The soldier was frightened of them. Many times he almost shot at them with the pistol when green and white tatters flapped suddenly in a shift of wind.

The fanatic hissed at him: "Coward!"

They crawled on hands and knees through a bamboo thicket; they lay on their stomachs and looked out across an open space.

A few big boulders, a crowd of eerie *tahu-tahu*, and a narrow, steep strip of beach separated them from the shallows where *Indigente* was anchored.

The soldier mouthed words in what was not even a whisper: "The ambush is behind a boulder or on the boat."

"*There is no ambush.*"

"Then you go first."

The fanatic said nothing; he lay in the bamboo, the submachine gun aimed forward into the open space; he gazed at the boulders and at the boat; the boulders baked in the sun and the boat rocked gently. There was no sense of living presence. There was a remote and desolate deadness about the scene which was like the inhuman lifelessness of the silent stick figures.

He jogged the soldier with his elbow and they looked at each other, looking into each other's eyes, beginning to grin, grinning with smug elation.

They stood up slowly and stepped out. In the open they stretched their necks to look as far as they could both ways, up and down the narrow beach. Chortling, they hurried toward the boat.

In the middle of the open space one of the *tahu-tahu* came to life.

When the boobies flew up, Tcham Ahn acted with such speed that he both pleased and startled himself.

He stood up from his crouch behind the boulder, where he had waited for what seemed like hours without moving; he strode quickly out into the open space, already tugging at buttons and scarf. He took a new stand amongst the group of figures nearest the shore, bracing his legs very wide apart, the coverall yanked open to the waist showing a white undershirt, the white scarf wrapped around his face from bridge-of-the-nose down, its long ends flapping in the sea wind. The shotgun was flat against the front of his right leg, barrel down, muzzle resting on the toe of one black shiny boot; his right hand held it by the small of the stock; his left arm was pressed tight to his side, while that shoulder rose crippledly higher than the other. He lost all resemblance to a human being.

The voice of his thoughts sounded gleefully in his head.

Sham man amongst the mock men.

He did not know what he had done until he had done it. Slow, fragmentary thought caught up with the accomplished act as he stood totally still.

One more stick man. Green and white. Will not see.

He knew that the act must have been unconsciously planned well in advance; for good or ill, he had already decided to move, open the buttons, tie the scarf; had already evaluated his chances as a scarecrow standing amongst scarecrows but otherwise exposed in the open without a shred of cover.

But the reason?

Then the birds had flown up, and he had instantly adapted the circumstance to the plan. Perception, determination, action—it pleased him that he was still sharp; it had happened without thought, quicker than thought. Either the turbans were on the south tip of the island scaring birds or they were hidden somewhere else, looking south to see what had scared the birds; in the latter case their reaction time was all the time he had. He hoped he had moved fast enough.

They will come.

They would come from the south or from somewhere else;
they would see him first or he would see them first. He would
shoot them from a stand over bait, or they would stalk him from
afar and shoot him down from hiding. By his move he had made
it a whole new hunt.

And the reason?

Barraka.

He withdrew his thoughts.

It is well-known that for successful posting over bait the
hunter must camouflage himself perfectly, immobilize himself completely, and wait patiently. But even this is not enough. Often
the quarry seems to sense something it cannot see, hear, or smell,
something that is an emanation from life itself. To avoid betraying
his presence the hunter must also withdraw even his thoughts
from the scene, becoming only a mindless part of inanimate nature.

Tcham Ahn stood in his crippled posture amongst the *tahu-
tahu* for an endless time in the white sun.

The bamboo stirred.

The right hand jerked the shotgun level, the left seized the
forearm and aimed the short barrel. The gun fired and jolted up
with the recoil, cut downward a little to the left and fired again;
empties clattered on the rocks.

Twelve thirty-caliber buckshot slugs struck the fanatic in the
chest and knocked him down. At least eight hit the soldier in
the face and throat and he fell more slowly, dropping the automatic,
probably dead before his knees touched the ground. The range
was less than fifteen feet.

Tcham Ahn sprang forward and kicked the submachine gun
out of the fanatic's grip, and then stood looking down. The
concentrated charge of single-O buckshot had caused massive
damage to the lower chest and thorax; the lungs would fill soon.

Hard black eyes glared up at Tcham Ahn, eyes that had
never given mercy or asked for it. Eyes of a man who was born
to the wars and would make no protest now. Something from
the dark night of lost time passed between the two men, and
Tcham Ahn felt pride and grief.

He squatted down by the fanatic's head and spoke to him.

"I stood in the open. It could have gone the other way."

The fierce eyes looked over Tcham Ahn's shoulder, a last long look into a sky full of light.

"Milikan," he said in a thin and bitter voice. "What are you doing in our war?"

"It's the only war in town," Tcham Ahn said. "That is going to begin to hurt soon. Do you want me to finish you?"

"Go kill your own kind, traitor to man. Your own war needs you."

He closed his eyes and spoke a word, something Tcham Ahn could not catch; perhaps a woman's name.

"What war?" Tcham Ahn said. It was possible. "Who is fighting?"

He had not been home for many years, and he had heard no news from there for at least three.

After a while he said again: "What war? Is the United States fighting a war?"

The man was alone with his death.

"*Mudd yedák*," he whispered in Arabic: Reach forth thine hand.

He opened the undefeated eyes once more and spoke with a grin:

"The People's Freedom Movement declared a people's republic in the United States two years ago. You have been butchering each other ever since."

"I've been out of touch," Tcham Ahn said.

He thrust downward with the shotgun stock and stood up, looking out to sea, far away. The far place.

Civil war.

Dying men don't lie.

Tcham Ahn was thinking about the possibilities. The challenge.

Even if none of this was real, really real, it existed as an act of mind, and could not be less than what he made of it.

At his feet the dead man murmured: "I am cold."

When Red Teeth and the pirates came back in the pamboat at twilight, they found two hastily dug graves and two expended shotgun shells, but *Indigente* was gone and so was Tcham Ahn. They never saw him again.

CHAPTER TWO

Blue S.T.O.P.

Mertensia

"I told him! I said to the crazy cocksucker: 'Why, you screwy son of a bitch—this is a twenty-five-million-dollar United States nuclear submarine, and we are thirty fucking fathoms down!'"

Captain Boyd C. Linebarger had already testified with professional dignity and military decorum before a board of inquiry, an evidentiary hearing, and his own court martial. The repetition was getting to him.

Colonel Volpe touched the tape recorder, adjusting the volume. "And he replied?"

"And he replied, 'And this is four pounds of Tovex with an electric detonator, and thirty fathoms puts us well below the waterline.'"

"And what did you do?"

"What the fuck *could* I do?"

Captain Linebarger's ordeal was mostly over. He was now in casual status pending reassignment to Menial Services Administration; no further harm could come to him, at least from S.T.O.P., whoever they were—some kind of subsection of Counter Insurgency Command. Colonel Volpe was in the Polwar Division of CIC; the others were nobodies, a Navy commander, an Army captain, an Air Force major, four or five civilians. They all had eyeglasses and ballpoint pens. They probably didn't even liase with anybody important, or why would they need to hear the whole thing all over again?

The whole thing all over again caused Captain Linebarger to clutch tightly the leather arms of the orthopedic chair.

"Thirty fathoms down and hydrogen feeders in my overhead!"

Acute aggravation lent his voice a ragged edge like a rusty razor.

"I only did what any responsible officer would have done."

Sensing devices in the chair recorded sullen pulsebeats and sweaty palms.

"All I did was save a twenty-five-million-dollar sub and God knows how many more millions in sophisticated ELINT aerial/ coastal spy equipment from a maniac with a fucking *bomb!*"

Colonel Volpe's eyes narrowed wincingly; he tuned the volume lower. "So we understand."

"Not to mention four cobalt SBM's in the war bucket!"

"There was also a crew of one hundred and eighty personnel."

"Not to mention *me!*"

"So you did as you were told."

"You're fucking *ey!*"

The ballpoints poised, writing nothing; eyeglasses glinted. Colonel Volpe prayed with his thumbs tucked under his chin.

"Captain Linebarger. We sympathize with your feelings, but our effort here is concerned with facts. The facts we are hoping to elicit do not relate to your grievance. We do not have influence with Fleet Command. Our effort as an advisory group to Counter Insurgency Operations is to elicit facts relating to the acts and tactics of the individual who stowed aboard your craft. Could we get on with that? And belay the salty sailor talk, would you kindly?"

"Yes, sir."

The commander from the Office of Naval Intelligence was intrigued by the question of dockside and shipboard security.

"How did he ever get on board?"

"How the fuck should I know?"

Yawning and relaxing after the business of casting off, putting out to sea, and submerging for the first leg of the run, Captain Linebarger had stepped into his private cabin to find a hallucinatory figure sitting on his bunk, holding a greasy bundle in one hand and a contact detonator in the other. It said:

"Come in and shut the door."

Mertensia had just spent six days docked in Cavite on a TR mission, entertaining dignitaries and the press and flying the flag to show U.S. solidarity with the righteous government in its battle against leftist-inspired Moslem separatists.

Flagship of Submarine Division 152, Squadron 9, U.S. Pacific Fleet, the 380-foot *Mertensia* weighed 4000 tons surfaced and 4500 submerged, with twin reactor engines, eight torpedo tubes, and eight missile ports. It was the pride of the command.

Then the first hour out of Manila Bay on a goodwill tour there was a scarecrow with a bomb in the captain's own cabin.

"Lock it, and assume the position."

Thinking back on it, Captain Linebarger touched the tip of one finger to the tip of his nose, sniffing.

"Of course, he could have swum in from seaward—he could even have bribed his way aboard, all that gold . . . then just hid out till we dived. Come to think of it, I *was* going to check on that—all those days, now I remember, I *thought* I smelled something funny in my cab—"

Suddenly he sat up straight as a stake.

The chair recorded icy prickling hackles.

"How many nights was he hiding under my fucking bunk?"

"Come in and shut the door. Lock it, and assume the position."

Captain Linebarger's head jolted; the totally unexpected sight was a shock that came like a leap at his face.

It was an hallucination dressed in green coveralls, a long winding white silk scarf and a slouch hat; it had pistols in twin shoulder holsters; it had black shiny boots; it had sun-bleached whitish short hair, a curious dull tan over dead white skin, and pale oyster-blue eyes.

The eyes were wide and wobbly and demented, but the voice was mild. But then it changed, an eerie thin squeak in the tiny compartment.

"Leviathan! Beast of the deep! Behold your doom!"

Trembling hands with dried blood under the fingernails held up the detonator and the greasy bundle like offerings.

But then the voice changed again, to an amiable murmur.

"Hey. Yoo-hoo, pay attention. Come, come, Captain."

The captain was standing staunchly spread-legged, grasping the binoculars on his chest, staring jut-jawed and indomitable, as though into the hell of battle. When the figure moved, he continued staring at the same place in space.

"Cataleptic paralysis," he heard the voice say.

He felt himself urged gently aside; his door was closed and locked; he was guided to the wall and leaned there in the position, hands flat, feet spread apart; he was quickly and deftly patted down.

"Who—"

"We'll talk in a minute. It isn't going to be as bad as you think. Please hold your hands down low, the right hard to port in front, left hard astern, if you will. That's right. Just to make any heroics the more difficult. Now you've got it."

"How—"

A friendly arm across his shoulders pressed the captain vertically downward, knees and back bent in a crouch, his hands positioned. With a click his wrists were cuffed together between his legs.

"What—"

"Sorry to put you in a stooped position for a man of your standing, but we're going to be roommates for a while, and I want you hors de combat. It might get very bad for you before it's over, cramps and so on. Let me know if you'd rather be killed. I can manage either way."

The captain gazed up sidelong. His mind began to function; he was, after all, an officer. The greasy bundle was high on top of the chart locker; it was tight up against the overhead with its hydrogen feeders; the detonator was in the man's hand. The man grinned.

"Now we can talk."

The captain squirmed, testing and trying his bonds; he was beefily built; there was no chance of lifting his leg over, slipping the cuffs under his heel. He shuffled tentatively, as though puzzled by his awkward posture; he had suffered a fright at the outset, and already there was a question. He stood pensively still, hunched half over. The amiable voice chatted to him, and the question grew more pressing.

"Who? How? What? Fair enough. Who am I—I'm the new commanding officer. How did I get here—by fishing boat from Rop Island. What do I want—a fast trip to the States or I'll blow the bejesus out of this pigboat as quick as it takes me to press this button. Any questions?"

Captain Linebarger's head hung upside down as he gazed perplexedly at his two wrists close-cuffed together in his crotch.

"I have to go to the bathroom. I don't see how I can."

Pause; a moment of head-scratching silence, then a puff of laughter.

"I don't either. Tough shit, as you might say. Let's get down to business. *Now hear this.*"

The changeable voice became as hard and cold as rock.

"This is the new commanding officer speaking, and here are the new Ship's Articles. Article One: My slightest wish is your command. The first attempt to thwart me in any way, the first hesitation in obeying any order, and you will instantly and painfully be shot in the kneecap. The second such attempt, either by yourself or any member of your crew, or any outside agency, and you will be killed. Have not the slightest doubt. Make not the least mistake."

He pointed a big-bore pistol at the captain's knee and then at his head.

"Say, Aye, aye, sir."

"Aye, aye, sir."

"Article Two: All communication between this cabin and the conn or whatever you call it will be via your intercom on the wall. No one is to enter or leave this cabin at any time. Your executive officer will drive the boat. Present with him in conn at all times will be the navigation officer and the sound and communications officer. For the duration of this voyage their single and sole duty will be to obey orders from you, dictated by me. To save your life. To save their own. Say it."

"Aye, aye, sir."

"Article Three: Standing orders are that the entire voyage shall be accomplished submerged, using the snorkel; snorkel depth to be maintained at all times after the new course is laid on; total radio silence at all times; signaling to other vessels or shore installations forbidden; relevant information to be forwarded to COMSUBFE by you, dictated by me; deviation from course or delaying tactics forbidden; no false moves; except for routine operations, absolutely no action or maneuver permitted unless on orders from this cabin."

"Aye, aye, sir."

"Article Four: Any action of commission or omission, any occurrence, mischance, consequence, or circumstance whatsoever, at any time, for any reason, that tends to disappoint me in my hopes of reaching San Francisco in fine fettle, solid comfort, and full command, will be firmly dealt with. I will firmly press this button. Have you got it all?"

"Aye, aye, sir."

"Are you ready to put it on the intercom?"

"Aye, aye, sir."

"Congratulations. You have just been hijacked."

Then for one instant the hallucination was back again as the incredible figure danced a sudden exhilarated hornpipe.

"I did it! I can do anything!"

Captain Linebarger glared up sidewise and deformed in outraged comprehension.

"Why, you *bastard!* You aren't a lunatic at *all!*"

"No, but I had you going for a while there, didn't I? Leviathan-behold-your-doom!"

"Why, you screwy son of a bitch—this is a twenty-five-million-dollar United States nuclear submarine, and we are thirty fucking fathoms down!"

OP URGENT SS(N) MERTENSIA SENDS TO COMSUBFE PEARL HARBOR STOP UNIDENTIFIED PSYCHOPATH WITH BOMB ADJACENT TO VOLATILE HYDROGEN FEEDER PIPING HOLDS CAPTAIN CAPTIVE STOP DEMANDS HISTORIC INFORMATION ON AMERICAN LIBERATION MOVEMENT STOP DEMANDS SAFE PASSAGE TO SAN FRANCISCO STOP DEMANDS JET LINER TO WASHINGTON STOP DEMANDS PENTAGON CONFERENCE WITH US CHIEFS OF STAFF STOP UNDER

PSYCHOPATH COMMAND PROCEEDING BASE STOP
REQUEST INSTRUCTIONS STOP

OP URGENT COMSUBFE PEARL HARBOR SENDS TO
SS(N) MERTENSIA STOP FOLLOW ALL REASONABLE
PSYCHOPATHIC DEMANDS STOP SAVE SUB STOP

"Cataleptic paralysis," Colonel Volpe said.

Just at that point the door burst open and a sergeant-at-arms poked his head in.

"If you men are finished with your interview, there's other people would like to use this facility too, you know."

He saw Colonel Volpe's gold eagles.

"Who are you people?"

"Special Tactical Operations Planning of Polwar Division of Counter Insurgency Command," Colonel Volpe said in only one breath. Formerly a Military Police sergeant, a CID officer, a stockade commandant, an MP company commander, and a division level provost marshal, he was a big, barrel-chested man, accustomed to loud commands and long sentences; but the sergeant-at-arms had a clipboard, symbol of authority.

"Well," the sergeant-at-arms said, "there's no priority overtime on that chair today. National Police is waiting to interview six recruits and State has a PFA defector. There's a war on, you know."

"We will adjourn to our offices," Colonel Volpe said.

He rode a rubber-tired golf cart down endless hallways. One of the civilian members of his team, the DIA representative, rode with him and said:

"What's it all about, Tim? Navy matters, Pacific Theatre, stowaway lunatics. Why didn't any of our agencies ever hear about this? Who sat on the lid? And where does S.T.O.P. fit in—what's hijacked submarines got to do with our guerrilla friends in the hills?"

"All in due time."

"What's it all about?"

"Operation Kalitan."

Then they came to corridor B-19, level 3, room 40036, the office of S.T.O.P. They parked and went in.

It was a small, windowless, lead-shielded room, secure but in no way luxurious; the amenities were few: two filing cabinets, a desk with telephone and typewriter, a drinking fountain, a hot plate, a big mahogany conference table with ten chairs, and a map. The map covered one whole wall and was flapped with many transparent acetate overlays.

While waiting, Colonel Volpe stood with hands clasped behind him in parade-rest position and studied the map. The map was to Colonel Volpe the official insignia of S.T.O.P.; without the map to prove their vital involvement in the war effort, he and his team members might as well be clerks in General Services. Only vitally involved sections got to have their own copies of the master map that hung in the War Room of the U.S. Chiefs of Staff; Colonel Volpe's map put S.T.O.P. right up there in the front lines.

Studying the map sometimes made Colonel Volpe feel like a field general with a riding crop planning his next slashing attack.

"Hold onto your hats, you Commie rats!"

The map was useful also as a short graphic course in the history of the war; marked in blue and red for Us and Them, the successive acetate overlays showed combat areas and occupied zones; starting from the last or top overlay, they went all the way back to the beginning.

The map itself was of the territorial United States with details of northern Mexico and southern Canada. Here and there on the first or original overlay were tiny red speckles entirely encircled by massed blue battalions, regiments, divisions. The second showed more speckles, and the third, speckles connected by lines. Then speckles and lines forming into spiky little rowels, stabbed at by broad blue arrows, and next, little, thin red arrows stabbing back at broad, split blue arrows. And then red veins and root systems, and soon the first tentative pink areas, like new skin under a scab, turning bright red, extending, blunting and bending the blue arrows, gaining everywhere like an itch or rash or a widening pool of blood. Colonel Volpe knew the tale by heart, right down to the newest overlay, the most recent spreading of the blotch, the latest victory of the triumphant People's Freedom Army.

"Niggers, crooks, and Commies," Colonel Volpe said to the map.

The other S.T.O.P. team members were arriving by cart or on foot.

Colonel Volpe sat down at the head of the conference table, sorting papers. Besides himself there were eight people on the subscription list: Lieutenant Commander Richard Rooney, representing the Office of Naval Intelligence; Captain John Makedon, representing Department of Army Intelligence; Major Miles Clifford, representing Air Force Intelligence; Preston Baldwin, from the Defense Intelligence Agency; Robert Walbridge, from the National Security Agency; Harrison Wylie, from the State Department's Bureau of Research and Intelligence; Wade O'Leary, from the Federal Bureau of Investigation, and a saturnine man known only as Kaul, from National Police Headquarters.

Their job, the job of S.T.O.P., under the leadership of Colonel Volpe, was to devise, contrive, or otherwise provide plans for possible special tactical operations to be mounted against the domestic foe. Their proposals and recommendations, in the form of work papers, were used to assist Polwar Division to assist Counter Insurgency Command in its weekly deliberations on how to achieve the overall mission goal: Scotch the Blotch.

Sometimes S.T.O.P.'s plots were used, sometimes not; when they were, Polwar mostly took the credit.

The team members settled in their seats, and Colonel Volpe replayed the tape thus far.

"... *fucking fathoms down!*"

Colonel Volpe switched off.

"In short, gentlemen, this, our Captain Linebarger, is a poltroon and a fart. I think we need concern ourselves no longer with him, but leave him to his place in naval history, along with the eminent Captain James 'Don't-give-up-the-ship' Lawrence, who, in 1808, surrendered the USS *Chesapeake* to the British frigate *Shannon* within sight of Boston Harbor."

The commander from ONI popped to his feet at attention; though very young, he wore bifocals.

"Sir. I object to that in the name of the United States Navy. Captain Linebarger is a responsible officer with an excellent record. *Mertensia* under his command won the FECOM Submarine Battle

Readiness Award for two years running. Besides which, the order from Pearl clearly ratifies his cowardice."

"Objection overruled," Colonel Volpe said. "However, since you are already on your feet and talking, you may recapitulate for the recorder the sequence of events on board following the captain's capture and the exchange of messages. I assume you have contacted JICPOA as per my instructions?"

"Sir. Joint Intelligence Center Pacific Ocean Area refuses release of any material on submarines now on active duty. It's a cover-up, and you know it. The stowaway said radio silence and all hands turned to, from Cavite to Washington. It was a perfect excuse to make believe it never happened. Not even the press heard about it. But I have found a secondary source of information direct from God."

Colonel Volpe painfully pinched the bridge of his nose.

"Go ahead. Say it."

The commander giggled.

"Sir. Lieutenant Commander Jim Bob God, USN, the executive officer who took over after they got the okay from COM-SUBFE and drove the boat home while Linebarger was loading his pants down in the cabin with that psychopath."

"*Shit!*" Kaul, the National Policeman, exploded.

"Sir. I have here the verbatim transcripts of Lieutenant Commander God's testimony at Captain Linebarger's court martial. What could beat that? May I read?"

"Proceed."

Colonel Volpe switched on.

"Sir. Lieutenant Commander Jim Bob God, being legally advised that he need not make a deposition, that any deposition he makes may be used against him—in any proceeding, civil or military—and who affirms that the following deposition was made freely and voluntarily, without offer of personal benefit, and without application of illegal force or duress, does proceed under oath to state the following:

I had the conn after we left Cavite. Lieutenants Stevenson and Rich were there. We never even known anything was wrong till the captain come on the intercom. And we didn't know what to do. We were going to send a message to Pearl about it, but the nut did. That was his own message, the captain read it out to us over the intercom. Then COMSUBFE said do what the nut wants, and the nut said set a course for Pearl, and we set a course for Pearl. It was scary. We didn't hear nothing all night. Then the captain come on the intercom. He was groaning. The nut wanted another message sent to Pearl, with our ETA. We wasn't to go in, we was to stand off, and them to bring out library books and newspaper files. It was about the rebellion at home, Kudelak and the People's Freedom Movement and the guerrilla stuff. The famine and the meltdown, the Terror and all that, about how it all got started. Captain told him all he knew, but he wanted it all, and then the People's Freedom Army and the war and where they were fighting and everything, right up to the minute. We were on patrol the last six months, we didn't know that. He said radio Pearl and put some researchers on it, or fly out the whole file from Washington, or get up two years' worth of *New York Times*, he didn't care what. Or else! Captain said, Do it, for Christ's sake! COMSUBFE said, Go ahead, it's public record, they would do it.

So that's what they did. When we got to Pearl there was this launch with a carton of books and papers and microfilm printouts and we was allowed to open one hatch to ship it on, and then Captain hollers, Crash dive! Crash dive? What the hell does that mean, like the movies? Captain screams, Crash dive, you bastards, whatever he wants, or he's going to shoot my fucking kneecap off! So we go downstairs—we almost drown the guys off the launch from Pearl. That's it, set a course for San Francisco, Captain says. He was groaning very bad all the time now. Cramps and things. All full ahead, he says, get me there! He wanted to get out of those irons. Belay that, he says after a minute. Oh, God, cruising speed—he needs time to study the material!

So we did. But he wouldn't let us bring the material down to the cabin. Read it over the intercom. Good-bye, boys, I can't stand up anymore, Captain says. So that's what happened. For the rest of the trip we took turns reading books and stuff over the intercom. We could hear Captain groaning in the bunk. The nut made some noises, like snorts or laughs at stuff we read, but he never said nothing. We kept on reading. This was like days! We never known if he was listening, sleeping, what. They weren't eating either. The steward left sandwiches outside, they never took them in.

Then the last day out of San Francisco Bay, Captain come on. I'm dying, boys, follow orders exactly. We was to pull right into the slip before the nut would get off, Captain with him, and books and stuff too. Staff car with one driver in it to take them to the airport and board them on a plane to Washington. No false moves, no funny business. COMSUBFE said humor him, we might as well find out what this is all about, he got his free ride, no harm done, all they were worried about was their submarine anyway. Let Air Force take it from here, let him blow up a jet for a change. Let Washington worry about it, let him blow up the Pentagon. Meanwhile they had forwarded his last message to the War Department. I remember it every word, we laughed our asses off. Dear Sirs, Request meeting with U.S. Chiefs of Staff at earliest convenience. Thank you.

Then we surfaced and drove in and moored up. Nobody allowed to crack a hatch until he was long gone. We never even saw the guy, all the way across the Pacific. Who's to say he was there? Maybe he was never real. Further this deponent sayeth not."

"Balls!" Kaul, the National Policeman, said. "He's real. We know all about him."

Colonel Volpe switched off.

Apodixis

Kaul dressed always entirely in black except for a red necktie of the snap-on type; its factory-tied permanent knot was grubby. He carried a black briefcase, holding it in his left hand. He held it even when sitting at the conference table. A zipper closed three sides of the briefcase, but on one side there was an additional closure; it was a Velcro strip which could be pushed open with the fingertips and the hand inserted inside, like a muff. Kaul could reach in at a moment's notice to either draw his gun or fire it through the briefcase, as warranted. He wore an N.P. shield on his vest beneath his coat. Kaul was one of the reasons the National Police were popularly called Nazis.

Colonel Volpe gazed at him with dry revulsion.

"Thank you, Mr. Kaul. Indeed, the man is not entirely unknown to all our various agencies, as you will see. But neither is it accurate to say that we know all about him. Rather, that several among us know something about him and have already been consulted, with a view to pooling our parts of information. You will all hear all."

Colonel Volpe switched on.

"By way of preface I might remark that the individual in question gave his name to the platoon of U.S. troops awaiting him at Dulles as Rainsford Zaroff. A piece of harmless whimsicality which we need not take into account, except insofar as we are dealing with a nut. Also, he described himself to a chief U.S. marshal as a secret weapon. His identity, of course, is known to us, together with additional particulars relating to his origins and early life. Since Mr. Kaul apparently desires to be the first to speak, we will call on him for a summary of the facts available through the archive banks of the National Police central computer, *sanctus et omnipotens*. Mr. Kaul."

Kaul could talk without moving his lips in the slightest.

"Think you're pretty smart, don't you?"

Actually, what he said was, *Hink you're tretty snart, don-yew,* as earlier he had said, *Dalls, he's real, we know all adout hin.*

Kaul slid his hand inside his briefcase, as if to draw power from the warm-walnut checkered grip.

Colonel Volpe was passing the first of the photographs around the table; it was of a boy blond to the point of albinism; he was staring into the camera without visible pupils; Shaman at age thirteen.

"First came to police attention in North Dakota," Kaul said, masklike (*Hurst cane to holice,* et cetera). "Suspect in the death of his guardian. Coroner's jury later ruled it a hunting accident. Old man wasn't his guardian, just took care of him. Lived forty miles out in the wilderness, hunter and trapper, lived on an old ranch. Found the kid lost. Never reported it. Never knew who he was or where he came from. No record of birth or parents. Data wasn't like it is now, we got compulsory input, centralized retrieval. Couldn't happen today."

Kaul glanced down at his notes without moving his head.

"Remanded to juvenile authorities. Placed in Bismarck or-
phan asylum. Kid was a savage. Ran away in midwinter. Found
him living in a Mandan earth-lodge village in the Medora badlands.
Father José Cassedy's Home on the Range for Boys took him.
Bean soup and hard labor. Left there two years later. No record
after that."

"No record after that," Colonel Volpe repeated, "when in
point of fact there was no *prior* record either, was there? No
criminal record at all?"

"No criminal record," Kaul said.

"Yet I have the distinct impression you are reciting a 'rap
sheet,' a profile of a criminal, whereas I understand quite the
contrary. Did he not become a serious student and a remarkable
overachiever?"

"He shot that old man," Kaul said.

"*Non demonstrandum est*," Colonel Volpe said. "Mr. Baldwin
has for us some facts relating to the period following the two-
year stint at Father Cassedy's boys' town. Mr. Baldwin?"

The man from the Defense Intelligence Agency said: "He
worked for the CIA at one point."

"Who didn't?" the FBI man said.

"Not as an operative. He was still a schoolboy, this was back
in the days of Princeton Ooo. We usually kept pretty close tabs
on them, so when we learned they were opening files on certain
students, we researched them too. By the time we heard of the
kid, he had developed into quite a brain. Two years at Father
Cassedy's and two more years in Richardton Public School—
where they boarded him with some Benedictine monks at Assumption Abbey—and there was nothing else they could teach
him. The monks sponsored him for some kind of tests that
qualified him to skip high school, and he was entered in a special
program for gifted teenagers at the University of Chicago."

The man from the National Security Agency remembered
something.

"That's right. He's in our files too. I forgot because it never
came to anything. Chess champion and linguist. He's got eidetic
memory, or whatever you call it. Photographic mind, total recall
of anything and everything."

"That's what got him the job with the CIA," Baldwin said.

"After he finished the program, he went to work at the CIA-funded cryptology lab at California Institute of Technology."

"That's right," the NSA man said, "we tried to swipe him. We got the Defense Department to offer him a four-year scholarship at the University of Illinois, so NSA could recruit him. But it seems he must have refused it. We have no file after that."

"Because he suddenly deserted the groves of academe," Colonel Volpe said. "I wonder if it was not the result of decoding all those reports from far-flung spooks living dangerous and glamorous lives. At any rate, his formal education completed, he thereupon abandoned tranquility for a life of action and violence. Captain Makedon?"

The second photograph was now circulating; it was a boot-camp mug shot of a pale young man with a shaven head; Shaman at age eighteen.

Captain John Makedon, representing the Department of Army Intelligence, reached under his chair for a musty bundle of papers. "We're lucky to have these at all. Old Army records are always getting stored away in Tennessee warehouses that burn down."

Colonel Volpe eyed the bundle. "We must wade through all that?"

"No. You know how it is, they include everything in your two-oh-one file. This is mostly junk. Shot records and shipping orders. Anything with your name on it, in it goes, even if it's just lists. I got a memo on him from the Adjutant General's Office. I only brought his file along for proof—because you aren't going to believe it, you aren't going to *believe* this memo!"

"Begin slowly, read chronologically, and we will try," Colonel Volpe said.

"Well, just for starters, he enlisted in the infantry, E.R. two. Code expert, chess wizard, top student, language major, he wouldn't have it any other way. Went through basic like a house afire. Soldier of the Month every month. He was a born combat type. There wasn't that much competition, though. The Volunteer Army program wasn't doing all that well. Most of the Vol units were pretty low quality. He was too gung ho for his barracks mates. Had a lot of nasty fights. All that ended suddenly, however, when one big son of a bitch up and died. There was some bad talk about Shaman, but the inquiry ruled it was one of those training-camp tragedies."

"*Another* hunting accident," Kaul said.

He reflexively inserted his hand in his briefcase.

"Anyway, he was a hot property, for a Vol," Makedon said. "At the end of Basic he put in for paratroop school and Ranger school and Special Forces, and zipped through them too. But instead of shipping him out with any of them, they sent him to Leadership School. See, it was Second 'Nam times then, and they were pushing them through pretty fast. They needed officers. Especially second johns with a high waste rate."

"Can we skip the disloyal PFM propaganda?" the FBI man said.

"Can we get through a little faster?" Colonel Volpe said.

Captain Makedon read from his memo.

"Served Second 'Nam as second lieutenant. Eleven battles. Distinguished conduct. Commanded special jungle platoon. Destroyed battery of enemy artillery. Detached service, led two-man long-range extended reconnaissance team, photographed enemy supply bases and staging areas in neutral territory. There's more, and it gets better. He stayed on roving service after that, practically lived off the land. Outside on his own, he hardly came in at all. Had his own hard core of hard-case undesirables from recon units, plus anywhere from a dozen to a hundred indigenous cutthroats as he needed them. Jungle bushy-wushies and uplands headhunters. By the time Second 'Nam spread all over the map of southeast Asia, he was everywhere. Finally they grabbed him coming in for money and supplies, made him a major and gave him half a dozen citations, and put him in command of counterguerrilla operations from Saigon to Rangoon, the whole peninsula. In two years he mounted seven hundred major and minor operations with eighty-two percent operational success. The only thing they couldn't make him do was to stop going along. He was hooked on it. He was their top expert on unconventional warfare at the age of twenty-two, and they were afraid he'd get snuffed. He was a hero. That is, he would have been a hero if we'd won the war, but we pulled out."

"A war to the finish, and we finished first," the FBI man said bitterly.

"Shaman wasn't finished yet," Makedon said. "When the U.S. forces pulled out, he didn't have enough. He resigned his commission, as light colonel by then, and took his discharge in Hong Kong. Forfeited repatriation, bought a sampan full of illegal surplus weapons in Macao, and disappeared. That's the last the War Department knows about him, officially. There were some reports. Then no more. Written off as dead."

Colonel Volpe leveled his ballpoint.

"Mr. Wylie."

"We pick up from there," Harrison Wylie said; he was the representative of the State Department's Research and Intelligence Bureau; he was looking at the next photograph: Shaman in Tu Do Street dressed in natty pinks with a major's leaves on his collarpoints and a Lucky Bar girl on each arm. "And I believe I am beginning to get a glimmering."

"So am I," said Baldwin, from the DIA, who had ridden with Colonel Volpe in the golf cart. "Especially the part about eighty-two percent operational success."

"We pick up again back on the peninsula," Wylie said. "Sorry, but this is the most detailed report we have. Or perhaps I should say the least fragmentary. He seems to have become progressively more skilled in covering his tracks. Well. After Macao our young man went back to the peninsula and linked up with the Montagnards. These are highlands elephant drivers and mountain hunters, quite fierce. In particular, a Cham tribe that continued its resistance after the war. I'm told that the Cham were at one time promised their own autonomous republic under the old regime, which may account for their tenacious hostility to the new regime. In any case, our young man fought with them for two years against the Reds, and has been credited with certain fiendish excesses perpetrated in a good cause. At the end of which time, the Cham butchered and roasted a buffalo in his honor and bid him a ceremonial farewell with many presents of silver and brass bracelets and anklets."

"We get the point," the DIA man said, looking at his watch. "This is too long."

"The rest are shorter," Harrison Wylie said coldly. "I believe I said this is the most detailed report we have, the remainder are fragments. They come from a variety of sources, not all reliable.

If all are to be credited, our young man has appeared and disappeared a dozen times, anywhere and everywhere east of Suez, and south too. I will simply pass on the reports and leave their evaluation to the infinite discernment of our impatient colleague."

"This is too long," Kaul said.

Wylie shut his eyes and shuddered.

"Six months after the Cham affair a man answering Shaman's description appeared at the head of a small assault force in one of those new radical-nationalist African nations and literally, à la Skorzeny, kidnapped the generalissimo. The body was never found. A democratic government was instituted. There!"

They were all grinning at him; he flushed and smiled.

"One report said he was hired as a consultant on terrorism, ambush, and torture by the Mossad Alyah Beth, but I think we can discount that. Another appearance was supposedly in Formosa, where he was engineering commando raids on the mainland just for the fun of it. Another and entirely different report had him recruiting crews to sail up the Yellow River in junks, on the theory that where river pirates could manage to evade Chiang's armies, modern-day irregulars could harass the ChiComs."

He went on for some time in a fragmentary fashion.

"Tentatively identified as a mercenary officer in Mozambique.

"Possible organizer of death squads for the Maharaja of Bhutan.

"Reported captured attempting to penetrate Ailul al Aswad.

"Leader of punitive expedition against West Irian bandits.

"Reputedly organizing right-wing coup in Pyongyang.

"Bodyguard with West Pakistan government in exile.

"Refused commission in Sierra Leone Creole Guard.

"Military advisor to the Sultan of Brunei.

"Wounded in the battle of Kuala Lumpur.

"Rhinoceros hunting on Kalimantan.

"Reported in Tonga Islands.

"Paid assassin.

"Hired gunman.

"Bank robber."

Several of the team members were openly laughing.

"Of *course*, it's obviously preposterous, or State would have pulled his passport quite a while ago, revoking his citizenship for serving a foreign power—except, in the main, why? The man seems to be involved generally in quite AntiCom activities. Who are we to object?"

Baldwin, the DIA man, stood up and tapped his ballpoint on the conference table.

"Gentlemen, I can add to this, and shorten it too, for that matter. I said earlier we buy our crap from the same people CIA does, and probably State too. We don't have to go into all these details. We know that ever since his discharge, Shaman has been knocking around, looking for fights. There's some like him after every war. Maybe not the usual mercenary, because he's a free-lancer, but the same idea. A trained professional soldier exercising his skills. As the colonel said, he's already in most of our files for one reason or another—we just didn't know he was the hijacker. Now we do. As a matter of fact, our agency knows even more, because we never retired our file. We knew he wasn't dead out there. Ours is recent poop on him because for the past several years he's been dealing in smuggled arms with our man Chien S'al in Dawitan. I have copies of the latest report for each of you."

"This is shortening it?" Wylie said acidly.

"In short, we all have a pretty good idea what Tim has in mind for this man. And I for one think it's well worth looking into. So let's quit fooling around and just *hear* about his Operation Kalitan. What have we got to lose? S.T.O.P. could *use* a coup."

"Those opposed?" Colonel Volpe said.

In the silence Kaul's hand rose slowly. He spoke slowly.

"The man is a murderer."

(*The nan is a nurderer.*)

Kalitan

Shaman stood in the doorway.

Two enormous U.S. Marines urged him a step forward and crowded in behind him; they flanked him; the S.T.O.P. team fixed him with stares ranging from censorious interest to gaping fascination; Colonel Volpe sighted on him with a ballpoint.

"I think were his wrists shackled, we could dispense with

Gog and Magog. No doubt they've got clearance, but the fewer ears, the fewer mouths."

"Less lips, less slips," the NSA man said. "Need-to-know, right?"

One of the Marines fumbled for handcuffs. Shaman obediently held his fists in front of him. He appeared innocuous enough in badly fitting khaki shirt, beltless trousers, and laceless shoes. Only Kaul noticed that his right fist was gripping his left thumb. Only Kaul saw the white knuckles and tensed arms, and shouted:

"Watch it!"

The tension broke like a cable snapping, and the two fists hit the two Marines in their two groins; they doubled over uttering identical exclamations; the backs of their pistol belts were grabbed and heaved as together they dove headlong at the table, arms and knees of seated S.T.O.P. members rising fendingly to meet them. Shaman was yelling:

"*I will not be bound!*"

Colonel Volpe blessed the air with three fingers, halting the Marines as they regrouped, clutching their truncheons.

"That will do." He jerked his head. "Dismissed."

"Don't need guards," Kaul said, hand inserted in his briefcase.

It was noticed that Shaman could not immediately readjust himself; what color there was in his face had drained away; he stood in an odd, compressed crouch.

The Marines were gone. Shaman sat down at the table without waiting to be invited; he was visibly controlling himself.

"Who are you people?"

"Special Tactical Operations Planning of Polwar Division of Counter Insurgency Command," Colonel Volpe said.

"Oh well. I never really expected to reach the Chiefs of Staff."

"We would like you to tell us about yourself."

"That would be bragging."

There was a stir and murmur. The reply seemed to tickle Harrison Wylie. He said: "We just heard all about your *exploits*."

"The floor will be open to random comments in due time," the colonel said severely.

Silence.

Colonel Volpe prayed with his fingertips propping his nose.

"Your *exploits* as a scholar, cryptologist, chess player, linguist, infantry soldier, combat commander, unconventional warfare expert, intelligence officer, staff tactician, freelance adventurer, rhinoceros hunter, pamboat pirate, et cetera, are known to us. We have all read the reports on you."

"Then they've done my bragging for me," Shaman said.

"Taking your scarcely credible dossier at face value, we must concede you a measure of expertise in both guerrilla and counterguerrilla operations."

"Isn't that what this is all about?"

"Also we have now all studied your plan which you style 'Operation Kalitan.' "

"Good. When do we start?"

"It is not up to us. S.T.O.P. proposes, CIC disposes. But we will return to Operation Kalitan in due time. First we will open the floor to general questions from those who require further information, as well as to random comment by those who find you simply intrigant."

Wylie blushed furiously. Some grinned. No one spoke.

"You don't have to mind this high-handed old Malaprop," Shaman said kindly. Wylie smiled at him.

"Informal conversation may also be of help to us in any decisions hinging on the open issue of your sanity," Colonel Volpe said sharply.

In the amused silence he prompted: "Gentlemen?"

The NSA man raised his hand.

"It is not necessary to raise your hand."

The NSA man said: "You invented this whole operation—this whole Operation Kalitan thing—yourself? And wrote it out on the sub?"

"That's right," Shaman said.

"What does *Kalitan* mean?"

" 'Shark' in the Bajau language."

"Would it be fair to ask, which side are you really on? Considering that a shark has no friends or foes, just victims?"

Shaman shrugged. "Call it something else, then. How about Operation Mertensia?"

Speaking of *Mertensia*, the commander from ONI was having difficulty sitting still.

"How the hell did you ever *dare?*"

Shaman grinned. "Is that a question or a reproof?"

"A twenty-five-million-dollar nuclear submarine! A United States Air Force jet! A conference with the Chiefs of Staff!"

"Audacity is what makes it work. Anything less and I wouldn't be backing my *barraka* all the way."

Then the questions came thick and fast.

"Were you really a pirate?"

"How many languages do you speak?"

"Whatever happened to your bomb?"

"Where the hell is West Irian?"

"Do you really expect us to buy Operation Kalitan?"

Shaman said: "That's why I came home."

"Did you really *not know* about the war?"

"Not until I heard about it."

"And that's when you decided to come home?"

"Somebody has to keep the world safe for whatever."

"All you know about the war is what you learned there on the sub?"

"What I learned on the sub is all there is to know about the war."

"Do you think they're beating us?"

"Not if I can stop them."

"What makes you think you can do any better than the U.S. Army?"

"What makes you think I could do any worse?"

Harrison Wylie said: "Considering your *vivid* reaction to those boys and their manacles, would you care to explain your unnecessary inhumanity to poor Captain Linebarger?"

"He could have managed. You can even take your pants off, once you get the fly open."

"Yes, but how *do* you get the fly open, and the *belt buckle?*"

Colonel Volpe raised a stern hand. "Let us suppose that you, Mr. Wylie, would have been pleased to help him. The subject is wholly irrelevant in any case. Let us continue."

The Army major was flapping a magazine in the air. "Didn't you use to write about urban combat in the *Infantry Journal?*"

"Years ago I heard they published some of my staff reports."

"About burning down the city to cover guerrilla unit movements?"

"Only the slums."

The NSA man was holding up his Xerox copy of Operation Kalitan.

"Why do you call it American Revolution Two?"

"Look around you."

"Who says it's part of a World Civil War?"

"Look around you."

Kaul said: "You kill that old man? You kill that son of a bitch in Basic? How many human beings have you killed? You enjoy killing?"

"To kill his enemy is the soldier's reward," Shaman said.

"Like to get *you* in that goddamn chair once," Kaul said.

The FBI man was without faith. "What if the PFA takes one look at you and swacks your head off?"

Shaman became all business.

"The transmissions from submarine to COMSUBFE, COMSUBFE to San Francisco, San Francisco to Washington, were all on PCM, the pulse-code modulator radiophone. If the PFA tapped that, all they know is that I am a hijacker. If they've tapped your agencies' files, which they doubtless have, all they know is that I am a former Army officer and later a freelance guerrilla. An ideal recruit for them. There's no reason for Red to suspect that I am a Blue infiltrator."

"Our man Salvatore infiltrated PFA Strategic Command. They chopped his head off."

"I'm all right unless they tap into Operation Kalitan."

Harrison Wylie made gestures of graceful horripilation. He said incredulously: "Even supposing they don't, how can you really think for a moment that one man, alone, single-handedly, could possibly escape from our side, cross no-man's land, penetrate Red lines, join their army, infiltrate their high command, and attack them from within?"

"Destroy them utterly from within," Shaman amended.

"It's one chance in a million."

"All it takes is one chance."

"Why would you take such an awful risk in the first place?

I mean, why should you do it at all? Don't tell *me* you care about keeping the world safe for whatever!"

"Let's just say I'm an old-line oligarch, trying to prevent the fulfillment of the promise of the machine age: the Urschleim shall inherit the earth."

To other questions he gave other answers.

The DIA man said: "I understand that you were able not only to penetrate Cavite in a sport fisherman, transship onto *Mertensia* unperceived, and stow away in the captain's cabin, but also to bring aboard your bag and baggage, personal weapons, and a small fortune in gold."

"What's the question exactly?"

"Well . . . where did you get all the gold, I suppose."

"That was only travel money. The rest is banked in Hong Kong."

"I gather you don't do all this fighting and killing for nothing."

"No, but I don't do it for the money."

"You do it just for the fun of it?"

"What else is there?"

"The floor is *closed*," Colonel Volpe said.

He switched off.

"Sly!" Wylie winked admiringly. "You didn't *say* anything."

"What happens now?" Shaman said.

"Unless you have some final remarks," Colonel Volpe said, "a transcription of this tape with a written report on our evaluation, plus a copy of your plan, go to Polwar Division, thence to Counter Insurgency Command, for its decision."

"I have some final remarks," Shaman said.

He rose from his place and walked around the table; their eyes followed; the briefcase was aimed at him as he moved; he stood staring at the map. Colonel Volpe switched on.

Shaman looked at the territorial United States and the details of northern Mexico and southern Canada, committing red and blue patterns to memory. He spoke with professional, no-nonsense calm.

"The United States Army has about nineteen divisions available for domestic counter-insurgency activities, also one air mobile and two paratroop divisions plus nuclear and miscellaneous arms.

All this in inventory at least, if not in actual action. Not even counting all your command genius and intelligence savvy in the White House, the Pentagon, Fort Meade, Langley, Warrenton, and umpty-umph places underground. The most powerful power on earth.

"The People's Liberation ragtagbobtail fighting it to a standstill has an unknown number of men, women, and children. As irregulars, they can be formed from innocent bystanders and helpless civilians into anything from snipers to guerrilla bands to fully manned battalions. And back again. Which is why you can't shoot the big guns. You can't fission-bomb them, you can't saturation-raid them, you can't bacteria-war them, you can't hammer-and-anvil them, you can't scorched-earth them—because they're the public. They are the American people.

"Nor can you defeat them in conventional ground war, assuming they would hold still for it. Remember our own government estimates during Second 'Nam? It cost us forty-five-thousand dollars to kill each Cong. Remember the British studies in Malaysia? It took ten to a dozen regulars to neutralize one guerrilla."

He looked at the blue map blotched with red like an itch or a rash or a widening pool of blood.

"You're all familiar with the tactics of World Civil War as raised to the status of high art by people's revolution after people's revolution in our century. Uproar east, strike west. Retreat, harass, raid, evade. You have studied Blitzkrieg and Volkskrieg. You have read Mao and Ho and Che and Chu Te and Giap. You know that Kudelak and the PFA have gone beyond them all. And yet you still sit around trying to hit smoke with a stick."

His voice became impassioned, apparently.

"The only way to fight guerrillas is to fight a guerrilla war with guerrilla tactics! The only way Blue is going to stop Red is with terror and double-cross and murder!"

The voice changed again; it had already changed a number of times, they realized. Now it was like a shrug.

"Operation Kalitan is a start. No risk, no cost to you. Just one man, one plan. If I succeed, you can close with the PFA and destroy it. If I fail, you'll never hear from me again. What have you got to lose?"

Colonel Volpe switched off.

"We'll be in touch," he said.

"The meeting will come to order," Colonel Volpe said. "All right, gentlemen, what's the consensus?"

"Preposterous. This man appears out of nowhere, with a ridiculous plan not just to infiltrate, penetrate, the rebel army, but to literally destroy it. Except he can't say how he intends to go about this until he has maneuvered himself into the right position—which he hasn't any idea about yet, but he'll know it when he sees it. I find it very hard indeed to swallow."

"Also, very complicated."

"And far out. Audacity is one thing. This is crazy."

"On the other hand, what if it works?"

"There is that. Even if it works limitedly. Who knows— maybe he could get lucky and do them some real damage before they chop off his head. We've sent out saboteurs before and lost them. Sometimes they blow up the ammo dump first."

"That's right. He said it. What have we got to lose?"

"*If* he has any intention of carrying out such a ridiculous scheme in the first place. Remember, this man is a maverick, an exile—very possibly a traitor or a lunatic. He hijacked a combat nuclear submarine. Maybe he dreamed up the whole thing to get himself off the hook. Wouldn't you?"

"It could be just a trick to escape from us and join the Reds."

"Yes, but what if it isn't?"

"It could be nothing but a pack of lies."

"Yes, but what if it *isn't?*"

Kaul suddenly exploded. "I'd like get *hin* in that goddamn chair!"

Colonel Volpe, fingertips to nose, assumed his pose of thoughtful prayer. "As a matter of fact, before taking the trouble to call this meeting—before simply dismissing him out of hand, in fact—I *did* put him in the chair. He was required to read the entirety of Operation Kalitan out loud, while being monitored."

"Yes? Well—what?"

"Rather inconclusive, I'm afraid. He wasn't lying, but he wasn't telling the truth either. Oddly enough, he didn't appear to register at all."

"Why not?"

"Probably a malfunction." Colonel Volpe prayed up at the ceiling. "The techs claimed no one was there."

Three days later Shaman was again escorted to the S.T.O.P. office. S.T.O.P. had submitted the plan to Polwar, and Polwar had submitted it to CIC under the title: "Proposed Counter-Insurgency Offensive Operation (Operation Kalitan)."

"What's the decision?" Shaman said.

"You're under arrest," Colonel Volpe said.

"Fifteen years," the judge said.

CHAPTER THREE
Passing Through

39618

Shaman was dreaming about boots.

In a dream that became more and more relevant as it went on he was waxing and buffing and spit-polishing a pair of old style combat boots. Spit-polishing boots was part of his being Soldier of the Month as was the white silk scarf he was entitled to wear instead of a necktie with his Class A uniform. Besides, he liked polishing boots, sitting there on his bunk after a long hard day, working along relaxedly with an empty mind. But neckties who were never Soldiers of the Month were beginning to gather around in their unpolished boots.

"Gung ho motherfucker!"

In the dream there was his unsurprised acceptance of being finally surrounded and trapped and bayed by wolves after a weary chase. It included a prior awareness of persecution and harassment: mess-hall jostlings, shortsheeted beds, sabotaged equipment, pilfered belongings, latrine fights, threats, and general abuse, all under the ringleadership of a big cracker son of a bitch named Yancy. Yancy with his I.Q. like his hat size and his fist size bigger than either.

"Stick them shahny boots right up yore ay-uss!"

In the dream was also his unsurprised awareness of the next, inevitable scene: Yancy and a posse of his Dixie degenerates beating up on the Soldier of the Month.

"Frail hell out of the brown-nose bastard!"

Relevant because when Shaman woke he realized his subconscious had gone digging in the time-suspended past looking for clues to a present problem. Last night before falling asleep he had been remembering Yancy in terms of Torox, the Super Patriot.

Same problem: same solution.

Enemy harassment: attack and destroy.

Yancy was dead now. One day near the end of Basic the company had walked out through the piny woods to the combat course. Everyone had to run the combat course at least once a week. Start off and sprint a few yards, crawl under barbed wire, jump up and shoot rifles at pop-up targets, dance over logs, climb a board wall, leap over a stream, duck under machine gun fire, charge up a slope, and throw hand grenades into a pillbox. Usually there were a few duds among the hand grenades, and Ordnance came by to sweep the pillbox area after the exercise was over. That day Shaman threw a hand-grenade-sized rock. Then the company was route-marched back to barracks through the pine woods in the deepening twilight. The field jackets the men wore, like the combat boots, were old QM style. They had hoods. Since helmets were worn on combat course days, the hoods hung down the trainees' backs. Guys were always putting asshole stuff in other guys' hoods on the march, stones, empty cigarette packs. Shaman walked silently on the fallen pine needles behind Yancy. He held the grenade under his coat and pulled the pin and counted seven and dropped the grenade in Yancy's hood and dove for the ditch. He saw Yancy's elbow in the air and his hand groping back irritably. Then the white flash and bang and gray smoke. No one else saw anything exactly. Later the investigation ruled somebody's wild throw on the combat course must have landed there unnoticed and hung fire unaccountably somehow, tragic mishap. No testimony was taken, or some of the trainees could have told a thing or two. The Dixieland band vowed vengeance but left the Soldier of the Month alone after that, with Yancy gone.

"His back was all over his front!"

* * *

Shaman woke after his dream, refreshed to the task. Instead of the stinking slab in his cell, he was on a soft white hospital bed. He was in the hospital where they had stitched up his scalp and held him overnight for observation, a routine precaution in case of concussion. He had a bulging forehead like a baby's and a whispering void that felt a yard wide between his ears, but the night had been good.

"Fake nausea, double vision, dizziness, and loss of memory," said a voice from the next bed, "and maybe we can work this thing for another good night's sleep."

Ralph Elf also had a cut on his scalp. They had shaved his topknot and stitched it and kept him overnight too. Shaman knew nothing about him except that he was a wiry little brown man who could move with eye-baffling speed.

"You saved my ass," Shaman said. "I owe you one."

"Don't mention it," Ralph Elf said. "Who did you say I saved?"

"Shaman. Three-nine-six-one-eight. You came in handy."

"I was really only field testing my calliocracker."

"So that's what that was."

"I was really only brushing up on my tamishiwara."

"So that's what *that* was."

"I'm a fourth dan Shotokan karateka," Ralph Elf said. "Why was it you said those guys were gang-stomping you?"

"They don't like my politics."

Ralph Elf rose on one elbow and peered.

"Wait, man, now I know you. You're the one that didn't want to be searched and got put in Maxwing for it. This time you're bucking for Polwing. Are you crazy?"

"I'm trying to get in with the Polfolk," Shaman said.

Polfolk were the political prisoners, in a separate wing, isolated from the Confolk in the other wings. The next step required Shaman to be in Polwing with the Polfolk, or it wouldn't work.

Ralph Elf said: "Man, don't you know, it's gruesome in there."

"I'll worry about that when I get in there."

"What's the bust?"

"Hijacking."

"That's not subversive activity, man."

"It was a submersible submarine."

"I mean, it has to be a political crime to get you into Polwing."

"What do you think I was trying to commit when you saved my ass?"

Then the trustee came with breakfast. Dry oatmeal and wet toast.

When he wasn't in the hospital, Shaman was in Two Wing with the Maxfolk. These were Confolk or non-political prisoners, but distinguished from their fellow felons by their violent ways and kept caged separately in the maximum security wing.

Shaman had earned his place in Maxwing his first day in the joint.

"Drop your pants and bend over."

He had already gone to considerable trouble to convince his escort party of two marshals that handcuffs were unnecessary and unacceptable. Now a guard with a rubber glove was proposing to search him for contraband.

"Come on, pretty boy, I ain't got all day."

His papers had been received, cross-indexed and filed, his new number assigned, his prison denims issued, his head shaved. All this in the reception center. Then next he had been led down concrete corridors and across an open space to the Spider.

The Spider was a huge hundred-year-old blackened brick building at the center of the prison complex. The center of the Spider was a vast green dome covered with a century of pigeon shit. The central hall under the dome was called the Rotunda and was the hollow body of the Spider. The five radiating wings were its legs. Around the inside circumference of the Rotunda were steel doors that crashed and clanged open and shut. Slouching files of men crossed and recrossed the circular space in chords and secants. Guards bellowed, guns glinted, bells rang, whistles blew.

In the center of this center of everything was a wooden table. On it was a jar of Vaseline.

Shaman stood goggling in nightmare disbelief at the guard with the rubber glove.

Passing inmates jeered and giggled.

"Inish-ee-yay-shun!"

"Save some for me!"

The guard with the glove bawled: "*Move*, you mother, or I'll search your mouth *last!*"

Shaman did not move, although his body seemed to have shrunk, coiled slightly, and his hands had flattened out, fingers tight together.

"All right, officers. Grab this fairy fuck and elevate his ass to the rafters."

It took eight guards five minutes. In the end he was stood on his head and searched for capsules of drugs, money, or other contraband anyway. But four of the eight were injured, three severely, one critically, and he had won his place. A loudspeaker voice from the height of the dome blared down:

"Put that fool in Maxwing! Christ on a crutch! Better soften him up first, for Christ's sake, before he mangles you all!"

"Croton oil," Shaman said. "It's a fixed oil, a vesicant, a pustulant, and a cataclysmic chemical purge. It takes a strongarm squad and a funnel to force-feed it to you. Then they lock you in the Box with a bucket. It all comes out in the end."

"I don't want any of that. I don't want any Boxlock or Maxwing or Polwing either," Ralph Elf said. "Man, you must be crazy."

Shaman came out of solitary five days later, feeble and docile and almost fatally dehydrated. After a turn in the hospital he was assigned to a cell in Maximum Security Two Wing, block 4, company B.

He was the sixth man in a six-man cell. As cellmates he had three muttering Hispanos who had started a mess-hall riot, a melancholy black embezzler who had fits of fury, and a fat man who had attacked a guard. All five were shanked down with sharpened screwdrivers, whetted pieces of steel, honed-down hacksaw blades, et cetera. Shaman crawled immediately into the empty bunk. The fat man would have tried to bugger him the first night, but the others were disgusted. The Hispanos said:

"*Pero, aún está corriendo caca, marano!*"

The next day he began learning the ropes. Bell at six, rise, wash, shave, clean cell. Wait. Breakfast bell, trick locking devices

crashing and clanging steel doors open tier by tier; walk to mess
hall guarded by guards with clubs and whistles. Bell, back to cell,
wait. Work bell, crash-clang, file to Rotunda, fall out for tag
shop, tailor shop, craft shop, laundry, kitchen. Eleven o'clock
bell, back to cell, wait. Lunch bell. Back-to-cell bell. Wait.
Work bell. Three o'clock quit bell, back-to-cell bell. Quad-out
bell, file out to yard, rest and exercise, socialize. Quad-in bell,
back-to-cell bell, supper bell, back-to-cell bell. Eight o'clock quiet
bell. Ten o'clock lights-out bell.

"Maximum monotony," Shaman said.

"It's better than interrogation pits in Polwing," Ralph Elf
said.

"Not if you know the answers," Shaman said.

He exercised. Up at five to do sit-ups, five, ten, fifteen as
his strength returned, then push-ups, knee bends, plus isometrics.
In the plodding lines he jogged in place, shadow boxing. In the
yard he raced around and around, sprinting, broken-field running,
broad jumping, high jumping over nothing. He joined other
exercise freaks and played handball with them on painted courts
and boxed and wrestled with them. In the overcrowded yard
their group was regarded with annoyed derision by the run of
Confolk, busy about their dealing and trading, courting, coquetting,
influence peddling, and drug pushing.

He worked. From eight to eleven o'clock each morning and
from one to three each afternoon he worked for thirteen cents
an hour in one or another of the work areas. From the kitchen
he stole a little vial of green food coloring, the stuff used in cake
icing. From the printshop he took a small quantity of red ink
and a stencil brush. From the tailor shop, where the prisoners'
uniforms were made, he took needles and thread and a square
of fabric. He completed his project secretly, cutting and hemming
the fabric in the tailor shop, washing, bleaching, and coloring it
in the laundry, painting the design in the kitchen, hiding in the
meat locker or in the dim-lit, cavern-vast potato cellar, where bats
lived in the ceiling. Eventually he was ready.

The exercise yard was an acre of hard-packed dirt, oiled down
each day to lay the dust of thousands of shuffling feet. It was
surrounded by four steel walls. At the four corners of the walls

were gun towers cased in armor and bulletproof glass and manned
by men with automatic weapons, horns, and searchlights. The
walltop walkways between the towers were manned by men armed
with shotguns and tear-gas grenades.

The Confolk called the yard Deathtrap. Against one wall
was a big box with a hinged lid. In this box were kept chess
and checker boards, handballs, softballs, bats, mitts, boxing gloves,
and other sports paraphernalia. The box was haunted. Once a
young con had grown tired of having his cellmates tie his hands
to the faucets of the sink and take turns fucking him every night.
Watching for his chance, he had climbed into the box. A guard
in one of the towers saw but slyly said nothing. To blow the
horn now would be merely to turn the boy out like an idiot.
Biding his time, the guard waited till after Quad-in, when the
yard was empty, then trained the tower's thirty-caliber machine
on the lid of the box and fixed it tight, screwing down the
versing wheel. Six o'clock supper bell. It grew dark. Eight
'ock quiet bell. Bedcheck time in the Spider. The boy thought
would be safe to come out. No one ever knew what the rest
of his plan was. The guard heard stealthy sounds. In the dim
glow of the security lights he saw the lid rise up about an inch.
"Escape! Escape! Escape!" he whooped, and hacked the boy's
brainpan off from the eyes up with an eighteen-round burst.

Now, Shaman stood on top of the haunted box.

It seemed an appropriate podium for a speech on the subject
of the wretched of the earth.

Spread across the acre of oiled dirt of Deathtrap were the
Confolk. Murderers, kidnappers, bank robbers, racketeers, swin-
dlers, tax evaders, gangsters, rapists, forgers, arsonists. The
wretched.

Strolling, gossiping, arguing, whispering, smoking, swapping
creep comics and jack books, kissing and rubbing in corners,
boxing, playing handball and stickball, or just standing and staring.
His audience.

A few nearby eyes looked up incuriously as he stood elevated
a few feet above them all. A few more glanced as he bellowed
in his loudest voice over the general noise:

"*Victims of fascism!*"

He reached under his prison jacket and brought out the flag

of the People's Republic of the United States, spreading his arms wide and unfurling it across his chest.

The green field symbolized the birth of the new freedom in forests and mountains. The red fist signified proletarian solidarity and blood sacrifice. The flag was visible from every point in the yard.

"How long will you let the pig hacks of Whoramerica climb to power and wealth on your backs?"

That was as far as he got. It took less than fifteen seconds to discover that he had made a serious miscalculation.

The immediate result was not an onrush of armed guards and his summary transfer to Polwing. The immediate result was Torox the Super Patriot.

He happened to be standing near the box, a thick, red-faced man with his cap on backward. At his first sight of the PFM flag he let out an outraged roar of militant Americanism that echoed across the yard. Instantly all eyes looked and saw, not him, but the flourished flag. Men came running from every direction.

Torox was screaming something over an uproar like the snarling and barking of dogs: entirely without distinguishable words but totally unmistakable in meaning. He stood at the head of the pack and tore his shirt wide open, scattering buttons. Tattooed across the full breadth of his chest was Old Glory, and the motto: Love It or Leave It.

A moment later Shaman was being gang-stomped.

"It still might have worked, except for you and your crazy calliope cracker."

"Calliocracker. That's cal-*li*-ocracker. It's my latest invention," Ralph Elf said. "Damn you, how the hell was I supposed to know it was a political demonstration? Man, you'd be in the morgue now except for me and my calliocracker."

"It wasn't supposed to be the star of the show. My flag was, till it got ripped to bits. I don't think the guards ever knew what was going on. Now I've got to start all over again."

Instead of riot squads charging in to grab him up and put him into Polwing for flying the PFM flag, Shaman had caught a fast glimpse of a wiry little brown man appearing out of nowhere to save his ass.

The man was lighting the fuse of what appeared to be a firecracker. Lighting and throwing and fighting all at once, moving with phenomenal rapidity, a whirligig of rabbit punches and karate shutos, his fizzing missile still in trajectory and then dropping among the scuffling feet of the patriots.

"You must have hit twenty guys just while the fuse burned," Shaman said with admiration.

Then the calliocracker, Ralph Elf's latest invention, ignited. It lay spinning on the ground, shrieking like a banshee and belching a yellow cloud of thick, stinking smoke. Amid the tangled knot of patriots absorbedly stomping Shaman and fending off the inexplicable little man, the effect of the smoke and noise was blind, howling panic.

Then the horns hooted, the sirens screamed, the whistles blew, the gas grenades fell from the walls, and the riot squads came charging into the yard to rescue Shaman and Ralph Elf and remove them to the prison hospital, where their scalps were stitched, and they were held overnight for observation.

"Excuse me for swearing at you like that just now," Ralph Elf said. "My head hurts worse than I thought."

"I guess that was some calliocracker after all," Shaman said speculatively. "What did you mean by your latest invention?"

"It's my trade," Ralph Elf said. "I'm a mad bomber."

Ralph Elf had made his first bomb when he was twelve. He was a kid with a chemistry set. He did all the kid experiments and then, when the chemicals that came with the set at Christmas ran out, he bought more by mail from a hobby supply company. There was no place on the order form where his age was asked. In due time a stink bomb exploded in assembly at his school. What made it a bomb was the little tin tube, emptied of bouillon cubes and filled with ammonium sulfide and a little wax-dipped firecracker, its fuse sticking out a hole in the cap. The explosion of the firecracker vaporized the ammonium sulfide and made the whole assembly hall uninhabitable for days. Ralph Elf's amazed sense of power and pride was too overwhelming for his twelve-year-old mind, and he was warped for life.

He made only two mistakes in his career. The first was when

a law-abiding chemical supply house in Pompton Lakes, New Jersey, reported a dangerous order to the authorities: nitric acid, sulfuric acid, and glycerine. Coming as it did at the end of a series of violent explosions in Ralph Elf's hometown, the report pointed more than a finger of suspicion at Ralph Elf. There was no hard evidence, but he was forced to take his hobby underground.

In the army he learned about hand grenades and satchel charges and C-4 and incendiaries and sabotage and demolitions. He served with the Special Weapons Section of the Ninth Volunteer Infantry in the Chilean Intervention, was a good soldier and drew no notice. Back again in civilian life, he studied up on radio and electronics and found a good job as arsonist for the Syndicate, devastating competitive enterprises all across the country with elaborate devices such as counters, photocell switches, moisture sensors, heat and cold sensors, capacitively operated relays, and multiple-pulse sequential systems.

"The second mistake was taking on freelance jobs," Ralph Elf said. "Don't ask me why, I never needed the money, and I'm not one of those kinks who gets his rocks off burning or blowing things. To me, it's the professional challenge. It was all right when it was just an odd job or two on the side, a store, a dry cleaner now and then. Accounting departments for embezzlers covering their tracks, a couple of factories for the labor organizers, no harm done. But then they started this People's thing, I swear I never had anything to do with it. I'm a technician, not a revolutionary. But there I was, somehow, with this beautiful plant in the Pittsburgh National Guard Unit motor pool, all laid in to torch their tanks and ammunition. It was lovely, a beautiful setup. Battery radio receiver with an initiating relay and heating coil activated by the relay, powdered magnesium piled around, and PETN primacord running to the ammo dump. And me a couple blocks down the road in a van with the transmitter, and twenty skillion SWAT cops with walkie-talkies and tommy guns. I didn't even know what happened until my trial. They snitched me out. It wasn't even a spy or an FBI agent. It was the PFM's. I will never understand it. Paid me in advance and then snitched me out. So there it was. And here I am."

Shaman said thoughtfully: "I was having a dream this morning just before I woke up. I owe this man Torox one too. How would you like to come in handy again?"

"Meaning what?"

"Can you make a real bomb, besides those calliocrackers?"

"I can make any kind of bomb, anywhere, anyhow, any time," Ralph Elf said. "If you don't think so, just help me work this concussion for one more night so's we can sneak into supply and check out these lovely chemicals hospitals always have."

Then the prison doctor came on his rounds.

"I have got nausea, double vision, dizziness, and loss of memory," Shaman said.

"So do I," Ralph Elf said.

The prison doctor was a mottled, red-eyed, alcoholic-looking man with many weary years' experience in first aid to traumatic injuries. He looked at them with sad exasperation.

"Are you both perfectly certain that you do?"

"I certainly do," Shaman said.

"I do *too*," Ralph Elf said.

"The funny thing is, I *really* do," Ralph Elf said when the doctor had left. He began laughing immoderately.

Two days after they were discharged—Shaman to Maxwing and Ralph Elf to the psychiatric ward for further observation—Torox the Super Patriot was having a smoke in Deathtrap surrounded by his buddies.

"I just came to say no hard feelings and God bless America," Shaman groveled.

There was a large hole cut in his pants pocket.

"Fuck off, you dirty fucking red Commie afterbirth. You're dead. God can't help you now," Torox said.

Shaman opened his hand and the bomb slithered gently down inside the leg of his loose prison pants and fell gently on the oiled dirt.

"Good-bye, then."

Shaman was gone.

It was potassium chlorate. Made from bleach and Sani-Flush from the hospital supply room, crystallized into pearly scales in the hospital lab, and decanted into a urine-specimen bottle. Torox glanced down to see it between his feet. It exploded and split him from the testicles almost to the sternum. Several of his buddies were slightly hurt by flying glass.

Everyone knew who had done it, and the Confolk thought Shaman was on his way to a murder trial when guards led him away to the Rotunda. But the evidence was slim and circumstantial, and there was enough to do without following up on every corpse in Deathtrap. The loudspeaker voice said:

"What's he doing in Maxwing with loyal Americans, anyway? Christ on a crutch! Wasn't he the man with the PFM flag? Put him into Polwing where he belongs, for Christ's sake, before he turns this place into a commune."

ABCD-ETC

The steel door slid closed from left to right with a crash behind him. Two athletic young men in tee-shirts like camp counselors close-marched him down a hall. On either side were solid steel doors with judas slots. Up an iron staircase. Down another hall. Blazing wire-caged light bulbs in the ceiling. More steel doors in diminishing perspective. One door stood open. Cell 266.

"Good evening."

The heavy steel door, concrete floor, windowless walls, welded slab bed, flush toilet, and small sink were standard strip-cell equipment in solitary-confinement blocks. The table and chair, coffee containers, transistor radio, and red and blue file folders were not.

"Welcome to Polwing."

He was an unnaturally clean and austere-looking young man wearing a kind of blouse with a high neck. He had large grave eyes the color of tombstones, and his sparse hair was slicked back flat. Cool, small pale hands lay on the table like slim, twin fish.

"My name is Spofford. I am your adjustment officer."

The two camp counselors let go of Shaman's arms, smiled at him, then turned and went out, shutting but not locking the door.

"I try to make first interviews as informal as possible. You can say anything you like, and so can I. It's all off the record.

We're not being monitored. If you want, I'll turn on the radio, and there's a way to jam the toilet so it flushes continuously, in case you don't believe me. We'll be bugging you most of the time hereafter, but not this time. I'm on my coffee break. I brought one for you, cream and sugar, if you want it. Sit down. Sit on the bunk."

Shaman sat on the bunk. Spofford sat at the table.

"Please don't think I'm threatening you, because I'm not. It's a help to both of us if you know certain basic facts immediately. As a new student you're probably wondering just what kind of place this is and how much you can get away with. The answer is *nothing*. Security is very tight, you'll be in close custody at all times. Don't be misled by appearances. For one thing, this cell, like all our cells, is a solitary-confinement cell, but you won't be in solitary, unless you break the rules. Then it becomes an *oubliette*. Let me show you what I mean."

He rose and went out, locking the door. He was gone five days.

He came back and sat down.

"Gradations of corrective counseling only begin with this type of isolation. They range from Contemplation, which consists in revoking the student's Convocation privileges, to Expiation, which consists in revoking blanket, mattress, light, clothing, food, and water. That is, from being alone for a while, to living like an animal starving in the dark. As a last resort there are also the pits in the subcellar. I hope it doesn't become necessary in your case. You should be getting food soon now. Students are served individually in their cells twice a day. Although there aren't really any *days* here, are there?"

Shaman's face was a little haggard, and he had grown an etiolated fuzz of beard.

"That was Contemplation?"

"No. Contemplation is for students who need time to sit down and think things out, ask themselves why they aren't responding better to their educational opportunities. They aren't allowed radios and reading matter. I hope they helped pass the time, by the way."

"The radio doesn't work."

"No, transistors rarely ever do in here. You could have listened to our news reports about guerrilla bands being annihilated, couldn't you? But you read the files, didn't you?"

"I read them."

"The blue folder contains abstracts from your military record and the presentence report provided to your trial judge. You're lucky he gave you *only* fifteen years. The red folder contains our information, with many of the particulars you'll be confessing to."

Spofford was sitting behind the table. Sometimes as he spoke his hands floated up, curving and darting gently. Shaman sat cross-legged on the bunk.

"I confess," he said. "Where do I sign?"

"It's a little like psychoanalysis," Spofford said. "You have to really *believe* before confessing means anything."

He seemed to sigh at the long job ahead. The hands were hovering over the folders, fingertips nibbling.

"A confession wouldn't interest us at this point. It wouldn't be sincere. It wouldn't fool us. As for me, I have some strange doubts of my own."

The hands settled weightlessly on the folders and lay still.

"We've got quite a jacket on you. I've been reading it all. But we'll come back to that later. I didn't finish telling you about Polwing."

"You didn't even finish your coffee."

"As I said, I'm your adjustment officer, and this first interview is to help me assess your case so I can recommend the correct rehabilitation procedures. You'll be seeing me from time to time as you progress. That's my job. But there's another reason. I'm also here to tell you there's no hope. As an intelligent, educated man, certainly you can understand that. Then *why?*"

"I don't understand that," Shaman said.

"Let me put it another way. Let's talk about Maxwing, the Spider, the whole joint. Six men in a cell designed for two. Thugs, killers, rapoes, pukes, and punks. Souls and bodies bought and sold for a pack of cigarettes or a pinch of dope. Riots, rapes, knives, razors, rats, cockroaches, beatings, monotony. A penal philosophy designed to emasculate strong men and destroy weak ones. But there's one thing about it. It's legal. It's constitutional. Imprisonment is an expression of the just censure of an ordered society. That society reserves for itself the right of ruthless suppression but *within* the law, and you can survive. Build your rep, show guts and cool, and probably the inmates will let you live. Do your own time, keep your nose clean, and probably the authorities will let you out some day. There is hope."

The slim, twin fish swam slowly together, clung, mated, and sank to the tabletop.

"But that is not Polwing. Here we have no overcrowded cells. No riots, no mess-hall murders, no sodomy, no drugs. Here, instead of solitary we have Contemplation. Instead of punishment, corrective counseling. Instead of screws, pig hacks, and bulls, we have sociologists, psychologists, and educators. We have convocations and adjustment seminars. But what is the one thing about Polwing? It is *not* legal, it is *not* constitutional. It may be the inevitable response to the political needs of our time, but it is *not* within the law. It is an illegal circumvention of the problems caused by overloaded courts, stupid or lazy judges, corrupt lawyers, negotiated justice, preposterous civil rights legislation, and obsolete law enforcement policies. Legally we can do nothing to you. *Illegally* we can do anything we wish! And that is why there is *no* hope here."

Shaman stretched and sighed. "So I've heard."

"Exactly!" Spofford exclaimed. "You *know* all this. You *know* we can keep you in Polwing all your life till you confess—and when you do, it's a *life sentence!*"

"What's the point of this?" Shaman said.

"The point is: Why? You wangled your way into Polwing on purpose. You're no revolutionary, let alone a suicide. Why, then? *Why?*"

"Just passing through," Shaman said.

"Very funny. It doesn't matter. You'll confess soon enough."

"I told you. I read it. Where do I sign?"

"Yes, that too, subversive activities, PFM flag, Torox." Spofford sighed. "But not yet. We'll be needing a little more confession than that now, won't we? For example: *What's behind all this?* I'm afraid it's going to take a whole new bill of particulars before you even go to trial, isn't it?"

"What trial?" Shaman said.

"Article Four, Trial by Jury. You want your rights, don't

you? Incidentally, the prescribed penalty for failing to shave during Contemplation is three days on Expiation. I'm sorry about your meal. They don't seem to have come around yet, have they?"

Then the two camp counselors came in, and this time took away the chair, table, radio, old coffee containers, blanket, mattress, pillow, towel, soap, razor, everything, and shut off the light and the water.

He was alone. Not even the sound of footsteps going away.

Without warning something came at him out of the blackness. Cold as ice. *You could die.*

Laugh it off, fool. Nothing is real.

Shaman lay in silent darkness, frightened at how frightened he suddenly was.

Dark blank blind black.

Fight it!

Control.

Think. What do you know?

Stygian. Cimmerian. Camera obscura. Eyes light retina. The human eye weighs about a quarter ounce, diameter about an inch. Light comes in through the cornea, through the anterior chamber, through the pupil. Pupil from *pupilla*. They used to think the tiny reflection in someone else's eye looked like a little girl. Through the iris muscle and the lens, through the camera obscura to the retina, upside down and smaller. In the human eye there are seven million cones, a hundred million rods, to see light. Light. When there is none—

Cold black ice. Death. You could die.

I never knew that.

Fight it!

Mind's eye. Use the time. Concentrate.

Drop tables. Hollow-point 165 grain boat tail 3006 over 57 grains of 4370 in 26-inch barrel zeroed for 300 yards shoots above and below line of sight as follows: 2.3 inches above at 50 yards, 4.5 above at 100 yards, 5 at 200 . . .

Good.

Memory. Review. Reflect.

Use the time.

PFA battalion combat team setup, about one thousand men:

three infantry rifle companies, one heavy weapons company, one field artillery company, headquarters and headquarters company, medical section, intelligence section, political section, all under tactical headquarters of sector command.

Good.

Fight it.

Control!

"You had it easy," Tronche said. "Every time they put me in Expiation they spray my hands with fluorescent stuff. They come around all the time with a black light, is my dong lighted up? The prescribed penalty for jerking off in Expiation is three more days in Expiation, for God's sake! What else is there to do?"

Tronche had been the head of a Bonnot-style gang, bank robbers for the PFM Expropriations Committee. Eight or nine other men were in the room, sitting on the floor or leaning against the white walls, looking at Shaman, not talking. It was a large, square room with no furniture or equipment except a television camera with a fish-eye lens in the exact center of the ceiling. There were no guards.

Shaman sat on the floor in a corner, his back in the angle, squinting up. He had had food and water, but not enough of either yet. His vision was blurred and he spoke with difficulty.

"Convocation?"

"Happy hour, that's right," Tronche said. "Watch out what you say, though, there's mikes."

Shaman shrugged, sticking his tongue out, oversized and discolored. He made deaf and dumb gestures.

"That's no dice," Tronche said. "You got to talk or it's the pits. We're supposed to drop stuff."

Another man straightened himself off the wall and approached. Shaman recognized him too from the fast briefing delivered by Spofford in a painful blaze of sudden light. This man said:

"What Tronche means is, Convocation is supposed to be unstructured conversation, but on topics of interest to the Nazis. Everything said is recorded and meticulously collated by intelligence experts for valuable information, and also by your adjustment officer for incriminating evidence. You must talk, but try not to say anything damaging to your own interests or traitorous to the Cause."

"Don't know anything," Shaman said.

"That's too bad. We were hoping for news from the outside."

The other men were moving in close to listen.

"How's the war?"

"Who's winning?"

"Most of us have been here quite some time," the man said. He was a tall, glossy black with steel spectacles. "This is Tronche, Charley Prinx, Senator Williams, the rest of the Polfolk on our corridor. I'm RAM. We'd really appreciate anything you can tell us."

"I was overseas. Then Maxwing," Shaman said. "You tell me."

He was swallowing painfully. The men looked at each other and nodded. They closed ranks, bending over him, backs to the TV camera, and one man produced an orange. RAM smiled, his glasses winking.

"Proletarian solidarity."

Shaman understood that it was offered as payment.

"I saw a map," he said. "Give me a minute."

He ate the orange.

An old man, flimsy and fragile, his face like a gray cardboard cutout, sat down beside him slowly and carefully. His left leg was strapped into an orthopedic brace to the knee, his foot in a metal stirrup.

"I am Senator Jay Walker Williams, I'm sure you remember me. They keep us in total ignorance here. We are cut off from public life, the need for news is a ravening hunger. New arrivals are our only source."

A toneless voice spoke from nowhere in particular.

"Students will talk at all times on approved topics."

The senator had been whispering, the men listening silently.

"The topic is Convocation, for the new man's benefit," RAM said in a loud voice, apparently addressing the camera. "You know, recreation, free time, social therapy and all that. Anyone care to comment?"

"I'm just glad to be here!" the man named Prinx said fervently.

"Charley's a coopérant." The others laughed. "Old Charley, always bucking for parole."

Prinx was the campus radical, caught picketing the NPROTC building with pockets full of PFM flyers and a bottle of acid. Not really hard-core.

"It's the old good-guy, bad-guy crap," a man said bitterly. "Your adjustment officer slaps you in solitary, MacBitch lets you out to Convocation, until they slap you in again. In and out, in and out. It's to brainwash you crazy."

"MacBitch?" Shaman said.

"The top Nazi, we call him that. He runs the evaluation team. We call it interrogation. He asks the questions. You'll see soon enough," the bitter man said. Vice president of a small sporting goods company, he had been caught with a Coupe de Ville full of unregistered shotguns and was still trying to reverse his conviction on a technicality: illegal search. The others called him Writ Writer.

He roared at the camera: "MacBitch, you bastard! You don't fool me!"

Another man had been a counterfeiter for PFM Economics Section. "Convocation is where, if they don't know already, you're supposed to hang yourself out of your own mouth."

Another was a deserter from INTERFORCE, trained in counter-guerrilla techniques at the Escuela de las Américas in Panama and sent south as politico-military advisor to a series of caudillos, comandantes, and presidentes, until he cracked under the strain of burning villages and tying people's heads up in bags of quicklime. He was appealing to the ceiling:

"A chance to atone! To unburden the heart!"

"That's enough about that." RAM smiled. "Sometimes it gets like a regular hallelujah meeting in here. How about that orange now, wasn't it refreshing?"

Shaman said: "I saw a map."

Everyone became quiet to listen.

"I can't tell you much. There were overlays, and I saw the latest. You seem to own everything higher than thirty-five-hundred feet. The Cascades, the Sierra Nevadas, the Rocky Mountains. In the East, parts of the Alleghenies, some of the central Appalachians away from the population centers, practically all the New

England mountains above Boston. Plus sanctuaries in Canada and Mexico. You also own most of the woods, swamps, and deserts. When I say own, I mean control. I'm not sure you could call them occupied zones, just big red blotches. You raid roads, cut powerlines, blow bridges, railroads, ambush Vols, hold a few towns, probably run things pretty much your own way. But the blue arrows and blue hedgehogs are everywhere too, and a map shows only a given moment. Guerrilla wars aren't fought for territory anyway. That comes later."

"But we're winning!" someone whispered.

"You've won a lot of frozen peaks and wild wilderness, damp swamps and dry deserts like what's left of southern New Mexico since the Meltdown," Shaman said. "Don't forget, the mid-continent was mostly empty in the first place; only about a seventh of the population lived there anyway. The U.S. is its coasts. You can fight a guerrilla war in the bayou backwoods or in upper Montana, but you can't win a revolution."

He slumped back in his corner and rubbed his eyes. "I can't talk now. My throat hurts. I'm hungry and thirsty."

Immediately the toneless voice from nowhere in particular said *"Meal time."*

The Polfolk stared from Shaman to the ceiling in startled surmise.

Shaman ate in his cell.

He looked up to see large gray eyes the color of tombstones at the judas slot. He said:

"What the hell did you do that for? Now they think I'm a plant."

"The map, that was the important thing. They were very interested, weren't they?" Spofford said.

The slot slammed shut.

No one spoke to him.

But it was that afternoon, if it was afternoon, after lunch, if it was lunch, that he found out what Convocation was all about.

"The topic is, the progress of the Revolution," RAM said. "Anyone care to comment on that?"

"I would," Writ Writer said to the camera. "Shaman two-six-six appears to think the Revolution is a bunch of robber bandits in the boondocks—he seems to think they're dragging ass! In my experience I would have said exactly the opposite. I wish *we* went to the mountains! In my day the mistake we made was Immediatism. The goal was mount more and more military actions right away. Strike at the nerve centers! Build up more and more strength! More and more powerful forces! Unite in the final attack! Our trouble was, we were so Immediate, we never waited to consider the strategic or political realities. All we knew was Down with the Government!"

"How true, how very true," Charley Prinx said. "Who can tell what might have happened if the PFM had truly sought the support of the people in the areas of their operations? Instead, they and their Immediatistic military forces have constantly resorted only to indiscriminate violence, rapine, extortion, robbery, assassination, reprisals, kidnapping, and terrorism. I am constantly amazed that I was an associate of persons capable of such deceit. I broke with them when it became obvious that their only plan was chaos! It was then, it was then," he sobbed, "it was then that I was arrested by a terrible mistake!"

"I am Senator Jay Walker Williams, I'm sure you remember me." The senator was making an oration. "I supported Mister Nicolai Kudelak as Liberation Party candidate for the presidency before the party was outlawed. You all recall the elections, I am sure. The last gasp of the democratic process. Forty thousand demonstrators in the capital, marching against the famine and demanding modifications in an electoral process keeping the same old elite in power. Firehoses and mace and tear gas, followed by elections with doctored voting lists, armed guards at the polls, electoral police reading everyone's ballot, boxes filled before the voting began, ballot counting in the Pentagon—"

"Yeah, and how *about* this Kudelak anyway?" Tronche said. "The big savior and like that. He's supposed to be George Washington and Simón Bolívar and Stalin and Mao and Ho Chi Minh and Che Guevara rolled into one—what's *he* doing nowadays? Last I heard, he was only a Liberation Party figurehead the PFM put up, supposed to be up in the mountains doing great things. Anybody heard from him, except manifestos and guerrilla manuals and stuff? Anybody *seen* him? Not me!"

"Oh, Kudelak—I never even *heard* of him!" the deserter said. "Happiness, peace, no more blood, no more torture, is all I wanted. Haven in my own native land. But I came home to violence and upheaval everywhere. Cities burning. Entire communities destroyed. New widows and orphans every day. Mysterious struggles and vengeances. Men abducted from their homes, never to return. Mutilated bodies in dark alleys and sunlit meadows. Anarchy! Apocalypse! I didn't understand. I *don't* understand. I never *will* understand! Why am *I* in Polwing?"

"You? You? *I'm* innocent! Sweet Badass's song!" RAM limped, shuffled, grimacing and grinning. "All I done was forge a check. I was a *ree*-porter. I was a maga-*zeen* writer. I told them, man, don't pay no mind to that Comminist line. It's the wave of the *past*. I wrote, 'The People's Liberation Movement must fight for class solidarity over race antagonism independently of the bourgeois democratic electoral appeasement politics of the CPUSA.' Said that! Said that, yes I did! Motherfuck Nazis rolled down on me anyway! Hoo-eee!"

Shaman said: "What the hell is this?"

It went on.

"My only crime was . . ."

"The mistake I made was . . ."

"I have never advocated . . ."

"I am not now nor ever have been . . ."

"Terrible, terrible mistake . . ."

Shaman crossed the room.

He held Senator Williams by the shirtfront, kicked his legs out from under him and lowered him gently, carefully, to the floor, an old man amazed and paralyzed with fear. Shaman loosened the brace at knee and ankle. The Polfolk saw and fell silent and looked on, but did not become involved.

Shaman stood under the camera.

"Spofford, get me out of here!" he croak-shouted upward. "What is this shit? Where's the Revolution?"

He swung the brace with its tangle of straps and buckles and smashed the camera in an eruption of sparks.

Shaman sat cross-legged on the bunk. A lamp shone in his eyes. His face was a white mask. It showed no sign of plans gone wrong.

Spofford sat at the table. His hands undulated aqueously.

"So you didn't think much of our revolutionaries."

"Losers. Cheese eaters. Comedians. That's not who Ho meant."

"Ho who?"

"When the prison doors open, the real dragon will fly out," Shaman quoted. "Ho Chi Minh. Prison writings."

"I see. Real dragons like Senator Williams, or do you mean Torox?"

"Real revolutionaries. The general jail population."

"Niggers, crooks, and Commies," Spofford said. "That's PFM recruitment policy anyway, isn't it? Jailbirds of the world, unite, you have nothing to lose but your chains."

"When the system's a prison, everybody's a jailbird."

"Good heavens, slogans! It's no good trying to sound as if you're a *real* rebel, you know. I don't believe a word of it. You're no revolutionary, you're a loner."

"I don't listen to losers talking about lost causes."

"Obviously you don't share their viewpoint."

"What viewpoint? If all you really know about the People's Freedom Movement is what those poor feebs tell you, no wonder you thought they could make me believe Red can't win."

"Do you?"

"Don't *you?*"

"Should I?"

"Hold it," Shaman said. "Who's asking what, exactly?"

"Oh, we're not bugged, this is purely informal. Go ahead, tell me, it's fascinating. *Can* Red win? Why do you call it Red that way, like a roulette game?"

"Red-force, Blue-force, why not? It's handy. It's map talk, movements, positions, tactics. Not politics—that's not my business. I'm a soldier, remember? I don't give a rat's ass, just so I'm on the winning side."

"Your comrades don't think you are, do they?"

"Those poor bastards gave up when the Revolution didn't succeed in one attack on the palacio. They think it failed. But it doesn't work that way. People's revolutions don't go from A to Z overnight anymore, if they ever did. But they don't fail either. They go from A to B to C to D, et cetera. It takes small gains, long years, and Asian patience. But they don't fail. Not anymore. Not in our century."

"Though, of course, *you* don't give a rat's ass."

"I see what I see."

"Tell me, convince me. I'm fascinated."

"Take that goddamn light out of my face," Shaman said. "Is that supposed to make me talk or something? Why the hell do amateurs think they always have to shine a light in your face, would you mind telling me that?"

"You've got blackheads," Spofford said, "all around your nose."

"No kidding?" Shaman said. "Also dandruff, dermatitis, prison pallor, halitosis, body odor, iritis, muscae volitantes, malnutrition, advanced ketosis, and general debility. What did you expect?"

"Tell me about the winning side."

"I'm here to learn, not teach. Put me in with the hard-core, hard-case guerrilla fighters you haven't castrated yet, and maybe we'll both learn something."

"Don't I just wish I could, though?" Spofford sighed. "It's out of my hands now. You've been turned over to MacBitch."

The white mask. The white mask showed no sign.

"Good. I'm way behind schedule already. Let's get this trek back on the track."

Black ice.

5,4,3,2,1,0

MacBitch had no feet. They had been shredded by the detonation of a homemade booby trap in the White Mountains. He still had the shaven-skulled, lean and ready look of a combat field commander, but shadowed over now with bitterness.

Other soldiers and civilians were in the room, but Shaman could not see them clearly because of the light shining in his face.

MacBitch said: "Officer Spofford tells us you are playing a clever game."

Shaman said nothing.

"For one thing, he tells us you are not known to hold any

position or rank in the People's Freedom Movement. In fact, you do not seem to be known to the PFM, or to anyone else. For another, he says you show little or no political knowledge, and less ideology. For a third, you have been in Asia and Africa for many years, and have never so much as seen our war. Officer Spofford is mystified. He does not believe you are a revolutionary at all."

Shaman said nothing.

"Perhaps you are a good soldier misled by ignorance or romanticism."

Shaman said nothing.

"Perhaps reinstatement at your former rank with full pay and allowances would restore your primary allegiance," MacBitch said.

Shaman said nothing.

Shadows came and went on MacBitch's embittered face.

"Let me explain this war to you, as one soldier to another. As an infantryman and an officer, you will understand. It is a strange, sad war, and you cannot fight it as war should be fought. The enemy is no enemy as you understand it, yet you know he is your enemy, you know he is there, everywhere."

Aching knobs fidgeted prosthetic contraptions beneath the table.

"You receive reports, and you go to investigate. You find burning buildings, dead policemen and soldiers. You see crude posters and slogans on the walls. Equipment has been stolen. There are no young people anywhere, only old people and children. No one knows anything, it is all over, you are too late, there is nothing to do now. You return to your base. It has been attacked during your absence. It has been destroyed, and fellow soldiers are dead, friends are dead."

Outside the focus of light was an uneasy shuffling and mur-muring.

"It is the same every day, growing worse. In the country, no road is safe from ambush. Your convoys are fired upon from nowhere. There are rockslides in the cuts and bombs under the bridges. In the cities and towns, explosions kill and wound people, and incendiaries set fire to houses and automobiles. But the enemy is gone. He has escaped, or has become part of the population again. He has vanished, like a leaf in the forest, or a droplet of water in the ocean."

MacBitch had begun to speak in a piercing, saw-toothed voice. The others murmured soothingly: Now, now. MacBitch said:

"It is strange. You have a complete modern war machine, the enemy has nothing. You have bombers, helicopters, rockets, artillery, tanks, everything. The enemy has hunting rifles, sticks of dynamite, and obsolete Antonin-K submachine guns. You have superior ground forces, superior weaponry, superior organization. Yet you are fooled and defeated everywhere, at every turn. Why?"

He was not looking at anything. It used to be called the thousand-yard stare.

"Why do you permit these things to happen? Why do you permit such tricks to succeed when they can be prevented? Why do you not execute whole towns? Why do you not hold hostages and take reprisals for each rebellious act? Why do you not use torture, terror, and murder against an enemy who uses them against you? Because you are an *idealist!* You are an *American!* Even if you had the troops to occupy and mop up this vast land of mountains and valleys and forests, what then? Mop up who? The American people?"

Then he was yelling.

"But then one day something happens, and you think, Yes! Why not? Destroy them all! Your modern war machine is not modern after all, in this newest kind of war which you must fight against an entire population, innocent and guilty alike. *Kill everyone!*

"Too extreme? Too drastic? No, no, no! Not at all! Let me tell you about this war! You find a bunker! For once you engage the enemy, the foe run to earth at last! You attack, you charge! You are a hero! You fight, you win! You capture the bunker! And now you discover why you must never stop until you have *killed them all!*"

He was whispering.

"You find seven corpses in Woolrich hunting shirts. Their weapons are gone. They fought to the end to allow one survivor to escape with the weapons, to use again another time. They died unarmed, booby-trapping their own bodies—to blow your feet off at the first kick!"

Shaman said nothing.

MacBitch shrieked: *"The curse of God on them all! No mercy!"*

A hand appeared horizontally, glowing in the light, patting him on the shoulder: There, there.

MacBitch spoke aside: "Let the record show that appeal was made to military honor and camaraderie. Let the record show appeals were made to patriotism and reason. The response was nonchalance."

Somewhere out of the light an old typewriter chunk-chunked a dozen or so laborious words.

"Officer Spofford has grounds," MacBitch said. "We will help Officer Spofford to discover what is behind all this."

First came the pits. The pits were in the subcellar, under webby, dusty, stone cross vaults. In the stone floor, steel lids like manhole covers. Under the lids, manholes, or almost. Almost man-sized, but a little too narrow, just a little too shallow. Shaman's hole was cylindrical, like a sump tank, lined with boiler plate. It held his arms to his sides but not too tightly, kept his knees and his neck bent but not too much. With the lid bolted down he could almost straighten his back, but not quite. With the lid down there was little air, less sound, and no light at all. In the darkness he crouched crippledly with his knees and neck and back bent. The steel lid bore down on his skull, his feet shuffled in filth. Sleep was fainting from suffocation and exhaustion. Waking was the agony of new cramps and spasms from fainting and falling with no place to fall. Excreting was adding to the filth that splattered his feet and legs. Hunger, thirst, and weakness were other problems.

In the kishka, or blind gut, no one pain is unbearable, and none is worse than any other. The pain is general. But it never stops, and in the kishka there is no end of time.

Can't breathe.

Fight it.

What do you know?

Strangulation asphyxiation choking. Only 4.2 pounds of choking pressure to block the jugular veins. Eleven pounds of squeeze to close the carotid arteries. Thirty-three pounds and up

to throttle the windpipe. Use a rope. Jump off a chair. As an intelligent, educated man, you can understand that there is no—
  No!
  Concentrate.
  Speed of sound 1087 feet per second, for arty purposes, 365 yards a second, mile in 5 seconds.
  To orient a map that does not have a pivot-point protractor, align compass sighting wire over north-south gridline and rotate map and compass using declination diagram.
  Tracking over dry grass, leaves, lie down at ground level and look across for dents. Look see eyes sight blind—
  Fight.
  Eyes embryonic two lateral stalks and bulbs from the brain, vestigial third eye remnant in human pineal stalk, three-eyed lampreys, eels, cyclostomes, primitive fish—
  Water.
  No, no!
  Waves deeps drops darks.
  Ocean.
  One-hundred-forty-million square miles of ocean as compared to 57 million square miles of continents and islands. That is, 71 percent and a bit more of the surface of the globe covered by water, or 14 times the amount of land above sea level. The deepest place is 35,400 feet. Down, down, down there's only mysterious lights. Lycoteuthis with long tentacles glimmering blue and white. Lamprotoxu with feelers glowing gray-green. Lophius anglers with luminous cartilaginous rods. They make light with luciferase, an enzyme, and go drifting by in the dark. Down, down, down below where no light ever was, vipers, dragon fish, gulpers, swallowers, eaters of what sinks dying down. Down at last, down, in the canyons of the unimaginable bottom, unknowable in stone cities and immemorial bogs of slime—what? What kind, what design, what size and shape? Formless then, unformed, unforming, eyeless-sightless, mouthless-soundless, limbless, mindless, hopeless plasmodium forever awaiting the light—
  Control!

  He was lifted out blind and gasping and thrown naked into a holding cell. Someone was there before him. RAM.

RAM's body lay at gangling angles, his purplish skin swollen up and burst bloodily in places. He looked dead. Shaman could not move.

RAM had ended up a Maoist. Years ago he had taken a trip or two to Cuba, but Castroism was not the answer. He had been a reporter for *People's Labor*, a member of the Liberated Labor Party, a member of the LLP National Committee, and editor of a magazine called *Watt's Up*, its name later changed to *Eat At Chou's*, still later outlawed and published anew as *The Cat's Mao*. In between times he had been associated with the Panthers, the Muslims, New Africa, People's Party IV, and the Black Time of Power Party. Finally he had joined a black activist Maoist group known as It's On! and had been arrested for complicity in a scheme to derail the 6:05 commuter train out of Manhattan at 125th Street and detain its cargo of Connecticut-bound advertising and businessmen for ransom.

The sally-port door and bar grate clanged and crashed. Two counselors in tee-shirts entered, clubs in their hands, spray cans in holsters on their belts. They bent down by RAM.

"See, he's not dead. Look at the spit bubbles."

They poked him. RAM's pulped face muttered:

"—*zeen* writer."

They nodded and straightened, turning to Shaman, smiling. "Just wouldn't confess," they said. "You're next."

The voice meant to sound scoffing rasped like cinders in the wind: "Who'd fall for that?"

They took his arms and marched him out. Evaluation time.

"Name? Service? Grade? Serial number? Date of birth? Place of birth? Race? Religion? Height? Weight? Color hair? Color eyes?"

The typewriter chunk-chunked words whether he answered or not.

He had been skin-searched. He was bound. He stood naked. *Hold out.*

It would not work if they did not believe it, and now was still too soon. He bore the bonds and the nakedness and the scorching light and stood with rubbery ankles and jiggling kneecaps for hours while voices from the shadows read aloud and MacBitch appeared and disappeared like an optical illusion.

Not yet.

Not yet and not for a while yet. He was not ready yet. He thought in terms of days, though there weren't really any days here, were there? The endless hours under the light were the days, and the black drowning hours in the pit were the nights. He recalled the first day perfectly. They took turns reading from his dossier over and over again.

"Have you anything to add?"

"No."

Chunk-chunk.

That was the first day. A few preliminary questions. He recalled it all perfectly, standing wobbling with general debility for seven or seventy or seven-seventy hours while relays of readers read from files and folders. And then the pit. The night. And then the day, and the night again, then the day.

Hold on.

Not too soon. Not too quick and easy, or they wouldn't believe.

But it had better work!

He recalled the odd hypersensitivity to sound that came perhaps as compensation for being blinded by hot painful light striking into weeping eyes. *Strrrip* as typed paper came out of the typewriter, *rattatat* as blank went in. Chunk-chunk.

Every so often he would go off on a long swoop, and then jerk back with whited-out eyes and saliva on his chin.

Too soon.

Not until they believed. Not until they were certain he must know something and would have to save his life.

Let them see him totter and wobble. Let them see him beginning to break down already just from the lack of sleep and food and air and light and water.

It was the fifth day or the fiftieth or the five hundred fifty-fifth.

He heard coughs, chuckles, chitchat, and the fidget of MacBitch's boxes of leather and plastic and gristle beneath the table.

"A few preliminary questions."

"Name? Service? Grade? Serial number? Date of birth? Place of birth? Race? Religion? Height? Weight? Color hair? Color eyes?"

He grinned up with mouth open and eyes shut.

"Sign . . ." He groped.

A counselor in a tee-shirt knocked his hand down. Shadows towered into the light, changing shape and hiding MacBitch.

"We have previously noted your eagerness to sign confessions relating to (one) PFM banner, clandestine fabrication of, public display of; and (two) James T. aka Torox White, by lethal device, slaying of."

Bulbous shadows haloed with fuzz leaned around him.

"Your history as lieutenant colonel in the U.S. Army, as guerrilla fighter, as irregular warfare expert, as double agent—"

"Executioner for the notorious Tcham Ahn, smuggler of arms to leftist Moslem rebels on Mindanao—"

"Highjacker of U.S. nuclear submarine *Mertensia* for delivery to secret PFM forces in Manzanillo—"

"Who cares?" a familiar voice said. "That's not the confession we want at all, is it?"

"Hey, Spofford!"

"Surprise, surprise. Thought you had us fooled, didn't you?"

The shadows leaned out of the light, and only MacBitch's vague form was there, glistening through streaming tears.

"Officer Spofford is here and he has the first question," MacBitch said. "One which he feels holds the key to the entire mystery."

"Yes, we don't know what you're up to, but you made one fatal slip," Spofford's voice said.

"Proceed," MacBitch said.

Cool dry fingers touched Shaman's arm, pinched his wrist, took his pulse. A watch was ticking. He could hear it.

"Now you will tell us," MacBitch said.

Camp counselors in T-shirts held Shaman still. Cool dry fingers gripped his arm, flexed his elbow, palped and patted, thumbed the vein.

Slow-spurting honey, needle-tipped with ice.

"Now you will answer," MacBitch said.

Cool dry fingers swabbed. "Give it thirty seconds, then start."

The watch ticked.

"Fifteen seconds."

I have to tell, I can't tell, the two halves of his brain said.

"Five, four, three, two, one."

Cool dry fingers tipped his chin up. "Go."

Ogo-ogo-ogo. Echo.

"Weewee," he said. And did.

Spofford's face appeared, drifting, splitting, like cell division: two faces. They spliced together: one face. It spoke. It said huge droning words reverberating vast volumes of hot empty air.

"WHERE . . . DID . . . YOU . . . SEE . . . THAT . . . MAP?"

Hah hah!

Tell them that and they'll know everything.

Have to! I can't!

No mercy.

It was time.

And it better work!

Shaman swallowed his tongue.

The chief medical officer was the same mottled, red-eyed, alcoholic-looking man who had stitched him up before. "I stitched you up before," he said. "More than once, didn't I? How many times is this?"

"It worked!" Shaman said. He woke in a white bed. Tubes were in his arms, his throat hurt, his mouth tasted sweet and acid with blood and medicines, and his head ached. But that was all. He wasn't dead. It had worked.

"It got you out of interrogation, is that what you mean?" the doctor said. "The hard way. You almost strangulated. A couple minutes more and you would have been dead or brain-damaged. As it is, you almost cracked your skull when you fell. On top of extreme physical exhaustion. You were blue! You've been out for forty hours! What the hell did you think you were doing?"

"Call it a timely tactical extrication," Shaman said.

"You swallowed your tongue on purpose, for God's sake! Roots and all, don't tell me! I didn't know anybody *could* swallow their tongue on purpose!"

"Neither did I," Shaman said, feeling gabby and giddy with relief and success. "You just fold it over and jam it back down your throat. Up and over as far as it'll go. Tongues are strong. That's the easy part. The hard part is making yourself swallow. Try it once."

The doctor tried it, lips closed and moving slightly. The expression on his face was thoughtful and mumpy. Then it dissolved in shudders.

"You must be crazy!"

"It got me out, didn't it?"

"Out where? With guards on the door? With MacBitch just waiting for your medical clearance? It didn't get you very far out, did it?"

"No, just to the infirmary," Shaman said deliberately. "The next step is yours."

The doctor looked at him.

"That's right," Shaman said. "It's all arranged."

The doctor opened surprised eyes like mottled egg yolks.

"You've got your instructions," Shaman said.

"Wait a minute! Wait a minute! Are you trying to tell me what I think you're trying to tell me? Because if you are, give the countersign."

Solemnly Shaman held up one deformed-looking hand. Second finger over index, third over pinky, the sign of the double double-cross. He spoke with painstaking distinctness.

"The nan is a nurderer."

"So you're the one," the doctor said. "What happened? They told me somebody was coming through. I got the papers right here. Transferred to Northstate Institute for the Criminally Insane. Hell, that was weeks ago! I almost forgot! You've been in and out of here ever since—how was I supposed to know? What were you doing all this time, for God's sake?"

"Improving my education," Shaman said.

CHAPTER FOUR

Ex Machina

Frenzy

"Grenade!" Ralph Elf screamed.

Ralph Elf wasn't crazy. He had been a prankster as a boy, a demolitions expert in the service, and a Syndicate torch in civilian life; also, in Maxwing he had made bombs, such as the calliocracker that had saved Shaman's ass and the potassium chlorate petard that had neutralized Torox the Super Patriot; and even in Northstate he had contrived at least once to make simple explosives out of wood ashes and his own urine. But he wasn't crazy. "I'm not one of the kinks that gets his rocks off burning or blowing things," he always said. "With me, it's the professional challenge."

"Then what are you doing in here?" the attendant said.

"I got hit on the head," Ralph Elf said. "My head hurts now. My memory goes blank. I don't mean I forget the past, it's the future I forget. I mean, I remember everything before they hit me on the head, I just forget things ever since. Any minute now I could forget what we're even talking about."

"That's called retrograde amnesia," the attendant said.

"What is?" Ralph Elf said.

The attendant rolled his eyes, turning away in disgust, and Ralph Elf screamed "Grenade!" and sprang on his back, knocked him sprawling on the stone floor, and bit a piece of his ear off. The attendant jumped up bleeding, hit Ralph Elf in the eye, and got a kick in the crotch in return, then two more attendants came running and together they beat Ralph Elf unconscious. They threw him into a Special Treatment Area. STA's can be cells or toilets or heavy wooden crates like abbreviated coffins, but this one was just a small stone room with nothing in it except a mattress that smelled like piss. Ralph Elf woke up in darkness with his top front teeth knocked out. After four days they released him, but strapped his arms up in a camisole and put him in one of the back wards. Back Ward 4. And there was Shaman with his arms strapped up in a camisole.

"What are you doing here?" Ralph Elf said. "I thought they buried you in Polwing?"

"It's all arranged," Shaman said goofily. "Once in the slam, all I've got to do is report on sick call. Our man on the inside has the certification and commitment papers ready. The next move is up to me. Mental institutions are easier to escape from than federal facilities."

"They forgot to tell you about Northstate," Ralph Elf said.

"Every soldier's duty is escape and evasion."

"They forgot to tell you about the back wards. This is Back Ward Four."

"That's forward back," Shaman said wonderingly.

A vast green room with steel-screened small windows, ring-bolts on the walls, dim, caged bulbs high up. Quiet except for moaning and jabbering and occasional thin, cold screams. Empty except for dozens of men, most naked or almost naked, some dressed in restraining garments, some wandering around slowly, a few chained to the ringbolts.

Shaman sat straight-backed against a wall, his arms strapped tight, his feet sticking out. Ralph Elf bent down to peer in his eyes: salt-white irises and pinpoint blue pupils.

"Man, what happened to you?"

"I almost pushed it too far."

"Pushed what too far?"

"*Barraka* too far. I didn't know I can die."

Ripped out of his mind. Chlorpromazine II.

"I'll be back to see you when the gong wears off," Ralph Elf said, and walked over to one of the warders.

The warder observed his approach and said: "If you want to talk to me, keep back ten feet, or I'll club you on the head with this stick."

The warders were beefy, brutal, terrified men, outnumbered twenty to one by homicidal maniacs. With the war on and the world falling apart and the system going to hell, there were fewer warders every day, and more and more vast green rooms full of maniacs ready to go at any moment.

"What's my friend over there doing in restraints?" Ralph Elf said.

"He was sent down for fighting. He beat up a doctor and three attendants in Ward A," the warder said. "He's a maniac."

"I don't believe it," Ralph Elf said. "I knew him in Maxwing, he isn't crazy. He's an exercise freak, he was always exercising in the yard. He probably only wanted to get some exercise. Why didn't they just let him exercise?"

"Get away from me, or I'll club you on the head with this stick," the warder said.

Ralph Elf went back to Shaman and made him stand up, walk around and around and around, then faster and faster and faster. Then knee bends and hip bends and squat jumps and racing in place and straining against the restraints. "It works the shit through your system quicker," he said. "If you can work it out before they come around again, you can get your head straight, for a while, anyway, before they gong you again."

After a long time Shaman said: "What happened to me?"

"When you were fighting those people, did they give you a shot?"

"I fought . . . That's what the fight was about."

Ralph Elf nodded. "You probably got the works—chlorpromazine injected and a couple of spoonsful of chloral hydrate to crash you down. Behave yourself and they won't do that again, but you'll probably get Deep Dose for a week."

"Deep Dose . . ."

"Mellaril, a hundred milligrams, three times a day—Valium, five milligrams, three times a day—phenobarbitol, two grains, three times a day—diphenylan sodium, one and a half grains, three times a day—"

Shaman staggered and sagged; the sound alone drugged him, a chant to put him to sleep. They sat down against a wall.

Ralph Elf said: "Guaranteed to turn you into a living corpse. Or they can always pump in more chlorpromazine and knockout drops. Anything to keep you quiet. Marvelous advances in psychiatric treatment nowadays. But if you behave yourself, you'll only get Daily Dose, like everybody else."

"Daily Dose . . ."

"Couple of hundred milligrams of chlorpromazine three times a day, maybe twenty grains of Valium three times a day, two grains of phenobarbitol three times a day, plus a couple of hundred milligrams of Dilantin three times a day. They don't want any trouble."

Shaman was working his face violently, grinding his jaws, bulging his eyes at nothing, trying to wake up, shake it off, stay alert. He seemed to glare maniacally at Ralph Elf.

"Tell me everything about this place."

"This is it. A dayroom full of guys doped down like low-grade retards, sitting around in their own crap, or tied up in straitjackets. You line up for pills and meals, at night they stash you in the cribs. What were you expecting, man, Freudian analysis?"

"How did you get here?"

"I've been here ever since," Ralph Elf said. "They put me in psychiatric observation when they sent you back to Maxwing, then sent me here. I'm not all there. Mostly I behave myself, or they just crash me down and throw me in STA. I don't always wear this thing."

He writhed his elbows under the canvas.

Shaman was already working on that, trying to remember the way escape artists did it. "How are these sleeves tied behind me?"

"With great big knots," Ralph Elf said. "Nobody gets out of Back Ward Four."

"How do you know till you try?"

"Oh, wow! Have you got a man on the inside here too?"

"If I have, are you with me?"

"You can't escape," Ralph Elf said. "You can't get past the warders. If you could get past the warders, the halls are full of attendants. If you could get past the attendants, all the doors are locked. If you could unlock them, there are guards with walkie-talkies on all the grounds. If you could get past the guards, they've got dogs. Vicious, hungry Dobermans."

He began to cry.

"My head hurts."

Shaman was noticing that most of the patients in Ward 4 seemed to be either bald or wearing shocks of hair like horses. The wandering ones muttered to themselves and took slow, shuffling steps. The naked ones had thin arms and shins, but round, pale-gray bellies. An old man sat patting a puddle of urine between his legs with soft plapping sounds. A man near him sat twisted into some incredible kind of yoga position. Others sat sluggish with amentia or lay motionless on their sides in fetal obeisance. Here and there in the vast green room were gibberers, groaners, and shriekers.

"For something that isn't even real, it sure as hell keeps getting worse," Shaman said.

"What does?" Ralph Elf said.

"Show me around," Shaman said. "Tell me all about this place."

"Behave yourself," Ralph Elf said. "Let's go, we can walk around. Look out for the warders. Keep away from them—they're scared to death, they'll kill you. It wasn't so bad when they had real warders. These are just screws. It wasn't so bad when they had real doctors, professionals. They had social workers. Psychiatric care. It wasn't so bad when they had qualified professionals. It was an institution, but it was run by civilized modern society. Now it's nothing but a dump. It's a dispose-all. Hello, Mr. Mokie Marco. This is my friend. He's not violent. Meet Mr. Mokie Marco, my friend the screw—all the screws are friends of mine. Hello, Mr. Mokie Marco. We're only walking around."

The warder was an Asiatic-looking man in a steel Wehrmacht helmet. He twirled his stick at them.

"Just *watch it!*"

Ralph Elf and Shaman walked together across the floor. It sloped down slightly toward the center. In the center was a drainage grate, stained and stinking.

Shaman said: "It's a fucking zoo!"

"Be careful you don't step in it. They flush the floor sometimes. They ought to ring a warning bell when they do. Anything you want to know, ask me, I know all about this place. I talk to the warders. I talk to the doctors too, but they all speak Pakistan or something now. Come on."

Shaman followed. In some places men were chained to the walls; a chain ran from one wrist through a ringbolt to one ankle; the patient could move but not wander. In a corner was a man entirely wrapped in a heavy canvas sheet and belted in. Even his head was wound in thick bandages. He was completely immobilized. His face was a death mask.

"He's dead."

"No," Ralph Elf said. "They feed him, and he eats. They lay him down, and he sleeps. Sometimes he hollers."

"How long does he have to stay like that?"

"For the rest of his life," Ralph Elf said. "He's a headbanger."

Another man was wandering freely but with his hands manacled to a heavy leather belt at his waist. His ears were scabby nubs. "That's another nut. It's for their own good," Ralph Elf said. "Hello, Tom."

"Hello, Ralph."

"Tom's a picker," Ralph Elf said. "He tears his ears up with his fingernails. He eats the bits. Ask me. I know all about this place. You think we're all maniacs here, but we aren't, not all of us. They don't have as many maniacs now. Only the worst ones. They let a lot go. They had to. My God, what else? How could they handle them all now? They gave them lobotomies and Pentothal shocks and sent them on home. They gave them chemotherapy, they gave them uppers and downers and mindbenders and what-all. They gave them a pill diet to take and threw them out, released, back on the street, walking around, hanging around out there. You'd be amazed at the people in here that aren't maniacs. Or they are now."

The headbanger and the picker were examples of hard cases. There were other hard cases, but most of the vast gloom was filled with men just wandering slowly with hangdog heads. A few combative types were in camisoles. Some others just sat or lay on the stone floor. Ralph Elf called these last the mopes. The mopes were moist and rubbery to the touch, and seldom moved or spoke. Many of them showed signs, new marks or old scars, of human bites.

" 'Namheads too," Ralph Elf said. "Depressed, alienated, addicted. Wounded and hooked on alkaloid morphine. They came home and tried to rob somebody, or killed somebody, or tried to fight the war, join the PFM or something. And the Nazis hit down on them. They've been here for years. They'll be here forever. They broke something."

A naked man with curly white hair on his belly and balls approached them, all smiles.

"Man, we've got every kind," Ralph Elf said. "Meet my friend Ray Sheares. Hello, Ray Sheares. Hello, good boy. He can't talk. They say he was all right when he came. Somebody's experiment didn't work. They've got secret labs, secret experiments on your brain. Sometimes they don't work. Or he used to be one of their agents that turned unreliable, or sold out. Or when the Nazis took over the CIA files and found something, nobody knows. They wanted him to forget. He forgot, all right. Good-bye, Ray Sheares. Come on. Meet a friend of mine."

Back across the room he had spotted a man in a white smock watching three warders beat an emaciated man on the head with their sticks. The warders were yelling disgusted at the man:

"Now *eat* it!"

"Hello, Doctor," Ralph Elf said.

"Hello, Doctor," the man said.

"He did it again?"

"He did it again."

"Meet my friend, Dr. Shaman. Meet my friend, Dr. Friedkin," Ralph Elf said.

"Hello, Doctor," Friedkin said.

"Hello, Doctor," Shaman said.

The warders were now handcuffing the emaciated man's hands behind his back and stuffing a cotton gag in his mouth. Ralph Elf explained: "It's for his own good. He's a regurgitator. He'd die of starvation. They make him eat it every time, but it doesn't help."

Friedkin said: "He inserts three fingers down his throat and triggers his gag reflex. Up comes everything. Meals, medication, everything."

"It's a thought to remember," Shaman said.

"This he does constantly, repeatedly," Friedkin said, "compulsively, I might add, as a gesture of relinquishment, rejection—rejecting his own life, as it were—ejecting it."

"Doc knows all about psychology," Ralph Elf said. "We don't care about that, Doctor. Show my friend Dr. Shaman the Penfield Finger. Let's see the Penfield Finger, Doctor."

Friedkin looked speculative.

Ralph Elf said: "It's okay, I vouch for my friend. He's not crazy, he's a political."

Friedkin said: "Are you familiar with Dr. Wilder Penfield's pioneering work in electrical stimulation of the brain, particularly in artificial evocation of buried memory 'bits,' by sending electric currents into certain areas of the cortex?"

"Definitely," Shaman said.

"His discovery was largely accidental. In the time since then we have learned that with ESB, patients can vividly remember long-forgotten episodes from the past. There is, of course, a redundancy factor that causes a random effect. Nevertheless, my contention is that inducing certain patients to relive specific experiences can have positive psychotherapeutic benefit in cases of neurotic repression."

"Show him the finger, Doc," Ralph Elf said.

Friedkin held it up, smiling: an ordinary right-hand index finger.

"Named in honor of Dr. Wilder Penfield, as a handy, descriptive nickname for a technique which I am developing," Friedkin said. "Are you familiar with the work at Newark College of Engineering in photographic measurement of the 'aura' or psychic discharge emitted by the forefingers of certain psychic healers during the act of healing?"

"Thoroughly," Shaman said.

"The similarities with the well-documented fingertip incisions of the psychic surgeons, as well as the 'spirit injections' accomplished merely by pointing, are too significant to be ignored," Friedkin said.

"Obviously," Shaman said.

"I do not suggest that the human index finger has magical powers," Friedkin said. "Simply that it can, and does, serve as an instrument for the aimed discharge of certain emanations that may be electromagnetic, bioplasmic, or even etheric in nature."

"Oh, get on with it," Ralph Elf said.

"Combining these two concepts, we find that the Penfield Finger can be used, in place of complicated ESB generating equipment and implanted electrodes, to stimulate the cortex and recall to the patient vividly intense memories. A handy 'spirit electrode,' as it were."

"Oh, man, why don't you just *do* it!" Ralph Elf said.

Friedkin lowered the finger, watching it all the way, and holstered it in his smock pocket.

"He makes you remember past things you forgot," Ralph Elf said.

"Not *me*, he doesn't," Shaman said.

"We have ample suitable subjects," Friedkin said. He turned slowly on one heel, scanning the room. "There is Professor Legge, one of our most interesting cases. One of our most frequent, and satisfying, subjects as well. We have an established rapport."

Professor Legge was a ghostly white figure, tremendously tall and slim, nodding and drifting in the dim green gloom. Scarecrow tatters draped his form, carpet slippers slapped the damp floor, lantern jaws grinned. He said:

"I'd like to go home."

"You are making wonderful progress, Professor. I'm sure it won't be long at all now," Friedkin said. "See, this time I've brought the review board to show them the wonderful progress you're making. Come sit down now, so I don't have to stand on my tippy-toes."

Collapsed, Professor Legge was like a broken scaffolding of spiky elbows, peaked shoulders, and great knobby knees. Friedkin stepped behind him, unholstering the Penfield Finger.

"The poor soul has a brilliant career behind him," he said sorrowfully. "It's difficult to believe now that just before commitment he was senior consultant to the internal affairs subcommittee of the Senate Judiciary Committee. Ph.D. from Yale University, author of several works on socioeconomic questions, faculty of Princeton University, head of his own investment firm, board member of several major corporations, founder and president of his own bank, founder of two savings and loan companies, president of Eastlands Mutual Funds society. Too bad he got mixed up in politics."

"What did he do?" Shaman asked.

"He wrote the Legge Report, the first subcommittee report ever to become a nationwide best-seller."

"He wrote what was really happening," Ralph Elf said.

"The Nazis said it was pro-PFM propaganda, but they let him plead insanity," Friedkin said.

"Oh, get started!" Ralph Elf said.

Friedkin pointed the finger at the top of Professor Legge's skull. "The emanations are stimulating your mind. Tell us what you remember."

"Chicken pox," Professor Legge said.

"Tell us words from your writings. Remember words from your writings. Your writings are very important. You were a prominent writer."

"Old forms of government finally grow so oppressive that they must be thrown off even at the risk of reigns of terror."

"Bullshit," Shaman said. "That's Herbert Spencer."

"There is a redundancy factor which causes a random effect," Friedkin said testily. "Often cell groups producing entirely different memories are only fractions of a millimeter apart."

"Smegma!" Professor Legge said.

"Let's hear something from the Legge report," Shaman said.

Friedkin shifted position, stabbing downward. The Penfield Finger at no time touched Professor Legge's head, however.

Professor Legge jolted.

"—vain efforts to halt the inevitable total disruption of United States society as we know it. Like a runaway train plunging to disaster while passengers and crew debate management policies versus coach-class conditions even as bandits lie in wait in the hills to loot the wreckage."

"Once he told us about his first piece of ass," Ralph Elf said.

"This is a moment of history," Friedkin said. "Back at the beginning. Tell us the way it all started, Professor."

"—internal problems aggravated to the final critical point," the professor said in a sleepy-groggy voice. "Ninety percent of the population living in or near complex urban centers, clusters, entirely unable to produce for themselves directly in terms of foodstuffs, clothing, heat, light, police protection, medical care, medicines, communication, transportation, even the bare necessities of life. Sustained only by a complex, precarious, symbiotic social ecology ever more dangerously on the edge of collapse. Quantum growth in government spending over many decades. Federal budget increasing three times as fast as the gross national product. Recipients of welfare et cetera added to government employees totaling over fifty percent of the population. Deficit spending pushing inflation to the point of bankruptcy and monetary collapse. Corporations averaging profits less than three cents on the dollar. Free enterprise needing ever larger federal subsidies. Personal income reduced to nothing by confiscatory taxes. Banks failing like rows of dominoes. Flat money flooding from government printing presses. Bank deposits, cash instruments, paper money increasingly worthless. American dollars refused by foreign vendors, including oil-producing nations. Petroleum-based fertilizers and pesticides in short supply. Farm profits inadequate to pay the cost of seeding the next year's crop. Wheat, rice, corn, and potato shortages. Incipient famine. Gasoline and diesel fuel reserves drained. Rail and highway food-distribution system crippled. Social Security and welfare funds exhausted. Unemployment riots, pension riots, union strikes, old-age marches, youth revolts. Fifty percent of the population under twenty-five. Veterans' protests, consumer rebellions, hunger riots. Cities across the nation starving in cold and darkness. No electricity. No water. No telephones. No food in the stores. No heat in the houses. No gas in the pumps. No answer, help, or hope. And the first maddened mobs gathering in torchlight, looting and burning . . ."

Professor Legge's bony bald head lolled, drooping dozily. He fell asleep sitting there. Friedkin holstered the finger.

"And that's the way it all started," he said.

"It's easy when you know how," Shaman said.

Far away in the green gloom and thick stench, double doors

opened, admitting a white blaze of fluorescent light. A hand bell
rang loudly: Oyez, oyez.

Hoarse voices began bellowing: "Up against the walls! Up
against the walls!"

"Feeding time at the zoo," Ralph Elf said.

"Gentlemen, it has been a pleasure," Friedkin said.

Dozens of terrified warders poured through the doors, flourishing sticks. They helped the inmates line up against the walls.
The hard cases were set free from their chains and restraining
garments, Ralph Elf and Shaman among them. They were released
and shoved away: Next! A few inmates could not or would not
stand; they were jerked to their feet, carried by their arms to the
walls and leaned there, where they slumped and sat. Then everyone sat.

"Down! Down! Down!"

The warders inspected the lineup along the walls. They
walked around pounding their sticks on the floor and flinching
jumpily at sudden movements. Shaman heard scattered shouts,
thumps, muffled grunts. Soon everyone was in his place. Then
came Daily Dose.

"See?" Ralph Elf said. "But at least they let you have your
head straight for a while."

A rolling cart came jingling and jangling with basins and
bottles of pills and syrups. Here and there mouths slacked open
at the sight: mopes and 'Namheads reacting passively and auto-
matically. A few hard cases resisted. More shouts, thumps, grunts,
and retching sounds.

"Behave yourself," Ralph Elf said to Shaman.

The hard cases who were taking their Daily Dose docilely
were not being strapped back into their restraints.

"Nice as pie," Shaman said.

When the cart came, he swallowed his pills and sipped his
syrup from the spoon nice as pie and waited till the warders went
on. Then he turned surreptitiously around, stuck three fingers
down his throat and triggered his gag reflex. He regurgitated
neatly and catlike behind him, where no one would see.

Then the food came. Stainless steel vats and tottering stacks
of plastic plates on rolling carts, trundled in through the double

doors by coopérants, trusted inmates from the front wards. They ladled and served. Some of the mopes and 'Namheads had to be fed. A few of the hard cases ignored the food, or threw it, or smeared it on themselves. In general the patients ate quickly and quietly, with little plastic spoons, or their fingers, or their mouths. Then it was bedtime.

"Crib call! Crib call! Crib call!"

Ankle deep in mess, the patients rose (or were yanked up, propped) and in single file were marched (or pushed, prodded, poked) out of the room, through the double doors, across the white blazing hall, through another door, to the cribs. The cribs were narrow cots with stiff little mattresses and high barred sides. The cribs of the hard cases had also barred lids and padlocks. In the room were dozens and dozens of cribs as far as the eye could see in the shadows. Between cribs there was barely room for the warders to walk, swinging their sticks and rattling the bars. In the ceiling overhead was a sprinkler system, adapted to deliver tear gas.

"Beddy-bye! No talking! No moving! No noise!"

Before they were separated, Ralph Elf managed to whisper: "I saw what you did. That isn't any good. You'll just lie awake all night listening to the lunatics. This is Back Ward Four. Nobody gets out of here."

"It's all arranged," Shaman said. "Are you with me?"

Ralph Elf secretly squeezed Shaman's hand. "Just tell me what to do!"

"Fake nausea, double vision, dizziness, and loss of memory," said Shaman. "I'll handle the rest."

Fantasy

"Go on," Friedkin said.

"Ten miles off Tawitawi with a following wind," Shaman said. "I'm sitting on the flying bridge. I am cutting a notch in the stock of my oh-three for a brave enemy. The sea is running and the sun is shining, but not for him."

"Go on," Friedkin said.

"Rhino!"

"Go on," Friedkin said.

"I can smell the jungle, I am sitting among the Cham," Shaman said. "I say nothing, it is not correct to speak. My talisman speaks for me. The chiefs pass my necklace around the circle, they count the dried-up little ears, curled like caterpillars. They smack their mouths in stupefaction, they give me the war baton. I am the new war chief."

Friedkin said: "When did you first discover this mystical power in the taking of life?"

Emanations streamed from the finger.

"Horse Blister!" Shaman said.

"How old are you now?" Friedkin said.

"I'm thirteen," Shaman said. "I'm pitching my camp. I unload Pony and put him on a long line to graze. It's late in the afternoon. I'm going to unpack and eat my supper and go to sleep and hunt in the morning. Around here is where I saw the biggest buck of them all last summer, his antlers in the velvet, his eyes like a cow's, standing in the raspberries."

"Where are you?" Friedkin said.

"I'm at the south end of Muqh Lake," Shaman said. "Climb the hill and look around. The setting sun is glowing on the water. Forests of trees for hundreds of miles. Ash, birch, hemlock, hornbeam, bass, elm, and oak all the way to the mountains. Swale with cedar and spruce and tamarack. Hazel bushes and beech trees where deer and bears feed. Nothing but wildwood everywhere except over by the lake is the Homestead, all fallen down. Somebody's farm a long time ago. Now there's only a rotten ruin of a cabin and an old apple orchard full of 'coons and rabbits and ruffed grouse. Deer and black bears come there too. The sun is sinking down over the mountains."

"You are pitching your camp," Friedkin said.

"I'm pitching my camp," Shaman said. "I'm going to unpack and eat my supper and go to sleep and hunt in the morning. I've got bread and sausage and bacon and jerked venison and coffee, and a hun partridge I shot on the way today. I've got my lean-to tarpaulin and a dried deerskin for a groundsheet and a buffalo robe to wrap up in and Pony's saddle for my pillow. I've got woolen socks and underwear and a flop hat and my moccasins and my buckskin trousers and hunting shirt he made me, and my Green River knife, and my Model 1892 Winchester he gave me, and twelve thirty-eight–forty cartridges we loaded last night in the kitchen."

"Who is he?" Friedkin said.

"He's an old, old man. I can't remember anybody else. For a long time I didn't know there could be anybody else. Horse Blister, I live with him. We live on the only ranch anywhere in forty miles. He hunts and fishes and traps, and makes splint baskets and moccasins. We have Pony and two work horses and a dog, Brother, and chickens and pigs and a garden and a cornfield. He is very, very old and works all the time. Sometimes he goes to town to trade baskets and moccasins and hides for flour and sugar and gunpowder and primers, other things we need. Sometimes he goes out alone in the forest and turns into different animals or trees or other persons. He is teaching me."

"The sun is sinking down over the mountains," Friedkin said.

The sun is sinking down, Shaman said. The first job is to make up my bed before it gets dark. The sky is clear, I don't need my lean-to. It's nice to lie looking straight up into the stars, till it makes you dizzy, maybe you're upside down, all that's holding you on is the flat of your back, or you might fall off into space. I'm so happy. I hope I can sleep. I cut poles to peg on the ground for my frame, I fill it with boughs of balsam fir and spread my deerskin hair side up. Then I make a little fireplace and light a little fire. The firelight turns the night dark black around me. I make my supper on roasted partridge and bread and coffee. The wind blows,
                   it gets colder, Pony stamps and snorts, I wrap up in my buffalo robe. It's stiff as canvas first, but my body warmth softens and molds it to me, and I lie in bed on my side and go to sleep watching the fire die. Up before the dry, windy November dawn, and bacon and bread and coffee for breakfast. In the dark I rub Pony for a while and put my robe over his back and give him corn to eat. He eats out of my hat. Then the stars
          pale away, the sky is powder blue with gold streaks like

banners, and I take my rifle and scout the brush and gullies on
the way to the lake. The sun rises, gold banners turn like spokes,
and the frost steams. It's so early, partridges are flushing everywhere, they're pecking for gravel on the ground, and I chase
them into the trees. I shoot two, both clean head shots, this side
of the ridge. I dress them and bury the insides under stones and
scatter dust on the blood to

                              leave no mess. I clean my rifle with
the pull-through, so it won't foul and shoot wild. Then I climb
the ridge. I reach the top and lie hidden to look down at the
Homestead where the old orchard is. Maybe there are deer feeding
on frozen apples. But I don't see anything, just the black rotted
logs of the cabin and frosty briar bushes. The trees still have a
few leaves and a last few bright apples hanging. The apples on
the ground are gone brown and black, and if you bite them, they
will taste like cider. I don't go down, I scout along the ridgeline,
working north

                      toward the head of the lake, seeing fresh deer
tracks where there's dust, but nothing big. Ahead is thick woods
and more partridges flying noisily up into the trees, but I want
a deer. I follow a well-used trail with droppings and rubs. Step
and stop, look all around. Step and stop, quietly, in soft moccasins,
all the way across the top of the lake, the wind in my face and
the sun on my shoulders, perfect for stalking. Slow and careful,
all through the morning, but I don't see anything, except

                                          a fox.
It sits gazing at me. I don't shoot. Maybe it's old Blister, watching
out for me. He disappears without a sound, and I walk down
to the lake, where I find a dry log in the sun and rest awhile,
then hunt back toward camp. Walking with the wind now and
making noise, so I won't see a deer if there is one, but I startle
a rabbit and shoot it. I don't like rabbits and won't shoot them
just to eat, but Blister has killed thousands and can see all around
him without moving his head. Rabbits and owls are both good
for this. In my camp

                      I gut and skin the rabbit and hang it up
to chill. Brother will eat it back at the ranch. Then sausage and
coffee for me and corn and a new patch to graze for Pony, then
clean my rifle in the dead silent noon, and a nap till it's time to

go out again. Up at the head of the lake I saw freshly browsed
hazel this morning. Now I go back there, moving very quietly
and slowly, and find a good stand, and wait there all the rest of
the afternoon. But nothing comes along, not even grouse. Not
even the fox, who could have warned me
                                                                   about the sky. The
sky at sundown is scarlet red in the west like blood, and in
November this can bring big wind, cold, maybe snow. The fox
would say: Head back to the ranch fast. But I am tired of seeing
nothing much except sign, and I am going to hunt this woods
tomorrow. After supper I lie in my robe watching the fire die,
and I go to sleep wishing I could kill predators
                                                            for their skill in
finding game. Blister has been killing hawks all his life and can
see antlers in a brush pile over half a mile. He has killed bear
and lion and never misses a stalk. Suddenly I am looking at the
Dipper and it must be three o'clock in the morning. I don't
remember sleeping, but a freezing wind has come up and my lean-
to tarp is flapping loose like a flag. Clouds from the west are
blacking out the stars. Before I can roll my robe and pack my
traps, whirling snow is everywhere. Pony whistles and kicks in
the wind, and then turns his tail and suffers while I saddle up
and tie on my bedroll and packsack. I can't ride, I lead him,
stumbling blindly up and over the low ridge, into the flying snow.
We are going
                        to the Homestead, there are walls still standing,
some protection from the storm. It takes almost forever because
I am lost half the time, but we find the lake and work down the
shore. I lose my flop hat, Pony has ice in his forelock and
eyelashes. Ahead is the wrecked cabin, we can shelter by the
wall. I can light a fire, roll up in my robe. Pony stops, he balks.
I yank him, he makes a noise like a scream, thin in the wind.
He shivers all over. We are ten feet from the cabin. It's a jumbled
pile of rotting logs. Pony won't go near it. Something
                                                                    is there,
something is in the cabin, he smells it. I can't see anything, I
can hardly see the cabin through the blowing snow. Pony kicks
and rears. I am trying to reach my rifle, hanging from the
saddlehorn by its leather sling. Something in the cabin is watching

us, and I yell into the wind. Maybe it's old Blister, but that wouldn't scare Pony. I don't know what it is, and I can feel my hair stand up. It's something big and strong. I'm afraid of it. I have never killed a predator or even a moose or an elk, and I don't have enough power. Whatever it is, it scares me, and we retreat. We turn and go back up the shore and I have to hold Pony hard or he'll bolt. A mile north we find

some rocks and spruce trees behind a bluff, and here we stop. Pony is quiet, exhausted and half frozen, and I tie him to a tree. He turns his tail to the wind and suffers. For a while I try to light a fire, but the icy wind blows the flames and the tinder away and I can't. I fold my deerskin and sit on it and wrap myself in my robe and spend the rest of the night with my rifle ready, listening to approaching footsteps and stealthy breathing that are only just the wind. Morning comes suddenly and the wind dies down to almost nothing and there's hardly that much snow after all, barely an inch or two. A great morning for hunting. The snow is good for tracking and spotting both. Pony is fine now. I feed him again and leave him there with my traps. This time I start up from

the edge of the water and scout till I find fresh prints, then follow them uphill into the woods toward the browsed hazel bushes. I'm tired and cold but the day is beautiful and they are big respectable tracks. When you are tracking a buck, he will know it and travel into the wind. If he has been feeding early in the morning, he will lie down now and again to watch his backtrail. Every so often I step off the trail of his hoofprints in the snow and circle ahead and cut back again with my rifle cocked and shouldered in case I can catch him

lying up with his nose pointed the wrong way. I move only a little at a time and I look very carefully all around, since with snow on the ground I can see him easier, but so can he see me. So far when I come back to the trail it's still there, it still keeps on without stopping. I see a place where he was pawing up snow and leaves under an oak tree. He's still traveling into the wind, and his big hoofs sink in straight and deep. He doesn't seem to smell me closing in, and I know he doesn't hear me. I am going crazy with excitement because I am me, but at the same moment

I am him too, because I know what he's doing. I know now. He's down and watching his backtrail, and if he sees me or scents me, he will sneak off on his belly in the other direction. But I know now. And I cut across the wind for a hundred yards and hurry upwind for a hundred yards and creep back across the wind for a hundred yards. The last takes longest. A step and stop, and look around. A step and stop and strain to see him before he sees me. Then back on the line of his travel, but there's no tracks. He isn't there yet, I'm ahead of him. I'm uphill ahead of him, waiting, and the wind is wrong but I don't care, he can scent me now, just so he moves. I'm behind a beech tree and my heart is hammering and below me is an open place and nothing is there, but then

I see him. A gray-brown shadow only thirty or forty yards away. He is sneaking off with his flag down. His head is turned so he doesn't see my movement as the rifle comes up, and the ivory bead settles low on his neck at this downhill angle. I can't remember squeezing, just the hard flat whack echoing back, and the thump. I drop on my heels to see under the black powder smoke. He springs up running with his flag flying. His front knees buckle and he slides on his face. I am already running and reloading, but he's down and stays down, blowing blood froth in his nose, his tongue sticking out. Blood and cut hair show on the snow where the bullet hit him and he made his spring. The wound is farther down the back than where I aimed, but he is dying. His hooves kick out and scatter powdery snow and black dead leaves, and I squat down by him and gather in his death.

"What's happening now?" Friedkin said.

Horse Blister is in the kitchen, with a fire in the woodstove roaring, Shaman said. He is clattering pots and pans. He knows it when I come onto the ranch and put Pony up in the horse barn and feed him and rub him down and tie his old blanket on. The sky looks like more snow.

Horse Blister is a huge furry bundle of shirts and greasy

sweaters and leggings and rubber boots under the low ceiling in the glow of the coal-oil lamp. He knows it when I stand behind him with the liver and heart in a sack, and he says:

"You certainly shot a lot of partridges."

"I shot a big buck too."

"One buck, with all those shots fired? You are a famous killer of partridges. Maybe you want to learn to eat gravel and nuts."

He is not joking. He is teaching me.

"I brought you something."

"I know that." It's why he lighted the stove and is clanking his pots and pans. Old Blister loves to eat deer liver fried or fricasseed and make stew with the heart. He still has teeth in back. His wooden old face is up there in the oily drifting smoke. His hat almost bumps the ceiling. I don't have to tell him anything, but I do.

"I was the buck. I became him when he turned off his trail."

"That's right." He is not teaching me now. He holds the heart in his hands, hefting it. "He will go almost two hundred pounds. It's a good buck. How many points?"

"Twelve." I watch him put the heart in a tin box and carry it out to the pantry to keep cold, then come back and start to cut up the liver to fry. I say: "It took me all day. He's gutted and hung in an oak tree way over on the northwest side of the lake where the old road comes out."

"I know that." He knows I dragged it the whole way around the top of the lake because the old logging road is the only way in there with the jumper, our homemade sleigh. Old Blister can't ride horse anymore, he has to take the jumper. I think he knows why he has to go bring in the buck alone too. But we don't talk about it till after we eat.

While we are eating, Brother slinks in the doghole low in the door and gallops all over me. He has smelled the chimney smoke and come in from far off. Big and black but with white hair all around his muzzle, just like the old man. I give him his rabbit cut up in chunks.

I am cleaning up the table and the stove.

Old Blister is standing behind me. He says: "Tell me."

I tell him about the Homestead, and the wrecked cabin in

the black night, and snow and wind, and the thing that was inside. "What was it?" I ask him.

But he's not there.

I scrape grease off the tin plates and wash up, while he is gone about time enough for a nighthawk to fly out and back. Then he comes in and says:

"It's a bear."

"I thought so."

"He ate apples all fall. He's eating them still. He denned up in there for the winter."

We sit at the table, with the lamp between us, and shadows leap up the walls. He coats lard on his fingertips and works the burrs out of Brother's ears, and I load cartridges. I seat number two primers into my fired cases with the tong tool. I fill the cases with powder, using the dipper that's supposed to measure forty grains. Cast lead bullets greased with beeswax and tallow are waiting, and I seat them on the powder and crimp them in. Outside it starts to snow again lightly, drifting on the freezing wind, and the windows rattle.

"Horse Blister," I say, to let him know that I am speaking seriously. "I can't go with you tomorrow to bring in the buck."

"Yes," he says. He knows. He wants to know what I know.

"I have to go back to the Homestead. I have something to do."

"Yes," he says. "What?"

"I was afraid. I have to find the bear."

"Yes," he says. "Why?"

"I want to kill him for his medicine."

The wind blows down the chimney. The stove smokes. I am cleaning my rifle. I cleaned it in my camp and I cleaned it after I killed the buck, and now I am cleaning it again, with only the least oil, because of the cold weather tomorrow. Blister is looking at me over the smoky lamp. He knows.

I have killed bugs and birds and mice and chipmunks since I hardly remember, and frogs and lizards for their patience, and snakes for cunning and striking speed, and squirrels and crows and hawks and badgers for nimbleness and wariness and eyesight and fight, and now deer for a year or two, and it's time. I don't have to tell him.

"Bear medicine is big medicine for a little boy," he says. "Maybe it will burst you."

"You have taught me."

Marksmanship and tracking and stalking and woodcraft, but it was always more than that. Taste the wind, read the dust, become the quarry. Clean up your mess, kill sick animals but never touch them, don't kill females, leave them for seed. But always something else too, and now I know what it is. Don't kill the female, give her life, but kill the male. Kill him for his horns, his teeth, his claws, his size, his strength, his speed. Hunt him for his meat or his hide if you want it, but kill him for his power, his savvy, his medicine. I know now, it's time.

"I believe you," he says. "Now tell me. If bear medicine doesn't burst you, what comes next after that?"

He is teaching me.

"I don't know."

"You don't know," he says. "After this bear, what is there to stop you from killing me and taking it all at once?"

Horse Blister has killed every animal there is. Bear and lion, elk, moose, wolverine, wolf, and man too. He has all their medicine and can become them all, and also other things, smoke, a jackstraw, a devil. I know this too, in a flash as amazing as lightning in the winter dark and storm.

But there is more. Horse Blister has taught me this too: He is all there is. Only he is real, alone there in the wilderness, in emptiness, nothingness. He made me. I wasn't born, that's where I came from. He is the dreamer, I am the dream. But what happens when he dies?

"I am afraid," I whisper.

"Why not?" Horse Blister says, pretending we both don't understand. "I think a bear is waiting for you tomorrow."

"Did you kill him?" Friedkin said.

My heart is hammering my whole body. I can't breathe, Shaman said. Bear sign is everywhere, his five-toed spoor in the night's fresh snow. Claw scratches on the apple trees, broken branches where he climbed up, fur where he rubbed his back on low limbs. Applesauce everywhere, old piles black under the snow, new heaps fresh as yesterday, soupy yellow puddles dropped this morning. It's noon, he's fed, he's holed up. He won't come out. He's under the fallen-in roof, down in a burrow under the trash, rotten logs, old boards, dried creepers. He knows I'm here, he growls and groans. I can't

see into the hole, I can't see much, my eyes are dizzy. My eyesight's as bad as his. He can smell me. I can smell him, I shiver all over. Squat down and peer, five feet from the hole. Hot in there, vapors coming out, like breath on cold air. Come out and fight. The gun is aimed, I can shoot into his burrow, like an open mouth. That's not the way. He has to come out. I back up, move off, hide behind an apple tree. I wait. The growling changes, it rumbles and buzzes, it stops. I wait, I wait, I wait. He won't come out, he won't move. I feel around me, I make no sound. I find apples, little hard frozen apples, under the snow. Moving slow as the hands of a clock I pick them up, I crush them

against the tree. Only the outside is frozen. The juice inside is fermented, hard cider, it can't freeze. Outside the apples are like nuts, but inside is winy juice. It smells. It smells like ripe rotting autumn all over again. It's stronger than my smell, gun metal, smoky clothes, fear sweat. The cider smell drifts and blows around the orchard. He can't smell me, I'm gone. I've left, nobody's here. Only a partridge. I'm a partridge. I am all the partridges in the cold, in the winter, pecking at the snow. I'm pecking at the snow. The bear listens. He hears a partridge pecking at the snow, scratching in the snow, for bits of apples, spilled seeds. He hears it stop. It starts again. Little chuckling partridge cries, and silence. He listens. He hears a soft sudden flap, partridge flapping up a tree. He waits, he listens. The partridge sits in a tree. It flutters down again. It pecks apples. The bear can smell apples. He hears another sound. It flops and hops. It's a partridge with a hurt wing, hopping and flopping. It makes faint pain chuckles. Its wing drags, it can't fly. It whirls little circles in the snow, one wing beating. It's dying. Chuck, chuck, chuck,

it weeps. The bear peers out. He's big, a big black bear. Big hard head,

broad heavy skull. White teeth, black lips, red tongue. Lighter
brown around the muzzle and little pig eyes. Shading darker back
over head and shoulders, white blaze on his breast. He comes
out. He comes out low, lumbering, humped as a grizzly. Huge
head sways in a loose inverted arc like a hammock. His shoulders
roll him forward, he lumbers forward, he stops, he points his
nose straight up. Nose smells apples, ears hear partridge, eyes see
nothing. Shoulders roll, he wallows one step, two steps, three
steps toward the tree. Shape moves, he sees it, gun metal and
buckskins. With a bellow like a bull he stands upright. He
towers up
                six feet tall, ruff flared, neck swelled, barrel-chested,
blaze-breasted, arms spread apart, claws like harrow hooks. I blow
his brains out. He's one step away. I am not afraid, I am not
afraid at all, it's something else. I don't know I did it. The bear
stands there in the smoke, sparks singeing his fur, face scorched.
He looks at me, a small hole under his chin. He bawls once,
spraying blood. He drops on all fours, then sits back like a dog
and falls over on his side. The little bullet went in the little hole
and blew the top back of his skull off. Light dry flakes of snow
eddy and settle on his fur. Some melt from his heat and turn
quicksilver. His tongue sticks out and he lies still. I jack another
cartridge in and touch his eyeball with the muzzle of my gun.
He doesn't blink. I put my hand on his heavy shoulder. I can
feel a deep-buried quiver like a motor running, slowing down.
It stops. He was fat and happy and full of apples. They can run
twenty miles over the hardest terrain and rip apart a dog pack
at the end of it. I felt his power when he reared up and bellowed.
I felt all his strength. I'm feeling it now, like heat off a fire. I
have to hurry, before
                he turns cold. I lie down in the snow on
my side, we lie face to face. He must go three hundred pounds,
I can't turn him over on his back. Working face to face with
my Green River knife I start at the neck. Fur like a wire brush,
but underneath it's downy. Under his fur a bear is made like a
man, skin, muscle, and bone. Blood pours out but doesn't squirt.
The arteries still. After he's cut from jaw joint to jaw joint, I
start the long cut, top to bottom, slicing and sawing through folds
of fat. From the little hole under his chin down past his man's

larynx, because I want the tongue too. Down the centerline
between the huge round arms, down the barrel chest, dividing
the blaze, down the vast belly, apple guts blurting out, down and
around his man's parts because I want it all, tongue and heart
and liver and kidneys and pecker and balls. Hack and stab and
rip. I use knife, hands, nails, elbows, knees, feet. Lying face to
face, half in the bear, half in the sodden bloody snow. I am
smeared with blood and waxy grease, gasping, freezing, sweating.
Hours go past, the sky says late, I have to go. Blister is waiting,
he heard the shot, he's up at the head of the lake. My packsack
                         reeks and drips. I can hardly rise,
I can hardly stand up. I can hardly walk out of the orchard,
climb up the ridge. Behind the ridge Pony is tied to a tree.
Before I even approach him he is blare-eyed and crazy with fear.
He rears and plunges, he's going to break the rope. I can't get
near, I can't touch him, he will kill himself. I can't ride him, he
won't be ridden by a bear. I take the rifle only and run. Run
like a bear, long cumbersome strides, thick heavy legs, heavy
lumbering body smashing straight through trash and thickets. Top-
heavy crouching running that's half falling down. I am at the
water again, it's two miles north and around the head of the lake
to the oak tree and the logging road. All my power is in my
legs and rolling shoulders. Breathing is a kind of whining buzz
like a saw in my throat. Rocks and tree trunks loom up, I'm
half blind, it's getting dark, but I can

                         smell. I smell smoke. I
stop. I'm there. It's only late afternoon. I breathe, my eyesight
comes back. A creek runs down through birch trees, into the
lake. Across the creek is the road coming out of the woods and
the oak tree and the horses and the jumper with the gutted buck
tied over it, and old Blister sitting by a little fire. He hears me.
He is turning, twisting to look over his shoulder, straight at me.
He sees me coming. I'm running. I'm running through the creek
and stamping in the icy mud, slow as a nightmare. I'm black and
spattered and mottled with mud and blood and filth and he's
rising to meet me. He knows. At the last moment he touches
his two hands to his chest and then flings them out at me: Take
it all! The rifle jabs at his heart like a stake. It fires. The horses

scream and jump, and he falls. From the woods Brother comes whining and I kill him too.

"Where are you now?" Friedkin said.

"Back Ward Four," Shaman said. "Where the hell did you think?"

"Fascinating, utterly fascinating," Friedkin said. "Am I to understand that by murdering me, for instance, you could thereby assimilate my physical attributes and possibly my medical and professional skills as well?"

"Your medicine, as it were," Shaman said.

"Astonishing. Incredible," Friedkin said. "That old man actually considered himself a magician, a sorcerer?"

"No, not exactly. You see, his idea was that he had created everything. Alone there in the wilderness, in the world, if not in the universe, he made it all up. Through his thoughts alone all things lived and had their being and did his bidding. Bear, deer, partridges, cabin, woods, mountains, storm, everything. Even me. He dreamed us. He was the creator."

"Amazing! And then you killed *him!* And took *his* medicine!"

"I wouldn't swallow too much of that Hunkpapa horseshit, if I were you," Shaman said. "The point is, can you order me sent down for electroshock therapy, or can't you?"

"Why not?" Friedkin said. "God knows you're crazy enough."

Just then, however, the double doors crashed open and a clamoring goon squad of a dozen warders charged in, brandishing sticks, billies, mace cans, straitjackets, straps, belts, handcuffs, leg irons, ropes, chains, and cattle prods. The House Rules Committee, looking for violators. But first they beat hell out of Friedkin.

Fugue

"Good old Friedkin, he never quits, he never gives up—ain't he a gas and a half?" the warder wheeling Shaman said. "One time he dressed up in that goddamn smock—he was following the *real* doctors around! Followed them around on grand rounds! He almost walked off the *floor* with them!"

Warm chuckles of admiring appreciation.

"Oh, we cooled him that time, we broke six ribs. He thinks he's some kind of crazy-nut faith healer."

"Thinks he is?" Shaman said. "Did anybody ever check it out? Didn't you see the aura around him while you bastards were beating him up? Like a stoplight in a fog."

"Aw, he always does that," the warder said.

The warder was pushing a gurney bed down a blazing white fluorescent-lighted hall. The gurney had Shaman on it, strapped down and buckled. There was a small sandbag under the back of his neck for a pillow. By raising his head a little he could see his feet, bare and pale and defenseless-looking. His head was all he could move. The goon squad had picked out half a dozen inmates and knocked them down and rolled them away to various destinations, accused of various infractions. Shaman's was barfing his Daily Dose. He wasn't the only one, but the others were merely being wheeled away to be given suppositories.

"You're a special case," the warder said, jockeying him into the elevator. "You're going to get it."

"Get what?"

"Electroshock," the warder said evilly.

"Oh, that's all right, then," Shaman said.

Lying prostrate looking at the ceiling while descending rapidly in an elevator was the oddest sort of sinking feeling, he noted. When the door opened, a guard with a shotgun looked them over and passed them on. They were in the labyrinthine basements of Main Building. The hall here had a lyart concrete floor and smelled of disinfectants. Small handtrucks with bottles and bed-pans lined the walls. Male nurses carrying clipboards wandered in and out of open rooms where there were mostly beds but sometimes glass cabinets and stirrups and stainless-steel sinks and apparatus. The gurney rushed on, making several turns. Shaman's chilly feet led the way.

The green steel door of Treatment Room 6T9 was closed and locked. Another patient was already there waiting, strapped to a gurney bed, parked in the hall. His warder was leaning against the wall, smoking. Shaman's parked and joined him, lighting up. The gurney beds touched side by side. Shaman turned his head and looked into a pale, pockmarked face inches from his own. For a long peculiar moment they exchanged expressionless stares. From behind the green steel locked door came a deep horrible sound like a man mooing.

"It's been banned by law for decades! It never cured anybody! It destroys brain tissue!"

Pockface began talking suddenly and animatedly as though to drown out the sound behind the door.

"They use it for punishment! It's illegal, but they do! Step out of line—shock treatment! They do it all the time! I get it all the time!"

"What for?" Shaman said.

"Punishment! I'm next! Then you! This way, instead of electrocuting me once and getting it over with, they can do it to me all the time! I'm a presidential assassin. What did you do?"

"I'm innocent," Shaman said.

"I'm not. I was on Death Row. Did you ever see Death Row? You go in a gate, down a fifty-foot corridor. There're cells on both sides. That's where you wait for your turn. At the end is a green steel door, just like that one. Dark green door, dark green room. They've got wooden bleachers for the spectators. Closed-circuit TV."

With his head turned like that, facing Shaman but trying to watch the Treatment Room door at the same time, the man was wild-eyed and dribbling from the corner of his mouth.

"Out the window you can see the telephone pole, with the wires running in. Big green insulators. The chair is up on a platform. A big dark oak chair. It buzzes all the time. It sits there like a judge with his hands on his knees. Come sit in my lap. There are stains from shit on the seat. Everybody does. They all do. A padre says, *Requiem eternam dona eis, Domine.* It's all over. It's merciful. How long have you been here?"

"Just passing through," Shaman said.

"I've been here two years," Pockface said. "Oh God! Oh God!"

The green steel door opened and a warder pushed a limberly unconscious post-convulsant patient out and rolled him away, saying: "Next." Pockface was next. He was still talking while his warder came and wheeled him into the Treatment Room.

This time the door was not closed. Shaman craned his neck to see why.

A pink, handsome man with a stethoscope around his neck was standing in the doorway. The therapist. He looked across the hall at Shaman with contemptuous icy eyes and nodded, as if to say: look and learn. The door remained open.

Through the door Shaman heard Pockface still talking. He was crying a message:

"If you ever get out, tell them I tried, code name Oswald, I'm still alive, they won't let me die!"

In the white tile room two large male nurses positioned the gurney bed and locked the wheels. The therapist took a jar from a shelf. He applied gunk to Pockface's temples. He pasted on electrodes. When the electrodes were placed, he pushed in a plug. He turned away and adjusted switches on a black box. Pockface said:

"Even Damien when he tried to assassinate Louis the Fifteenth—tied to four horses—he wouldn't come apart—they sent for an ax—"

Between them the two male nurses held his head still, stuffed a wad of gauze in his mouth, then stepped back.

The therapist looked up from the black box and out into the hall, staring at Shaman again with grim scorn, and nodding again, as if to say: see for yourself.

Shaman was puzzled. The bought bastard, he knows who I am. What's it about?

Activating a stopwatch with the thumb of his right hand, the therapist turned up the rheostat with the thumb and forefinger of his left.

Pockface hit the straps so hard the gurney bed jumped and jolted. His body writhed all over like a rubber bag of snakes. It went on an on.

The therapist shut off. Instantly Pockface collapsed flat like a dropped marionette. Instantly he was in a deathlike sleep, face sunk in, eyes rolled up, toes turned out. The therapist removed the electrodes. Gingerly he retrieved the gauze wad with a forceps. The two nurses unlocked the wheels, and Pockface's warder stepped forward and took the bed, backing it out, starting it away.

"See you," he said to none and all.

The therapist stood in the doorway. He seemed to be looking at Shaman with intense hostility: Now you get yours!

What the hell?

Shaman's warder wheeled him in. The two nurses positioned the bed and locked the wheels. The therapist took the jar from the shelf. He applied the gunk to Shaman's temples. He pasted on the electrodes. When the electrodes were placed, he pushed in a plug. He turned to adjust his switches. But he wasn't watching what he was doing—he was keenly, hungrily watching Shaman's face.

Shaman suddenly understood. And it was like relieved laughter.

"Why, you sadistic son of a bitch! You're trying to make me sweat!"

The therapist's pink face flushed red. He grabbed up some papers from somewhere and began to read, not looking at anybody. One arm waved widely at the warder and the two nurses.

"You men—get out. Take ten. I forgot, this one hasn't had a medical yet. Got to do a workup first. Leave us alone."

It was so implausible that all three stared in perplexity at him. Both of the nurses said: "What?" Shaman's warder said: "Alone?"

"Don't I just wish he'd try!" the therapist said confusedly, answering before he was asked, drawing his coat back to pat the butt of a forty-five-caliber snub-nose revolver, fat as a bullfrog, in a hip-hugger holster.

"What's he laughing at?" the warder asked.

"What *do* crazy people laugh at?" the therapist said, blazing fiery red. "Go on, get out, I told you. I'll call you when I need you. Don't you understand English? Wait in the hall."

They were alone. Shaman chuckled. "What was I supposed to do, beg and cry?"

The therapist was regaining his composure. "You murdering freak! Wouldn't I love to *really* burn your brain out!"

"If you didn't have your orders."

"That's right. I've got my orders. I don't have to like it, but I'll do it—I don't want Kaul sending lunatics like you after *me!* But don't expect any special favors."

"Take this crap off and let me up," Shaman said. "What's it about?"

"I know *you*, that's what," the therapist said. He detached electrodes and unbuckled straps. "I saw your file. I know who you are. But more important, I know *what* you are. A murderer and nothing but a murderer! You aren't even on our side!"

"It's supposed to be a secret," Shaman said.

"I'm not that stupid. I can put things together. I'm ashamed we have to use murderous outlaws to fight this war. It demeans the whole struggle. You're no patriot. You're a *sociopath!* I know what I know."

"You shouldn't even know the name Kaul," Shaman said. He stood up and stretched, working his muscles. He was generally feeble, worn out, wasted. Complete physical collapse wasn't far away; he had to work fast. It wasn't going to be easy. "What else do you know?"

"I know what they *used* to do with animals like you in places like this. Electroshock's nothing. They used to torture them, drown them, heat their heads in ovens—anything to drive out the evil demon. Personally, I'd *love* to do the honors in your case. Except in your case I wouldn't even allow you the benefit of the doubt. *You* aren't possessed—"

"I was a *dakma* once," Shaman said.

"—you *are* the evil demon!" the therapist said excitedly, past hearing, carried away as though by revelation. "That's what makes it so horrifying! You're a portent, a sign—something—the retribution for what we've become! You and your kind had to happen! And now you have! Don't you see what it means?"

"We're wasting time," Shaman said baffledly.

"Man has finally outdated the Frankenstein legend." He was whispering intensely with total belief. "Innocence—that's when he only *accidentally* created evil. Now he *is* the monster!"

"You're nuts," Shaman said. "Down to business. Are those three in on it?"

"What?" the therapist said.

Shaman was standing by the gurney bed. With both hands he hoisted one end in the air and slammed it jarringly down, at the same instant uttering a deep, horrible moo. In case they were listening.

The therapist was startled out of his absorption. He stared nervously.

Shaman said: "The three in the hall. Come on. You sent them out."

He was moving around the room. Besides the gurney bed and the electroshock equipment, there was only a filing cabinet and a desk with a typewriter. The therapist had the only weapon, the pistol. But something could be improvised. Shaman pecked idly at the typewriter. It was screwed fast to the desk.

"No, they don't know anything," the therapist said, "that's why I sent them out. The fewer, the better. I'm the only one who knows anything. I wasn't allowed to tell anybody. Need-to-know, the orders said."

"Tell me the orders." Shaman was idly pecking words on the typewriter, no paper in it. A terrorist slogan: There are no innocent victims.

"After the phony shock treatment, you fake unconsciousness," the therapist said. "I tell them to park you in the hall, then I call them in and hold their attention while you sneak away."

"That's it?"

"No," the therapist said grudgingly, "I'm supposed to slip you the key to the infirmary pantry down the hall. You hide in there, then sneak your way to the loading dock and smuggle yourself on the food-service van. It goes to town every day. It's the only way to get off the grounds."

"That's all?"

"I didn't write the orders."

"You couldn't have done much worse."

"I told you. Don't expect any special favors from me."

"That's right," Shaman said agreeably. "I'm supposed to be resourceful. I'm supposed to improvise as much as possible. That way if the enemy ever checks up on my story, nobody can tell them much. Nobody but you. You already know everything, don't you? You saw my file. That changes the game a little, doesn't it? Where did you say the infirmary was?"

"What?" the therapist said. "You're in it. All the rooms on this corridor are part of the infirmary. Why?"

"I was wondering about a patient named Ralph Elf."

"I don't know anything about admissions. Is he sick?"

"Nausea, double vision, dizziness, and loss of memory. He was supposed to turn himself in this morning."

"Then he's here somewhere, so what?" the therapist said. "Look, we've been quiet in here too long, they're going to wonder. You better get back on the bed and get on with the plan."

Shaman pecked at the typewriter. He spoke as though to himself:

"Stalking is the hard part. The approach is everything. Just getting into range. Using every bit of cover you can. I've already made mistakes. Spofford got the scent, all right. Lucky he didn't know which way the wind was blowing. And now this lousy plan."

"What?" the therapist said. "What's the matter with the plan?"

"Nothing that wouldn't spook the quarry from here to the horizon."

"Nobody said it would be perfect. Red spies could get in here too, remember. It's supposed to look like a real escape— how much help do you expect? You'll just have to do your best and take your chances."

"I can't take any chances," Shaman said.

The roller, the platen, lifted out with a little jingle. He turned to face the therapist, holding it in his hand. Hefting it in his hand: about a pound. It would have to do. The therapist looked blankly at the roller. Shaman glanced absently down at it, then turned half away, as though to replace it. From the half turn, feet firmly planted, he spun back swinging.

The roller hit the therapist under the ear, on the sterno-mastoid. He stumbled against the gurney bed. Shaman uttered a deep, horrible moo—in case they were wondering. The therapist's legs buckled.

Down he went. Not out yet. Big bastard with a fat neck. Shaman bent over and struck him again on the same side of the head, just above the ear. The therapist relaxed. Out.

Quick. Revolver first. Fat, froggy forty-five, cylinder full of lead points. Frisk. Nothing else. White coat off, aloha shirt under. Slacks, loafers. The therapist lay on his back in socks and shorts, no undershirt. Shaman got dressed. Wallet, keys, money, I.D. card folder with badge: U.S. Police Reserves. He yanked off the shorts. Pink all over, baby fat. But at least his sphincters hadn't let loose. Shaman knelt between the spread legs. He inserted the barrel of the revolver.

The barrel was four inches long with a ramp front sight. Relaxed, the therapist accepted it. Carefully Shaman levered it to full depth, face of the cylinder flush against the perineum, muzzle buried in the anus, aiming along the long axis of the trunk. He cocked the hammer.

"*Requiescat in pace,* torturer."

It was not the perfect silencer, but it came close. The explosion convulsed the body but made only a smothered thumping sound in the room. The jacketless bullet, big as a jelly bean, mushrooming still larger, ruptured organs and burst tissues, splintered ribs, and lodged somewhere behind the breastbone. The therapist's mouth flew open, his eyes bulged, and he died. All with no more noise than dropping a book or bumping a chair against the wall.

Shaman was already crouched, listening, at the green steel door. Whatever the three in the hall might have heard, if there was any reaction, it was not alarm.

Dressed in a white coat, with a stethoscope around his neck, and gripping the revolver in his right hand, Shaman unlocked the door.

One gurney-wheeling warder and two big male nurses bound and gagged in a storeroom, one elevator guard knocked cold by his own shotgun stock, one doctor, three medical-staff personnel and two infirmary attendants drugged with their own medicine, one gravely injured pantry steward, one dead food-service van driver and two dead loading dock security guards later, Shaman and Ralph Elf were traveling north toward freedom along deserted back-country roads. Ralph Elf was driving. Shaman was in a long-delayed coma.

"The meeting will come to order," Colonel Volpe said. "All right, gentlemen, you've read the memo. Our agent has successfully escaped from custody and is now at large. Phase One of

Operation Kalitan is now completed. Any comments or questions on that?"

"Refresh my memory. What's Phase Two?"

"Phase two, as you might have been expected to recall, requires him to disappear into the underground, make contact with Red elements, infiltrate the People's Freedom Army, penetrate the higher ranks, and maneuver for advantageous position. In this he is on his own. We can provide no further aid. In fact, according to the plan, we will not know where he is located or receive additional reports from him till such time as he is in position to initiate Phase Three."

"Which we still don't have the faintest notion what *that* is."

"This point is clearly covered in Operation Kalitan. At the proper moment he will give us our cue. First he must orient himself, evaluate the circumstances, watch for the correct moment, and select the optimum target of opportunity, before making his move."

"If he makes any move at all. I still think the whole operation was a smart way to get out of jail for stealing a submarine and trussing up poor Captain Linebarger like that."

"In fact, we may never see hide nor hair of him again, now that we let him get away. That's my opinion."

Colonel Volpe said: "Agent Shaman may be likened to a self-placing bomb. If he is to function as we hope he might, he must be allowed his own discretion in placing himself where and when he can do the most good—or the most harm, I should say—to the enemy. Meanwhile, since this phase of the operation is outside our control, I suggest we limit our comments and questions to Phase One, as I previously stated."

Kaul said bleakly: "I have a question. How many men did he murder?"

(How nenny nen did he nurder?)

"Yes, that's right. Was so much killing and violence really necessary? I don't mean fellow inmates and guards and others so much, but wasn't that electroshock person one of our own operatives, planted there to help with the escape?"

"Little breach of security there," Colonel Volpe said. "Agent Fosbert was not supposed to know anything about Shaman or his mission, just handle him through. Shaman took on-the-spot steps."

"He sure did. He took a lot of others too."

"I trust no one here was under the illusion that for a mission of this type we were sending a Sunday-school superintendent," Colonel Volpe said.

Harrison Wylie spoke suddenly: "*And*, of course, no one is bothering to see *Shaman's* side of it."

Smiles all around.

"Tell us, Auntie."

"Certainly it's none of my official business," Wylie said, turning red. "But I couldn't call myself a fellow human being if I didn't say a word at least. I mean, God help him, the poor man! I don't blame him a bit, whatever he had to do. He didn't know what he was letting himself *in* for."

"Didn't he? It was his own plan."

"He couldn't! If he really *was* away there overseas all that time, how *could* he know? What it's *like* out there! How it *is* now! My God!"

"He knew it would be rough."

"Did he? How could he? My God! Don't you see? He sat here, in this nice, clean, safe room, and plotted himself a course he couldn't even imagine! Jail! The madhouse! The way *they* are now! Like a sick man's nightmares! Then out into no-man's-land—no-man's-land! The world, or the horror that's left of it! Human garbage dumps! And from there through enemy lines! Into *their* world! The new democracy of fanatics, perverts, and cutthroats! He's going the whole way! We only know by reports how bad it is now, but he's going to see it *all*! Do you know what I'd call that?"

In startled silence they listened.

"A pilgrim's progress through living Hell," Wylie said with unexpected impressiveness. "It's a journey no sane mind could stand."

After a moment Colonel Volpe broke the spell.

"Well, we picked the right man."

CHAPTER FIVE

No-Man's-Land

Zombies

All around, in the dim-lit, strange, high room, they sat or lay on
the gritty floor, some awake, some asleep, like bundles of old
clothes in the equivocal light, gathered around an unplugged
hotplate. It was mealtime, but they had no food. And Shaman
still slept. They were waiting for him to waken and think of
something. But he slept on, shivering, and dreamed, and it was
winter.

Gulls cried; sea mews cried on sharp rocks the dull color of
dunes and grasses, sky and waves; seals roared on bare shingle.
Pack ice driven on by black upwells from the lifeless deeps piled
up, shattering in stone inlets. Aurora borealis streaked across the
vault, glimmered down on water, ocean, created before light, and
algae, comb jellies, glass worms sank in snowfalls into thousand-
fathom trenches; thousand-fathom worms writhed in the bottom's
ooze, and spores froze on the surface, rocked in gray, whitecapped
furrows of wind.

"Shaman," they urged softly. Their last food had been a
carefully dissected chicken, its blue veins taut as wires, cooked
on the hotplate wrapped in aluminum foil, eaten a little at a time,
and its bones and insides boiled in soup for many days. "Shaman."

"Black night black dogs run black pad paws mark light swift dry blown snow," he said loudly when they touched him.

"Sha-man! Sha-man! Sha-man!"

"Click clank the warder weapons gleam cold lights their barrels creak," he said in his sleep. "Soft tread in snow hush walk."

Their queer, misshapen figures crouched around him, bending to listen. He was dreaming, and it was winter. In the sky the stars were clear, cold steel; the earth was barren iron covered with snow. Trees cracked, broke, in the forests; spangles of moisture froze like lichens on volcanic rocks. Below the bluffs were long leaden waves and gray sand, jagged ice in dark inlets, and wind in dead dune grass.

Shaman cried and shivered in his sleep; blue cold crept up his thighs. Superstitiously they crouched near to hear if he would speak some word of answer, sense, or meaning to their situation, and some were afraid that he was dying. He dreamed that it was winter, and in the cold gloom saw them, crouched together, faint and freezing, fugitives at the end of the earth, and this time he heard them chanting:

"Lost we hide we nowhere no we cold white hide we hide we hungry hungry hide we cold white dark and cold and cold and dead all dead all dead."

His voice rose to a shout; he sat half upright, slack-jawed and wide-eyed, as though about to scream, and then he woke. Their dim bone-sharp faces were close around him, their bony arms across his shoulders in the greenish light. "You dreamed," they said when he looked at them. "You almost died."

He covered his eyes and his face with his hands.

Afterward he knew that he had come near to death, because pain or illness dreams were of deeps and darkness and drowning, but death was always cold white ice.

Somebody was feeding him Cup-A-Soup, a banana, and peanut butter on a spoon. It was Ralph Elf.

Voices drifted in and out of his sleep. Phantoms came and went, passing by, talking—asking, answering, arguing, confessing, supplicating, explaining, orating—sometimes to him, sometimes to one another, or to themselves, or to no one. In the near and far reaches of the loft were empty silences and sudden commotions. There were daylight hours of tall shapes in dusty shafts of light, and black hours of invisible stealthy bustle.

He raged and swore and kicked off the rags and fought to get up; they gave him the revolver and he slept again. He held it and slept, woke and slept again, peacefully, then woke finally and saw the gun gripped in his fist, opened the cylinder, saw the empty chambers and grinned wryly.

The phantoms and commotions became people and events: people like ragbags, a dozen or so of them all in a long, low loft piled high with props and artifacts, lighted by shattered glass skylights; events in random sequence as they moved and met, conversed, scuffled, bargained, coupled, declaimed, hallucinated, kept house, or cooked up and shot.

The gnarled, knobby minotaur became a hunchbacked man named Diosdado; the woman in Indian skins was Lunares; the others were Peterwell and Ward, the homos; Whitelaw, the black pimp; Tex, the white one; Subway Conductor, Fried Fat, and Smith, the muggers; BP, a gibbering little girl of thirteen; her one-legged father; several Vol deserters, and the rest of the Zombies.

When they saw him awake, they crowded around him, talking, asking, answering, arguing, confessing, supplicating, explaining, and orating. Ralph Elf chased them away.

Shaman said: "What do they want?"

"Salvation," Ralph Elf said. "I told them you were God."

"I've been beat up, starved, drugged, locked in a cell block, or solitary, or a crib, or the kishka, or a straitjacket, ever since I hit this beach," Shaman said. "I'm no good to myself, let alone anyone else. Why did you tell them that?"

"I was listening. You told Friedkin," Ralph Elf said. His eyes were odd. "Isn't it true you're dreaming all this? You thought everything up? You're the creator? Then why don't you fix it?"

"Don't believe everything you hear," Shaman said.

"Why don't you make everything right?"

Shaman was sitting up, sipping soup. He looked narrowly at Ralph Elf over the rim of the cup. Ralph Elf was going fast.

"Good question," Shaman said. "There is such a metaphysical concept—I think it's called solipsism. But it wouldn't work like that in reality, would it? Probably gods and playwrights have the same problem. Creative consciousness in a vacuum is one thing, but people and objects and events once created have a way of getting out of hand. Then what's real? Who's in control?"

"You're in pretty bad shape," Ralph Elf said. "Maybe when your power comes back."

"I need a six-month rest cure. Food, sleep, vitamins, exercise, sunbathing on the Riviera."

"This place was the best I could do. It'll have to do. I don't know the city anymore, it's all so weird out there. Everything is gone, everybody I knew is killed or gone. Man, it's Freaksville!"

Ralph Elf looked peaked and taut and frightened.

"It's like Hell," he whispered.

"Where are we?" Shaman said. The loft was filled with props and artifacts: furniture, stacked flats, free-standing doors, windows, and archways, an elephant houdah, a cardboard fireplace, heaped-up drapes and rugs, and mountains of crates and boxes. Everywhere were little nests and campsites where the Zombies lived.

"I call them the Zombies, the city's full of them. They can't go anywhere, nobody wants them," Ralph Elf said. "The Nazis and the Vols shoot at them, so do the Reds. They're all over underground and in these lofts and places. This used to be a shooting gallery, a junkie hangout, it's my old neighborhood. It used to be the African Center for Dance, Music, Culture, and Magic. Some are just crippled or old or crazy, there's no place to go out there. They're not all dopers, but mostly. What else is there? Leftovers, you could call them, odds and ends. Left over when everything went weird out there. Remains. They just don't know they're dead yet."

He explained that in normal times the Zombies would be hanging out in the street or in detox centers or hospitals or old-folks' homes or rehab centers or flophouses on the margins of society. But these were not normal times. There wasn't any society. Some of what he said was difficult to follow. Ralph Elf was getting worse. He was a Zombie too.

"They yell and puke all night."

"How did we get here?" Shaman said.

"I thought we could just lie up somewhere. I didn't know. I ditched that van. I dragged you around all day, looking for some kind of hideout like this. It'll have to do."

"You saved my ass again," Shaman said. "Still coming in handy."

"Man, we're friends, aren't we? What's friends for? Hey, we must've known each other a couple months already. That makes us *old* friends, the way things are now," Ralph said. "It wasn't easy, though, the city's not like it used to be, everything has gone to pieces, it's all changed. You can't just walk around with no place to crash, until somebody picks up on it. I used to know plenty of characters who would hide me out, where did they go? We're lucky we found this place, we're lucky we found these Zombies. Tell them something."

"Tell them what?"

Ralph Elf laughed. The Zombies heard and came closer, appearing from the shadows, trying to listen, coming back again. Chased away repeatedly, they kept coming back. Ralph Elf began laughing immoderately.

"I told them you were God. Didn't you hear them, praying and confessing?"

"I heard."

"They took us in, didn't they? They pulled you through, didn't they? They don't even have any food, you're lucky they didn't eat *you*! All the time I wasn't here, they took care of you. I got a workshop, I make some bombs for Machete and the Reds, then I deliver downtown. I get some food, that's where the food's coming from, the little we got. They let me feed you, they let you eat it. They didn't even *kill* us for it."

Shaman sat up and looked at the Zombies. They nodded and grinned.

Ralph Elf said: "Their main man went O.D. and out. He was their main man, he led them on little rat raids, for food and dope. Now they've got nobody, nothing, nowhere to go, what to do? They needed a god. A god of food, junk, and hope. You're it, they love you. Salvation."

"They believe that?"

"When you've got nothing, you believe anything."

"What do they want from me?"

"I told them you're a big PFA general with a connection. Help me fix you up and you'll lead them all to the mountains, where mankind and smack are free."

"Forget it," Shaman said. "I've got things to do."

"Yes, but not till you're well again."

"Let's get down to business. Where are the bullets for this revolver? What happened to that elevator guard's shotgun?"

Ralph Elf dug secretively in his shirt. "Here's the bullets for your gun. The shotgun I traded for blasting caps."

"Who are Machete and the Reds?"

Ralph Elf became intensely serious and sententious.

"They are the PFA guerrilla force left behind in the city to harass and terrorize," he said. "That's all I know and all I want to know. I don't have anything to do with this People's thing. I'm no revolutionary. I'm a technician. If they want bombs and chemicals and such, that's my bread and butter, but don't expect me to take sides. I may be crazy, but to me, what's the difference? I don't see any difference just because you write *freedom* on your flag and kill people. What's the big difference between the liquidation of the kulaks and the crematoriums and Hiroshima? What's the difference between killing to keep America free and killing to make America free? I can't even remember which side is saying what."

"Never mind that," Shaman said. "Can you get me in touch with the local PFA or can't you?"

First, he lay on or in or under a pile of tattered mock-velvet drapes, rugs, costumes, and miscellaneous rags for another four days, eating Ralph Elf's hard-earned Cup-A-Soup, bananas, peanut butter, cheese, raisins, and canned fruit, while improving his education.

"Tell me all about it," he said to the Zombies.

A couple of the Vol deserters were high on something, capsules out of a mixed hatful, any- and everything. They tried to give him some, or anything else, whatever he wanted, offerings at his feet, intoning, goofing:

"Sham! Man! Sham! Man!"

In a dusty shaft of light from above, Peterwell and Ward were dancing together, a dreamy foxtrot, humming music, touching tongues. The others were more or less somewhere nearby. BP's one-legged father sat in a nest of rags and cried. Subway Conductor, Fried Fat, and Smith were conspiring. Tex was nodding out in a corner. Ralph Elf had gone downtown.

Diosdado came to sit by Shaman. Running nose and watery eyes and uncontrollable twitches, but apart from that and signs of malnutrition, an unusually handsome, curly-haired, long-lashed, faunlike young man, beautifully made except for one thing. Diosdado said:

"You see this honch? You know what is a honchback in this city? That's *no chance*, hermano! Forget it! Go drown yourself! But I tell you something. I make it anyway! In the old days I make it, I make it *big* like I don't *got* this honch! Because I am a *brains!* You take me with you, I be a brains for you too. I make it big in the city with my honch and my brains like you never saw! I don't feel like a honch, nobody know I got this honch. The chicas they don't say, Get lost, *jorobao!* They say, Oh, Dadi! I was the *big* time! With my brains! Only eighteen years old!"

He rocked his buttocks on the soot-drifted floor. Tears leaked from his eyes. He lived it again. Big time was *la tecata*. Heroin meant big money, fine cars, fancy girls, no hunch.

"The paisans, they got the smack. They don't give you only a little. You get too much, maybe you take over. Don't push, don't push the organization. But I *think!* I think, they got fights! They got trouble with the Cubans and the coloreds. Talk to *them!* A piece costs maybe two hundred, two fifty—I got a thousand! Me and Rudi, my friend, we spread it around, piece here, piece there. We go out of the neighborhood, we even go out of the borough! Paisans sell us a little, coloreds sell us a little, Cubans sell us a little. I got a *stash!* Dadi is dealing! Next we got pushers! Next we got pipeline! Big Time!"

Sitting in the soot on a yardbird's nutmeg-high with a headache, nausea, tears leaking down his cheeks. What happened?

"One year. My whole life. One year. I got a Cadillac brougham. I get up every morning, I got satin sheets. Chicas kiss my cock. Walk my streets, people say, Big Dadi! I tell you something. Honch is gone! I *got* no honch! One year, one *bendito* year of a *life!* Charmaine she move in with me, the most best thing I ever have. Arrogante, black like silk, silver hair. She teach me everything—smoke, snort, screw. Every night we are in the moon. I love her! I am screwing like loco, I am stuffing all the time. White horse. Two weeks *embalao*. Strung out like you never saw. Wake up in the satin sheets—*tutzones* all around the bed. Charmaine, that black motherfuck puta! Paisans send her to *set me up!*

Too big too fast, don't push the organization. *Cosas de la vida.*

"Wha? Wha? Wha? I say. No think, no brains, just white horse crazies. I find out soon. Big black *cabrones* all around the bed. My honch is back. One year, one year of a whole life. Black cocksuckers whip it. They got a whip, bunch of aerials. Blood all over, meat strips. I look at Rudi, my friend. Rudi's in the bed. Rudi's dead. Face all cut open, neck all cut open. Stomach cut. They put the whip in Rudi's hand. Put the knife in my hand. Police was there already, writing notebooks. You know. The paisans got the cops too. I don't feel nothing yet, too much horse. Tomorrow I feel it. Cops whipping it, big bloody honch. Lawyer says, Welcome to the big time. I got a deck and a half. Fifteen years."

Poor Diosdado, poor Dadi. A young-old crippled faun dumped back fifteen years later on the wild streets of a city he never knew. Exploding bombs, fires, soldiers, guerrillas, shootouts, snipers. Supplies dried up, and the last few pushers dodging mobs of ferocious, panicked addicts, and PFA death squads too. Hiding out in a loft full of junkies with his mangled back and screeching skull. Trying to feed a fifteen-year prison habit on nutmeg, Nyquil, and worm pills, choking on his own pus. Lunares tried to take care of him sometimes, as they were both from Arecibo, but he had had enough of women, and screamed: Get away, you black motherfuck whore!

Peterwell and Ward danced past, dipped to a halt, stood still embracing, playfully: "We're the two-backed beast!" The beast swayed and clung, each contour and surface touching. It simpered and mocked: "He thinks you're going to save *him*! Just because the PFA takes jailbirds! Isn't that redick? Don't you just come? He sniffs ammonia! He eats worm pills! Antihelminthics, like a doggie! For the harmine! He really thinks you'll take *him* to the mountains! Imagine! *We're* under no such delusions. We *know* the awful things the Reds do to us. We know where *we* belong. *Some* of us at least still know how to score!"

And whirled away, humming: "All You Need Is Love."

The two-backed beast and BP, the baby prostitute, were the only ones who could still score regularly off the strange armed animals in the wild, shattered Freaksville streets, and then only at night, in the dark, amongst the blasted walls, hiding from the Vol patrols, the Red marauders, the gangs, the madmen. When BP went out, she gibbered and gobbed from dim doorways: Blah, blab, blap! She couldn't talk anymore. When she came back with a stick or a fistful of 222's or bennies, her one-legged father would stop crying for a while about the awful thing he did to her when she was eight, and they would nestle up in the rags together and swing.

BP's father would not be around much longer. He had lost all his coordination and staggered and fell down and dropped food out of his mouth and fell asleep in the middle of things, and sometimes stopped breathing and turned cyanotic from too many bennies. Poor BP's one-legged father.

Subway Conductor, Fried Fat, and Smith were conspiring. They had not made a grab in weeks. It wasn't any use talking. They gave up and came swaggering and complaining, tough and aggrieved. "Nobody can't score if there ain't nobody left to score off!"

Tell me all about it.

Subway Conductor, Fried Fat, and Smith said:

"Not like the old days!"

"You should have seen us in the old days!"

"In the old days, we was a team!"

Three shivering, bony, baldheaded old men with body bugs.

"See, we all turned out in different ways. Back in the *old* old days he was a numbers runner, he was a car thief, I was the only one into mugging. And juicy too. I would go down to midtown, midtown money. Only it got too crowded. There was whole packs. They'd just as soon mug you as a tourist. You'd hit a mark, they'd hit you. I needed backup. The shit was starting, this revolution shit, and I needed partners."

"He needed partners, I needed a new thing. The shit storm,

you know. It was getting bad. I used to boost cars, you know, I had my own tricks. Always work alone. Way out on the Island, farout places, ain't no cops in a mile. I had my own ignition switch, complete ignition switch, with a key and all. I just pull the wires, put in my own switch, turn my key in the box, and away we go. Back to town, drive into Cisimo's, he would sell some of them if they was a Ford—just tear those door tags off, and they never stamp their engine block either. But mostly rip it down. I never saw nothing like it. So fast you wouldn't believe. *Bang* goes the hood, *pow* goes the jacks, *slam* goes the blocks, and *whoosh*, out comes the guts. Engine, transmission, differential, batteries, tires, radio, stereo, air conditioner, bucket seats. In half an hour there's nothing left but a hunk of junk. He towed them away somewhere. He handed me two hundred a car. I was making out. But then they started the shit storm and then they started the gas rationing, and then the essential driving, and nobody had much money anyway, and then they started the shooting, and nobody was driving no place. It happened so fast. They was commandeering cars, and the others was blowing them up, and roadblocks and tanks, so I said, Piss on this noise, I don't need no war! Cisimo got shot by white dudes in hunting boots—what *is* this shit? No more car clouting."

"Not much numbers then either. Oh, not right away. People will always buy, but it's hard, right in the middle of everything—busting and shooting. The whole barrio was a battlefield all of a sudden. Incidentally, I wasn't a runner, by the way. I was controller, later district collection, for a wheel we had. The Holy Oriental Lucky Room Bank. It was in a funeral home. We covered thirty-two blocks. But the shit was already starting. Oh, not right away, just Racial Pride and Oppression and White Devil stuff. Bet on Brotherhood, not on the Bolita. Players giving their money to those gangs instead—Palante, Time of Power Party. Or buying guns. Then the Reds put out a reward on runners, our runners were getting beat up. Banks getting raided and robbed. They were handing out propaganda. Numbers, gambling, booze, dope—the Man is cutting your balls off. We heard the People's Freedom or whatever was going to stop crime. Oh, we laughed. Stop playing, boozing, and stuffing? What will they *do* with themselves? Well, it happened, all right. They stopped everything! You can't go out in the street! It's murder!"

"Same here. I was into mugging all my life. Regular mugging, like in the *old* old days, midtown money. It seems like years ago. But even after we teamed up, it was getting hard. Declined right down the line. No more fat cats, no more out-of-towns, no more movie managers, no more pimps, no more finance collectors. Cops and Vols all over, anybody has a bill has a gun. Uptown just as bad, no more unemployeds, no more welfares, nobody with a dime. Not even hardly a pusher, stuff all cut off at the source. Silver City, New Orleans screwed up too, fighting wars. We made it awhile when they had the dole, government food. Hitting people coming off the handout lines, for the groceries. Like it's the end for us, man. Soaking beans and rice off old ladies. Then they cut out that, no more dole. Those that still eats are out at night shaking the city for dogs and cats and rats. Those that stuffs are out dealing and dying for the last six codeine pills in the world. And that's where it is. That's how it stands."

"We haven't made a grab in weeks. Nothing to grab."

"But we still got the cods. Give us a chance."

"Like, you know, man, we've been thinking about it, we wouldn't say no, we wouldn't mind, what we mean, branching out a little, freedom and like that, it sounds good to us, we like your operation, we got lots to offer, you help us, hit on the right people, get together on it, we got a dynamite deal, right?"

Everybody wants to go to the mountains.

Poor old Subway Conductor, Fried Fat, and Smith. Strummed up on the last six codeine pills in the world and nowhere to go. They just didn't know they were dead yet.

Then came Tex, the white pimp: "Has that hoity-toity black buttfucker been talking to you? God damn a nigger, shorting me out, beating my time! Don't listen to him! I always loved freedom! Take *me!*"

Then came Whitelaw, the black one: "All right. I don't argue. You got to take only one. Take the best. I prove it to you. Don't answer me nothing. Just say to me: Go! I cut his honky heart out!"

And Lunares, hauling up her Indian skins, to show him where she got her sobriquet: spots and sores and yellow stuff. "I cannot do straight tricks anymore. But I can do French. Give head, you say. Up the back. Hand jobs. Freak tricks. I dress up. You hurt me. I hurt you. What you want? You don't have to pay me nothing. Help me. I need help. I need help. I need help. I need help. I need help. I need help."

All in all, education and all, when Ralph Elf came back and brought Machete with him, it was soon enough.

Lieutenant Machete, Rob Williams Company, Inner City Task Force One, Metropolitan Sector Headquarters, Northeast Tactical Command, People's Freedom Army, U.S.A.

Vampire

"We risk our necks getting here. Maybe we got to battle our way back," Machete said. "Let's see this wounded PFA general you talk about."

"Oh, I just said that," Ralph Elf said. "To get you to come."

The muzzle of Machete's BAR scribbled on the air, including Ralph Elf, Shaman, and the Zombies in one quick motion. His voice snapped with anger.

"I got authorization to execute all here!"

Flanking him were two assistants with automatic shotguns.

"Not me!" Ralph Elf said. "You can't execute me!"

"You useful, bomb man. The rest comes under Desanctification."

Machete was tallish, thinnish, oldish; the BAR looked outsized on him, but he handled it with ease. His irritable, bloodshot eyes were the eyes of a worrier.

Shaman said: "What's Desanctification?"

"Who you?"

"I'm that wounded PFA general."

"You better be, or you dead too."

The guns aimed.

One of the Vol deserters broke and ran for it. An assistant took two quick strides and tripped him; he scuttled on hands and knees; the assistant clubbed the nape of his neck with the butt of a shotgun; the Vol fell flat on his face; the assistant hammered his skull three times hard; bone cracked and crunched;

once more for good measure; the head was dented all out of round, bleeding from eyes, ears, nose, and mouth.

The assistant was a muscular pug-nosed blond with forearms like thighs. He said lucidly to Machete: "We don't want any shots up here. It's still daylight. There might be patrols outside, right, Lieutenant?"

"Right on," Machete said. "Watch out the rest of them."

The assistants took up positions guarding the Zombies. The second assistant was as big as the first, or bigger; he wore crisscross cartridge belts and bandido mustachios. He took out a big knife.

"Say the word."

"I don't know," Machete said. "That was back when the Terror. Maybe it ain't Discipline now."

Shaman remembered. Desanctification was standard operating procedure during an early phase of the Revolution; it was based on something in the manifesto: "We call an end to the sanctification of the useless. No more shall society's misfits, morons, psychopaths, and criminals be coddled and cosseted at the expense of the People."

It was one of the more ambiguous passages. Moderates took it to mean no more bleeding the worker to support the non-worker in costly charitable, mental, or penal institutions; extremists interpreted it to mean an end to parasitism of all sorts via summary executions; the fanatic fringe extended the meaning of useless to include everyone from Mafia kingpins through politicians to mongoloid idiots.

During the Terror, along with open warfare by the PFA against the fat cats and their military and police lackeys, there were also massacres and assassinations by death squads not only of Syndicate gangsters, drug traffickers, vice lords, purveyors of pornography, gambling operators, et cetera, but also of addicts, alcoholics, rapists, child molesters, pimps, madams, whores, homosexuals, the mentally ill, even cripples, the aged, infirm, and retarded—the fargone as well as the farout. To the wall.

"It was never rescinded," Mustachios said.

Ralph Elf and Shaman stood together. Ralph Elf clutched Shaman's arm.

"Not me! Not him!" he said. "You said you'd take us to headquarters!"

"He don't look like no PFA general to me," Machete said.

Mustachios cachinnated. "What he looks like is a sick doctor."

Shaman still wore the white coat, now ragged and filthy.

"I'm a courier," he said. "I just escaped from Northstate with a top-secret message for Metropolitan Sector Headquarters."

Mustachios cachinnated. "Northstate is right. The fucking funny farm."

"Waste the fucker," Pugnose said.

"I ain't going to mess with this!" Machete said irritably.

Shaman still wore the white coat; he reached under it, brought out the forty-five revolver and stabbed it in Ralph Elf's belly button; Ralph Elf turned the color of cream cheese.

"We go to sector headquarters or your bomb man goes to join the majority," Shaman said. "I've already pulled the trigger. All that's holding the hammer back is my thumb. Shoot me, and it slips."

Machete's bloodshot eyes did not so much as look at the revolver.

"Slip away," he said. "There's plenty bomb men."

Mustachios cachinnated. "We shoot you and get him for free."

"What an asshole," Pugnose said. "Waste the fucker."

Shaman said: "Aren't you going to save him?"

Machete leveled the BAR. "Who cares?"

Ralph Elf shut his eyes.

"*You* better," he whispered. "I got half my stock in trade in a money belt around my waist and the rest in my pockets. Enough high-power explosives to spray the whole bunch of us all over the block, if a bullet hits me."

Machete made a quick command decision.

"Brother, don't get so edgy," he said. "Let's talk."

So then they all went together to Metropolitan Sector Headquarters.

"Only it ain't just that easy," Machete said.

"Discipline," Machete said. "We move when it's safe, that's how come we lived this long. Discipline. Bide by the rules, that's what they got them for. Don't make sense—Discipline say, do it anyway. That's why we an army now, not just mobs. Discipline is the faith of the Cause."

They were crouched on a rooftop, behind a parapet, looking out across a city smoldering in sad sunset light. Shaman and Machete kept watch; Mustachios and Pugnose dozed; Ralph Elf was muttering to himself. On the roof were a shattered water tank, the remains of dozens of television antennas, clotheslines, old tar buckets, and two passed-out winos wrapped in ragged overcoats. Machete said about the winos: "Ain't no place for such in the New World to come."

The roof was not high, but the building was perched on high ground; it made a good vantage point. There was a horizontal view of the city under a canopy of pollution, and a vertical view of the darkening streets below. The city smoked in a hundred places like a dump heap; actual fires burned in several tall buildings. There were some sirens and bells, every so often a gunshot, once an explosion, but the general effect was silence. An airy, abandoned silence. No traffic noise. Down below, the streets were empty of people but jammed full of cars, parked, fuel-less, stripped, forgotten. The sidewalks were piled high with festered mountains of garbage, and the curbs, the streets, even the cars, were covered with it. Nothing seemed to move except the slow smoke and the distant flickering flames.

Right now was the magic hour. The Vols and police owned the city during the day; the rebels, the gangs, the marauders, and the madmen owned it at night. Machete was waiting out the twilight.

"Makes no never mind to me," he said about the winos. "I wouldn't be bothered with them. Ain't my job. I was never Morals Squad. They would waste anybody, their job was killing Useless. Crooks, junkies, fags, kid gangs. I never done that. Same reason I don't kill them poor old freaks in the loft. Why? In the Terror I was Crimes Squad awhile. We kill lawyers, bank officers, loan-company guys, that's different. That's Enemies of the People. Some we shoot, some we bring to People's Court. I always like Assaults Squad best. Telephone exchanges, TV, radio stations, power plants, police stations. That's fighting! That's Cripple the System, Defeat the Oppressor! I don't say nothing against killing Useless, if it's Discipline. I just say I'm glad it wasn't never my job to do."

Except for when he was sent out on false leads about stray wounded PFA generals, Machete's job was a daily round of sabotaging utilities, disrupting communications, wrecking police vehicles, ambushing Vol patrols, booby-trapping bridges and tunnels, starting fires and cutting the firehoses, et cetera, as part of the PFA guerrilla force left behind in the city to keep it in a constant state of anarchy and panic.

"Eddie, now, that's different," he said, pointing his chin at Pugnose. "He was Morals Squad. He was Euthanastes. Like as not he drops them two winos over before he leaves, I bet. That's his Discipline, he likes it."

Pugnose was the one who had torched the rubbish-piled building with a thermite grenade when they moved out, leaving the Zombies to roast in the loft. He was also the one who dropped the passed-out winos over the parapet before the group left the roof. They never woke up; dived in silence into the dark.

"What the hell kind of war is this?" Shaman said.

"You didn't know?" Ralph Elf said bitterly.

Machete signaled: *Down!*

They ducked, hid behind heaps of garbage or derelict cars; ahead was an intersection; the narrow street opened on a broad avenue; lights were moving on the avenue.

The narrow cross street was in complete darkness; up ahead the intersection was like a stage. Enter left, crossing from north to south: the enemy. First scouts on foot, wearing flak vests and carrying submachine guns, then an armored car, then two troop carriers filled with men, then a flatbed truck with a searchlight, last a half-track bristling with twin fifties. The searchlight revolved slowly; powerful spotlights and flashlights probed the darkness; headlamps lit the way ahead. Walkie-talkies and radios crackled. The column went on; the lights faded away.

Columns like this one passed up and down the main avenues throughout the night. In addition, there were foot patrols in the side streets; in addition, heavy weapons companies strategically located; in addition, reinforcement groups including troops, tanks, and heli-gunships armed with rocket launchers, anti-personnel bombs, and hopper-fed, laser-sighted Gatling guns.

The mission was to hold rebel operations to a minimum from curfew until dawn, when the police took over the city.

It was a long way downtown to Metropolitan Sector Headquarters on the lower east side.

Shaman wanted to know why they crept along penned into narrow canyons instead of using the subways, sewers, underground pipelines, and other tunnels beneath the city.

Pugnose whispered: "Electrified, mined, poison-gassed, bugged, TV monitored—you name it. They ain't *that* stupid, asshole."

"How about the park?" The park ran north to south, miles of it, gone wild; he would have felt more comfortable amongst rocks and trees, rather than boxed in a cross street. But the park had been off limits for years.

"It's a fucking *mesh* of trip wires," Pugnose explained.

Machete wormed his way back from the point and hissed with rage: Shut up! Shut up! Didn't they know every other lightless lamp post was now a listening device?

He was staring worriedly at Shaman's white coat.

"You awful visible, ain't you?"

Under it were a decomposing aloha shirt and a pair of oversized pants. Shaman said: "Do you think HQ will believe I'm a PFA officer?"

Machete and the others were dressed in dark clothes, with caps pulled low. Ralph Elf too. Machete said to him: "Where you get them clothes?"

They had to jog him; Ralph Elf seemed in a state of abstraction. "In a store. It was empty. It was wrecked."

"Good idea," Machete said. "There's lots of stores, we could keep an eye out."

They moved on. One at a time they crossed the avenue. Machete first; count fifty; Mustachios; count fifty; then the rest. Running, Shaman glanced south and saw taillights, searchlights, spotlights far away. They entered another cross street, ran along, turned several corners. A ruddy glare lighted the walls. Machete signaled. They all dove for cover.

Down the street a doorway was burning. It was choked with rubbish and seemed to have vomited rubbish onto the stoop and sidewalk, and the rubbish was blazing like a bonfire. People were watching it; there were people in windows and on fire escapes and nearby roofs. In the firelight Shaman saw abandoned cars and mountains of garbage and quiet faces glowing red.

"I wondered where everybody was," he said curiously.

For the first time he had a sense, not of deserted ruins, but of hived and hidden life all around.

Ralph Elf was crouched hugging his knees, muttering:

"No, they're all gone. Old ladies, sick people dying in rooms, burnt buildings, basements, no water, no light, no food."

He was more than abstracted; he appeared dazed.

Mustachios came crawling through the filth.

"Machete says split out of here. That's going to draw a patrol, maybe helicopters. And quit that talking, he says. No more talking."

They doubled back and ran. Ran and ran. Machete led them south, east, west, north, jogging through deep canyons, dodging and darting across open spaces, sprinting across intersections.

Shaman was lost, turned around, disoriented; still weak, he puffed and panted, slipped and stumbled. All the streets were the same, cars and garbage, stoops, smashed storefronts, broken or boarded windows, gutted buildings, bullet-pocked walls.

He was reading the walls; all the walls had graffiti. He had not been able to read them in the darkness; now he was reading them: STEEL KNUCKLES. WHITE DEVIL BEAST OF THE EARTH. HORSE IS BOSS.

They were splashed or spray-painted on all the walls; some of the more recent, in red paint, were PFM slogans: UNITE OR PERISH. FIGHT OR DIE.

He saw them clearly. He was seeing something else too. Where was the light coming from?

It was, or had been, a narrow cross street like any other, but the canyon wall on one side had been blasted to rubble, bulldozed off like a firebreak. One whole side of the street was open to the sky. High in the sky over the nearest rooftops hung a blue-white flare. Far away, but it lighted the garbage underfoot. There were tracks in the garbage.

"Hold it!" he yelled in the eerie quiet.

In the lead, Machete jumped as though goosed, spun around and came charging with his head down; he stopped with his face inches from Shaman's face, his BAR in Shaman's stomach. His big teeth gleamed and gritted, and he hissed like a steam valve:

"You make *one more noise!*"

"All right. But you're walking into an ambush."

Machete peered. "What you mean?"

"Look," Shaman said.

The tracks in the garbage were as clear as though stamped in fresh mud. Heels, wheels, and slip marks. A squashed juice carton was still dribbling a last few drops. A ridge of ooze was leveling out, and a crushed plastic bottle was just regaining its shape.

"At least a dozen men and one truck," Shaman said. "They went through about two minutes ago. If you can't see them a hundred yards ahead on the street, they're not on the street. If they're not on it, they're deployed off it, ahead of us, waiting for us."

"How you know that?"

"It's what I'd do," Shaman said. "I'm an old bushwhacker myself."

Left alone at the point, Mustachios suddenly jumped up, fired his shotgun, and came running back.

"*It's fucking Vols!*"

Lights blazed on; among the derelict cars was an Army truck; headlamps and spotlights briefly silhouetted Mustachios. Whistles blew; several of the Vols got off fast shots, taken by surprise, and then the truck's fifty-caliber machine guns came on with a mind-numbing roar like an avalanche; but it was too late. The ambush had failed.

The heavy bullets blew up garbage in fountains, smashed into walls and cars. Too late; a hundred yards away—Shaman and Ralph Elf first, Pugnose and Mustachios right behind them, last Machete, pausing to check them past—all were entering the first available doorway.

They were in an apartment building; by the vague light from the street they could see a wall of mailboxes and buzzers; beyond that total darkness. Machete felt his way ahead, led them straight into the building, trampling in the trash. He turned on a penlight. Red rat eyes looked up at them and bugs crawled the walls.

At the end of the hall was a fire door, burst outward; Machete crept on all fours and looked out. Behind the apartment building was an areaway, a pit at the bottom of an airshaft; overhead were fire escapes, clotheslines, and dead wiring. Machete led on, without the light. They followed across the open space, entered another building via a rear door, went along still another infested hall, and emerged on a street again. And ran like hell.

"You done us a favor. We almost walk into that. Now I do you one too," Machete said. "You know where this place is?"

It was some kind of underground arcade. In midtown, south of the park, off one of the main avenues amongst tall buildings, an arcade or underpass just below street level. The dim glow of Machete's penlight partly illuminated the remains of shops and snack bars. Underfoot was a mess of shattered glass and cracked tiles. The tiles were from the walls and ceiling; in some places whole chunks of the ceiling had fallen in. Short side tunnels were either choked with debris or completely collapsed. Machete led on to where the wreck of a newsstand leaned against the wall.

"Right around here somewheres, I remember."

He went poking off with the penlight. In the dark, the others sat down, breathing noisily. Shaman found Ralph Elf by feel and patted him. Ralph Elf muttered dazedly: "My head hurts." Shaman relaxed and listened to the other two: Mustachios on his right drawing his knife from its self-sharpening scabbard; Pugnose on his left unloading and reloading his shotgun blindly. Then they all shut their eyes in the dark and waited, glad of the rest.

The newsstand was a flimsy bolt-together structure like a child's playhouse. Across the front a few old magazines still hung from bulldog clips strung on wires. The inside of the stand was stuffed full of crumpled and shredded newspapers, heaped up and hollowed out to form a soft burrow. In the darkness no one saw this, or knew that the inhabitant was at home.

Machete came back. "I find it. Come on," he said to Shaman, and took him along the arcade; they passed a booth, turnstiles, and a dark stairway down to the subway; they came to a storefront,

smashed plate glass and mutilated mannequins. A sign read:
HABAND.

"Fine clothes. I fix you up. Said I would." Machete chuckled
richly.

By the glow of the penlight Shaman saw smashed fixtures,
toppled racks, piles of clothing.

Back at the newsstand, newspapers rustled quietly. Mustachios thought it was Pugnose or Ralph Elf stirring. Pugnose
thought it was Ralph Elf or Mustachios. Ralph Elf didn't notice.
It was so black he couldn't tell whether his eyes were open or
shut. He was trembling all over.

In the store Machete said: "What you looking for now?"

Shaman had already found a sage-green denim coverall, a cap,
underwear, socks, and a pair of work shoes; had dressed in them,
discarding the white coat, aloha shirt, pants, and loafers; but he
was still searching the place for something: a white silk scarf. It
was the wrong kind of store. "Shoo, man, we find you a ladies'
wear," Machete mocked.

In the vampire's burrow were pigeon feathers and feet and
sucked bones. It crouched on all fours; it listened and smelt and
felt; prey was only an arm's length away.

Ralph Elf sat trembling. He felt like weeping without knowing
why; he yawned and stretched instead, making a faint moaning
sound.

In the pitch-dark something landed on his back; it gripped
and hung on. Hot, wet, and hairy, it nuzzled his neck and
bit in.

His scream filled the whole arcade.

A few feet from him Pugnose convulsed with fright and fired
his shotgun accidentally, startling Mustachios out of a light doze.
In the store Machete switched off the penlight and froze; Shaman
took one step and flattened against a wall. Up above on the
avenue a passing Vol patrol heard the scream faintly and the
gunshot loud and clear.

Running, Shaman and Machete heard Ralph Elf scream again.
Draw breath and scream again. He was lying on his back in the
mess of glass and tiles. Blood ran from his neck. His mouth
gaped as he sucked breath and screamed again.

"Shut him up!" Machete hissed.

Shaman bent over and stunned Ralph Elf with the butt of his revolver.

In the glow of the penlight something struggled feebly. Pugnose and Mustachios held it by the arms, yanking its head back by the hair. Long, dirty hair growing down the back of the head. The bony head had a white bulging forehead and the eyes were sunk in deep pits. The nose was missing, ulcerated away by cocaine or possibly cut off, but the flesh around it had healed, leaving a triangular hole. Together with the gritting, grinning teeth, the effect was skull-like.

It was naked and filthy. Blood ran from the jaws down between sagging black-veined breasts. The body was scrawny, the arms and legs sinewy, the sex withered, the hands and feet equipped with claws.

Mustachios held its head yanked back by the hair. "Watch out. This is going to gush."

He stabbed his long knife straight into the throat. Pierced the hyoid bone, thyroid cartilage, ventricular and vocal folds, cricoid and tracheal rings, arytenoid muscles, larynx and ventricle. Then slashed outward.

Ralph Elf's mouth gaped and he screamed at the ceiling.

Machete said: *"Shut him up!"*

Pugnose tried to kick him in the head and missed. Shaman knelt, touched his hand to Ralph Elf's lips, and hushed him. Machete switched off the penlight. They listened.

Distant clattering sounds echoed through the arcade; back in the direction of the entrance the walls glowed; the beam of a spotlight zigzagged down the stairs.

"Move out," Machete whispered.

Shaman hoisted Ralph Elf to his feet by the slack of his shirt. Ralph Elf screamed.

"Cut *his* throat," Pugnose said.

"Shut up, shut up! Grab belts!" Machete led the way; Mustachios grabbed his belt in the back; Pugnose grabbed his; Shaman grabbed Pugnose with one hand and dragged Ralph Elf with the other.

They moved this way for a dozen or so yards. Glass and tiles crunched underfoot. Whistles echoed. Lights glimmered behind them. "Aw, fuck it," Machete said. He switched on the penlight. "Might as well see. They know we down here. Got both ends shut off too, what you want to bet?"

They ran, following Machete's little light. Behind them men in steel helmets and flak jackets filled the arcade. Far ahead in the dark shrill whistles sounded. Trapped.

"Aw, fuck it," Machete said; they had reached the change booth and the turnstiles; he crawled under a turnstile, dragging the BAR. They followed, and ran down the dark stairs to the subway platform.

Shaman said: "I thought these tunnels were wired?"

Machete jumped down onto the tracks.

"Stay here, then. Wait for the flamethrowers."

Mustachios was leaning out over the platform, twisting his neck to see into the dark tunnel where the tracks led away.

"What if we step on a third rail?"

"Asshole," Pugnose said. "There ain't any juice since the riots."

They followed Machete; the tunnel entrance was blocked by a wooden barricade with a yellow lightning slash and the word DANGER.

Shaman said: "Hold it a minute."

Machete turned the light on his face.

"Don't quit thinking yet," Shaman said. "What happens now?"

"It comes up top by the bridge," Machete said. "Maybe they ain't plugged up that end yet. It's about a mile."

"Can we get through?"

"We can try. It's half fell down in places. I don't know."

"They'll follow us in," Shaman said.

"That's right. They'll catch up. We got to step slow, watch out trip wires, mines, claymores. They can step in our track. We got to creep and feel—they can run. They'll catch us up in two minutes. If we don't blow ourselfs up first. All right. But it's better than the flamethrowers. I going in. You do what you want."

Shaman spun the revolver on his forefinger. "What if we could stop them right here?"

"How?"

"Keep them from following us into the tunnel. What then?"

"Shoo, man. We're in headquarters, almost. It's by the bridge."

Shaman was looking at the arched roof overhead, just inside the tunnel mouth. Water running, wires and conduits dangling down, enormous slabs of stone cracked and heaved by past explosions up above.

"Great place for a cave-in," he said.

The lights and clatter were at the turnstiles.

"You go on," Shaman said. "Trip those wires, or leave me a safe track to follow, I don't care which. You've got about thirty seconds."

Shaman was alone; he had withdrawn some twenty-five yards into the tunnel; he lay on his stomach with his elbows propped in the muck, the revolver held tightly in a two-hand grip.

Flak jackets and steel helmets were on the station platform.

Spotlights and flashlights flickered this way and that. Then they all came to focus on Ralph Elf. Handy to the last.

Ralph Elf hung upright on the wooden barricade, his arms hooked behind him over the top rail; he was facing into the tunnel, away from the lights. His head was lifted, turned toward Shaman, but from that distance the staring, empty eyes weren't visible.

Shaman steadied the front sight on Ralph Elf's midriff, where the belt was, under his shirt.

"Old friend," he said.

The blast brought the entire arched roof down.

Revenant

Brigadier General Coldebeefe, PFAUSA, was a six-foot-three, 290-pound professional soldier, and one of the top combat commanders in Northeast Zone.

Formerly a U.S. Army career man, he had been among the first to join the PFM's secret cadre after Second 'Nam; as junior officer and later as infantry commander he had spied, proselytized, and agitated for the Cause. Following the famine, the riots, the Meltdown, and the outbreak of actual armed revolution, he had been a key figure in the famous "colonels' coup" which had turned the entire 509th Regimental Combat Team over to the rebels, lock, stock, and barrel.

Since that time he had fought his share of battles, had been promoted and decorated, and was currently assigned to the staff of Northeast Tactical Command. At the present moment he was on detached service, traveling incognito, halfway there, sitting on his duffel bag eating Reese's peanut butter cups and drinking warm cream soda.

He wore tailored green fatigues, black boots, web belt, and pistol; on his shaved head was a peaked cap with a gold star. Everybody else in the dead-burned place was out of uniform.

General Coldebeefe was old army, with the regular's contempt for guerrillas, maquis, and other raggle-taggle. He was mildly but basically contemptuous of Metropolitan Sector's mission in the first place, more so of Inner City Task Force, with its haphazard bombings and assassinations, ambushes and suicide raids. Forget unconventional warfare; give him disciplined, uniformed troops, with standardized weapons, every time.

He was even more contemptuous of Rob Williams Company, a typical guerrilla mob with its headquarters in a dead-burned dockside godown. Rat shit and pot smoke and scummy bastards in rags and sneakers. Only one man wore anything like a uniform, a sage-green coverall, and he had demonstrated he was nuts already, flipped out, freaked out, spaced out, whatever. All the rest were the usual cutthroats, like dead-burned street rats. Unsoldierly, irresponsible mugger-buggers that ought to be liquidated before they contaminated the Cause.

The general ate his ninth peanut-butter cup.

On the other hand, let's be fair. Guerrillas had their uses, and they were expendable. While the armies in the mountains were building up, they did a job that was necessary; at least they were on the right side, and usually liquidated themselves in the process anyhow. Furthermore, it wasn't his problem, they weren't his men. He was just visiting.

He was on his way elsewhere. Rob Williams Company Headquarters was only a waystop anyhow, a place to rest, eat, pick up messages. Except there had been no messages and no place to sleep or even sit, and nothing to eat but candy and soda pop.

Let's be fair, though. He was on a top-secret mission. They were not supposed to know he was coming, or who he was when he got there.

Just prior to General Coldebeefe's arrival, Rob Williams Company's C.O., Captain Carelli, a scar-faced ex–labor organizer, had told his men: "Shape it up, you shitepokes, there's a real live PFA general coming through here tonight, traveling incognito on the underground. It's that big Coldebeefe prick, all the way down from Canada to take over command of the Bugleburgh Enclave, but don't mention that, because it's supposed to be a secret."

Enter General Coldebeefe, with his escort, two huge PMP's, one a former ISU pistol champion, the other a Euthanaste karate killer, both dressed in crisp, creased fatigues, white scarfs and bush hats, both armed with automatic pistols and Skorpion submachine guns.

Immediately the whole pack of them had come loping, goofing, bopping around, with moron grins.

"Hey, man, what's the word on the Bugleburgh situation, mon général?"

"Cheese and crackers got all muddy!" General Coldebeefe exploded in a long blast like a rocket. "What kind of dead-burned security is this?"

"That's all right, we heard about it already . . ."

"We heard on the radio, we ain't stupid . . ."

"How many times is this that we held Bugleburgh?"

"And the Vols come and took it back again?"

"Like, we heard Colonel Lysander went crazy."

". . . refused his orders."

". . . going to stand and fight."

"And you're going in . . . relieve him . . . court-martial . . . we heard . . ."

One by one they stopped.

General Coldebeefe stood six-foot-three and swollen.

He nodded left, then right, to his two PMP's.

"The next man who asks a question about Bugleburgh or any other top-secret information, shoot him. Shoot him down

dead in his tracks as a security risk. Don't wait for a signal from
me. Just fire."

The PMP's slipped their safety catches.

Silence.

But something else odd was already happening.

The man in the sage-green coverall was getting up. He had
been seated slumped against a wall, but now he was climbing up,
laboriously, like scaling a cliff. He was balancing weightlessly on
his feet and coming toward them. Soon everybody was watching,
in the silence.

Somebody snickered. General Coldebeefe saw whited hair,
sunless-white skin, eyes that looked all white. Freaked out, all
right. The man seemed to tiptoe-shuffle toward them, kept coming.
He stepped right up to one of the PMP's, stopped inches away.
Gently he touched the tip of one finger to the PMP's white scarf.
He hooked the finger, flipped the scarf out. Flipped it out of
the shirt. The scarf hung down the PMP's broad chest like a
dribble bib. Somebody burst out laughing.

The PMP shook his head addledly—woke up. In startled
anger he raised a fist the size of a beer stein, swung a short, hard
cross with the weight of his whole body behind it—meant to
take the fool's head off at the neck, but the fool blocked it. He
blocked it! General Coldebeefe blinked. Not only blocked it,
but struck back. A hand, fingers—something—slid inside the
PMP's right cross and turned it aside, and the hand or fingers
went on and poked the PMP in his thick throat, just under the
jawbone, faster than the eye could follow.

The PMP was clutching his throat with both hands, saying,
"Glok, glok," his eyes bulging, his tongue sticking out.

"*As you were!*" General Coldebeefe roared at the other PMP,
swinging his Skorpion up.

Frozen motion.

"I'll say when to shoot," the general said.

Something about the man's face . . .

The man looked at the general with frost-colored eyes, shrug-
ging.

"I only wanted to see if it was silk."

Now General Coldebeefe had finished off the peanut-butter
cups and had had his fill of soda pop, as well as of Rob Williams

Company's hospitality, and was awaiting his transport, sitting on his duffel bag gazing fixedly across the room at the figure lying slumped against the wall again. "Who's the scarecrow?"

"Aw, a recruit, who knows?" Captain Carelli said. "They said he's supposed to've escaped from the federal funny farm and wants to join up. Why not? Hey, man, never mind him. Don't you want to know what goes on here?"

"What goes on here?" the general said absently.

Something about the white-eyed face . . .

Carelli was saying:

"I know it ain't real military fighting, with deployed actions and all that, but nobody can say we didn't do our job. When I came down here from Monongahela, I took over a company with a hundred and seventy men, and now I got forty left. But there isn't a power relay, a telephone exchange, police station, motor pool, television, or radio station we haven't hit. Rob Williams and three other companies are keeping four regiments of Vols tied down." He went on talking about the job of Inner City Task Force; the general wasn't listening. "I was in the union since the first job I ever had. I put up dead-or-alive posters on the Conglomerate Bloodsuckers, and then I was in jail three years, and I joined the PFA in the riots. Now I been in the city since the Breakout—they gave me Mao on urban guerrilla war, they asked me to fight from within. I did, I been ripping the guts out of this city for two years. Even in the Vols they pull you off the line sometimes. I got to get out. I don't mean quit. I got lots of fight in me. But I'd like to get into the regular PFA. Up in the hills. Out west. Bugleburgh. Anyplace. I don't have to be a captain. Lately I get this ache in my kidneys. I'm not that young—"

"That's *it!*" General Coldebeefe said. "Pyidawtha Beach!"

Back then he was only a company commander. Second 'Nam was spreading all over the map, and U.S. forces were evacuating everywhere. The bay off Pyidawtha evacuation beachhead was full of ships, the troops were on board, and only an Engineer combat battalion was still inland, in the steep hills behind the waterfront, with orders to destroy the railroad. General Coldebeefe was Captain Michael Riley then, commanding an infantry company, with orders to protect the engineers. The enemy was so close, they could smell him. What's that smell? *Ngapi-htuang*. What's *ngapi-htuang*? Dried fish.

Actually, the whole coast smelled like blasted coal dust and the smoke of burning warehouses and factories. They watched the engineers finishing up. The last bridge, a long one with twenty or so spans, largely built of wooden-tie cribbings, was being blown. The last rolling stock, seven locomotives and about a hundred cars, had been assembled. Backing across, the engineers blew the farthest span first, and dumped as many locomotives and cars as possible into the gap, before retreating to blow the next. The locomotives all had steam up, and started fires in the wood cribbing as they crashed down. The climax came when they ran six tank cars loaded with gasoline into the gorge and drove a fired-up locomotive in after. The bridge began burning so fiercely that whistles on the wrecked locomotives started blowing by themselves.

That's it, that's all, they're done. The engineers left running, just about the time the enemy was arriving—advance parties firing down at them from an inland ridge, also from somewhere to the south. Captain Riley and his company withdrew slowly after the engineers, fighting a brief skirmish or two, and that would have been that, except they got into a firefight on the way through the burned warehouses to the evacuation beachhead. It was only a patrol at first, but the more shooting, the more enemy came running.

By the time they broke free, twenty minutes had passed, they were down to a dozen men, and worse was in store. They raced out onto the beach and stopped cold. The troops were gone, the engineers were gone, all the LST's were gone. Worse still, they must have had to depart in a hurry—the dead were still there. All along the sand a hundred or so casualties were lined up in rows, all in green plastic body bags, except for a hastily abandoned few, hideous lumps of mangled butcher's meat, speckled with flies, without even GRS tags in their teeth.

Captain Riley and his deserted dozen faced outward—seaward—gazing at the ships in the bay. They might have seen something that might have been an LST turning back for them, but it was too late.

They faced inward—inland—dropped their weapons and raised

their arms high over their heads. Out of the burned warehouses, creeping across the shoreline trash, came enemy soldiers, two platoons at least, with guns leveled. An officer in a toupee led them, cautious but grinning. Merikan, you die.

But the LST *was* coming.

And the dead were *not* dead.

Captain Riley heard the chug of the LST edging shoreward. He couldn't understand it. Didn't they see? The enemy soldiers advanced. Only yards away now. They were creeping between the rows of bodies—the green, soggy bags and the unwrapped corpses steaming in the heat.

"I thought I was going insane," General Coldebeefe said. "I thought I was having psychic hallucinations."

Hit the dirt, the dead whispered.

A whistle blew muffledly.

The dead screamed! Captain Riley almost did too.

The body bags, previously slit open from top to bottom underneath, were rolling over, jerking up, jumping in the air, screaming. Each was a green cowled thing, like a mad, hilarious insect in a pod, horned and spined and berserk, exploding in red fire and stinging smoke.

The metallic roar dwindled away raggedly. The roar of whooping, triumphant laughter went on. The rush into the surf began. The LST pilot said the enemy looked like men fed through a shredder.

Shaking jubilant fists at the sky among his bellowing, crowing, shoulder-punching, knee-slapping, foot-stomping men, was the white-eyed commander of the rescue force.

"I would know you anywhere," General Coldebeefe said.

"My head's all right. Mostly it's just exhaustion now," Shaman said.

"That's a nice piece of custom pistol you've got there," General Coldebeefe said. "You can take your hand off it. We're on the same side. You wanted to join up, didn't you? Well, I owe you. Now you can join up with the regular outfit instead of a mob of dead-burned guerrillas. Lucky I happened along. Maybe for both of us. See what I mean?"

"I remember you," Shaman said.

"Horse chips. We only met the once."

"I have one of those trick memories, like an idiot savant," Shaman said. "You had a mustache. You chewed tobacco. Your name was Riley then."

"Everybody has a new name now," the general said, "to prevent reprisals. Or party names, or jail names, or just for the halibut. Everybody does now, it's the Revolution. New world, new beginnings, new names. I thought mine was a famous old British guards regiment, and now I'm stuck with it."

"So you're a big rebel brigadier general now," Shaman said.

"And you were the youngest U.S. colonel in FECOM," the general said admiringly. "Do you know, I kept track of you for years after that? So did a lot of other people. Including the brass. Far East Command—the War Department. You were up and coming. Right up the rungs. And now I'm a big rebel general, and you're a busted-out defector looking for a billet. And we meet again *here*! That's no accident. That's too much co-incidence. By jeebers, I think it was *meant*!"

He was so in earnest, his boots creaked. Shaman motioned to his side. "Have a seat. Tell me all about it."

The general glanced absently at the dirty floor, then went and dragged his duffel bag over and sat on it. He spoke vivaciously.

"That's why I said, maybe lucky for both of us, see what I mean? Heck, I found out who you were as soon as we got back on the ship. As soon as I realized. I wanted to transfer. I wanted to *join*! Any outfit that could pull off a stunt like that! What lunatics! They told me about you. Some kind of specialist in operations like that. You organized this bunch, but the trouble was, it wasn't your command. You didn't even *have* a unit, you were on your way somewhere else."

"West Irian," Shaman remembered.

"Later on I heard about your combat record, the recon teams in the Delta and what-not. Organizing special jungle platoons. Long-range infiltration units. I must have put in for all of them, all I heard about. Every time I heard of a command you had, I put in for it. I had a reason. Then they gave you counter-guerrilla operations for the whole peninsula. There was a lot going on down my way too. But every time somebody pulled off a stunt like that, it reminded me of you. Anywhere in the theater

there was a swifty, I wondered if it was you. And so did a lot
of people. You were pretty famous."

"That's what comes of leaving witnesses," Shaman said.

"Out East, at least. Famous in the service, anyhow. You
were a maverick. There aren't many. A few try, but they bear
down and bear down until they grind you under. They never
did you. But here's the main reason I kept track. I always
followed your career. Because I was into the Movement ever
since Second 'Nam. And I knew some day we'd be fighting our
own army. I'm pretty good at standard military tactics. I win
my battles, I say so myself. And I always thought if ever I got
the chance to work with you, I'd learn about unconventional war
too. I used to keep track because I always knew we'd need your
kind of rotten war when we came home to fight. See what I
mean?"

Shaman rubbed his eyes tiredly. "So you sold out to the
PFA, and brought along the 509th RCT, and came to be a big
rebel brigadier general."

"Yes, well. After that I kind of forgot about it. I thought
you were dead, out East, if I thought about it. We had our hands
full, getting the PFA under unified command. Workers. Politicals.
Crooks. Revolting Army elements. And the people! Half didn't
believe it was happening here, and half thought it was black-
versus-white and didn't know who to join. Until after the Breakout, I remember. We were up in the mountains. I picked up
the paper. It was a propaganda paper Agitprop put out. 'Government Killer Hijacks.' Sub thief sunk, it said. Fifteen years.
Even the tyrannical oppressor's own murderous lackeys are turning
against them and going to jail for the Cause, it said, but I was
fascinated. Not that I figured I'd ever see you again. But all
those years, I used to wonder—which side would you be on when
the shot hit the fan?"

Shaman said: "Just so it's the winning side."

The general was so animated, he punched himself in the fist.

"Exactly! It's like a miracle! It was meant to happen, don't
you see? From halfway around the world—to escaping from
there—to showing up here—right down to my dead-burned PMP
you knocked out of action. Who *else* is going to take his place,
one of these civilian mugger-buggers? And who else do you know

that owes you his life just when you need a favor? See what I mean? It all fits!"

"That's what worries me," Shaman said.

"It's for our mutual benefit," General Coldebeefe said. "Look, I have this little trip to make. I'm waiting for my transport now. Come *with* me! You wanted to join up. I need an aide. You'll get a commission, the best rank I can swing, we'll put you on my staff. See what I mean? You get to join the winning side— I get my unconventional war expert. Mutual benefit, by jeebers! What do you say?"

Shaman scratched his head bemusedly. "Let me think this out. It fits too well. Never trust a pat hand."

The general stared, disappointed. "How's that?"

"I'm supposed to improvise. But that usually means making the best of bad breaks, not good. Manipulating circumstances, not having them play into my hands. Like fate bait. That's what worries me. When is a shortcut not a shortcut?"

"You're talking in riddles," the general said.

"When it's *au poteau,*" Shaman said. "Don't mind me, just let me think this out. Go on, tell me about Bugleburgh Enclave."

"Well, I don't know what that means," General Coldebeefe said, a little nettled. "Bugleburgh is just the mission I'm on, that's got nothing to do with it."

"Maybe it fits too."

"It's just a little town along the Delaware," he said, and when Shaman raised a brow, he added: "Actually, it's Nicolai Kudelak's birthplace, but except for that, it's nothing. Just a little jerkwater town. It might be the county seat. One movie, two five-and-dimes, maybe ten thousand people. Not near anything, no tactical value, no industries, no nothing. Even the railroad quit on it before the war. We occupied it without a shot. We've held it ever since, but we don't even use it as a base, or a showcase either. There's wilderness areas we hold that's better for the one, and towns and occupied zones out west that's better for the other. Anyhow, the dead-burned place is indefensible without artillery to keep the hills clear all around."

"Not to mention air cover."

"No, they don't bomb. Because of the Bugleburghers. They're

the only target. We aren't even there in strength. A couple of battalions. Waste of time, see what I mean?"

"Until the enemy attacks."

"Well, that's the idea. Every once in a while the enemy comes through en route somewhere, or their high command gets a bug up and they take the place over. They can have it. We draw back. Booby-trap everything, bushwhack a few patrols. I don't have to tell you. Withdraw from the enemy's strength, attack his weakness. *Tam dong, yu chi chan*, and what-not. They leave sooner or later. Because Bugleburgh doesn't have any more strategic value to them than it does to us. Then we occupy it again. But only till next time, see what I mean? It's happened three or four times already."

"And now it's happening again?"

"That's right. The U.S. Ninth Division is coming upriver from Camden, with tanks and artillery. Time for our little disappearing act, like they say. Fish in the sea, smoke in the fog. Except for one thing. Northeast Tactical Command starts getting nutty messages from Bugleburgh C.O. Lysander, the commander. We thought they were in code. Then he sent a lock of his hair. Then we knew. One of his political people got us by radio. Lysander went nuts! He refused to accept the orders. He doesn't agree with the PFA timetable. Now is the time for a full-scale confrontation, a test of strength. He's going to meet the enemy! He's going to stand and fight! He's going to engage! He's going to win the war! I'm going there to cashier the stain-in-the-brass and shoot him! And if you're coming with me, I think that's my Major Pilsudski there now, with the transport arrangements, so you better decide—see what I mean?"

"Oh, I've decided," Shaman said. "My only problem was improvising the new elements into the basic plan. Not just you, but Bugleburgh too. I'll tell you all about it."

But first there was Major Pilsudski, from Metropolitan Sector G1, with the transport arrangements for traveling via the underground, destination Bugleburgh. The routes were so secret, never the same twice, that all the way down from Forest City, on the St. John River, General Coldebeefe had never known where he was; and leaving Rob Williams Company Headquarters, he didn't

know where he was going. With Shaman and both the PMP's—
the stricken one had recovered, after all—he was shunted from
hand to hand, station to station; through back alleys, wrecked
buildings, dripping tunnels, out of the city. Hiding in a burned
marina eating canned corned beef and waiting for rain was one
experience; crossing the river in rubber kayaks three nights later
was worse; skulking through industrial wastelands and cattail
swamps in rain and dark was less nerve-racking but nearly as
dismal. Then a day in hiding with food, warmth, even some
whiskey, in a safe house, buried in a steel cave under tons of
jagged metal in an auto junkyard. Then, two nights later, a car,
whispered instructions, a full tank and extra can of gas, a harrowing
drive without lights along shattered country roads to the Delaware,
where they crossed on a one-lane bridge, high in the mountains,
and turned south toward the Water Gap, Washington Crossing,
Bugleburgh, before stopping. It was dawn. They swung off the
road and hid the car. One more night drive would do it. The
two PMP's, red-eyed from alternating driving with riding shotgun,
fell immediately asleep. Before going to sleep too, the general
gripped Shaman's hand, gave him a wink and a nod.

"Looks like we got it made, buddy."

They lay stretched on the grass. Bright summer morning,
green and sun-gold. Jaybirds said, "Thief!" A redheaded wood-
pecker said, "Fear!"

"I want to explain," Shaman said. "You were frank
with me."

"How's that?" the general said sleepily.

"About you and this shortcut business," Shaman said. "I've
decided it can't be a trap after all. On the contrary, I believe it
just proves that my *barraka* is still holding. I must have invented
you right when I needed you most."

"Invented . . . What?"

"You didn't think you were real, did you? It's too perfect."

The general's head wobbled with befuddlement.

"I'm sorry, I don't . . ."

"Operation Kalitan," Shaman said. "It was designed to establish me as an ex–army officer, hijacker, federal prisoner, escapee
and defector, so I could penetrate the People's Freedom Army."

"Well," General Coldebeefe said, "aren't you?" Then his

brows bunched, bulging at Shaman: Wasn't he? Certainly! But Kalitan? Penetrate? "What does that mean?"

"Not just to join, enlist, but to rise up through the ranks. Right up the rungs. To the top."

The general shrugged and grinned. "I don't get it."

"To cut its head off," Shaman said helpfully.

The general was bewildered by the eerie contrast between the manner and the content of the speech. He went over it in his mind. It became clear.

The two PMP's were asleep in the car. Without changing the position of his body, General Coldebeefe sent one hand creeping toward his pistol belt. Shaman sat up on the grass. His pale eyes gazed at the hand, and the hand stopped. The general lay frozen.

"You're an infiltrator!"

"That was what I had to work out," Shaman said. "How to improvise you and Bugleburgh into the basic plan. It's a shortcut. If it works, and it should, the stalk is over. I've got the quarry in my sights. By jeebers, now we're getting somewhere!"

"If this is true," the general said shakenly, "why are you telling me?"

Shaman smiled oddly at him. "You should be wholly aware of everything. Strong and alert and ready. Are you at the height of your powers?"

The general goggled in total discombobulation. "What the hail are you talking about?"

"That's part of it. I need the orders you're carrying, and your maps, situation reports, et cetera. I need your authority as a general and your authorization from Northeast Tactical Command. I also need your savvy and your star and your status. In short, I need your medicine."

"My med—"

"I need it to take command at Bugleburgh Enclave."

"Over my dead body!"

"See what I mean?"

CHAPTER SIX

Red Blotch

Masquerade

Lysander, the commander, stood chest deep in a foxhole on High School Hill. Pink dawn lit his baggy, sagging features. Stubbled cheeks, sleepless eyes. He tried to see his watch; he held it above his head to catch the light; his forearm was a dark shape against the sky. He stood facing roughly east; the enemy was approaching from the east, with the sun. The sun was already lighting up the green hills all around, but the valley below was still in shadow; a few nightlights gleamed in the town. All calm, silent, sleeping.

He raised his bottle to the peaceful scene. Salud.

Bridge Street, Main Street, State Street. Business center, First People's National Bank, River Hardware, Hattie's Millinery, Methodist Church, Immaculate Heart, Bugleburgh House, Bijou Palace, Moose Home, Woolworth's, Bratt Brothers. Town square, city hall, police station, firehouse, veterans' monument. Commandeered shopping center, where the troops barracked in empty stores. Two-lane steel bridge over the fish-belly-colored Delaware in the damp dawn. River Road running south past brick buildings and garages to the railyard, north past streets of old-fashioned tree-shaded homes to the outskirts: factories and cemeteries. A small factory town in a river valley, in a hollow of hills, and the enemy coming. He raised his bottle. Salud. Here's to it. To Bugleburgh Enclave. Salud.

He spoke aloud:

"Here's to the crud-sucking cowards afraid to stand and fight.

"I don't care . . .

"Here's to igno-minious de-feat number . . . ? How many is this?

"Here's to that big Coldebeefe prick."

He drank each time.

Once in the old days he had held out six days in a union hall against Pinkers and Burnses and State Guards till all his men and ammunition were gone, and then against billy clubs, blackjacks, soldering irons, and water cures till they couldn't wake him up anymore, and he never once gave them anything. But now he was fifty-eight years old. Lysander, the commander, relieved for insubordination.

He snarled a snarl of grim and bitter disillusionment.

"Fuck 'em all."

He realized that he was watching moving lights down in the town—headlights were coming across Bridge Street and turning up the hill; they got bigger and paler as they climbed the long driveway into the morning light, and a car stopped in front of the high school. The car's door opened and he knew who it was. "I'm over here, shithead," he grunted in his foxhole, one of a row dug across the crest of the hill. He hoisted his bottle and drank. "Here's to you too, shithead."

Shithead was Captain Posey Wells. Supposed to be his intelligence officer, was really a PIS operative. A snoop, a politruk, keeping track of everybody's political morals and revolutionary orthodoxy. Lysander watched him step away from the car and stand peering around the grounds.

Sunlight lit the roof of the school. Down below, the town was waking; dogs were barking, and the river glittered with ripples.

Lysander did not move or speak, just sat in his hole, neckless and bullet-headed, looking like a sulky woodchuck. Eventually Captain Wells spotted him anyway and strolled over, saluted. "Good morning, Colonel, sir."

Note the malicious grin.

"Get out of here. Let me alone. As of oh-eight-hundred, I'm relieved. Go tell it to Coldebeefe."

"Golly, sir, I guess you didn't hear," Posey Wells said gleefully. "I looked for you everywhere, but you weren't in your quarters. Of course, I see your point, sir, I should have thought of it—a little private celebration. A little going-away party, relieved of command!"

"Hear? Hear what?" Lysander said.

"General Coldebeefe is dead. Ambushed in a Vol roadblock north of the Water Gap—him and his escort and his car, blown up and burned flat to the tire tracks. He won't be relieving you after all. I thought you ought to know."

He stopped and waited.

Lysander's head came up slowly.

"Coldebeefe? Dead?"

"Fried to a crisp."

Lysander lifted his face to the morning light. Exalted. Vindicated.

"I'm still in command!"

Posey Wells squatted down by the hole, the better to watch his face.

"Aw, gee, sir, I guess I forgot to mention it. There was one survivor. That's how we heard. He managed to escape with Coldebeefe's stuff, including his orders—and he's a one-star general too, so I guess that makes *him* your relief. You're relieved, all right. Relieved of command."

Lysander sagged back in his hole.

But Wells wasn't finished yet.

"It's queer, though. Nobody knows who he is—nobody ever heard of any General Shaman. No mention of him in the orders. No way to check, no way for Northeast to send anybody else in time. The enemy will *be* here in two hours! Too late to do anything about it—I just thought you ought to know. Isn't that interesting? You're relieved, all right, but who says by *him?*"

Still not finished.

"That's not all. Fact is, he's been at headquarters since a little before midnight—getting briefed, taking over, grabbing right on—but here's the peculiar part, sir. He's organizing something— sending out scouts and skirmishers, ordering fortifications, setting up perimeters, deploying the troops. He's even arming the Bugle-burghers—union members and unemployed, the firemen, even the sanitation crews!" Posey Wells suddenly laughed out loud. "It looks like he's planning to stand and fight—the very thing you got relieved for! Isn't that ironic?"

He watched Lysander, the commander, slump down in his hole and turn into an old man.

Or, as he later explained it at NETC general staff HQ: "Being the situation substantially what it was, of course, I can see his point. With the enemy already busting our outposts, it was too late to start arguing about who was in command."

Present at the meeting, held some weeks later and many miles northward, in the Adirondacks, were the general officers of Northeast Tactical Command, liaison officers from contiguous commands, General Soga of the People's Military Police, and a Mysterious Visitor.

The general officers said: "In short, Colonel Lysander made no attempt to verify the identity of the self-styled General Shaman."

"No, he was drunk," Wells said.

Captain Posey Wells then drove hurriedly back down High School Hill to Bugleburgh House, and never saw Lysander again.

General Shaman's command post was on the second floor of the two-story hotel. Wells arrived in time for the start. He was there till the end.

Shaman wore a peaked cap with a single gold star on it.

"It certainly wasn't up to me to question his authority."

"Thank you, Captain. We have your report. Dismissed."

As General Soga remarked to the general officers of Northeast Tactical Command: "Obviously People's Intelligence Service comrade Wells is young fool. Nonetheless well placed during engagement to make valuable observations."

From the personal report of Captain Posey Wells, PIS, to Major General Soga, PMP:

Oh-eight-hundred-thirty hours. I arrived at the command post in Bugleburgh House. By then the so-called General Shaman had taken charge—and I do mean taken charge! Right or wrong, fake or not, he was in command—and I do mean command! He already had a good start since midnight, and during the next two days he managed to organize and execute a perfect withdrawal—exactly according to Northeast's original orders. Two days later we marched out not leaving a sign of a man, a stick of matériel, or a stitch of evidence. It was beautiful!

The only difference was, those two days. He fought a defensive action. For two days until he withdrew, he flailed the snot out of the enemy. And that wasn't in the orders. But how can you hang him for that?

Oh-eight-hundred-thirty-five. He was sitting at Lysander's desk. Lysander's officers were briefing him, all talking at once. HQ clerks, memos, notes flying, runners popping in and out. Messages. Phones ringing, landlines, radios squawking. He was not only taking it all in, he was reading orders, situation reports, T.O. and E. books, battle histories, troop deployments, maps—never missing a beat.

I stared at him. I didn't know him, I never heard of him, neither did anybody else. We had radio calls in to NETC, but by the time we found out he was fake, it was too late.

He was wearing a dark green one-piece coverall. Long white silk scarf, actually two scarfs knotted together. Fat black revolver on his hip, in a G.I. holster, not a good fit. Skorpion machine pistol on the desk. Black sunglasses. He lifted them to look at me. Eyes like a venomous snake. I know how birds feel. I couldn't look away.

"Wells. Intelligence officer. Where the double have you been? Never mind. Down to business. Check me on this."

He proceeded to give me a detailed rundown on the whole situation—better than I could myself! He knew where every man, every weapon, every position was. Amazing grasp! As though he'd been studying it for months! I was listening with my mouth open. I couldn't move my eyes.

"Who *are* you?"

"Where *have* you been? Don't you read general orders? I am the new C.G. We fell into an ambush. Coldebeefe's dead."

I didn't say anything. That wasn't what I meant.

He then went on to brief me on the enemy's movements. And it was like listening to a playback of the whole night's intelligence reports—which I hadn't got myself yet! Amazing!

"The main body of the Vol Ninth Division is in transit thirty miles to the south of us on east-west Highway Sixty-five. The Third Infantry Regiment with two armored car companies has been detached and sent north to invest Bugleburgh Enclave. This force is now within striking distance and has already engaged our outposts. An assault team has crossed the Delaware at Yardley with orders to circle east and launch an attack from High School Hill. On the other bank of the river the balance of the regiment, with the armored cars, is presently moving into position to cross the bridge into town."

He seemed to be waiting for some comment from me. I said:

"Well, it always worked before."

"Meaning?"

"They always use the same battle plan. We always withdraw north."

"Lysander seemed to think he could hold against one regiment."

"They'd only send the whole Ninth as reinforcements."

But Shaman was smiling. It takes time to halt, turn, redirect a whole column in division strength.

"Two days!"

A runner hurried in with a message: The enemy regiment had drawn up on the far side of the river at the approach to the bridge.

Shaman talked on the phone: "Are they crossing yet?"

Vol reconnaissance teams were on the bridge, engineers were inspecting the spans and pilings, looking for explosives.

"Rinehart!"

A very young officer with buck teeth came to the desk and saluted.

"Get on the radio. Major Pravda to let the scouts cross. No shooting. Are the mortars in place?"

"Yessir."

"I'll tell them when to open fire. It won't be at the bridge. Where is Mr. Mayor?"

I saw now that the mayor of Bugleburgh, under guard, had been sitting hunched against the wall between a file cabinet and the water cooler.

Mayor Ott came forward wringing his hands: "If you'll let me ex—"

"When the People's Freedom Army requisitioned all private motor transport, you hid your car under a pile of coal. What is there to explain?"

"It's my wife's . . . It's a classic . . ."

"Where is it?"

The guard said the car, a vintage MG roadster, had now been resurrected, restored to operating condition, and was parked in the municipal lot.

"Arm this man and assign him to the rifle pits up on High School Hill," Shaman said. He was scribbling orders as fast as he could write, handing them to officers, assigning them here, there, everywhere. They left, running like mad.

He turned to me. "Come on. Can you drive four-on-the-floor?"

In the car we raced north on State Street. Shaman rode shotgun, Skorpion cocked and locked. He shouted: "The enemy isn't expecting a fight or he would have sent more than a regiment. It always worked before. You always withdrew north. Maybe we'll fool them this time."

"What about heavy weapons?"

"Nothing to worry about. Except for the cannons and fifties on the armored cars, they've brought only infantry weapons, machine guns, recoilless rifles, mortars. No artillery or air strikes because of the Bugleburghers. Neutrals. Civilians."

The MG skidded to a stop at the union hall on north State, where about two hundred men were standing around three trucks—workmen from the town's factories. PFA soldiers in fatigues were up on the trucks handing out weapons, mostly miscellaneous hunting or target guns, and hand grenades. The officer was a black man with an eyepatch.

"How many all told?" Shaman asked.

"Five hundred and eleven," Patch said. "The rest has already gone off to High School Hill under Lieutenant Bolivar. These guys is the holdouts. They don't want to get guns. They don't want to fight. They say it ain't no war of theirs."

"They're all union men, aren't they?"

"One union or another."

"Get among them. Spread the word. This time the enemy is coming with arrest orders from Washington. The name and address of every man who ever joined a union or worked in a union shop. It's a death list."

"Fight or die," Patch grinned. "I got it."

"Arm them and send them to Major Dalton, on the Main Street barricade, north of Bridge Street. Let's get out of here."

We raced back to the command post in the MG. He was smiling.

"That death-list thing also helped us to organize and arm the registered unemployed, the railway workers, and the fire, police, and sanitation departments."

"Is it true?"

"Agitprop swears it is."

He said this in a chuckling voice. Come to think of it, he had spoken in different voices before—he seemed to use different voices depending on what he was saying.

Oh-nine-hundred-fifteen hours. From the second floor C.P. in Bugleburgh House we could see smoke on High School Hill. From the distance the shots sounded like hammers hitting wooden planks. In the command post a courier was waiting. We'd captured the scouts who came across the bridge. Shaman scribbled a note and handed it to the courier: "Shoot the officers, men to work as forced labor on the Main Street barricade, shoot them later."

The phone rang. It was Pravda, commanding the bridge defense. Vol advance elements were starting to cross.

"You have to hold them . . . Hold as long as possible . . . No, they won't cross in force yet . . . Because they can't be sure what they're up against—they can't be sure we haven't mined the bridge . . . You'll be pulled out before that . . . Don't use the phone—matter of time till they cut the wires."

A radioman cried: "General, the first wounded are coming down off High School Hill!"

"Presbyterian Church!" Shaman yelled.

Applethorne, the supply officer, had come charging in, raging furiously, and was banging on the desk. Somebody took his squad of guards away from the armory, sent them out as riflemen. Worse than that, every last speck of his reserve high explosives had been removed, God only knows where, without advising him.

"That happened as of three A.M., and you're just finding out about it," Shaman said. "You're off the job. Draw a weapon and report to Lieutenant Bolivar's rifle company."

He snatched a note from a runner, read it, scribbled a reply on the reverse, handed it back to the runner: "Operation Charon all ready." He hurried to the window. Down in the street, pickup trucks, PFA soldiers with thirty-caliber light machine guns, twelve teams. Shaman leaned out and yelled: "Six teams and a lieutenant to Main Street barricade. Orders of Major Dalton. The rest with me."

He reached in a pocket of his coverall and tossed me a folded map. I caught it in the air. Started to open it, but he stopped me.

"Never mind that. Don't waste time. Take it to Dalton. It pinpoints where I want every man, every gun, to cover the barricade. Red A's: rifle teams. Red B's: machine guns. Red C's: rocket launchers. Red D's: demolition charges. Tell Dalton he is personally responsible for the element of surprise. If a single man in his command fires a shot, or lets himself be seen before the signal . . . Well! Don't take the car."

"Where will you be?"

"High School Hill—" He stopped. A very peculiar thing happened. In the midst of the uproar he stopped dead, a pivot in a pinwheel. He smiled, seeing something in his mind. What made me think of a man leaving the party at its height to go upstairs with a woman?

"We may get some fun out of this yet." His voice was gentle.

He turned, running already, out and down the steps. I went to the window. The six machine-gun teams were loaded into pickup trucks. Shaman appeared and jumped into the MG, yanked the starter, ground the gears, raced away. The pickups followed.

Ten-hundred-thirty hours. I was at the Main Street barricade. It was a strange sight, sort of spooky. More like a dump heap than an actual barricade—junk cars, broken furniture, lumber, cables, oil drums, mattresses, cinder blocks, garbage cans, park benches—everything piled up twenty feet high, blocking off the street. This was the business district just around the corner from Bridge Street and the bridge. Stores, offices, banks, restaurants. Plate-glass windows and brick and stone building fronts. Fighting around the corner, where Pravda's men were stalling the enemy's advance across the bridge, but silence here.

Dalton was about finished positioning the last of his men, weapons, and explosives. He told me the charges were mostly dynamite and gunpowder but laced with nails and scrap iron. They weren't in the barricade, they were in the buildings, hidden. His men too, once placed, had disappeared, gone from sight, bushwhackers.

A squad of soldiers led the forced-labor prisoners away, to shoot them in the alley. Dalton gave me a thumbs-up sign. "All ready."

I took a pickup truck and hurried across town via Bridge Street. In the mirror I caught a smoky glimpse of the bridge and worried about taking a shot up my tailpipe. On Park Street I left the truck and walked halfway up High School Hill to Major Mihailovitch's C.P., a small luncheonette where the kids used to hang out. He and his officers were in back, watching out the kitchen windows. The high school building had been under heavy attack for over an hour now; our men were waiting for the order to pull back into prepared positions in the rifle pits and foxholes. As for our new commanding general, where was he?

"Crazy!" Mihailovitch told me. "That son of a bitch is crazy!"

Mihailovitch was a soldier of the old school, once a Green Beret, then a mercenary, before the Revolution. He had Shaman's Skorpion—Shaman swapped him for a twelve-bore shotgun. Mihailovitch was pop-eyed with indignation. What kind of C.G. was this?

"That crazy son of a bitch went hunting!"

Shaman took the shotgun, a box of shot shells, and went out with one of the skirmishing parties. It came back without him and said he had gone on around the hill behind enemy positions. That was about an hour ago, so I didn't have long to wait. Shaman returned grimy with smoke and dust and grease. He gave back the twelve-bore, reclaimed his Skorpion, and stuck his hands into the cargo pockets of his coverall. Dug out two handfuls of small, soft things like bloody noodles and scattered them across the kitchen table. Ears!

"Back to business. All ready?"

Mihailovitch gaped. "Yes . . ."

We were all gaping at Shaman, but he hadn't stopped moving. He grabbed a pair of binoculars from one of Mihailovitch's officers, took a flare gun from another—turning to me: "Let's go."

We left there, hurried across the slope through the lumberyard into a field of weeds, tin cans, garbage bags, rotten crates. He bounced—rested, refreshed, relaxed. Not a man to explain much, but I understood now. Our new C.G. was a close-combat freak. They get off on it.

We took cover behind a large, old, rusty boiler tank. A few strays were whizzing around. From this point we could look up to watch the battle at the high school, or down to see the bridge and Main Street. He had the binoculars trained on the school building. The windows were all smashed but in one was some kind of banner. A signal.

"Operation Little Red Schoolhouse all ready," he said. "Report."

I reported: "So is Dalton on Main Street. So is Pravda at the bridge. So is Operation Charon. All ready. All ready for *what?*"

"*Counterattack!*"

He fired the flare gun.

I am in intelligence, not field operations. Here is the situation, as I saw it. The events as follows I observed, but only figured out completely later on.

The high school defenders were taking heavy fire. Soon they'd have to surrender the building to the enemy assault team.

About half the enemy regiment had crossed the bridge and was now turning up Main Street. Soon the other half would start across.

The flare soared high over town. Burned out, fell!

The high school defenders started pulling back to the foxholes. The enemy force prepared to attack the Main Street barricade. A rubber life raft, still inflating, popped up under the bridge. Shaman pointed with his arm. "Watch there."

The life raft was loaded with every last speck of Applethorne's reserve high explosive. It blew up. A ten-foot section of the bridge sagged into the water.

"In memoriam, Ralph Elf," Shaman said. "Watch there."

Two thirds of Pravda's men were packing up, pulling out, clambering into trucks and every kind of requisitioned vehicle. Rushing hip-hip-hooray toward High School Hill.

"Mihailovitch's reinforcements," Shaman said. "Watch there."

Up the hill, our men had walked out of—the enemy into— a building set on fire.

"Little Red Schoolhouse," Shaman said. "Watch there."

Along the river, spurts of smoke—our mortars opening fire. Pre-aimed, all right, but not at the bridge at all. They were pulverizing the Bridge Street/Main Street intersection.

"Rat trap," Shaman said. "Watch there."

Between the mortar barrage and the barricade: half the enemy regiment.

Simultaneously, Dalton's bushwhackers opened fire from hiding.

Red A's, red B's, red C's.

In the walls, dynamite and gunpowder, laced with nails, scrap iron.

Plate-glass windows, brick and stone building fronts exploding.

I couldn't see it all. Smoke, as always. Black from the burning high school, heating oil or something—drifting clouds from the blown-up bridge, the mortar fire, the charges at the barricade—rockets, grenades, and small arms—slowly filling up the valley, hiding the rest.

I couldn't see what was happening. But I could hear it. Over the row and racket—our men cheering, the Vols . . . dying!

It was fantastic! I never saw anything like it! We were slaughtering them! And that was only the first morning!

Massacre!

Coffee break.

Instant coffee and English muffins.

General Markhausen had pushed a button.

Orderlies trotted in—bustled with pots and packages, cups and saucers, sugar, milk, butter, orange marmalade—then left.

General Curcio thoughtfully dunked a muffin.

"Massacre, of course, is an exaggeration. Your Captain Wells seems to have been carried away by excessive admiration. I don't doubt the Vol forward elements were severely mauled at the barricade; but they did nevertheless manage to fight their way out and resume the attack. Also, the bridge was soon repaired, enabling the reserve and armored car companies to cross. High School Hill was, in fact, taken. Our troops were outnumbered, forced to withdraw to the north, as originally planned. There were other battles—in the town junkyard, for example—and several very impressive ambushes in the factory district, according to our reports. But the fact remains, the enemy took Bugleburgh six weeks ago and holds it now."

General Soga raised a finger.

"Notation please. Beg to remind, significance of performance of self-styled General Shaman not in did not what did not, but did what did."

"What?"

"Flailed snot out of enemy," General Soga said.

Major General Soga, commander in chief of the People's Military Police, People's Freedom Army East, was a full-blooded Chinese and a veteran of the Italian Red Army, but he had been born in San Juan Capistrano, educated at Stanford, and could speak ordinary English when he chose.

He turned to the Mysterious Visitor, a small, smiling man with a large head.

"The thing is, we may have a military genius on our hands."

The Mysterious Visitor was intrigued. His interest was immediately noticed, and the generals reacted with uncommon deference.

"Of course, sir. Any information—"

"Who is this General Shaman? Why have I never heard of him?"

"Well, sir, we never heard of him ourselves till he turned up at Bugleburgh. Apparently he was an impostor, an opportunist, taking advantage of the critical situation at the time. Not even a member of our army."

"Who, then?"

"Well, sir, apparently he's a former U.S. Army officer—the one who hijacked the *Mertensia*, if you recall. They put him in federal prison, then in Northstate, where he escaped. Somehow, he linked up with Coldebeefe in the city, and Coldebeefe recruited him as an aide. According to his story, when Coldebeefe was killed, he knew there wasn't time to send anybody else. He wanted to join us anyway, and this looked like his big chance. To show us his stuff. As simple as that. So he assumed command."

"And did a masterful job of it, it seems," the Mysterious Visitor said, laughing. "How much of this checks out?"

The generals looked at each other; tiny shrugs; they looked at Soga.

Soga took up a folder. "All objective data. Military record verified; we have access to pre-war U.S. files. Trial transcript, imprisonment date, commitment papers. Northstate escape confirmed; we had an emplaced agent. Statements from Lieutenant Machete and Captain Carelli of Rob Williams Company, Inner City Task Force. All checked out. See 'Extract Hijacker.'"

"It sounds straightforward enough," the visitor said. "Wouldn't he be a worthwhile recruit, assuming he's properly disciplined for impersonating a general officer?"

Soga raised a finger.

"Notation, please. Historical data checked out. Additional data still under consideration. Other factors. Worrisome stuff."

"I see . . . I think," the visitor said. "In the meantime, what?"

Soga consulted his folder.

"Subject arrested following Bugleburgh withdrawal, sworn in as private, People's Freedom Army, to facilitate court-martial for impersonation of officer. Sentenced to penal battalion during period of consideration of worrisome stuff."

"The Kamikaze Korps?"

"So."

"I see," the visitor said. "What's the rest of it?"

The generals looked at each other; frowns; they looked at Markhausen.

Markhausen said: "Well, sir, it may be a little premature . . ."

A silence fell.

The Mysterious Visitor smiled.

"Come now, gentlemen. Drink your coffee. Put aside your military manners for the moment. I know you are in a hurry to move on. I won't delay you long. Here is an extraordinary story. A man out of nowhere who takes unauthorized command of our Bugleburgh forces and inflicts heavy damage on a numerically superior enemy, then executes the original retreat orders to the letter. As Captain Wells has so acutely remarked, how can we hang him for that? Similarly, General Soga, who points out that we may well have a military genius on our hands. In short, a worthwhile recruit to our cause, who is in dire danger of death in the Kamikaze Korps pending your decision: What to do with him?"

He rose and moved easily around the room, clapping a shoulder here and there. Small, big-headed, smiling, he seemed to radiate a surprising power, not of compulsion, but of right and reason.

"Certainly he would be of more use to you as a troop commander than as a private in a penal battalion. Depending, of course, on what you mean by worrisome stuff . . . ?"

He spread his hands expressively.

General Markhausen said: "Well, sir, it comes under three headings, actually. Things we're worried about . . ."

"Firstly: personal," General Soga said. "Subject exhibits strangeness of personality and behavior. Coldness, silence, indifference, inhumanness. Impossible to evaluate in terms of sincerity, trustworthiness, veracity."

The visitor shook his head. "Would you summarize that?"

"Something stinks," Soga said.

"That's pretty subjective. What is your procedure?"

"Subject currently undergoing in-depth psychological/psychiatric examination by professional expert. Formerly emplaced agent at Northstate, familiar with case. Analysis proceeding under code name *Wei kuo jen*, meaning 'foreigner.' "

They smiled at this from a Chinaman.

"Beg to explain. Humble one does not suggest foreign origin or nationality, but foreignness to all. Apart. Alone. Alien."

"I see. So your professional expert is analyzing him not because he's crazy—though he may well be—but to discover if you can trust him. Still, there's obviously more to it than that, or why go to this much trouble?"

General Juárez spoke. "Yes, sir. Secondly, there's his recent

activities. As you know, we don't have jails or stockades. The
penal battalion is a regular combat unit, except for two things.
They lose their rank and privileges, and get all the suicide missions.
The dirty dregs of the army, you might say. Maniacs and incor-
rigibles. Use 'em up, burn 'em out, good riddance. That's why
they call it the Kamikaze Korps. Well, he just took over."

The visitor looked blank. "Took over?"

"Yes, sir. Colonel Oh, the commandant, reports that the
prisoners all nominally obey him, but they've set up their own
internal organization and this man Shaman runs it."

"How did he manage that?"

"I wouldn't know, sir. It's like Bugleburgh again. We only
know that in the five weeks he's been there, he's got the whole
scroungy bunch saluting him, sitting still for training sessions,
going out on combat missions, and bringing back ears."

The visitor made a grimace.

"I am beginning to see your problem. What to do with him,
indeed? You said three headings actually. Personality, performance
. . . what else?"

"Proposal," General Markhausen said.

The word hung in the silence.

General Curcio rose slowly to his feet. He sought his place
in a pack of papers, put his finger on it, and looked at the
Mysterious Visitor. He spoke reluctantly.

"You understand—special circumstances—his undeniable military expertise. His top-secret information from U.S. military
sources. Otherwise we would never even consider . . ."

"Go on."

"Private Shaman has proposed a plan. He says it will win
the war. He calls it Operation Kalitan. May I read from his
introduction?"

"Please."

General Curcio coughed, cleared his throat, and read as
follows:

"The United States Army has about nineteen divisions available for domestic counter-insurgency operations. Also, two paratroop and one mobile air division, plus nuclear and miscellaneous
arms—all there in inventory, at least, if not in actual action. Not
even counting all that intelligence savvy and command genius in

the White House, the Pentagon, Fort Meade, Langley, Warrenton, and umpty-umph places underground. The most powerful power on earth.

"Our People's Liberation ragtagbobtail fighting it to a standstill has an unknown number of men, women, and children. Being irregulars, we can be formed from innocent bystanders and helpless civilians into anything from snipers or guerrilla bands to fully manned battalions. And back again. Which is why they can't fire the big guns. They can't fission bomb us. They can't saturation raid us. They can't bacteria-war us. They can't hammer-and-anvil us. They can't scorched-earth us. Because we are the public. We are the American people.

"As a result, this is where we stand at the end of the second year of armed conflict. Stalemate. Which means, we are winning. In a real sense, we now own everything higher than thirty-five-hundred feet. The Cascades, the Sierra Nevadas, the Rocky Mountains. In the east, parts of the Alleghenies, most of the central Appalachians away from the population centers, practically all the New England mountains above Boston. Plus sanctuaries in Canada and Mexico.

"All we need now is sufficient courage to engage the oppressor in a major battle. If we win it, we can establish a free zone and a provisional government. This will legitimize our revolution. This will mean recognition by the uncommitted nations as well as matériel and assistance from every enemy the United States has ever made, from Novosibirsky Ostrova to Tierra del Fuego.

"This is what we must do to win the war. This is what we must do to establish the People's Republic of America.

"What are we waiting for?"

The Mysterious Visitor stood silent, thinking. There was no doubt now about his power, his authority.

He said: "I'll read this 'Extract Hijacker.' I'll read this *Wei kuo jen* file. I'll read Operation Kalitan. And I will meet this man."

He turned to study the big map tacked to the wall, marked with red and blue arrows and encirclements. He smiled a smile of shy whimsy.

"Let's see what this false-face, who pretends to be what he

is not, has to say to the false-face who pretends not to be what he is."

The smile went away.

"I'll let you know."

Excursus

"Go on," Friedkin said.

"The barrel of the Skorpion is burned out, I use my revolver. The revolver is empty, I toss some grenades. Vols are everywhere, falling all over themselves," Shaman said. "Open season and no bag limit."

"Go on," Friedkin said.

"Counterattack!"

"Go on," Friedkin said.

"I'm at the north end of town, ambushing the Vols we suckered into the warehouse," Shaman said. "The only line of advance they've got is through the junkyard, and we're waiting in it. Toppling stacks of car bodies forty feet high with steep aisles in between, and we're waiting there. They creep into sight, sick and sweaty, flogged along by their own battle police, and we're waiting for them. We murder them. Everything we've got pours down on their heads like shit from a chute. The sad bastards, I feel sorry for them, and help as many as I can to fuss and fret no more in this life."

"Go on," Friedkin said. "Where are you now?"

"Wait a minute, I know you. I'm in Back Ward Four. I thought you were a doctor, but you're just another one of the crazies. What makes you glow like that?"

"I can understand how you might think so," Friedkin said. "Actually, I wasn't either. Your friend Kaul isn't the only one who sends infiltrators behind enemy lines, you know. In fact, I was an emplaced agent, so to speak. But Northstate was a long while ago, and I am your doctor now. Trust me. You are at Bugleburgh Enclave."

"I am at Bugleburgh Enclave," Shaman said. "We're evacuating, moving north. We move up the river into the Poconos, then turn east. We walk for a day and a night. Posey Wells apologizes, he is embarrassed. I thought he was only Lysander's intelligence officer but he was doubling as a PIS-ant all the time."

Friedkin said: "When did you first begin to suspect things were going wrong?"

Emanations streamed from the finger.

"I'm under arrest!" Shaman said.

"You are moving north," Friedkin said.

"Guards," Shaman said. "They handcuff me at night. We are moving north again, miles and miles, days and days. Everyone from Bugleburgh at first, but then dropping off by squads and platoons. Fewer and fewer each day. By the time we cross the state line, east of Binghamton, there are only a couple dozen of us. A party of officers, soldiers, me and my guards, and Wells, who keeps apologizing—he talks to me, he hated to arrest me, he thinks it will be all right, they'll have to recognize the job I did at Bugleburgh. He gets me a spiral notebook, he gives me ballpoint pens. Every night we camp in the woods and I write, write, write. He promises to deliver it personally to NETC when we arrive. After Rome and Utica, we're safe. We're in the Red Zone. Mountains and forests. There are PFA forces in Nobleboro, on Little Moose Mountain."

"You are writing," Friedkin said. "What are you writing?"

"I'm writing in a spiral notebook by campfire light with handcuffs on my wrists," Shaman said. "Everything I know, and I have to prove I know everything. Everything about the PFA that NETC knows, more about the enemy than the enemy himself. It's top secret. I can't tell."

"That's all right," Friedkin said. "I'm quite familiar with Operation Kalitan. Captain Wells personally delivered your spiral notebook to General Soga at NETC. They have all read it, and were very much impressed. But they are wondering where you came by all this top-secret information. They can't understand how you can know as much about the PFA as they do, more about the enemy than the enemy does. Hence these little sessions. Now—what does the name Nicolai Kudelak mean to you?"

"The legendary founder of the People's Freedom Movement. Chairman of the Central Committee. Pro tempore chief executive of the People's Republic of the United States. Honorary commander in chief of the People's Freedom Army. The George Washington, the Joseph Stalin, the Mao Tse Tung, the Ho Chi Minh—the oracle and elder statesman—of American Revolution Two. Little guy with a big head."

"He was very impressed with you," Friedkin said. "He was there as a visitor, an observer. He does that, you know. Really he belongs at Central Committee headquarters, wherever that may be. But he likes to travel around in disguise, like Haroun al Raschid, as it were, keeping an eye on the Revolution, seeing things firsthand, so to speak. They say he pops up in the most unlikely places. On the ready line just before an assault, for instance, inspiring the troops. This time he was interested in the Bugleburgh post mortem—it was his birthplace, after all—so he came to visit us here at Northeast Tactical Command."

"I'm at Northeast Tactical Command," Shaman said.

"No, I'll tell you when. But he was impressed, and he was very interested in your Operation Kalitan," Friedkin said. "And he's very interested in these little sessions too. In fact, I'm wired. He's probably listening to our every word this very minute."

"Hello, out there," Shaman said.

"Concentrate," Friedkin said.

"I'm at Northeast Tactical Command," Shaman said. "I was arrested, I was tried. This morning I was at Kamikaze Korps HQ. Guards brought me here. I'm in your office, or whatever this is, some kind of lumber mill."

"No. You're traveling north," Friedkin said.

I am traveling north, Shaman said. We're high up, past Stillwater Mountain, past Coffin Mills. Old Camp Drum was somewhere not far west of here. We've been walking for days and days through miles and miles of woods. Millions of acres of green forest—hundreds of thousands of men. They're camped in little valleys, in deserted villages, in caves, beside hidden lakes, in ski resorts, summer resorts, abandoned logging camps. Here a few, there a few, everywhere a few more. Platoon-sized, company-sized units, never bigger. Communications must be astonishing. How do they do it? Discipline too. There are women! But Wells tells me no, no problem. They aren't whores, camp followers, they are wives, mothers, daughters—compañeras, south-of-the-border style. Soldaderas all. Officers and troops, organized as cooks, couriers, clerks—fighters too—reconnaissance teams, bearers, even guerrillas. We come to a deep, broad valley. Wells grins—I must be gaping. Heavy artillery is moving through. It appears and vanishes, like a mirage. We climb out of the valley, walk

into wilderness again, deep forest, alive with men. Green-garbed, armed, silent, rushing by, vanishing. With no more than whispers in the brush. Training, Wells says. We eat and rest at noon by a little lost lake. Muskrats, a doe and her fawn. I can't believe it's an engineer depot, tons of stuff, in pits, holes, burrows, caves—even underwater. Three hundred men live here, but I don't see a soul. Eat and rest and on again, north and north, till late afternoon in dim dark pines. A dirt road, a stone wall, a remote little overgrown tourist camp, with a dozen tumbledown log cabins—and a medium tank inside each one. Sleep that night in a bunker invisible from ten yards away—headquarters of a rifle company—and walk next morning through forests filled with men and machines and matériel. I know the figures, I know the facts, but the reality is astonishing just the same. Red marks on a map, stacked figures on paper, are one thing, this is another. I am in the Red Zone, occupied by the People's Freedom Army. Journey's end. Destination. Somewhere around here in this lost land of lakes and forests and mountains

is NETC Headquarters, but I never get there. Seven PMP's from the Provost Marshal's office are waiting for me. Walk some more. The holding cell is a mine tunnel in a hill under oak trees, no back door. Cavemen in there, dozens of men, hairy and muddy, stripped to their shorts, ankles chained—awaiting trial. The court arrives by camouflaged jeep every morning, and they are called out one by one and sentenced to punishment. Mostly for assault, murder, rape, or other offenses against their fellows, but some for cowardice in battle, others for using drugs. The cowards and junkies are shot, the rest taken off somewhere in their chains. My case comes up four days later, it's special. The court arrives by command car and includes General Soga, who swears me into the People's Freedom Army and calls me Tovarich. Posey Wells testifies and shrugs apologetically. The court-martial officers deliberate, deliver their verdict, pronounce the sentence, and want to shake my hand. PMP's unshackle my ankles

and lead me away through deep woods, stripped to my shorts. Walk some more. Penal Camp Four is in a valley two days' hike north. Eli Oh is the commandant and explains the situation to me. You may be a hotshot one-man blitzkrieg and the hero of Bugleburgh, but here you're just another Yelp. We don't wear prison stripes here, but your right hand will be dunked in yellow dye solution that will mark you wherever you go. We don't have cells or locks here, but this is PFA territory for hundreds of miles around and standing orders are to gun down escaping Yelps on sight. We aren't confined here, but the only way you'll leave will be in combat units when we send you out to die fighting. . . . Guards

lead me away. To a little wooden cabin under a cliff full of caves. Here my name and number are written down, I am issued boots, fatigues, mess kit, and my right hand is dunked in a bucket and comes up luminescent lemon yellow. Then to a clearing in a maple grove. Here cooks with yellow hands are manning a field kitchen, skulking figures gripping mess kits in yellow hands are gathering under the trees, and my guards leave me: You're on your own. Big galvanized cans are simmering, one with coffee, one with stew, another with soapy water, and another with boiling water, the last two for rinsing, sterilizing mess kits. Men are skulking, lurking, circling like wolves in the shrubbery. A whistle blows, a long line forms, I join on. We pass by another bucket and dunk, whether we need it or not. Then we dip coffee, dip stew, and wander away amongst the trees to eat, sitting down cross-legged anywhere. I meet my fellow Yelps. All have yellow right hands. It's better than branding with a red-hot iron, they tell me. Some battalions do that, some chop off a pinkie, that's permanent. We dunk to get food, dunk to draw weapons, but that's not permanent. We fade, if we don't cop a suicide mission first. Do good in a fight and they let you fade and your sentence is over, they send you back to your regular outfit. But usually you get killed. . . . My fellow Yelps are mostly criminals and just this side of feeble-minded. Maniacs, rapists, butchers, sneak thieves, perverts, drunks. Most have lived half their lifetimes in one prison or another, it's all the same to them. Strangely enough, there is great fervor for the Cause, and I think something can be done here. We live

in this valley, in these woods. Rude hutments and lean-tos and tents and dugouts. There are no guards except for one platoon of PFA soldiers guarding Eli Oh's headquarters tent and another of submachine gunners guarding the little cabin and the cliff caves where supplies and weapons are stored. There are no regulations except general orders to stay hidden and dispersed in the deep woods, forming up only at chow time to dunk right hands and eat, and sometimes receive assignments. Yelps who receive assignments report to the cliff, to draw weapons and be formed into squads, platoons, frequently companies, and be marched away, seldom to return in full force, sometimes not at all. A man named Bojorques—a Texan, an ex-prizefighter, and the presiding judge of the Kamikaze Korps Kangaroo Kourt—explained the situation to me. You may be a rip-snorting pizen-pure curly wolf and one-man massacree in a fair fight, but if you ever cop a mission in this here Korps, you can kiss your ass good-bye. . . . Yelps are

the scum, refuse, riffraff, worthless in the new society, useless to the army except as cannon fodder. The Red Zone under Northeast Tactical Command extends north from the Thruway to the Canadian line and beyond, east from Lake Ontario almost to Portland. The enemy attacks the frontiers constantly, the PFA retaliates with strikes at New England cities or the New York metropolitan area. At any given moment there is always some furious battle going on somewhere. Yelps are thrown into hopeless situations by squads, platoons, frequently companies, to die or desert or surrender, good-bye and good riddance. But I do not see why

it must be this way, I decide to change things. Something to do to pass the time. So far, since my arrival in the Red Zone, I have been amazed and impressed by the large amounts of war matériel and the great numbers of men available—a real army is bivouacked in these millions of acres of woods. Command competence is something else again. Enthusiastic amateurs are running NETC. Dedicated, brave, ingenious, intelligent. But amateurs. Not military, not professional. In short, I don't know about other commands, or the PFA as a whole, but here at NETC I have seen lots of slipshod shit. I decide to work on it. On the Kamikaze Korps, at least. Something can be done here, and it

will pass the time, something to do while waiting for the next step. First comes reorganization and reindoctrination of the Yelps, stiff discipline and some intensive battle training. There is no authority among them except the Kangaroo Kourt. Once this is adjourned permanently and replaced by a proper command structure, few obstacles remain. Feebs and criminals do not want to die uselessly—die at all, in fact—any more than do soldiers and revolutionaries. It is better to kill than to be killed. Victory is better than defeat. Survival is better than suicide. Life is better than death. My riffraff become victors, my scum of the earth become survivors, my dead dogs become live heroes—our suicide missions become proper professional operations, our hopeless situations become military triumphs, our Kamikaze Korps becomes an elite combat unit—and the yellow hand of the Yelp becomes a badge of honor.

Friedkin said: "Yes, we all know of your miraculous accomplishment in turning a filthy rabble into a crack special-operations unit. What we want to know is *how* you did it."

"Pride," Shaman said. "Nothing miraculous in it. Nobody had ever bothered. Eli Oh could have done the same, or any competent commander. First establish unquestioned authority— beat down a few, execute a few. Break bad habits, change their thinking—abolish defeatist names: Kamikaze Korps, Yelps. Standardize uniforms insofar as possible, organize proper units, appoint cadre, enforce rules, reward effort, punish slipshot shit. Above all, train them to fight—lead them out to fight and win, and march them back to strut and swagger. Call them men and revolutionaries. Pride."

"No, no," Friedkin said. "I mean how did you take command?"

"Every mob or prison population has its big bully or little Caesar," Shaman said. "Find him and shade him."

"I see," Friedkin said. "Interesting turn of phrase, wouldn't you say? Considering the man you *shaded* was a Texan, wasn't he?"

"Bulldog. Get the bulge on."

"Don't you mean he was in command, so you killed him—*murdered* him for his medicine, so to speak? Oh, I remember!"

"No, what medicine? He wasn't in command of anything; he was just popular. King of the Kangaroo Kourt."

"Then why are you talking like a cowboy now?" Friedkin said. "You are back in the Kamikaze Korps bivouac area. Again it's the first few days. Yelps are the scum, refuse, riffraff. May I remind you that Nicolai Kudelak and the generals of NETC are monitoring these little sessions? Trust me. Concentrate."

"I am back in the Kamikaze Korps bivouac area," Shaman said.

The boys hold Kangaroo Kourt on me because I am fresh fish, Shaman said. They fine me five dollars and all my worldly goods, but all I've got is my new boots, fatigues, and mess kit, so they think they'd better hooraw me a little, but it's all in fun. I just pretend I am broke to lead while they shirttail me around a little. Spin me around somewhat till I fall, then they're having too much fun to quit, and go to sneaking up behind one another and tearing their shirts off. Pretty soon I am forgotten and buttons are flying and most of them have no shirts on, laughing and hollering. I lie there and limit myself to tripping them as they romp by. One man incurs a broken ankle from it. Meanwhile I am looking Bojorques over. He is sitting up kingly on a box, with one of the compañeras, a woman named Janaloo Heaps, handing him drinks and smokes. He is a big strong man who

really was a cowboy, later a bronc rider in rodeos, later a pro football player who turned to ring fighting, and was pretty good, they say, but that was before the war—he is a lot older now, forty and up. So I come back the next day to see him preside again. He is presiding in top-dog style, with four or five of the women hanging on him now, with henchmen to do his bidding too, for so long as he provides the fun. These women, though not prisoners—at least not in this battalion—aren't from the regular milicianas, or the Librigades either. They are the kind of women

who would get into any jail if they could, to service the cons.
Bojorques likes them to call him Waco, but Janaloo Heaps tells
me the Hispano girls say it as "Hueco," meaning hollow, having
tried him. The henchmen are the worst bunch of raw, hard,
ragged rowdies. They are scarred and lumpy all over, and a lot
lack eyes or ears or fingers. Bullies and bums and bravos, hardly
a brain in their heads, and he is

not much better, but they follow
his lead. This day he has to castigate an old boy who insulted
him. Four hard straight lefts while the man staggers, and a
walloping right overhand that rips a flap of the man's forehead
down over his eyes, bloodying him blind. Old Waco Bojorques,
he lets smeared plastic wood on his knuckles dry and cake when
there is Kourt. The blood excites everyone, and they stomp all
the man's friends and run them off. Then Bojorques calls the
Kourt back to order and to the business at hand. One of the
Yelps got some cocaine somewhere and was snorting it, a poor
soul shot to pieces long before this. Henchmen bring him out
and everyone hoots him and they decide he's an enemy of the
people. Bojorques pronounces the maximum on him. If this
seems odd, remember

there is great fervor for the Cause here
and the Revolution was ever fanatical against drugs. They drag
him screaming and fish-flopping through the woods to the Kon-
centration Kamp, everyone tagging along to see the fun. It's a
picnic. Old Waco Bojorques swaggers and swanks, and if he isn't
top dog, you'd never know it. There's a ramshackle shack and
the busted timbers of a lost mine digs and the shaft. It goes
straight down. Caved-in edges, some trompled berry bushes, and
a black hole straight down, with an old board across it. The
Kamp is the Kourt's prison, and four men are already hung up
on various trees, dangling on ropes, looking white and sick, and
one chained by his head to a stump, but no one pays them any
heed. One yells, Sock it to him, Waco! Everyone crowds around,
having a good old time, and the henchmen drag the doper to
the shaft, holding him so he falls face forward and grabs the
board across the hole, then they let go his feet. He swings and
screams. Mercy! They get a pool going on how long he can
hang there. A couple of boys that didn't bet long enough try to

hasten matters by chunking rocks at him, but that's cheating, and a fight starts. In the middle of it all the doper loses his grasp. In dead silence, with everyone frozen,

you can hear him howl. All the way down, but nobody hears him hit. That hole is deeper than a sick man's nightmare. The uproar starts again, everyone collecting bets. I have already pegged the henchmen, eight big men with clubs on thongs, as my first cadre. I go to them and say, Tenhut! They look at me blank. Who the fuck are you? I pick one, a man named Matador, and promote him to sergeant. Orders: Keep the crowd back. The loser goes down the hole. And next time I expect a salute . . . He gawps. I am already on my way to Bojorques. He's too busy with his women and his admirers, I have to kick his ass. He turns around, unbelieving. Silence, everyone frozen again, a voice says, Uh-oh! Bojorques stares in amazement. I tell him I am half bull moose and half crocodile and I come to see how he does his own dirty work. What? I tell him loser goes down the hole. What? I tell him, sorry he doesn't understand, but I didn't come here to talk him to death. What? So I try a straight right. Up close he is mighty big, it only staggers him a little. The women hold him up, whether he needs it or not, and everyone is surprised. But he understands now, and he

shakes loose. He grins. He motions— everyone back. He balances on the balls of his feet. Why, you snake-eyed milk-faced shit-eating son of a bitch! He tucks his head down between hard round shoulders and comes on. I poke another straight right hand that he easily picks off in midair, thinking I am no boxer, but there is a left hook right behind it. His eyes cross and he sits down thump with his legs out, but only for a moment. He scrambles up shaking his head like a buffalo, and bellows. Hee-yee-yah-hah! And here comes all two hundred fifty pounds of him. I am backing, bobbing, bouncing, but I take a beating. He is hot and heavy and fast. Rights and lefts rip my lips and bloody my nose and one ear. It's the dried, caked plastic wood. Bob and back and bunch my shoulders and hide behind my forearms till the worst passes, then straighten up and left hook, hook, jab and jab, and right hand that jolts me as much as him. He rubber-legs backward, his hands drop, blood bubbles between his teeth. It looks like time, I move in for the kill, but it turns out

bad judgment on my part. Waco is faking. A fist hits me on the ear, then maybe a bag of cement in the belly, and then very likely a telephone pole across the back of the neck, and a voice says, When did you first begin to suspect things were going wrong? All I can do is back and circle, trying to shake the wobblies, but he crowds in and crouches, his bunched shoulder is under my chin, hammers hit my ribs and kidneys, his big head comes up, rears back, his forehead cracks into my nose. But he's not boxing now, it's all crush and kill. His own pack is howling, it could turn on him and he knows it, he forgets to box. I duck, seize his hair and one arm, and over he goes, flat in the dirt. Over the howl of the pack someone says, Ho, ho! Fair fight! At least it gives me a breather. I am set when he gets up groggy. Jab, jab, hook, hook, punch in the pit of his stomach, and he grunts and blinks and stumbles back, and his own pack hates him, and he comes in charging. By now my nose is streaming into my mouth and I've got two fat eyes and gashes everywhere from the plastic wood and I miss a counterpunch

and he nails me on the Adam's apple. Yee-hah-hah! He kicks. A mule shoe hits me high on my thigh and numbs the whole leg, and then a battering ram slams into my jaw and spins me around, and then a freight car thumps into the small of my back. Down, chewing dirt, his weight pinning me, his arms around my waist, I can't even wiggle, I can't move his weight. But he lets go one arm to grope for a stone or a stob of wood to cave my head in. Ho, ho! Fair fight! But I can move, and I roll and bring a knee up under his chin. Teeth fly. We both roll. We scramble up. We face off. Where is he? He's looking for me. Where am I? The pack howls, it's howling for a death now. When I can see, I see something, and it changes everything. Old Hueco is playing out of wind, I can hear it whistle. All those drinks and smokes. Faces masked

with bloody, sweaty, oily filth, we face off. He looks at my hands, trying to gain time for himself, feigning admiration. Hoo-wee, son! What are you hitting me with? His own pack jaws and jeers him. Turning on him, and he knows it. Windmilling, here he comes, now or never, do or die. Gets in some good licks too, one more time. He smashes my nose some more, splits my cheeks against my teeth, shuts one eye up tight, but it's over. His elbows are down, his fists droop, he can hardly lift his arms. I feint and fade, long lefts, jab, jab, he tries to grin and signal. Son, I got to admit . . . I watch for my chance and kick him in the balls. Ho, ho! He screams and grabs, I spin him around with a hook, and I

jump. I jump on his back, scissors around him, around both waist and arms, his hands clutching his crotch. My right arm around his neck, larynx in the angle of my elbow, my fist gripped in my left palm, both arms squeezing, and it's over. First he is panting like a steam engine, then I shut him off. In eight seconds he blacks out. The pack hoorays and hollers. I hold the hold. I increase the pressure. Strangulation, asphyxiation, choking, four-point-two pounds of pressure to block the jugular veins. The pack yells and yammers. Eleven pounds to close the carotid arteries. The pack gawks and grumbles. Thirty-three pounds and up to throttle the windpipe. I can hear them murmur and mumble, and hush. It's quiet. Four full minutes by the clock. The tongue falls out, eyes bulge, suffuse, spittle drips. In the quiet I can hear his silence. In my arm I can feel the pulse in his throat throb and stop. In my arms and my legs I can feel the shudder, the strange buried buzz, then cessation. In my embrace I hold his death. I let go

and get up. Stand tall, it's important. In the quiet, everyone stares at Bojorques. Slowly, then, everyone stares at me. The women move first, wet-lipped and walking funny. They want to touch me, wipe my face, tend my wounds. The men shuffle, grin, one says, Fair fight, one says Yeah, one says Yay. There's doubt and dumbclotz deliberation, but it's happening already, the king is dead, long live the king. Morality of the wolf pack. They move in, they clap me on the back, they smile, they truckle, they toady. Janaloo touches me, I mean touches me, to tell me, but that's for later. First comes Matador. He is grinning at me, and he has obeyed so far, he and the henchmen have kept the crowd back, so I nod. He shrugs and he and the henchmen pick up the loser and throw him down the shaft. Bouncing from side to side, but we can't hear him hit. A few pebbles rattle hollowly after him, and in the silence

Matador turns to me grinning and marches his men to me across the open space and halts. Everyone watching, I give him his orders. Disperse the troops back to their assigned areas. Get me some iodine and gauze and sticky tape. Stand ready for our first cadre meeting right here in one hour. What did you say, soldier . . . ? He knows, he grins, he says: Yes, sir! And . . . ? He is still grinning, and it's a sly, mocking grin, and it's a sloppy, slipshod salute, but it's a salute, and that's a start.

"Go on," Friedkin said.
"And so on," Shaman said.
"So you killed Bojorques too," Friedkin said, "when it wasn't really necessary. Whipping him in a fair fight would have won you his position as King of the Korps just as well. How many more did you kill?"
"We had to execute a few for insubordination at first."
"And turn the rest into an elite corps of murderers like yourself," Friedkin said. "Tell me, don't you ever feel guilt?"
"Guilt?"
"That poor electroshock therapist back at Northstate was a trained psychologist. When you murdered him for his medicine, didn't you thereby acquire any of his professional insight?"
"Insight?"
"Trust me. I am your doctor. There's a reason why you are a cold, calculating killer—a brutal, conscienceless murderer—expertly, mercilessly slaughtering everybody who gets in your way, without a qualm of compunction. We must drag these dark matters out in the open and face them frankly and unafraid. Don't you see it yourself?"
"No."
"No? Concentrate," Friedkin said. "Isn't it significant that during your entire career, whenever possible, you have somehow managed to bury, sink, cover up the corpses of your victims, as if they were merely so much *offal*? And isn't what this indicates also indicated by the way you use phrases like 'open season' and 'bag limit' when you talk about killing Vols at Bugleburgh? Even more significant, don't you frequently take trophies—ears, to be

exact? Why not heads, or skins? If yet more proof is needed, don't we have it from this Janaloo person, along with others of the soldaderas? Don't you customarily mount your women from the rear, as though they were *beasts*? And the final and most sinister clue of all—why Rainsford Zaroff? Do you honestly think it was merely coincidence when you gave a false name taken from a story about men hunted as *game*?"

"What's all that supposed to mean?"

"Great God, man, can't you see it? It's the whole pattern of your case! To you, human beings are only game, quarry—at best only cattle, dumb brutes—prey! Animals to be hunted and killed! Is it any wonder you haven't got any *empathy*?"

"I wouldn't swallow too much of that pisse-en-lit popsicology, if I were you," Shaman said. "The point is, is NETC going to accept Operation Kalitan or not?"

"How on earth would I know?" Friedkin said. "But these little sessions of ours are over, anyway. Kudelak wants to see you now."

Wei Kuo Jen

They crossed a high grassy meadow and the wind caught up with them, blowing as though to hustle them along, pushing at the PMPs' hats, tugging Shaman's scarf out in front of him as though pulling him along on a leash. The grass hissed, the trees ahead began to whip, thunder muttered, and they hurried. The path led down from the meadow into a dim forest, wound downward into a deep glen, and crossed a rocky stream. A ruin and a waterwheel appeared in the gloom. Beyond was a wooden foot-bridge and beyond that a round, terraced knoll under tall old oak trees. Hidden among the trees was a long, low, rambling structure all shingle roofs and log walls, as though half a dozen large cabins had been crammed together. A flagstone path led up to the main entrance. Over the porch hung a weathered sign: KUSH-NAH-NAGUA LODGE.

Shaman stood gazing. He had seen outposts and trip wires and other signs of a tight-woven defense perimeter all along the way. The woods were full of mines. On the roofs of the structure he saw radar spikes. All the doors were closed, and the windows were boarded. This time he had made it to NETC Headquarters.

His PMP's were not guards. They were escorts, not authorized to enter. They saluted, respectfully—this was the prisoner who had made a combat unit out of a Yelp battalion—then wheeled and left. High over the building the wind roared in the oaks, and the late afternoon light dimmed, then flickered with lightning.

Shaman stood on the porch as the sentries examined his orders. He felt his eyes widen and his nostrils stiffen with a kind of eagerness—a mental hunger too focused to be mere excitement.

A sentry said: "What does Kudelak want to see *you* for?"

"I never even seen him," the other said awedly.

Inside was a vast low-ceilinged hall with several stone fire-places. Once there had been partitions: lobby, reception desk, dining rooms, a bar with deer antlers. Now there were officers and office clerks, and card tables, picnic tables, boxes used as desks and chairs. A captain examined the orders too, and kept them, saying: "General Soga's compliments, sir. Over there."

In a dim corner General Soga was working by battery lamp. Shaman saluted, reporting as ordered. Soga looked up and stared at him for a long time. Other officers came to look. Clerks stopped to watch.

Soga said: "Chairman Kudelak will see you."

Shaman said nothing.

Soga said: "Worrisome stuff."

Shaman waited. He could feel his yellow hand and his smashed nose and the recent raw scars on his face and Soga and the officers and office clerks looking at them.

General Soga said: "Excuse, please, certain points elucidated before meeting. Firstly, Chairman Kudelak may appear gentle, polite, foolish, strange. Not case. Is man of great heart, mind, spirit. Most important man in world today—important man for new tomorrow. Point: Do not underestimate, misprize. Secondly, is People's Central Committee high ranking officer, commanding attention, obedience, and more—love, allegiance. Point: Do not attempt boldness, disrespect."

Shaman grinned at him. "Is bending the knee all right? Or should I try a formal *k'ou-t'ou?*"

"Thirdly," Soga said, "has read complete military history,

'Extract Hijacker,' plus details of submitted plan, Operation Kalitan, plus transcripts of recent psychological/psychiatric sessions, file *Wei kuo jen*. Point: Do not lie, do not deceive, do not evade."

"You've been listening to Friedkin's tapes," Shaman said.

"Yes. From now on, no more of your smartass non-answers or blasé bullshit," Soga said. "Not with him. Not with Nicolai Kudelak."

Soga stood up, a pidgy, pudgy, inscrutable man suddenly with a pistol in his fist.

"If you will follow me, I will take you to the chairman now."

Shaman followed. Four officers fell in behind him, sudden pistols in their fists too. They left a hall prickling with stares and breathing with whispers. Down a long dark hall with thunder rumbling remotely, through a door, and up a flight of steep, narrow steps to an unsuspected second floor somewhere in the rear of the structure. On a landing at the top, more guards, heavily armed. Soga, the officers, stood back while the guards searched Shaman, emptying his pockets, examining his shoes, patting down every inch of his body. It was a ritual, something religious. Shaman thought: Watch out, or they'll make a convert of you too. All these dark halls and hushed voices and reverent attendants. I'll end up another of this old man's disciples.

Then General Soga opened the door and ushered Shaman in ahead, saying: "Comrade Chairman. Here is the man."

Shaman looked. And in that instant everything changed.

Across the room, silhouetted in the dimness against a large window, almost a glass wall, stood what seemed to be a small, misshapen figure, dressed in a monk's robe.

Then the sky split and flashed, the glass blazed, and all light in the room seemed to flow and center on the little body and big head, as in the grumble of thunder Kudelak raised one arm high, intoning with a shy smile:

"*Sta! In nomine Causae nostrae: dic mihi qui sis et quam ob causam veneris!*"

Except when the lightning flickered in the window, the room was dim and warm under a rough-beamed ceiling. A fire burned in the fireplace and two chairs were placed there. Books lay open on a desk with paper, pencils, and a candlestick. In a corner stood a wind-up phonograph, a Victrola. Shaman heard himself saying something, he did not know what. Nothing was real, except the little man, smiling at him, gathering all the light in the room. He was real.

But everything had changed. Nothing would be the same again.

"Thank you, General," the man was saying. "We'll be fine now."

And the voice was slow and strong too, heavy as gold is heavy, and as lustrous. Shaman heard Soga leave, closing the door behind him, and thought: It's coming. It's coming now. As though it were he, not Kudelak, who had been left in the room without protection.

"I think I can offer you something rare indeed," Kudelak said, and went on speaking, but Shaman hardly heard, watching intently—watching the man's every movement as though it were a dance, watching as though to memorize every gesture. Not till Kudelak had crossed the room to a footlocker, opened it, brought out a bottle—not till he had come back with the bottle and two glasses, and had led the way to the fireplace—did Shaman realize that he had been asked a question.

"Sir? I beg your pardon."

"I was wondering," Kudelak replied, "if you had understood my salutation."

"Sir. No, sir. Something about the Cosa Nostra."

"So much for my Latin." The shy smile was back. "I was trying to say Our Cause. But forget the military manners, please; consider yourself off duty, why don't you? Relax and enjoy; we've got all evening." He was busy with the bottle. "And I promised you something rare."

Shaman found himself seated before the fire, holding a glass. One part, at least, of the complex confusion he felt was a sort of stunned passivity, a lack of resistance. Kudelak was holding his own glass to the firelight. "Genuine twelve-year-old Scotch whiskey. To your good health. And to your release from the penal battalion. I've been told by the military people that the next step is the reinstatement of your rank."

Shaman swallowed. It burned all the way down. It helped.

"Sir. What rank is that, considering I was sworn in as a private?"

"I'm sure the military people will think of something. That would be part of the package, wouldn't it?"

"Operation Kalitan, yes, sir." His voice rang out suddenly. "Has it been accepted?"

Kudelak was staring into the fire, the light rosy on his face. It was impossible to guess what he was thinking, but the heavy voice came up as though from underground, from deep-buried places. "Military tactics are not my concern; I want other answers from you. Far different answers. Though I suppose we can start here. I have read your proposal, of course, as well as General Soga's report. And I will grant you that the astonishing amount of information you provide makes Operation Kalitan sound highly plausible."

"Plausible? It could win the war!"

"Or lose it. Don't play the fool."

"What's the matter with the plan?"

Kudelak looked him full in the face—like a glare of light.

"It calls for the massive total commitment of the entire People's Freedom Army. To one final battle. Winner take all. On the strength of a few pages scribbled in a spiral notebook by a murderer who may be a madman."

The fire crackled. Shaman felt dazed, defenseless. It was coming, the time of nakedness. He spoke, trying to turn the talk away from the subject of himself, but Kudelak's deep eyes held him, making his voice sound confused and unconvincing: "What does that matter? Isn't it the plan alone that counts? Whether it will work or not? Isn't that what your general staff has to decide? Not who or what—"

"*Sta!*"

But the voice was gentle. Although with a kind of vibration in it, so that Shaman's mouth stopped, open, and he found himself tensely listening.

Kudelak said: "What else are we accepting with this plan?"

Shaman stared at him wordless. Other answers. Far different answers.

Kudelak said: "Our Cause. When it brought us here to meet in this room, I spoke to you in the flash of the lightning."

"Yes."

"In the name of our Cause: *Tell me who you are and why you come.*"

And nothing would be the same again, and anything could happen now. In the fantastic room with the storm outside and the firelight flickering on the ceiling and walls, only Nicolai Kudelak was real.

"*Qui sis?*" Shaman said. "Who are *you?*"

"Fair enough." But there was no smile now, nothing but power. "I am the conscience of the Revolution, and I come to hear the truth."

Shaman could not look at him. He gazed into the fire. "I will tell you," he said, "all the truth I can."

Kudelak nodded.

Shaman said: "I don't think anything else is possible."

And then the rain came washing down the great glass window, and intermittent flashes threw writhing boughs and water shadows on the ceiling and walls, and the room became even more dreamlike with soft words and soft steps and domestic sounds and scents as women came with linen and plates and pots and set up a card table and served dinner: venison/pork meatloaf, canned corn, biscuits, peaches, coffee. Kudelak in his monk's robe with a shine of gravy on his upper lip, apologizing for the poor fare provided by the ladies of the Librigade; Shaman almost drunk with fat and butter sauce and sweet syrup, protesting so much rich food after months of penitentiary, institutional, field, and catch-as-can rations and penal battalion stew: "I may get sick." Then the women softly moving, clearing up, withdrawing, closing the door, and Kudelak shyly producing a box of blond cigars, gift of the Cienfuegos Cuban Volunteers, and the Victrola wound up and playing *Les Eolides.*

Shaman began.

"If you've read the file General Soga calls 'Extract Hijacker,' then you already know my past history—in the U.S. Army and as a freelancer. I was in the Sulu Sea when I first learned about your Revolution. The fastest way home was by nuclear submarine, and you know about that too. You know that I went to the pen, that I escaped, that I linked up with Coldebeefe, and that I took command at Bugleburgh."

Kudelak smoked thoughtfully. "Truth is not facts, but what lies behind them."

"What truth? Why even bother about it? What is there to doubt or disbelieve? I came back home to join the Revolution— what do you care on which side? I have a plan and it will work— what else matters? Accept that, for the sake of argument, and the rest follows. I invented the original Operation Kalitan on the submarine, for the simple reason that I needed some way to beat a hijacking rap. When they fell for it, part of the deal was to arrange an escape from the pen, via Northstate. Kaul set it up. I made it as far as the city, stumbled into the Bugleburgh situation, took advantage of it, and here I am."

"You make it sound very simple."

"It *is* simple. To get out of jail, I offered to pose as a traitor and a fugitive, and to join your Cause."

"In order to double-cross us."

"That's what *they* were supposed to believe."

"But now you are double-crossing them."

"That's what *you're* supposed to believe."

Kudelak stared with wry startlement. Grinning, Shaman held up one deformed-looking hand. Middle finger over index, ring finger over pinky.

Kudelak said: "How shall I know *what* to believe?"

"Exactly," Shaman said. "Why even bother about it—what's the difference? Leave me out of it. Back to business. The plan."

Kudelak rose. The phonograph had wound down, with horrible noises. He lifted the needle, wound the machine, started it over: Oh, floating breezes of the sky, sweet breaths of fair spring that caress the hills and plains with freshest kisses.

Shaman said: "If you've read my spiral notebook, you've seen every detail spelled out for you."

"I am not a military man," Kudelak said. "The general staff is in a far better position to evaluate your information and judge your plan. If you're determined to tell me about it, I will listen. But you must explain it as simply as you can, from the beginning."

"All right. From the beginning. I sold Special Tactics and Operations Planning of the U.S. Counter-Insurgency Command a bill of goods—called Operation Kalitan. Phase One: I would be convicted and sent to jail as a hijacker, but an escape route would be rigged for me. Phase Two: I would cross over, join your Cause, and infiltrate your high command. Phase Three: I would work from within to destroy you."

"How?"

"I left that part blank. Because I didn't know—I didn't have any idea—except getting free. They had to take that part on faith."

"Which they did? It's hard to believe."

"Why? What did they stand to lose? At worst, one escaped con out of a jailful? One blown agent never heard from again? At best, an infiltrator placed where he might get lucky and do some good?"

Kudelak threw his cigar in the fire, reached under his chair, drew out the bottle and poured them both a drink of twelve-year-old Scotch.

"I see," he said. He sipped. "So now Phase One and Phase Two are done; you have escaped and joined us; simple as that. And to suit the new circumstances, you have rewritten Phase Three."

"That's right. In a spiral notebook," Shaman said. "Although rewritten is wrong. I would say completed. Operation Kalitan was never complete before. Now it is. And it will work."

"To Operation Kalitan." Kudelak raised his glass. "Tell me how."

Shaman stared soberly into the fire, drinking.

"Certain points elucidated first, as Comrade Soga would say. One: I have seen the shit they've made of everything, with their jails and madhouses and famine and freaksvilles and National Police and nuclear accidents. Point: I'm working now to destroy *them*— to this extent at least I have joined the Cause. Two: The top-secret information in my spiral notebook, on U.S. Army strength and troop deployments, is accurate and complete, straight from S.T.O.P. in the Pentagon. Point: In the right situation, you are *stronger* than they are—able to meet and beat them not only in guerrilla warfare, but in an open battle. Three: They have had no report of me since Northstate, and all their intelligence can tell them is that I was at Bugleburgh—as a *general*."

"The point being . . ." Kudelak said.

"That they think I have succeeded. That they think I have joined your army and infiltrated your high command. And that soon I will be in touch to tell them about Phase Three."

Kudelak saluted ironically with his glass. "Which, little though they know it, has changed radically."

Shaman looked up, surprised. "No. What makes you think that? It's the same thing I'm telling you."

Kudelak shook his head. ". . . telling me?"

"That it's time for the U.S. Army and the PFA to meet in open battle," Shaman said.

The music was over, the record hissing monotonously. Kudelak went and stopped the machine, then tossed some wood on the fire, then walked to the window and stood looking out at the storm.

"As the thunder follows the lightning," he said. "Excuse me if I seem a little slow to catch up; it's the distance that gives that effect."

"I wasn't trying to puzzle you," Shaman said. "I may slither but I don't lie. You wanted the truth."

"Nor am I so far behind as we approach it," Kudelak smiled. "Now we are all but simultaneous. Isn't what you are telling me that your next move is to go back? To return to S.T.O.P. as a successful infiltrator of proven loyalty?"

. "I said it was simple."

Kudelak came and sat down; he filled their glasses. "What will you tell them?"

"The truth—exactly what I've told you. The pen, Northstate, the city, Coldebeefe, Bugleburgh, the Kamikaze Korps, Nicolai Kudelak, and Phase Three of Operation Kalitan."

"And what will they be supposed to believe?"

"That I have completed my mission. That Phase Three is the way I have found to destroy you."

"How?"

"By selling you a bill of goods—by convincing you that it's time for the PFA to meet the U.S. Army in open battle."

Kudelak smiled at the ceiling, shaking his head again. "Explain."

"I will go back to S.T.O.P. of CIC and tell them I have talked the Red high command into launching a full-scale attack against Bugleburgh—the birthplace of Nicolai Kudelak. I will tell them that Kudelak, the Central Committee, and the general staff have agreed that the guerrilla fighting has served its purpose and the next stage must be conventional warfare, as prescribed by all the authorities."

" 'When the guerrilla army in its steady growth acquires the characteristics of a regular army.' Guevara," Kudelak quoted. " 'Gather the fragments into a whole.' Mao."

"I will convince them that you are determined to stand and fight—that you are willing to challenge the U.S. Army to a test of strength. That you are ready for it, and believe you can win. That you believe a victory will legitimize your Revolution, gain support from people's governments around the world, and enable you to establish in your own free territories the People's Republic of America."

"Will they believe it?"

"Yes. Because your Red forces will already be in action."

"Doing what?"

"Attacking Bugleburgh."

Kudelak laughed outright. "And what will the U.S. Army be doing?"

"It will be sending reinforcements to its Third Infantry Regiment, presently occupying the town. But more than that, it will be rushing all available forces to the scene—because, you see, I will have told it all about your plans. It will be jubilantly hurrying to see a conventional army's dream come true—an elusive guerrilla foe caught out in the open at last. The phantom adversary melting away no more, but standing still to be butchered by the finest modern weapons. It will be hastening happily to defeat you in the final battle, secure in the knowledge that you are a weak, poorly armed, slipshod rabble which it can easily destroy—because I will have told them so."

"And what will we be doing?"

"You will be attacking, but not too hard, to allow the enemy time to send his reinforcements, mobilize his defenses. You will be allowing him to dig in, fortify the town, establish supply lines, bring in whole divisions, consolidate his position in every way.

In fact, you will be giving him every possible advantage—to make his total defeat all the more resounding. Meanwhile, you will be drawing a siege ring around Bugleburgh, digging bunkers, tunnels, caves, laying mines, setting booby traps, preparing roadblocks, positioning artillery, arranging ambushes. But most of all, you will be gathering from across the length and breadth of the nation every man, woman, or child capable of firing a weapon or carrying a can of ammo. In short, you will be making ready to defeat the enemy in the final battle—secure in the knowledge that he is only a paper dragon, an outmoded, outmaneuvered, outnumbered array of lardass generals and reluctant conscripts, too weakened by sabotage and internal strife to resist any longer the will of an armed people—because this is what I have told you."

Kudelak shook his head with wry admiration, filling the glasses.

"And so is joined the battle of Bugleburgh," he said. "Which you believe that we—not they—will win."

"If I didn't, would I be here? I'm a soldier, remember. I don't give a rat's ass about politics. Just so I'm on the winning side."

Kudelak rose and walked to the window, looking out. "I will grant that the plan has all the virtues of audacity."

"Audacity is what makes it work. Anything less and I wouldn't be backing my *barraka* all the way."

Kudelak's shoulders shrugged. "I don't understand that."

"Why even bother about it? Leave me out of it—what's the difference? The plan is what counts, and you said yourself that was a military decision. Are they going to accept Operation Kalitan or not?"

Kudelak was watching the storm.

"I may have misled you on that score," he said after a pause. "I confess I did so to draw you out."

"I've told you everything."

"You've told me nothing," Kudelak said. "I've already studied Operation Kalitan quite carefully. As I said, I want other answers from you. Far different answers."

"What else is there?"

Kudelak came back and sat down, bending forward, hands in his lap, massive head nodding, deep eyes gazing into the fire.

Shaman watched him, then turned away, gazing down too, seeing skulls and flowers and jewels in the flames. He heard the heavy voice coming up from down underground, from buried bedrock.

Kudelak said: "Understand my meaning. As a boy I once watched a man, a strange man indeed, tie two cats' tails together and hang them over a clothesline—to see them tear each other to pieces."

Shaman thought: It's coming.

Kudelak said: "Professor Friedkin was wrong, wasn't he?"

Shaman gazed into the fire, feeling drugged, hearing the voice and thinking: No, not from underground, from inside, from inside me, from inside myself. He knows.

It was there in the files, the dossiers, the spiral notebook the personal reports, the transcribed tapes.

Kudelak said: "It is not because you think of human beings as animals that you kill them so easily and callously. You do so—you abolish, obliterate them, as easily as blowing out a match, or as callously as hanging cats on a clothesline—because you do not think of them as life at all. You do not believe in them; they are not real. Only ideas in your imagination, thoughts of your mind, projections by your consciousness."

The skulls and flowers and jewels glowed and changed. They might have been the glaring lights and moving shadows in MacBitch's interrogation chamber. *Now you will answer.*

"Solipsism," Kudelak said, "from *solus*, alone, and *ipse*, self, if my Latin does not fail me again. A philosophical theory holding that only the self exists, and its awareness constitutes the only reality."

Shaman said nothing. Surprise, surprise, thought you had us fooled, didn't you?

"To the solipsist," Kudelak said, "his own mind is the only thing in the universe. In fact, it *is* the universe, and all it contains is what he conceives in thought."

Shaman stared at the lights.

I have to tell, I can't tell, the two halves of his brain said.

"Truth," Kudelak said. "Silence is not truth."

Shaman raised a face of anguish.

"How can I answer that?"

"I think you know exactly how to answer."

"It's your theory, you tell me."

"I think you know exactly what I am talking about."

"Life is but a dream."

"Is it?"

"Merrily, merrily down the stream," Shaman said. "If you think I am going to admit to being crazy, you're out of your mind."

Now Kudelak was looking at him, and the smile was back.

"A solitary consciousness in infinite void," he said. "Please, I am not unsympathetic; I am not so foolish as to demand simplistic yes-no answers. I will grant you we are dealing with matters that are unknowable. Nor are we the first to find them so. Descartes and Locke laid the foundations for epistemological idealism—the theory that experience is the only world we know. Kant, and after him Fichte, tell us that the mind of the individual is the only existent, and produces or imagines the world as its assumption, or postulate, or projection—even its illusion. Everything begins with *cogito, ergo sum*."

"*Sum*," Shaman said, "*ergo sum, es, est, sumus, estis, sunt*. It's all bullshit! I can't talk about it!"

"Of course not. To whom?" Kudelak smiled. "Nonetheless, we have arguments opposed to this form of idealism: pluralism, transcendental dialectic, collective awareness, even Kant's own thing-as-such."

"But they don't prove anything—or disprove it either! Don't you understand? Formal systems are bullshit! If I'm creating everything, I'm creating them too! And you *telling* me about them! They never existed until you started to talk! And I invented *you!*"

Deep-set eyes of immense calm stared into tormented eyes the color of rain. Then Kudelak nodded. The fire was dying down. He went and threw some wood on. He sat down again, settling comfortably, seeming to fall into thought.

Shaman drank from his glass. He knew that he had said nothing in words, but felt that in fact admissions had been forced from him with needles and lights.

"I promised you the truth," he said. "I lied. I can't even talk about it."

"You already have," Kudelak said. "Surely you didn't think I was asking your opinion on subtle philosophical propositions. I know—we both know—what you believe. That is not the question. The question is whether you truly believe it or not, and if so, are you mad or sane."

"Yes-no answers?" Shaman said.

"Let's say a choice of possibilities." Kudelak smiled, acknowledging. "To believe without reason—in the bowels, as it were—that you are alone in the universe, is simple psychosis, and not uncommon. On the other hand, to arrive through rationalism, empiricism, even intuitionism or simple inductive logic, at the same position, is classical metaphysics. Which are you, a madman or a metaphysician?"

"I can't answer that either."

"But you can talk about it, can't you?"

"Of course not. To whom?" Shaman grinned. "Besides, both those possibilities imply a thing-as-such universe that has created a mind, mad or sane being irrelevant. Isn't there a third possibility?"

"Which is . . . ?"

"A thing-as-such mind that has created the universe, mad or sane likewise irrelevant."

Now it was Kudelak's turn to make a face of pain.

"Not so irrelevant," he said. "Insofar as I can think about such an idea at all, if the universe is an illusion, it's not the illusion of a metaphysical mind."

"You mean it's mad?"

Kudelak rubbed his pained face with both hands.

"Silence is not truth," Shaman said.

Kudelak sighed and put his hands in his lap.

"I know very little about submicroscopic particles or the far end of the red shift, but somewhere in between them lies the human world," he murmured. "I wish I could say it did *not* seem to be the creation of a disordered mind. Or even worse, the projection of a mind suicidal with hatred of itself and of life itself. A madman's world."

Shaman bent, found the bottle, and refilled his glass. He held it to the light. He was savoring the moment. He was feeling better.

"I wouldn't know about that," he said. "But I can see the problem. Wouldn't it be something if you and all of it were only a thought in my mind—and I was crazy?"

"There's a fourth possibility," Kudelak said.

The glasses were full again. How many times was this?

They sat in companionable silence, watching the flames.

Old friends now, Shaman thought.

"You haven't agreed to the third possibility yet. Neither have I," he said. "What's the fourth?"

"I will explain," Kudelak said. "Let me ask you first. Have you ever tried to test the solipsist proposition? Have you ever tried to prove it to yourself deductively if it's true, or rid yourself of psychosis if it's false?"

"You're the one who knows about assumptions and Kant and epistemological this and that. It isn't provable or disprovable either way."

Kudelak tapped a finger on the air.

"How could a man believe that the entire universe existed only in his mind—as an illusion, a dream, a projection of his consciousness—without attempting to test it?"

"How could a man test it? By ceasing to dream? Ceasing to exist? What would oblivion prove?"

"Simpler proofs," Kudelak said. "If a single mind could create a universe, then its prime function would be to create apparent reality, even if only in its own realm of perception. Can you do that?"

"Wait a minute," Shaman said. Calculation was in Kudelak's voice. "Do what?"

"Do it if you can," Kudelak said. "Create reality in this moment, as a solipsist must in each and every moment. Do something."

Shaman spread his hands. "Like what?"

"Anything. Turn the fire into ice. Give us two left feet. Make the sun rise in the west."

Shaman suddenly jumped from his seat and smashed his glass in the fireplace, all in one motion. Behind colorless eyes something seemed to detonate. He shouted:

"That's childish! You're talking about God—magic—bullshit!

It doesn't work that way! What's a dream, what's psychosis, what's *reality*, except waiting to see what in hell is going to happen next?"

He stood glaring.

Kudelak raised his glass. "My friend, I got you."

Shaman slumped in his chair.

Kudelak spoke as though to himself: "What loneliness!"

Shaman reached down for the bottle.

"Yes," he said. "But everything's changed, anything could happen now. That proves nothing. Get on with it. What's your fourth possibility?"

"One final question," Kudelak said. "When did you first begin to suspect things were going wrong?"

Shaman stared at him. He lifted the bottle and drank. As he lowered it he felt himself drift off in a long slide, jolt upright again at the end. How many was this?

Kudelak was prompting him.

"For a man who was not willing to give even his name, you have already told me much. Why not all of it?"

Shaman gestured widely with the bottle.

"Don't I wish I knew? Maybe Spofford. Something went wrong then. Polwing wasn't in my plan, MacBitch knew more than he was supposed to. I got back on the track again at Northstate, but then Friedkin got into it. If I projected him, why don't I know what makes him glow like that? Coldebeefe was all right, I invented him exactly when I needed him, and Bugleburgh—but Bojorques was supposed to be easy, and he almost got me. I can't account for that either. I don't know when it started, but things have been going wrong all along. They're still going wrong, and now it's you, and lately there's been *cold white ice!*"

Kudelak shook his head. "I'm afraid you've lost me."

"Well, I may be getting a little drunk."

"So may I." Kudelak smiled. "What about me?"

"Some solipsist!" Shaman said. "I don't even know how *you* got into this, much less what *you're* going to do or say! Let alone anybody *else* in the world!"

"Dreams are like that," Kudelak said. "What about cold white ice?"

"Maybe it all started with old Malajirin," Shaman said. "He told me I was going to die. I never knew that. I never believed that. I can't die, how could I? But then what about in solitary—the kishka—in the loft? Hallucinations, visions, fits. Where do they come from? From my mind, or from outside? Cold white ice means *death*!"

"The thing-as-such," Kudelak said solemnly.

Shaman shut his eyes, alone in darkness.

"That's right," he said. "I didn't believe in my death because I couldn't imagine it. Now I can."

"You've invented it."

"That's right. Does that sound like I could control what's going to happen next? As though I could do magic tricks, god tricks, like making the sun rise in the west?"

Kudelak reached out and took the bottle. "And then we shall discover what oblivion proves."

"What?"

"With your death, of course. Presumably all the world as we know it will vanish away. Like blowing out a match."

"Oh, yeah," Shaman said. "Well, why not? It's my dream, even if I don't control it. The world is tearing itself to bits anyway, like cats over a clothesline."

"Not necessarily," Kudelak said. "There is still my fourth possibility. We haven't considered that yet."

"Oh?" Shaman said. "What is it?"

"That you've made one little mistake," Kudelak said. He was holding his glass in one hand and the bottle in the other. He tossed the glass into the fire, took a deep swallow from the bottle. "*Wouf!*" he said.

"What are you talking about?"

"One little mistake," Kudelak said. "We are agreed, for the sake of argument at least, on a consciousness in the void whose prime function is the creation of apparent reality that consists of an illusory past leading up to a given moment of awareness. An awareness-as-such which we may call the solipsist mind. So far, so good."

"You *are* drunk," Shaman said.

"Now, then. What shall we call a mind that consists of an awareness of the given moment leading forward to the *future*? A mind that projects, imagines, perceives, invents a new and better world—wealth, peace, justice—the hope of humanity! A mind whose prime function is to create the Millennium!"

Shaman grinned. "You?"

"Why not? I believe in the future of man and his world. Perhaps the world *is* a dream in a single mind. But who says *your* mind?"

Shaman was laughing.

"That would explain my surprise when I first saw you in this room," he said. "For a moment I thought you were real."

"If I am . . ." Kudelak said, "you aren't."

Shaman stopped laughing.

Kudelak said: "Wouldn't that be something? If that's what it all boiled down to? Which of us is dreaming who?"

A yellow fork of lightning flashed blindingly immediately outside the glass window, and the thunder was like a cannonade.

Shaman jumped to his feet. *Who made that happen?*

"There's one way to find out," he said.

Kudelak sprang suddenly from his place and fled across the room.

"No, no, it's too late for that now. You might have had a chance when you first entered, if you had moved fast enough. We've been monitored ever since. There's a peephole, and a rifle aimed at your head right now."

The door burst open and General Soga with ten armed men rushed in.

"Oh, I didn't mean that," Shaman said.

General Soga said: "Excuse, please, perhaps overreaction of extreme protective surveillance. Comrade Kudelak most important man in world today, most important man for hope of humanity, Millennium."

"Good-bye," Kudelak said. "I have to go back to Central Committee Headquarters right away. As soon as I sleep this off. *Wouf!*"

"Good-bye," Shaman said. "I guess this means Kalitan is off."

Kudelak smiled shyly.

"I may have misled you on that score." He seemed apologetic. "I confess I did so to draw you out. As a matter of fact, that

decision was made some days ago, with little help from me; I told
you I wasn't a military man. Our general staff has carefully
considered your plan and decided that it'll probably work; what
do we stand to lose? I've brought a copy of our complete battle
strategy for you to read on the way. You leave tonight."

Three hours, four cups of coffee, and two bacon-and-egg
sandwiches later, outfitted with a new green coverall and a butt
pack containing odds and ends of equipment, six-foot-long white
silk scarf, and forty-five revolver, Shaman was on his way south
in a battered van marked Kush-Nah-Nagua Lodge.

Two weeks, four river crossings, seven underground waystops,
five nights-in-hiding, one Vol checkpoint, and one National Police
field HQ later, he was on his way to S.T.O.P.'s offices in an
armored car.

Colonel Volpe and his staff had been advised and were waiting.

"They fell for it," Shaman said.

CHAPTER SEVEN

Clothesline

Sitmap

The ungainly plane shook and shuddered as its engines revved, propellers flashing in the sun. A D-427, a flying boxcar, called a Turkey Buzzard, all rivets and sheet metal. It rumbled and bumbled working up flying speed, and lifted off exploding tongues of flame from its motors. A few minutes later it was at twelve hundred feet, hurricane winds howling through its steel belly, where the passengers sat.

Shaman was the fourth man in a stick of twenty, all officers. Major Chapin, the jumpmaster, moved down the line, speaking to each man, shouting over the din. To Shaman he said: "Not to worry, Colonel. Just like the old days." Then he went back to the door and leaned out dangerously, looking down at the countryside, slipstream sucking at him. The Buzzard banked, straightened up and reduced speed slightly, as the control board turned green.

"Stand up. Hook up. Check equipment."

The captains and majors and colonels stood in their bulky gear, ears buzzing, blood pounding, eyes foggy. Shaman heard them bellowing behind him, heard "Four ready," checked the chute of the man ahead of him, and bellowed in his turn: "Three ready!"

"Two ready!"

"One ready!"

"All ready!" the stick leader shouted.

"Drop zone approacheth!" Chapin yelled. "Suck in your guts and grab your nuts! Stick leader, take a tee on me!"

Chapin was standing in the doorway, battered by cold winds. The men lined up, each one touching the shoulder of the man in front. The board turned red.

"*Hit it!*"

Chapin stepped out the door and was whipped away.

Feet shuffled. Stick leader, number two, number three—fell, jumped, or were pushed—then Shaman.

The cold back-blast struck him. He was counting.

"Hut thousand. Toop thousand. Threep thousand. Fawp."

The harness jerked him erect, and he looked up at the beautiful white silken canopy.

He was floating, he was falling, he was rising, he was soaring.

He was utterly alone.

The scream that seemed to tear his mind from his body was the scream of his first jump and every jump since, and now it was brand new again—a scream of pure joyous exultation.

The apotheosis of freedom.

Then earth came up and hit him. He rolled into a four-point landing and collapsed his parachute. He was in the landing zone. In the mix-up around him were other jumpers with flapping chutes, medical personnel on standby, officers and sergeants from the airborne unit in charge of the exercise, observers from Counter Insurgency Command, and a man wearing a black suit and a red necktie of the snap-on type. The last was carrying a black briefcase, and was approaching. Shaman did not recognize him at first, but then he did.

"We meet again, murderer," Kaul said.

(*We neet again, nurderer.*)

Kaul had come with a staff car and driver. On the way back to Corps HQ he sat with his right hand inside his briefcase, gripping his pistol.

Shaman said: "Fancy bumping into you here."

"No," Kaul said. "The hospital told me where. Supposed to be there for nutritional therapy after your ordeal."

"I was till this came up," Shaman said. "The Airborne's been giving a refresher course for officers scheduled to be inserted into the Bugleburgh situation."

"That's you," Kaul said. "I saw your orders."

Shaman had requested a command, a battalion at least, possibly a regimental combat team, and had heard he was under consideration for the reconstituted Third Infantry.

"You didn't get it," Kaul said without moving his lips.

They entered via the main gate, past flapping flags and saluting sentries, and drove across the vast camp. Marching men and moving vehicles were everywhere, in clouds of dust.

Finally Shaman said: "You saw my orders?"

"Detached service," Kaul said. "Advisor with Colonel Double-toe's intelligence team."

"Intelligence." Shaman grimaced.

"What else? You're the expert. Inside info on the Reds."

"I wanted combat."

"You'll get plenty. On the front lines. Starting tomorrow. That's where you're going now."

"I am?"

"Briefing at fifteen hundred hours."

They drove in silence. The driver passed by Corps Headquarters without a glance. He drove unerringly to the BOQ and halted in front of Shaman's door. Shaman looked at Kaul.

Kaul said: "You'll want to get into Class A's for the briefing."

Shaman went to his quarters to change out of fatigues into dress uniform. Kaul followed him.

"What is this?" Shaman said.

Kaul said nothing.

"All right. You tracked me down for a reason. Let's hear it."

Kaul gripped his pistol in his briefcase and said: "Congratulations."

"On what?"

"Your successful mission into Red territory. Your return with their secret plans."

Shaman stopped with one leg in clean khaki pants. "For a man of few words, you don't say much."

"How does it feel to fool everybody?" Kaul said.

Shaman exploded.

"God damn it, I'm getting tired of this! All I did was exactly what I said I was going to do. Infiltrate the Reds and set them up for us to chop down. I've already been over it twenty times with Counter Insurgency Command and twenty more with the Chiefs of Staff. The plan's been in operation for three weeks, everything is working the way I said it would, the PFA is walking right into our trap, and we're well on the way to winning the war. Just who the hell am I supposed to be trying to fool?"

"Congratulations," Kaul said.

Shaman put on a clean khaki shirt and stuffed his scarf into the collar. "I heard you. But that's not why you took all this trouble to track me down, is it?"

"No."

"Then why did you?"

Inside the briefcase Kaul's hand gripped the gun with grim pride. "I'm a cop."

(I'n a cot.)

Shaman looked at him and turned away, sighing tiredly. "Relentless, righteous Inspector Javert," he said. "What is it now?"

"The murder of an old Hunkpapa Indian," Kaul said. "The murder of a soldier named Yancy. The murder of a prisoner called Torox. The murder of a therapist and three more Northstate personnel. The murder of Ralph Elf. The murder of General Coldebeefe. The murder of a Yelp named Waco Bojorques."

Shaman put his cap on and turned to the mirror on the wall. A metal mirror, hung on a nail. But he was not looking at himself. He was looking at Kaul's reflection.

"Prove it," he said. "They never existed."

He reached out his hand and tipped the mirror up. Kaul's reflection disappeared.

"See?" Shaman said. "*You* aren't even here."

Kaul's voice said: "I'm here. I'll always be here. Every time you turn around."

Shaman laughed at him. "Oh, yes, I remember that. Zane

Grey, wasn't it? Or Louis L'Amour? If you're going to give me a lift to that briefing, I think it's time we got started."

In the staff car he was still chuckling.

"At least I got you to say more than two sentences in a row."

"The only sentence I'm interested in is yours," Kaul said, clamping his teeth. "Life imprisonment."

(Life intrisonnent.)

Then came the briefing, although it was hardly a briefing; more a pep rally, with everything but cheerleaders. Assembled in the Officer's Club Lounge at Corps were two-dozen paratroop, infantry, artillery, and intelligence officers, all newly assigned to Bugleburgh, some waiting to drop in with their units, some with orders for the morrow to join outfits already in position. Coffee cups were in evidence; the infantry burrheads passed a bottle.

An inspiring message from Major General Cob of Counter Insurgency Command—who unfortunately could not attend—was read by a full colonel, who then made a speech of his own. He was a fat full colonel, whose face was flushed with happiness. Shaman listened to some of it.

"Gentlemen, you might think this is just one more battle, but believe-you-me, it's not! It's a historic moment! It's a dream come true! Ever since this war started, all we ever wanted is for the lousy Reds to stand and fight like a man. Come out of their holes and face us. Stick their necks out and try to hold their ground. We've all prayed they would. Because as of that moment, they've had it! It's all up with them! Because we can move more forces to anywhere faster than they can, and keep moving them in forever, and the United States Army can whip shit out of them any day of the week and twice on Sunday!"

Scattered applause and boos.

"And now that's exactly what's happening at Bugleburgh! Our high command has top-secret info that the lousy Commie bastards are going to come out and fight! We tricked them into thinking they're tough enough now to beat us, but we have top-secret info that they're still only a weak, poorly armed, slipshod rabble we can easily destroy. And that's not all! We also have complete and accurate info on PFA strength and troop deployment, plus even a copy of their complete battle strategy, which tells us exactly what they're going to do before they do it!"

Big finish.

"What they're going to do exactly is, play right into our hands, with you gentlemen in at the kill, and all I can say is, I envy you, and—good hunting!"

A question-and-answer period followed.

"Why pick Bugleburgh? It's just a little town in the boondocks, with no military or tactical value to either side."

"We didn't exactly pick it—we tricked them into attacking it because it's their top man's hometown and it would be a psychological and propaganda triumph for them if they could capture it from our forces—but they can't. Any place would have been as good. It's a set-piece battle."

"What's going on out there now? I mean, what are they dropping us into this time?"

"Our daily communiqués, operations and intelligence reports, show it's all going according to plan. Since the Reds attacked three weeks ago, we have been holding them off, and this time they're not Mao-melting away on us. They're moving in more and more men, and setting up a siege ring all around us, right on schedule."

"That's *good?*"

"That's the *plan!* As soon as we've got their whole lousy army in our trap, we break out and *blast* them!"

Shaman listened to some of it. He was more interested in the various maps pinned to one wall: topographical and tactical maps of Bugleburgh Enclave. He was memorizing them when the man next to him leaned over close and whispered:

"I know you. You were in jump training this morning. I know *who* you are too. You're the guy who got them all their top-secret info, and now they're the big masterminds and you're the forgotten man."

He was a young captain in razor-pressed suntans, tall, blond, extremely handsome, a movie star, except for one disconcerting walleye. He said:

"Would you tell me just one thing? Why in the name of God didn't you just assassinate Nicolai Kudelak when you had the chance, instead of this complicated business? Wouldn't that have had the same effect, like greasing Uncle Ho when he was still a waiter in Paris?"

"How do you know so much?"

"I'm on Doubletoe's team too, jumping in tomorrow. I've seen all the reports on you and Operation Kalitan."

"Maybe you know more than that fool," Shaman said, indicating the colonel. "I've got a question. Why is Counter Insurgency running this whole show? Why not the Chiefs of Staff?"

"Oh, you know the top brass. Wait till it starts looking like it's a success. It was CIC's plan, so they gave it to General Cob, so if anything goes wrong, it's *his* ass. Besides, Bugleburgh isn't the only fight going on, you know."

"It's the only one that counts."

"Yeah, well, the chiefs have got a couple of other fish to fry, right about now. Lately the PFA has been feinting at other cities and towns up and down the Delaware. Just raids and hit-and-run stuff, but it might be they want the whole river valley, not just Bugleburgh. That would tie in with their territories up into New York. They'd dominate everything from Canada to the Delaware Bay and cut off all the major cities from Philadelphia north."

He stopped, saw Shaman looking at him with disbelief, and grinned mischievously with one lunatic eye. "Of course, they're probably only diversionary tactics. Bugleburgh is what counts. But you know what I kind of wonder about your trap sometimes? Do you remember the story about Ernest Thompson Seton and the Currumpaw Killer?"

"No," Shaman said, baffled.

"Well, it seems down in New Mexico they had this wily old wolf nobody could nail for years and years. Dug up traps, sprung them, the whole bit. So Seton decided he would kill him with the bait to end all baits. Moldy cheese and kidney fat from a fresh-killed calf, stewed and cut into lumps, all untouched by human hands or metal knives. With enough strychnine and cyanide inside each lump to kill a dinosaur. Then he put them into a rawhide bag soaked in calf's blood and rode out ten miles, planting one bait every quarter mile, never touching them, never even breathing on them, to keep the human scent off. Know what happened?"

Shaman was laughing. "What?"

"All the other old trappers, they thought it was the finest work they ever saw, and just about gave him a gold watch. The Currumpaw Killer, on the other hand, he collected most of the baits together, in a little pile, and shit on them."

By now several other officers sitting nearby had begun to listen, and when the story was over, they laughed too. Heads turned: What's the joke?

The fat full colonel said: "Any more questions?"

By chow time Shaman had picked up his orders, drawn his weapons and equipment, and packed his personal supplies into a musette bag. He went back to the BOQ, showered, and slept till an orderly woke him.

At oh-four-hundred hours next morning he and his fellow officers assigned to Flight Firedrake were in a windy, cavernlike tin shed lighted by high, hanging fluorescent tubes. Airborne soldiers were buckling parachutes on them and Airborne officers were checking the fit. At oh-five-hundred hours somebody shouted: "Move out!"

Cool black winds blew gustily, and tower lights, beacons, spotlights flashed as they crossed to the waiting Buzzard, its props spinning. Shaman had a sudden primitive prickling and turned to look back. There was Kaul. He was standing in a lighted doorway with two men with clipboards. When their eyes met, Kaul raised one hand, fingers twined in the sign of the double double-cross.

The Buzzard shook and shuddered, taxiing, and the man in the bucket seat next to Shaman said: "What was that all about?"

"Well, if it isn't the Currumpaw Kid."

"Do you know who that guy is? He's one of the top honchos in the National Police Force. What's a top Nazi doing keeping you under personal surveillance?"

Shaman had to yell over the rising howl of the motors. "I'm the man that got them all their top-secret info, remember? But I had to do some spooky things to get it. He doesn't trust me."

"That's disgraceful!" The Currumpaw Kid was indignant.

"They ought to ask the Army. Doubletoe says you're up for a decoration for what you already did behind enemy lines. And now you even requested a Bugleburgh assignment. What more proof does he want? What else do you have to do?"

"Win this battle, I guess," Shaman said. "Which reminds me. I have things to do. Back to business."

He unstrapped and unbuckled till he was free to move, then stood and went forward, climbing over knees and bundles, staggering with the pitching of the plane. The hatch to the flight deck was open. The navigator and the engineer were drinking coffee in their little compartment behind the pilot. "I want to see the flight plan and your maps," Shaman said.

"Says who?"

Shaman pointed to the insignia on his helmet.

"Yessir. Want some coffee?"

The navigator, a lieutenant, shrugged, and handed him a sloppy stack of folded maps and papers.

An hour later he stood behind the pilot, gazing ahead. The copilot was listening to operational radio, ground calls. A patrol somewhere below was calling in to Bugleburgh Command Center, code named Hermit.

"Hermit, this is Probe Nine calling. Reply."

"Hello, Probe Nine, this is Hermit. Receiving you five by five."

"Roger, Hermit. We're approaching Pimple, four hundred meters. I'm deploying my platoons on the west slope, waiting for my barrage."

"Roger, Probe Nine. Barrage will begin at oh-seven-fifteen. Repeat, oh-seven-fifteen."

The copilot grinned at Shaman. "Some outpost got wiped last night," he said, and jerked his thumb out and down at the cloudy floor under the plane. "Bugleburgh coming up."

Shaman spoke to the pilot: "I want you to drop down under this cloud stuff. Fly north up the river at about six or seven hundred feet. Over the town and keep going. Five or six miles, then make a turn, come back, turn again, and get into your original flight path. Then we'll make our jump."

The pilot said: "What? I haven't got any such orders. Who the hell are you? Are you nuts?"

Out of the corner of his eye he noticed that his copilot had
turned deathly pale. He glanced quickly behind him and saw
nothing but eyes he would never forget in a face he would never
remember, and turned deathly pale too.

"I'll have to report this."

"Okay," Shaman said. "It's a reconnaissance overflight, or
whatever you call it. Understand what I want, and you'll do it
right."

Engines slowing slightly, the plane nosed down and skimmed
into the cloud cover. For half a minute Shaman saw nothing but
shining, blinding fog. Then the earth spread out beneath. He
saw the silvery river, winding north, high forested hills on both
sides. Here and there were small dark patches, cleared places,
raw dirt. More and more of them, and then they began to be
linked together, and soon both shores of the river were cleared
of trees. A broad swath, muddy-brown colored, with the river
in the center. It widened to include a straight gray streak—the
airstrip—and then the town.

Bugleburgh was a central cluster and outlying scatter of
buildings isolated in the middle of a vast mud flat surrounded by
a bowl of thickly wooded, steep green hills.

Shaman grunted deep in his throat. The buildings were
fortified, of course. The mud flat was actually a complicated
system of diggings—bunkers, earthworks, trenches, caves—linked
by paths and roads. Artillery was everywhere, sheltered in pits.
Armored vehicles were hidden beneath roofs and tarpaulins, rocket
batteries and recoilless cannon in revetted holes. The summits
of the nearest hills had been cleared and were bristling with wire
and weaponry. Thousands of armed men were down there, dug
in deep and waiting, and a hundred thousand more were within
radio range. But the initial impression was the strongest. Bugleburgh was a lonesome fold, and the wolf was on the prowl.

Then the drop—the floating, falling, rising, soaring.

And the scream.

On the ground he saw that they might as well have flown
in by transport. A huge cargo plane was parked on the well-
kept airstrip, unloading bales and bales of barbed wire.

What he hadn't noticed from the air was the old quarry not more than a thousand yards from the edge of the airstrip.

"Lieutenant Colonel Shaman, sir. Attached to Colonel Double-toe's intelligence team."

Command Center, the center of the web, code named Hermit, was in the basement of the First People's National Bank of Bugleburgh, below street level, down with the vaults and safe-deposit boxes. General Stavros and his adjutant looked up from some figures. Shaman said: "Just a courtesy call, sir."

They looked at him. The adjutant said: "What's that weapon, Colonel, is it issue?"

Shaman was carrying a short-barreled automatic twelve-gauge slung on his shoulder. The adjutant looked at it irritably. Then he noticed the green coverall with its many pockets. "That certainly doesn't look like regulation." Then he noticed the long white silk scarf, and his voice became peevish. "We don't mind a certain degree of individuality, Colonel, but I'm afraid you're out of uniform."

General Stavros said: "Who gives a shit, Frank?"

"Yes, sir."

Stavros stood up and put his hand out, smiling widely. He was a big man gone soft, with a barrel chest and a beer belly that made his shanks look spindly. His face was pink, jowly, and genial.

Shaman had to look twice to be sure. The general was chewing gum, a big pink wad of gum.

"Shake! I've been informed about you. Welcome to Bugleburgh. Meet my adjutant. Frank, this is the man who helped make this here operation possible, and if he wants to wear Air Force scarfs, he can. When we win this fight, it's him we have to thank. Colonel, we're proud to have you aboard. How's it going so far?"

"What?" Shaman said.

"Oh, you know." Stavros hushed his voice cunningly. "Operation Kalitan."

"That's what I was about to ask you, General."

"Were you? Well, I can't tell you much about the big picture, naturally. I command the defenses, but outside of that, the orders

come from Cob at CIC. We're just holding the fort, praying and
hoping they wait till Task Force Gralloch gets here to clobber
them. I thought you might have the latest word on that."

"No, sir. I just got here myself. Although, if I could poke
around a little, I might know more. I'd like to take a few scouts
out and look the situation over, with your permission."

"If it's all right with Doubletoe, it's fine by me." Stavros
grinned. "Just let me know if you find out anything."

Shaman disengaged as quickly as possible. "Just a courtesy
call, General."

Stavros was a lardass.

Shaman started out. Earlier he had noticed one man in the
room full of officers and NCO's. He was a colonel in combat
fatigues, bald though still young, and with a face hard as the blade
of an ax. He was holding a map case in his hand, and watching.
He seemed to be sizing things up.

This man now cut across the room and stopped Shaman
with a finger in his chest. "Kalitan, right? Complicated son of
a whore!" Then he said:

"Kyte. Don't worry about Stavros, he doesn't matter. We'll
win anyway. What's your drink?"

"Scotch," Shaman said. Why not?

"See you later," Kyte said.

"Lieutenant Colonel Shaman reporting for duty as ordered,
sir."

"You came in on Flight Firedrake," Doubletoe said, looking
pointedly across the room at the Currumpaw Kid, who had been
there an hour already and was hard at work with a decoder.
"Where've you been?"

"Paying my respects to General Stavros, sir."

Doubletoe kept shifting and fidgeting in his chair. Hemor-
rhoids maybe. Thin, dark, and nervous, with a crooked mustache,
he looked like put-upon Mister Taxpayer in the editorial cartoons.
People kept hurrying by, dropping heaps of papers on his table.
One of them was the Kid, winking and rolling his wild eye
mischievously at Shaman.

Doubletoe hadn't any time for anything. "You're supposed
to know it all, maybe you can tell me. Maybe you can tell me

what the Reds are hitting our planes with. Every once in a while they're hitting our planes. For a ragtagbobtail that's supposed to be armed with old hunting rifles, they're hitting our planes with something."

"A few of them are SAM-9 anti-aircraft missiles, but most are our own," Shaman said. "Read the appendices to Operation Kalitan. The guerrillas have been raiding our base camps, weapons dumps, and National Guard armories ever since the war started. That's where they get most of their supplies and weapons."

"Where are they getting the mines? Mines are all over the woods out there. Everytime a patrol goes out, somebody steps on their mines. For a bunch of raggedy-ass bandits that's supposed to have nothing but booby traps and pungi sticks, they've got some powerful mines. Where are they getting them?"

"They've been digging up our mine fields for years too," Shaman said. "You'll also find that a lot aren't mines at all, they're our own one-oh-five-millimeter shells with the nose fuse removed and an electric blasting cap used instead. Tell your patrols to watch out for the man with the igniter, hidden in the bushes."

Doubletoe was reading papers all the time, chewing his mustache. Instead of helping him with his too-many problems, answers to his questions seemed to fray his nerves to the breaking point.

"You know so much, maybe you can tell me. Maybe you can tell me this. Until lately we sent out probes with packs of Doberman pinschers. Attack dogs trained to track down Reds and kill them, and smell out traps and ambushes. But not anymore. The Dobermans won't go anymore. They'd rather lie there and whimper. Because there's only one thing that Dobermans are afraid of, and that's wolves. And the woods are full of wolf pee, splashed on trees, rocks, everything. The town's surrounded by wolf pee. Even the dog cages smell like wolf pee. Where the hell did they get wolf pee?"

Shaman was startled. Wolves kept getting into it—this was the third time in a row. Winter forest beasts, beasts of night and snow. He hoped it meant nothing. No more surprises.

The conversation was over. Both the phones on Doubletoe's desk began ringing at once, a call from Outpost Pimple and another from Hermit; then a radio message came in from Support Pluto, and a runner arrived from one of the artillery battalions.

"Team assignment—" Doubletoe tried to say, talking to several people at once. A couple of them seemed to be correspondents, with brassards on their arms and cameras around their necks.

"I'll be around," Shaman said. "First I have to get oriented, probably take some patrols out myself. Stavros says it's okay."

"*What?*" Doubletoe said. "Hello, hello, hello! No! No! Don't bring any prisoners here! This is an intelligence HQ, not a POW camp!"

Shaman saluted and left; time to find out where his quarters were and where the mess was.

The former were in the basement of the Presbyterian Church, in a room once used for Sunday school classes, strawberry socials, and other informal get-togethers. He was assigned to a floor space, a cot, and footlocker by the C.Q., a young corporal with a comic book stuck in his hip pocket.

The latter was in the shopping-center plaza where some of the infantry soldiers were barracked in empty stores. The parking area was full of tents, one of them signposted Officers' and Staff NCOs' Mess. The meal was boiled chicken, boiled potatoes, fruit salad, and date-and-nut bars. The tent was filled with men. Shaman sat with some junior officers bitching about waiting for the Reds: "Why don't we just storm out and wax their asses?"

Afterward he took a walk around, memorizing. The troops in the empty stores slept in bunk beds and kept their weapons locked up in arms rooms. He saw some of them hanging around, playing cards or shining boots. Most were still in the enlisted mess, or else finished eating and playing softball in the cool of the evening. Laundry was hung up here and there, and men with towels on their hips were coming and going from the showers.

He walked on and saw the tankers sitting up on their vehicles, smoking and talking, watching the airstrip. A transport was just taking off, rising into a spectacular sky: the earlier cloud cover drifting high up, now black on top and crimson underneath, like a magician's cape.

He saw lights on High School Hill and all along the eastern positions. Lights far across the river to the west. In his mind's eye he saw lights in long lines straddling the river and then converging to both north and south to form a long, ragged oval. The lights outlined Bugleburgh Enclave, showed the exact size, depth, and extent of the defenses. Not that the enemy didn't know anyway, but there were too many lights.

On the way back to the Presbyterian Church via the junkyard, he heard the big guns. The eight-inch howitzers, gigantic self-propelled vehicles like tanks, had a fire mission. They were directing a salvo of airburst shells at Hill 570 in Red territory to the south. The ground quaked, the guns roared, the retaining bands whooped dementedly in the air, and far away the shells exploded like pretty pyrotechnics.

Kyte was sitting on his cot waiting for him, wearing a flak jacket, a steel helmet, and a pistol belt.

"Eat yet?"

Shaman looked at his cot. It had been a long day.

"Think about eating in the mess," Kyte said. "Think about a few well-aimed one-oh-five rounds on that parking lot at chow-time. It hasn't happened yet, but it's coming. I eat C-rations in my hooch."

"Is that why you wear that flak vest?"

It was the latest issue, made of some new kind of super Fiberglas.

"Every time I got to go out. That's why I don't live in a church cellar with a hundred tons of masonry over my head and only one exit. Think about it. I came to offer you half a hooch. Follow me."

They went out and walked up north Main, away from the business center. Lights burned in many of the homes: billeted soldiers, Bugleburghers long since evacuated. They went on toward the outskirts: factory buildings and cemeteries.

Shaman noticed that Kyte walked peering at the darkness, crouched and wary as though on patrol in hostile country, except now and then he spoke.

"I have to spend some of each day in Hermit with Stavros and his folk, but at least there're tunnels and dugouts. Much as I can, I like to stay out in the open, where I can pick my cover. By God and country, nobody's killing me if I can help it!"

Farther on he said: "Don't worry about Stavros and those

HQ numbnuts. They give the orders, but I carry them out. They don't care how, just so I handle it. And as long as they let me handle it my way, I'll hold this hellhole till it freezes over, and then skate on the ice."

They walked past the Catholic cemetery and out onto a mud flat strewn with sandbagged mounds, each with a small door closed by a tarpaulin flap. They arrived at Kyte's own mound. He stopped and said: "This is my area. Officially, I'm in command of the Fourth Reconnaissance Battalion, but my exec runs it for me. Unofficially, I command the defenses. You know how it works?"

"Yes," Shaman said. "You start taking over the little jobs, the hard jobs, the dirty jobs, the dangerous jobs, until gradually you've got them all, you're doing everything, nobody else understands what's going on."

"Stavros needs all the soldiers he can get, and he knows it. I was a soldier all my life. It's my trade," Kyte said. "Do you know the reason I'm running things?"

His voice was as hard as the ax blade of a face Shaman saw in the dim green glow of a flare high up and far across the river.

"Because I *can!*" Kyte said.

Before going underground, he examined the entire area carefully, peering into every shadow, scanning the sky.

"Welcome to my hooch," he said, leading Shaman into complete darkness, scratching a match, touching it to an old-fashioned kerosene lantern on a table. They were in a ten-by-twelve dirt-walled room under a log ceiling with a foot of dirt piled on top. Two bunks were against one wall, several chests, boxes, olive-drab packs and bags against the other. The table and two chairs were the only furniture.

"Scotch, you said." Kyte threw his helmet and the flak jacket on the bottom bunk, went digging in one of the boxes, found a bottle, and sat at the table. He took a long drink, wiped off the neck with the palm of his hand, and passed it over.

Shaman took it, sat down opposite, drank deep, and looked at the kerosene lantern, thinking: except this time there isn't any Victrola or thunderstorm, the Scotch is awful, and I am not going to get drunk and answer questions.

Kyte was rubbing his bare bald head with both hands.

Shaman said thoughtfully: "So you're the key man. Most important man in Bugleburgh today. Most important man for triumphal defense of Enclave."

Kyte's glare had a whetted steel edge. "Say it funny if you want. I don't do it all. CIC has the plan, Cob sends the orders down, Stavros passes them on, I see that they're executed—because I can! There's some good men here. The platoon and company officers are as good as they come. The ranks are mostly silly shits—I've seen them blow thousands of rounds at one sniper. You know what we've got for soldiers nowadays. They just want to sit around reading jerk-off magazines and getting high. It makes me worry some. Too many people here think this is just some more guerrilla nonsense. God damn it, there are *army* units out there! Full-strength regiments! Divisions! Moving up to attack! It hasn't happened yet, but it's coming. I can't be everywhere, but when and where I am, I know what to do and how to do it. You could say that, yes. I'm the key man."

"Like an orchestra leader," Shaman said.

"Yeah. Cob and Stavros and the rest of them own the orchestra. They call the tune. But I'm the conductor. I'm the man with the baton."

Shaman indicated the bottle. "Is that what this is about?"

"I know who you are. I know what you did behind enemy lines. And before that too. Paratroops, Rangers, Second 'Nam, operations commander of the whole peninsula, youngest colonel in FECOM. All in the U.S. Army, as a soldier! A *soldier's* kind of soldier! That's what it's about. That's why you're drinking my Scotch. That's why I'm offering you half my hooch, a flak vest just like mine, and a chance to help me. I need you. We can do it. Let's *win* this fight!"

"All right," Shaman said.

Kyte was still glaring. "How's that?"

"All right," Shaman said. "Did you think you had to talk me into it? That's why I'm here. I don't fight except to win. Let's get down to business."

Kyte stared with steely eyes for a moment, then grinned ruefully and rubbed his bald, bony head. "I don't usually make speeches."

"Tell me about the counter-offensive," Shaman said. "I

haven't heard much about it. I wasn't in on the planning sessions back at Corps."

Kyte drank, wiped off the neck, left the bottle between them. Shaman did not reach for it.

Kyte said: "Officially, the defense mission is to resist. That's all. Hold Bugleburgh using as much force as we need, only gradually increasing force as the enemy increases the pressure on us. The longer we hold, the more troops they move into the fight against us, till we've got the whole PFA surrounding us. Happy day."

"That's the trap."

"We're the bait. The overall strategy is supposed to be that on that happy day, massive reinforcements get dropped into the Enclave, meanwhile Task Force Gralloch moves up the river. It splits, envelops the PFA, we break out, and between us chop their whole army into itty-bits. One enormous counter-offensive that finishes them all at once, forever."

He banged his fist on the table.

"God damn it, I don't care! It may be screwy. I don't believe about half of it. But it's the best chance we ever had, and I think it'll work. Don't you?"

"I wouldn't be here if I didn't," Shaman said. "First I need to know a lot more. I saw some maps back at Corps and got a look from the plane, but I'm still weak on the general setup. Check me on this."

He moved the bottle, took a map out of his shirt pocket and spread it on the table: a terrain map showing the town and the surrounding hills inside the long ragged oval, with the river running through the middle. It had blue lines and rakes and rectangles everywhere.

Kyte looked once and said: "Weak? You've got every defense position marked in, down to the last door bell and support post. God damn it, if the enemy had this, they'd be in our pants in a minute!"

"I don't mean our defenses," Shaman said. "Where's the enemy? Where are all those full-strength regiments and divisions? They weren't on the maps at Corps, and all I could see from the plane was hills, and treetops packed solid enough to walk on."

"You think *we* dig in? You think *we* camouflage?" Kyte said.

"There's thousands and thousands of men and guns out there—
miles and miles in any direction you want to walk—beginning
anywhere about ten feet outside our perimeter. They're *there*, all
right. You'll see soon enough."

"How about tomorrow?" Shaman said. "Stavros okayed it,
and Doubletoe didn't say no. All I need from you besides that
flak vest is the loan of one of your reconnaissance platoons."

Sitrep

First day: He went south, across the perimeter, heading out past
the last Blue defenses, past the last outposts, downriver into Red
territory. Not too far; just far enough to test his men, watch
them move, lead them in an assault, see them fight, then bring
them home again. They scouted twenty square miles of wooded
hills and valleys teeming with men and riddled with diggings,
stalked and ambushed an enemy security patrol escorting a work
party of men with bundled camouflage nets on their heads, and
were back inside the perimeter before nightfall. At the critique,
after chow, the platoon leader, Captain Caldwell, said: "Jesus
Christ, there's a million of them out there!" His respect for the
enemy verged too much on superstitious fear; he was sent back
to Battalion, along with several others who felt this way, together
with ten older men, two clumsies, and a machine gunner who
wore thick eyeglasses.

Second day: He gathered the men together under the trees
in the Catholic cemetery and talked all afternoon about night
movement; then in the twilight led them out. Wearing soft caps
and carrying only knives, they walked north, mile after mile,
deeper and deeper into steep, dark, enemy-held hills. Sneaking,
creeping on hands and knees, frequently squirming on their
stomachs, they investigated cookfires and nightlights, found en-
campments and assembly areas, spotted motor parks, ammunition
dumps, communications bunkers, and gun emplacements. Then,
near dawn, the long walk home, the dangerous reverse-penetration
of enemy lines, the wary approach to C Company's defense
positions, and the straggling hike back to the battalion area, where

Shaman weeded out a few more and sent the rest to get some sleep.

Third day: He took the remaining twenty-odd men west, leading them across the river on one of the submerged bridges, their boots sloshing in six inches of water. In thin, chill drizzle they passed through the perimeter and climbed into the hills. Progress was slow; enemy patrols were everywhere. From cover in a sorry pine woods they looked down on a road in a little valley, a crossroads with a ruined gas station and a deserted restaurant: gracious country dining. A convoy of trucks went by, and after it what looked like a whole battalion of men in PFA coveralls, carrying ammunition. They followed, up a steep ridge whose summit overlooked Bugleburgh; on the reverse military crest were earthworks and in them SK-Z recoilless cannons and 105 howitzers. Further along the slope were shallow pits containing 4.2 mortars. Parked under the trees were Stalin organs, mobile fast-firing rocket batteries. They crawled backward down the ridge and hid in the pines again, whispering: "The airstrip!" After an hour the drizzle turned into a downpour and they made their way back to the perimeter. An engineer captain met them at the bridge; the water was knee deep now, and he had strung a guideline on floats so that nobody would step off and drown. He chuckled with rain sluicing off his helmet: "We're in deep enough as it is." Shaman made his report by phone rather than risk running into Doubletoe at Intelligence HQ.

Fourth day:
He sat on a tombstone in the cemetery, scratching at the ground with a stick. His seven best men squatted in a semicircle, watching him, and he said:

"Here's our objective. It's only about nine miles east, but it's going to take us all of tonight and most of tomorrow to get there, because we'll be stalking all the way. Walk a step—wait and watch—walk a step. You deerhunters know what I mean. Nine miles of tiptoeing through enemy country. All right. Now go get some rest, and check your gear. You'll be carrying explosives on the way in, maybe fighting on the way back, so pack light— weapons and ammo, that's all. Report to me behind the field house at seventeen hundred hours."

He was busy for a while, arranging with Major Willie Lee Johnston for eight haversacks, each containing three kilos of plastic explosive. Willie Lee had them made up and put them in a jeep, but said: "Mother have mercy, Colonel! You going to blow up a whole frigging mountain?"

"There won't be time for scientifically placed precise charges," Shaman said. "Just hit and split."

Then he drove up the hill to the high school, parked where the guard at the door could keep an eye on the jeep, and went inside. Dark, empty, echoing halls, wrecked classrooms, broken windows, smoke and fire damage throughout. He ascended broad, littered stairs to the top floor, climbed iron steps to the roof, found two heavy machine guns, a dozen troops, two corporals, and a lieutenant sitting around doing nothing much. "What the hell is this?"

"Our position, sir. Third squad, B Company."

"This building is in direct line of sight from every Red-held ground elevation within ten miles. When the shit storm starts, the first shells are going to hit right here. Tell your C.O. to find you a better spot."

He watched them pack up and leave, grousing. The troops were groggy with pot and pills.

He walked around the parapet looking down at the Enclave, looking up and away at the hills. The afternoon sun was finally shining through, a dull paper wafer in the cloudy sky. Light on Plexiglas glinted below as a helicopter rose from the airstrip. Tail high, it climbed a hundred or so feet, then hovered, waiting, while four more joined it; then all five flew west across the river, big green bugs, double-rotor attack choppers.

"Stavros!" he said like a curse, watching, as they swung low, one by one, to strafe the steep ridge, 7.62 miniguns clattering in the distance, then disappeared behind the crest, landing to discharge their passengers. It had to be Stavros's plan, some kind of vertical envelopment crap, left over from First 'Nam. Kyte would have known better than to try to carry a ridge full of artillery with five choppers worth of infantry. Whether he doesn't know about it or was overruled, Shaman thought, either way, he couldn't be the key man he said he was.

But then things began to happen.

As he watched, he saw the helicopters lift again, high over the ridge, hovering—not leaving. They hung in the air as smoke began to drift up from behind the crest. Fifteen minutes later dozens of columns of smoke were rising from dozens of separate locations: grenade smoke, white phosphorus smoke, gasoline and fuel-oil smoke, plus just plain wood smoke, as though from numerous small brushfires. He could not hear small-arms fire, but there must have been plenty—the soldiers were running the length of the ridge, sending up smoke from every gun position.

A signal rocket ascended; instantly the helicopters dropped from the sky, vanishing behind the ridge. Long slow moments passed by. Then the first reappeared, loaded, a man's legs still dangling in the hatch. And then the others, pulling full pitch, jumping out of range of ground fire, tilting their tails in the air and flogging home fast, their job done.

Shaman knew what was coming; he scanned the southern horizon. There they were, flying low, straight up the valley: a group of seven Viper-22 raiders from Steelton Air Base, zeroing in on the smoke.

Like a box seat at the ballet, he thought, watching the planes swoop and spiral and soar and return, again and again. Nose cannon, wing rockets, napalm, twenty-millimeter explosive bullets at an incredible one hundred rounds per second. For ten minutes they devastated the west slope of the ridge, blasting and burning it to bare rock, where nothing could live. Then in a flash of silver and a scream of sound the leader chandelled skyward at five hundred miles an hour. The others followed, and a minute later all were gone.

Shaman watched the setting sun vanish behind a vertical wall of oily smoke hundreds of feet tall and thought: It was a good attack. Perfectly planned, perfectly coordinated from the ground, aggressive defense at its best. The way a soldier would plan it. A soldier's kind of soldier. So it had to be Kyte after all, and that was a help to know.

The seven men waiting behind the field house were frolicsome with elation: "Oh, man! Did you see that? We porked them! We cut off their credentials!" They sobered when he gave each a haversack, opened his own to show them the puttylike stuff and the wires and batteries.

"It's fairly safe to carry. No smoking, of course. And let's hope nobody takes a hit from a tracer."

In the dusk they descended the hill behind the high school and moved through a ranger battalion's area. Shaman stopped at the C.P. to ask about conditions; they let him listen to the radio; from all over the perimeter companies and outposts were reporting in: Sierra, Sierra, Sierra. Secure, situation same.

In the dark now, they walked to the line, to the last foxholes, where engineers waited to lead them through the labyrinth of barbed wire, mines, microphones, trip wires, claymores, and fougasse drums. "Line of departure, lock and load," Shaman said.

Two men were whispering about him as they loaded their pieces, adjusted their packstraps. "I ain't worried. He's a cold-blooded prick, but he gets us out and gets us back."

Shaman wished he was that sure anymore, thinking of Kudelak. It got harder and harder to know what would happen next.

Fifth day:

Morning came bright and cool. General Stavros thought of it as bracing. He bounced into Hermit at oh-seven-hundred hours feeling refreshed by a sound night's sleep—secure, situation same— and found himself in a nuthouse. Everyone on his staff was there, plus dozens of division and regimental officers, plus dozens of people he hardly knew by sight, plus other dozens he didn't know at all; and every one with a message or a request or a question.

The Reds had hit Doorbell Knob at two in the morning, their favorite time. Support Post Zeus on the far side of the camp was receiving mortar fire. An O.P. up north had seen enemy troops on the move in the vicinity of Teat Hill, not far from where yesterday's satellite photos had shown Red trucks concentrating. The chief medical officer had a problem; an air-control officer was bitching about ack-ack over the airstrip, and one of the officers from Doubletoe's intelligence detachment was yelling something about Day-Glo hats.

If General Stavros knew one thing, it was that confusion didn't help. The best way was to let things simmer down till they made sense. His orderly brought him coffee and a crumb bun, and he sat at his desk, listening composedly as they all talked to him and to each other.

"Aggressive patrolling is fine, as far as it goes, but it doesn't go far enough."

"It keeps them from digging trenches right up to our front door, doesn't it?"

"Sure, but it doesn't stop them hitting Zone B every time we send patrols out to patrol Zone A."

"It kills Reds, doesn't it?"

"Sure, if it doesn't get ambushed first."

"It's because we don't know where they are. We've got plenty of Red positions marked on nice overlays with nice red grease crayons. Too bad nobody's ever there."

"We got satellite photos that show us everything down to the license plates on their fucking hippie vans."

"Which is why they move every two hours, so we might as well be getting photos of Flodden Field."

"Didn't we booger them yesterday?"

"We boogered some guns maybe, but what's all this buildup around Teat?"

"I don't know, but if they're massing north, I'll tell you one thing. Watch out south!"

The chief medical officer explained that because of the recent heavy rainstorm, what with the town's system and the landscape's natural drainage having been disturbed by so much digging, the entire Enclave was now a foot-deep slough of mud, causing one sanitary problem due to that, and a separate and worse one due to rats. Rats everywhere.

The Zone C commander had cornered General Stavros's adjutant: "I have got to have at least another battalion to beef up my positions if you expect me to keep them from strolling up both sides of the river and knocking our bridges out and cutting off a quarter of our force. God damn it, Frank, attack is inevitable!"

"I hope so; that's what it's all about, isn't it?" the adjutant said. "Not yet, though; we're waiting for two more enemy divisions supposed to be coming overland from the midwest. We want to catch as many as we can in our trap, don't we?"

Shortly before eleven a loud series of explosions was heard

and the TV screens showed the Fourth Regiment's mortar company area being ripped up by shellfire. Incoming 105 rounds with delayed-action fuses, sinking deep into the buried bunkers before exploding. Somewhere in the western hills was an emplaced battery that fired three salvos of twelve shots before quitting. "Guess what," somebody said. "We didn't booger them all."

Half an hour after that, one of Kyte's aides rushed in with battle orders for the general's approval. Stavros read them:

> *Enemy sit:* Mobile Red ARTY pos. Hill 904 complex gc BP 763549. *Mission:* Seize, hold, mark, evac obj. BP 763549. *Execution:* ALT 9 land LZ ECHO at 755501, H-hour 1200. A Co. estab. LZ security LZ ECHO H minus 10, B Co. advance axis TIN H plus 5 est. block pos., C, D Cos. advance axis COPPER H plus 10. Freq. 4.89, shackle code TWO ACTUAL. Div. tacair dir. air spt. call sign GREEN HOUSE. Mark Red ARTY pos. WP.

"What do you think, Frank?"

"Looks good to me, Dom."

Stavros sighed. The division casualty officer was calling. "Regret to say we lost our men on Knob, sir, but Zeus went out after that mortar team and offed them all. A bunch of Puerto Ricans in leather coats with homemade sixty-millimeter mortars. Not PFA regulars, sir, but body count is body count."

An information bulletin was just in from CIC Headquarters back in the Pentagon:

> Since the largely successful effort to deny the insurgent forces gasoline with which to operate motorized equipment, the increased use of synfuels such as methanol has been observed, making it imperative for every unit in combat operations to include personnel trained to find, identify, and destroy such enemy installations as close-coupled gasifiers, lockhoppers, thermal-conversion equipment, and bio-mass sources.

The officer from Doubletoe's intelligence detachment was back again—a handsome young captain with one wild walleye. General Stavros was trying to watch the attack on the western hills on TV. "Day-Glo *whats?*"

"Hats, sir," the adjutant was explaining. "Cheap red hats, the kind hunters wear to keep from being shot by other hunters. Wear one and you can walk through enemy lines, sort of like a safe conduct, when you want to surrender or defect to the other side."

"We're finding them all over," the Currumpaw Kid said. "Somebody is handing them out in the enlisted barracks like propaganda leaflets."

A phone call from the airstrip: One of the morning's flight of supply planes, having landed a load of concertina wire, had been hit by a SAM-9 and had crashed into the adjacent quarry.

A radio message from internal security: The crash crew in the quarry had seen evidence of enemy diggings down in the bottom—tunneling in the direction of the airstrip—lending credence to previous information from PFA prisoners (see I.S. Report A-91: *Bunghole*).

A report from Operations: Teat was under attack by a large PFA force supported by eighty-one-millimeter mortars and 3.5-inch rocket launchers.

"All right. That's it," Stavros said.

He stood up behind his desk and rapped with his empty coffee cup for attention. Big, beer-bellied, barrel-chested, and pink with elation.

"Let's all simmer down now and see if we can nutshell this here situation. I've been observing this morning's activities and come to some conclusions. Taken all the bad with the good, I'd say we're in business. What we've all been hoping and praying for is about to happen. The Reds are starting their main attack. Which means at last it's time for us to launch the big one. Counter-attack!"

Smiling, he bent one knee and hooked his thumbs in his belt.

"In the next few minutes I'm going to be getting on the horn to General Cob at CIC to exactly that effect. You all know the drill. The code word is Phase Three. When we give that word, Flight Hardcore takes off from Steelton and brings our reinforcements—the whole Fifty-seventh Airborne! Simultaneously Task Force Gralloch moves up the river in full division strength.

Between us we clobber them. We smash them! We annihilate them! To the last man!

"Of course, I can't give the code word just yet. We have to be absolutely sure this is the real thing. But this Teat offensive looks it to me, and I am going to tell HQ to stand by to commit on a moment's notice. Meanwhile, I want every unit in Bugleburgh in position, every gun loaded, every man alert, ready to repel a Red assault from any direction."

He cocked his thumb and fired a finger bullet at his adjutant.

"As for this morning's activities, here are my orders. Colonel Kyte is taking care of that battery that fired at Fourth Regiment, and I want all my combat commanders to see what we can do about this penetration up at Teat. You better set a security guard to keep an eye on that quarry—I want an investigation into that, by the way. How did sappers get into our camp, and how much digging did they do under our airstrip? You unit commanders, see to it there's somebody in your outfits that knows what a gasifier and a bio-mass is, whatever the hell they are. Frank, let's remember when we get Cob on the horn to ask him how about my request to defoliate the hills, considering there's no civilian population to give us bad P.R. And—oh, yes—Frank, I want rat poison issued at platoon level right away. We don't want health hazards around here. That's it, right? Now if nobody minds, that Green House airstrike is about due, and I want to catch the show."

Late that afternoon Doubletoe emerged from Hermit and stood on Main Street in the last of the sunlight, cursing. He had hardly been able to get a word in edgewise. Stavros watching the action up at Teat had been like a kid at the Saturday movies. "Look at that! They're still attacking! Hot shit! This is it!"

Doubletoe had remained calm. "General, we're just not sure of that. That's what we'd all like to know. Maybe this Shaman could tell us. Maybe he could tell us, if he's supposed to know so much. Where the hell is he?"

"How should I know? He's on *your* staff."

"*You're* the one who okayed it for him to go out on recon."

"I did?"

Doubletoe had lost control, partly from severe bodily discomfort, if not pain. "General, I can't be responsible for that crazy man! I can't be held responsible because I haven't even *seen* him! I haven't seen him since Firedrake! He came in and went out, and the next thing I knew, he was working for Kyte!"

"Well, go ask Kyte then. Quit bothering me. Can't you see we're under attack? Hot shit!"

Doubletoe walked wincingly across Main Street, keeping a weather eye on the northern skyline. Distant rattling and banging, puffs and clouds of smoke up there. He hastened uptown. He didn't take his jeep; a lone pedestrian made a lesser target.

The electronics bunker was twelve feet underground, a reinforced concrete room full of taciturn technicians and chattering machines. Doubletoe hated the place. The piped air seemed to hum with the constant traffic of incoming and outgoing messages—bleeps and beams and pulse beats—making him feel dangerously irradiated, brain and organs bombarded by invisible emanations from television, radio, radar, vascar, geophone, even seismograph and other machines he knew nothing of. It was like being inside a microwave oven or a cyclotron.

Kyte liked it there. He could keep track of everything that was happening, without having to hang around Hermit. He was sitting at a table cluttered with telephones, field radios, walkie-talkies, microphones, and headsets. On the wall behind him was a bank of TV screens like Stavros's, showing overlapping views of the whole perimeter: east turned dark, west still glowing, south twilit and peaceful, north flickering with light in flares and flashes.

Apparently the fight was still going on, but not going too badly, because Kyte would know, and he didn't look troubled. He had time to talk, at least.

"Don't pay any attention to Stavros. He's a happy warrior," he said. "Didn't you see his face? Like a clock with no hands? It's that Valium chewing gum."

Kyte was wearing combat fatigues, a steel helmet, and his flak jacket. Doubletoe looked at them and said: "The general thinks this is it. The big push."

"Wishful thinking."

"Is that so?"

Kyte took off his helmet and rubbed his bony head, looking up with a positive twinkle of humor. "Stavros thinks Teat is swelling to a climax, pardon my pun. Just like a couple of days ago he thought Pimple was coming to a head. All he wants is to send that code word."

"Maybe you wouldn't mind giving a poor, ignorant intelligence officer some information on what to expect," Doubletoe said, and trotted out his own joke: "When it comes to intelligence, I've got piles."

Kyte swiveled around in his chair, pointing to the screen that flickered with flares and flashes. "I'll tell you one thing. When they come, it won't be some half-assed probe with stovepipes in support. They'll come all at once and everywhere at once, like a fire storm, like an avalanche, like a tidal wave. *He'll* know it. *Then* he can send his code word—*then* we can all relax while Hardcore drops in and holds our hand and Gralloch goes out and beats up the bullies."

But something moved his hard face even as he spoke. Doubletoe saw a thought glint once and vanish like light along a steel blade, and stared with surprised eyes.

"You don't believe it either!"

Kyte stared back bleakly. "Believe what?"

Doubletoe lost control again—he knew he itched; he suspected he was bleeding. "What if they don't come? What if *we* don't get help? Or not enough, or not in time? What if *none* of it works? That's what you just now thought, isn't it? Nothing has worked yet. None of it has happened the way it's supposed to yet, has it? Why should Hardcore or Gralloch?"

"What are you talking about?"

"The plan! The trap! The set-piece battle! The Reds coming out to fight! So far *none* of it has worked out the way it was supposed to. Or *was* it supposed to? Maybe it was not *supposed* to! Maybe it was not supposed to because that was the *whole trick!*"

"What trick?"

"How should I know? I'm only a poor, ignorant intelligence officer," Doubletoe said. "Why don't you ask *him?* That crazy man, that goddamn Shaman! If you can *find* him!"

"Oh." Kyte grinned, glancing up at one of the intercom loudspeakers high on the wall. "Yeah, I heard you bitching over at Hermit this afternoon. What's Shaman got to do with it?"

"It's his plan that isn't working. Or is it?" Doubletoe said. "Maybe it's his trick too."

"You're full of shit," Kyte said. "All he did was to help set it up, like promoting a fight or a ball game. He didn't plan the strategy, the defense, the counter-attack, or any of it. Cob and his numbnuts back at CIC did, for better or worse. And they don't know how anything is going to work out either, no more than any other battle. Because the enemy isn't just reacting to us, they've got their own game plan. They're here to try conclusions too. That's what it boils down to, just like always. Red versus Blue. Whichever side has the best plan or executes it better cops all the cookies."

"Is that so?"

"That's so," Kyte said. "Think about it. And as far as Shaman goes, if he's a crazy man, I wish we had ten more like him. You must not have been reading your daily reports, or you'd know. He's been running recon missions, bringing back more hard intelligence than all your cameras and satellites lately. Instead of sitting around wondering what's out there, he's been out finding out."

"What does that prove?"

"Here's something else you may or may not know," Kyte said. "The enemy has bigger guns out there than we thought. We don't know where they are, but we know they've got them, because Shaman spotted a truck convoy and a whole PFA battalion of bearers. They were coming in from the west with one-fifty-five shells. One-fifty-five shells! Looks like we're in worse case than we thought. However, our air observation thinks it spotted men and trucks about nine miles east, maybe hiding one-fifty-five ammo in the old railroad tunnel, so I sent Shaman to see. In fact, that's where he is right now."

"All I ask is to be kept informed," Doubletoe said.

"In fact . . ." Kyte said. He looked at his watch. He wheeled his chair to a control board, depressed a button, and got an exact time readout. "In fact, he's been gone since about this time last night and I'm expecting a signal from him at twenty hundred hours, if you'd care to sit down and wait a couple of minutes."

"I don't sit much," Doubletoe said. He watched Kyte flip over a row of toggles and turn a few knobs and dials, tuning in on the eastern quadrant. Darkness and silence: nothing to see or hear. The screens showed only the dim shape of High School Hill, behind it higher hills rising into a starry sky. The microphones picked up only night noises, rustlings and whisperings like leaves and wind and water.

They waited. Doubletoe felt bleeps and beams and pulse beats invisibly bombarding his brain and organs.

The readout said 2004.

"Well, it looks like—"

"Wait," Kyte said.

A soundless giant flashbulb went off behind the high horizon. An incandescent giant orange fireball rose from behind the hills. A rumbling, slow, underground thunder shook bedrock beneath the concrete room.

"He did it!" Kyte bellowed.

"What the hell?"

"A whole tunnel full of hundred-pounds-apiece artillery shells, like one contained charge!" Kyte said. "He must have blown up the whole frigging mountain!"

Sixth day: A little after midnight the enemy artillery opened up. A duel began, Division's eight-inch howitzers against at least three batteries of emplaced 155's. Kyte was in the electronics bunker; he left in a hurry to get to Hermit before somebody got panicky and forgot that a battle was still going on up north. On the way he had to jump for cover every few yards; he calculated the incoming rounds at about one per second and sixty per minute. Not just the heavy 155's, but also 105's, seventy-fives, and recoilless and mortar rounds too, hitting all over the Enclave as though the Reds were test-firing all the guns they had. Meanwhile the big howitzers were shooting back, practically blasting the tops off every enemy-held elevation within range. Most of the choppers were in the air, high over the hills, shooting rockets and dropping napalm. Kyte saw the dark sky lighted up different colors and thought Bugleburgh looked like Hell on fire.

Stavros was jubilant: "This is it!" But he saw the point: "Yeah, we *are* kind of in the spotlight." Kyte said: "Sure, we might as well share it with them, it's their battle too. And besides, maybe we ought to see what's going on before we send the code word."

So Stavros ordered every searchlight on the perimeter to focus on the hills, ordered the choppers to drop flares, the artillery to shoot illuminating shells and incendiaries, the line companies to fire tracers and rockets and to detonate all the napalm and fougasse pots on their fronts. "That's more like it," Stavros said. "Sure," Kyte said, "now we can see what they're really up to. Check your screens. This doesn't look like much of an attack to me. I don't see any ground forces, and the defense positions haven't reported any, except up at Teat, and we can handle that."

When the artillery duel ended, a silence fell. It seemed the attack on the northern perimeter had worn off too. The defenses had held. General Stavros watched his screens, saw fires burning but no sign of movement. Electronics reported no activity in any zone. The outposts, line outfits, and support posts began radioing in: Sierra, Sierra, Sierra. Adjutant Frank was on the phone with Zone A HQ: "Counter-attack successful; we beat 'em off with company weapons." Air control reported two helicopters damaged landing on shell-damaged helipads. Stavros returned to his desk. An orderly broke out coffee-and. Kyte left for his hooch, to get some sleep. He hadn't slept for a long time. But first he took a quick tour.

He saw the helipads; it looked as though the enemy guns had hammered them at short range, with never a miss. He saw the airstrip too, struck hard. He saw where several 155 rounds had landed among the M-129's, the armored, amphibious personnel carriers, in Fourth Battalion's motor park; five of them were totaled. He saw where the enemy had scored a hit on a dugout full of small-arms ammunition and M-92 grenades. He saw destroyed earthworks and caved-in commo bunkers and trenches and ex-ploded infantry positions. G.R. personnel were in these latter, gathering chunks and bits and putting them in body bags with green tags. He saw medics and casualty officers, and company officers reorganizing their units, and soldiers staring blankly at nothing. He went past a battalion aid station, heard men screaming and groaning. He went in and looked, and saw in the nightmare light the naked bones and severed limbs and bubbling holes, the ash-gray faces, the red rags, the grape-jelly blood of mortal wounds, and the knives and tubes and bottles. A corpsman glanced at him quickly, saw no mark on him, and said: "You want something,

Colonel?" Kyte said: "I was a soldier all my life, you can get used to it. I don't want to get used to it. Nobody has a right to get used to it."

The sky was still dark, but by the time he had reached his hooch, some of the smoke had drifted away and he could see icy stars. He went underground, pushing aside the tarpaulin, squinting blindly at the light—

At the *light!*

Too late, too slow, too sleepy.

Shaman had lighted the kerosene lantern and was seated waiting, half a bottle of Scotch on the table. He watched Kyte stumble in, halt, realize that he should have come in shooting—curse, squint blindly, claw at the holster on his belt—then shrug and relax. Grinning sourly, he came forward, put his fists on the table, and leaned his weary weight on them. Strain and sleeplessness were scratches on his hard face like file marks.

"Lucky for me it wasn't the enemy."

"You never know," Shaman said.

Kyte slumped into the opposite chair, staring curiously. Shaman was tattered, filthy, had lost both his hat and the whole left sleeve of his coverall; that arm bore a long ragged gash, and he was doctoring it with salve from the combat Medpak on his belt.

Kyte said: "Have a hairy?"

"We had to fight our way into the tunnel. Guards. Light machine gun and a rifle platoon. Dalrymble got the gun with a grenade, but it killed him."

Kyte dragged the bottle toward him but did not drink yet; he was seeing wounds and blood; he shuddered coldly. "I hope it was quick. Death is bad enough, but pain is the worst. Death isn't Hell, but pain is, or vice versa."

He shook himself and sighed. "Oh, God! A peaceful night's sleep!" Then he said: "I see you're wearing the flak vest—that mean you're going to take me up on the rest of it? Half a hooch?"

"I still have work to do."

"Not tonight, you don't. You did enough for tonight. You know that son of a whore registered on the Richter scale? Honest to God! Besides, you must be beat. You made a fast trip back. I wasn't expecting to see you until tomorrow at the earliest."

"We had to tiptoe in, not out. After we blew it, there was plenty of confusion. Reds running everywhere—shooting each other, more than likely. Meanwhile, the attack on the north zone had already begun—more confusion. It only took us a couple of hours. I came straight here."

"You haven't reported in yet?"

"That's the idea."

"Where's your men?"

"The LMG got Dalrymble; the rest will be along. I turned them loose before we got to the perimeter. Told them it was good opportunity for a training exercise—practice infiltration— each to find his own way home."

Kyte looked dubious. "Everybody is pretty alert tonight. You could lose some more men."

"But none of the good ones," Shaman said, waving his bare arm in the air as though to cool it. "Let me have your Medpak, will you?"

Kyte tried a glare of moral outrage, but couldn't manage it with red-rimmed stinging eyes. He rose and took off his belt, removed the Medpak, and threw the belt and holster on the lower bunk, followed by his helmet and flak vest. With a tired lurch he sat down again, stretched his legs out, tugged his top shirt buttons open. He saluted with the bottle, tipped it high, and drank deep. His jaws clenched, his cheeks grinned, and he shuddered. *"Brrrraa!"*

"Exquisito," he said when he could speak. "Listen, I was talking to your boss today. As long as you haven't reported in yet, give Doubletoe a thrill, why don't you? Show him you're still on his team. He worries about you. He thinks you might be a traitor."

"Doubletoe is next," Shaman said.

"Next what?" Kyte said, drinking again. "Jesus God, this piss would burn holes in a crocodile."

But he took another drink. Then put the bottle down and hunched his shoulders and crossed his arms low over his stomach and sat still, as if listening attentively. "I got to catch some zees," he said. "It's been a long day today. Not just the attack up north. That barrage too. It kicked the crap out of us. As if they knew right where to aim. We lost some vehicles and some equipment and some men. And we lost the airstrip too, as far as transport planes are concerned, till we get the engineers in to fix it."

"If they get the chance," Shaman said. "Don't forget Bunghole."

Kyte peered blearily, and shook his head to clear it. "I forget."

"We don't know how extensive that tunneling was or what they managed to bury under the airstrip before we noticed."

But Kyte was holding both hands in front of him, worriedly observing a gross tremor in the spread fingers.

"Damn, I better get some rest fast," he said. "One more thing I was supposed to tell you when I saw you, speaking of Doubletoe. His intelligence team took a casualty, a kid trying to reach the electronics bunker in the middle of the uproar. A young kid with a walleye, maybe you knew him. Flipped his jeep and cut his head in half with the windshield."

"I knew him."

"They found a note in his effects, a radio message he sent or was going to send by secret PCM, directed to ECCOM, NatPol, Kaul. It concerns you. You'll see it tomorrow, but what it says is you're a hero, a great man, a loyal American, and the kid requests relief from the dishonorable assignment of spying on you."

Shaman said nothing.

Kyte was watching him intently. "So Doubletoe's not the only one. Kaul thinks you're a traitor too."

Shaman said nothing.

"Now all of a sudden you've got locktitis?"

Shaman said slowly: "I was not going to bother you with it."

Kyte's puckered, intent eyes suddenly shut. He flung them open with a jerk of his head. Spit ran down his chin. He wiped it off. He remembered where he was and what he was saying.

"Well?"

"I'll tell you," Shaman said. He got up and walked to the bunk, put Kyte's Medpak in its pouch but kept the belt and holster in his hand, stepped behind Kyte's chair and stopped there, stood looking down at the bald, bony head. "The Currumpaw Kid was wrong. Kaul is right."

But Kyte was having a bad abdominal cramp. "You—"

"Take it easy. It's nothing you have to bother with now."

Kyte grunted. "What are you talking about?"

Shaman shrugged. "It's there to read in Operation Kalitan."

"I don't believe it! Kalitan—it was your plan, you set it up! You were working for me all week! You just blew up a whole Red ammo dump!"

The pain got bad. He crouched in his chair, stamping his feet.

Shaman said: "Remember the map I was drawing? You said if the enemy had it they'd be in our pants in a minute? It shows lots more now. All the defense positions, as well as the exact locations of Hermit, Intelligence HQ, Communications HQ, the electronics bunker—every supply and ammunition dump, every battery position and gun emplacement—zone defenses, armored deployment, wire, mine fields—all the rest of it. Every target in the Enclave."

Kyte was bent over, gasping. "I remember."

"The enemy has it now. I made a detour on the way in. We had a prearranged drop."

The pain was going away.

"When's the big attack?" Kyte said hoarsely, with closed eyes.

"Tomorrow. Today, I should say. In an hour or so. About dawn."

"Why did you come back here tonight? Why not just take your map and go back to your Red friends? Join the big dawn attack with them instead of being in here on the wrong end of it?"

"I told you, I still have work to do. The Enclave isn't going to be reduced in one day. When Hardcore and Gralloch arrive, there's going to be a full-scale battle. Red is going to need help— I have to be in position. Your position, more or less—in command of the defenses, unofficially, at least. I need your know-how to work effectively on the inside—sabotaging things. For instance, eliminating any officer who shows the least sign of competence."

Kyte nodded. "Me."

"You're the key man. The man with the baton."

Kyte's bald head was sweating; he was breathing deeply and rapidly. "And Doubletoe's next."

"Followed by whoever replaces him. Also your exec, and Stavros's man Frank. A couple of unit commanders I've noticed, good men. Trapnell of Division Artillery. I don't know who else yet. Have to play it by ear."

Kyte sat up straight and reached for the bottle. He took a big swallow, put the bottle back carefully on the table. He was fighting drowsiness and nausea at the same time.

"You slimy, scummy, stinking son of a whore," he said, "get out from behind me, or can't you face a man?"

Shaman walked around and sat again at the table, belt and pistol holster across his lap. Kyte was white-faced and stiff; his red eyes leaked like steam nozzles.

"Why are you telling me?"

"It doesn't make any difference now."

"Oh, no? What makes you think I won't kill you first?"

"I can't imagine it," Shaman said.

Kyte tried to get out of his chair and could not.

"By God and country, nobody's killing me if I can help it!"

Tears filled his eyes and ran down his cheeks.

Shaman picked up the bottle, and put it down again.

Kyte sat still, looking at it.

"You already did."

Shaman made a magician's pass.

"It was in the whiskey," Kyte said.

He turned aside and vomited. When nothing more would come, he stuck his fingers down his throat, retching and spitting.

"No wonder I felt sick."

Then, because he was a fighter, he got to his feet. Bracing himself with his fists on the table and pushing. Discolored saliva ran from his mouth and the tremor shook him. His idea was to pick up the bottle, hit Shaman with it, or failing that, knock over the kerosene lamp and escape. Shaman took the bottle away and moved the lamp out of reach. Kyte tried to move around the table and grapple with him, but his legs buckled. He said: "I guess not." He sat down hard.

Shaman said: "The salivation and hypotension and muscle weakness are because it's a fluoride-based rat poison. Worse is

coming—epileptiform seizures, dyspnea—no breath. Bad cramps
and convulsions. Eventual respiratory failure. I don't like this
any better than you do. There's only one thing I could do to
help. Do you want to go off turned on?"

Contorted with nausea, Kyte tried to say something.

"Your Medpak has a morphine syrette in it, and so does
mine," Shaman said. "You could shoot them both and go under—
no pain, sleep till it's over. Better than dying like a crushed
snake."

Tears poured down Kyte's cheeks; lacrimation was a symp-
tom too.

"I can't move. I can't do it. You do it."

He crossed his wrists on the table and put his forehead down
tiredly and his voice came up choked: "Maybe a nice dream."
Then after a moment he lifted his face and rested his chin on
his wrists, looking up.

"I was a soldier. Not *rat* poison! Oh, my God!"

"Think of it as a good night's sleep," Shaman said.

He had brought back with him two of the haversacks, dead
Dalrymble's and his own. He rigged the roof with one, stringing
the wire out to the nearest trench. Then he put on his flak vest
and helmet and sat down to wait.

At dawn the first enemy shells began to fall on the Enclave.

With scattered explosions sounding everywhere, he triggered
the plastique in the roof of the hooch, and buried the body under
a ton of earth and timbers and burst sandbags.

Then crouched listening to the roar that went on and on.

What the hell?

The hooch was down, its roof dropped in, smoke and dust
billowing up, dirt and debris settling back—but the roar went on
and on, growing louder and louder, coming closer and closer.

The enemy barrage.

His eyes went wide and white.

"What the hell is going on here?"

Shit Storm

Because everything was changed now, and anything could happen.

First it was the enemy barrage. He was running. Thunder

and lightning hammered him; the splintered steel or glass was like rain or sleet. Huge pressures swelled out at him and bumped him stumbling this way and that. Falling, he lay bouncing on jolting, surging earth. Sudden heat opened a mouth at him like a blast furnace, and fire on his gashed left arm made him shout. He crawled and hid, spat dust, got up and ran—the Enclave was exploding around him. He dove down an incline, slid on his hands and knees, fell against concrete. His ears rang; he lay battered and scorched, unbelieving.

I knew they had guns—

Nobody has that many guns!

The enemy has.

White anger rose up suddenly in a kind of cold flush.

"No more surprises!"

He was in the electronics bunker. Round-eyed technicians with headsets and microphones stared at him, his blackened face and bleeding arm. Two field-grade officers from Operations were there, trapped by the bombardment. "Where's Kyte?"

Tiny, tinny voices in the numbing uproar.

"We saw the flak vest, we thought you were Kyte."

"I'm sitting in for him." Shaman sat in the swivel chair, flipping and switching toggles and knobs and dials with Kyte's own easy mastery—but the screens reported only smoke and flame, the overloaded sound sensors only static. Operational radio jabbered messages between the line outfits and their C.P.'s: "We're pinned down!" From Hermit a PCM message was going out to Cob at CIC, a loop, repeating over and over:

"Phase Three! Phase Three! Phase Three!"

With a grating sound the buried concrete room seemed to jolt slowly like a ship's keel hitting bottom, and powder puffed from sudden cracks in walls and ceiling.

What was *that?*

Then he was staring at the screens.

"That was no artillery shell."

The screens showed nothing except smoke, but Air Control was calling Hermit: "We're hit! We're hit!" And then the smoke began to lift away on the early morning wind. Where the airstrip had been there was a volcanic crater still flickering with fire, surrounded by the strewn wreckage of transport planes and helicopters.

I knew about that.

Bunghole: the enemy tunneled underneath and planted mines.

Then why are you surprised again?

Something is happening here. What is it?

The wind was blowing and more screens were clearing to show various areas of the Enclave being shelled. It was unbelievable. Scarcely any buildings were left, and those still standing were burning like bonfires. There was no sign of life aboveground and nothing to see except churned mud and the gray-white flashes of explosions and the dark, erupting flowers of smoke.

Then it stopped.

All at once he was hearing a voice, close by, in the room: "Never get out of here alive—"

Silence. Even deep underground the sudden silence everywhere was a shock, an impact, prolonging itself into a hollow ache.

The shelling was over.

Of course.

Now comes the attack.

Immediately he was tripping switches, yelling frantically, reaching as many of the command posts on the perimeter as he could: "Alert! Get ready! They're coming now!"

Panic answered him: "We're blown all to hell! We're thirty percent casualties! They smashed our positions!"

"Hold on, hold on," he was muttering.

He was on the direct line to Hermit. Runners to the line companies. Infantry reserves stand by. Mortar teams, rocket batteries, artillery—shift to preregistered targets, saturation strike with VT fire. "They are going to be on our front step in about one minute!"

The speaker overhead spoke in Adjutant Frank's peevish voice: "On whose orders? Colonel Kyte, is that you?"

"Who gives a shit, Frank?" Stavros's voice said. "It sounds good to me."

"Who is that? That's not Kyte. Who is that?"

"Kyte had one drink too many," Shaman said. "No time now. *Look at your screens!*"

The Reds were attacking.

Overlapping views of Hill 601 on the northeast quadrant showed him a slope, and the slope was moving. Its crest seemed to bristle and its surface to crumble downward like gravel sliding and rolling.

"Nine—eleven—thirteen. Magnification!"

The movement was men. They wore green and brown and blue denim and plaid shirts and windbreakers and caps and helmets and carried shotguns and assault rifles and 'scoped sporting rifles and hand grenades. More and more were appearing over the crest and coming, stumbling and sliding down the slope toward the Enclave like a slow avalanche.

"North's where the fight was yesterday," one of the operations officers said. "We aren't reinforced up there yet."

"They'll take the factories and the junkyard," the other said.

Shaman was already on the radio talking to the executive officer of Kyte's Fourth Battalion: "Hold them at the cemetery."

"Who is this?"

Enemy infantry was approaching other points on the perimeter. What he could not see on the screens was reported by the unit commanders: "I got Reds on my front. They got mortars—"

The high school was burning again; by its red light the Red assault force could both see and be seen. PFA regulars using automatic weapons and grenade launchers were moving up the hill against machine guns. Suddenly Shaman saw a startling close-up of a man with a ponytail and bushy whiskers, and one of the screens went dead.

The Reds were shooting out the cameras.

Zone D commander was on the phone: "We're holding them." The enemy could not reach the river; the defense positions on the west shore were holding them. But the barrage had knocked out the Bugleburgh Bridge as well as two out of four of the underwater bridges, making resupply and reinforcements problematical. "We've taken a lot of casualties already, and our ammo is going fast."

Shaman flicked to Zone C, south. More cameras out. The valley was filled with smoke. He heard the commander reporting to Hermit: ". . . during the shelling. They were digging all the time. They were digging under fire, their own fire. Right up to our MLR. We've got Reds in trenches sixty meters from our MLR."

Reports were coming in from every sector: "Enemy attack."

"Hold on, hold on!" he was muttering. Too soon, too fast!

"Send reinforcements!"

"Artillery support!"

"Where's our choppers?"

Shaman sat back, watching screens wink out one by one as cameras on the perimeter were destroyed. The sound sensors transmitted a confused din of shots and explosions and cries of men in fear or pain or triumph. Soon there would be nothing but sound.

Like going blind.

Going blind was losing control. The realization stopped the breath in his mouth—suddenly he knew what was happening and what was wrong.

It's happening without me!

He shot himself backward in the chair. Buried underground in a concrete room with the lights going out one by one.

Helpless.

"*No!*"

First it was the unbelievable shelling, now it was the irresistible enemy forces attacking all at once, everywhere at once. But it was not too late. That had been a mistake, the electronics bunker was no good—buried away underground; he could not take Kyte's place, command, baton, from there, without taking part—and in so doing, taking control. *Control.* Before it was too late.

I have to *see!*

He was running, out in the open, in the early sun, scarves of smoke drifting, noise all around him. The town was unrecognizable—buildings smashed flat or still burning, groups of men hurrying by, vehicles roaring and stumbling in the shattered streets. Look up: steep green hills all around, moving slopes crumbling downward.

He saw the mess area in the shopping-center plaza—shell holes and heaved concrete slabs and the demolished stores and corpsmen carrying away the wounded and the dead. From a pole high overhead a PA speaker whispered a weird conversation, a freak fragment:

"What do you think, Frank?"

"Why don't we punch it up on the computer, Dom?"

Shaman shook his fist at the pole. "You lardass son of a whore! *Don't do anything till I get there!*"

He was halfway to Hermit when the sky leaned down in a steep bright slant and hit him like a rockslide. There was the disorientation of being turned upside down, end over end, the distant sensation of his body falling, grinding dirt. He was dazed and deaf and dazzled, lying still on his back feeling his heart stagger and then thump like an old engine. He hadn't heard the whistle or the whir. The shell had burst only twenty yards away. More were coming—the air was full of streaks and holes. The barrage had started again. He ran.

Take stock: His shotgun was gone and his left arm felt numb. Haversack still there, didn't blow up—good. Revolver in holster. Eyesight and hearing coming back. Legs okay.

But I am not going to make it.

Hermit was too far.

He knew from the gathering rhythm of the shelling and from the fact that Hermit was the center of the web and a marked target that he would never reach there alive. A solid wall of explosions stood blocking off the way to the center of town. He would be killed.

"That's not in the plan."

The enemy was shelling again to cover the next stage in the advance of its infantry troops. Nothing to worry about, he wasn't the target.

No need for fear—

But something in the sky was waiting to fall on him.

He was running crosstown, clambering through the wreck of shops and businesses, toward refuge. He knew where to find refuge. The bouncing of the earth was scaring rats out of the ruins, sending them scampering in all directions. Refuge was across the mud flats where once had been a park opposite the town hall: the field hospital.

Tents were aboveground, tunnels and deep chambers below. The enemy took great care never to shell hospitals; it was against

PFM policy—because dead men were dead men, but wounded men were an inconvenience and a liability and a drain on U.S. resources. The hospital area was safe—the shell bursts seemed to track him to within sight of the metal buildings painted with crosses, then shift away as he dove into a hole. Shaman yelled and kicked desperately. The hole was full of pieces.

He crawled out shuddering—safe—and sat looking into the hole with horror, his back skin creeping. Shells were dropping all over the town but not on the hospital area. Two orderlies emerged from a tunnel dragging a tarpaulin that sloshed with blood and sagged with small bundles—pieces of flesh with skin and hair and nails.

Shaman roared in fury at the orderlies: "You're supposed to bury that filth!"

Astonishment. Not until it's full. Chief surgeon's orders. Otherwise they'd be digging fresh holes every couple of minutes.

Another hole was nearby; other orderlies were emerging from tunnels, bringing bodies in green bags up from underground, dumping them; a bulldozer stood waiting. There was traffic in the opposite direction also—wounded men, bodies not dead yet, were being brought in from every part of the Enclave and taken underground. Shaman followed a file of litter bearers down a steep ramp lighted by hanging bulbs. They came to a dim cave full of casualties waiting for surgical attention. There were hundreds of them, lying on the floor, lying in rows, crammed together with barely room for the doctors and corpsmen to move among them.

Shaman looked around him—he was expecting nothing—and suddenly he was in Hell.

Pain is Hell, or vice versa, Kyte's voice said.

Screams and blood and agony made a kind of chaos, and the chaos was inside his own brain and body.

A young Vol lay propped against the wall pursing his lips and uttering soft puffs of air: "Oooh-oooh-oooh!" as though trying to blow smoke rings. He was crushed from the waist down. Shaman turned away.

A face looked at him with no jaw, a bloody hole in place of a mouth, long ropes of mucus hanging down, an incision at the base of his throat and a trocar inserted, a silver tube, clogged with coagulated blood—he was strangling.

A man with no back was sitting up; his lungs were visible, working—he was whimpering. He was singing; he was scraping up handfuls of dirt from the floor and dumping them into the gaping stomach of the man next to him, like a child playing on the beach.

From end to end of the dim cave were men were being tortured to insanity by damage to their bodies.

Shaman shut his eyes as the chaos tried to swallow him.

Fight it.

Control.

It isn't real.

But Kyte's voice said: *Pain is the worst.*

Someone was talking to him; a voice had spoken to him several times already; it had said: "You get used to it, it's not so bad, imagine how it must have been before anesthetics."

"I can't take this."

The doctor said: "That's just empathy, shows you're human."

"Not me! I'm getting out!"

"Better let me take care of that first."

Shaman looked down at his left hand. The hand leaked slow blood, a fragment through the palm. It was numb.

The same arm!

Listen.

The shelling had stopped again.

Immense quiet.

Hermit. The way was clear.

The doctor was trying to wrap his hand. "You're WIA now, you don't have to go out—"

His voice stopped and he disappeared like an image on a shot-out TV screen. The whole cave was gone. Yellow filtered sunlight.

Shaman was running up a ramp into the open.

Hermit!

But it was too late.

He was outside and the surprise was still out there waiting, and the fear like something hanging in the sky, and now the chaos was part of it too, all mixed together with what was happening without him, out of his control.

Too soon—too fast.

He needed a point of vantage to see from, but the cameras were shot out and the electronics bunker was going blind. Hermit was too far, the town was a maze of smashed or burning buildings. A blistered half-track appeared, wrecked by a shell, abandoned in a crater; he climbed the cab and stood as tall as he could, stared in all directions, saw only ruins and mud flats, movement in the smoke: men running, a few vehicles racing past. Where is everybody?

He knew the enemy was closer; the Red infantry had used the barrage as cover to leapfrog closer, close the ring—by now they must be attacking the inner defenses in dozens of places. But where were the battles? The wind had stopped; the sky hung still like a sheet of glass; no helicopters, no Vipers from Steelton, no Buzzards filled with Hardcore paratroops either. Gunfire and mortar or grenade explosions here and there in the distance, but not much, not enough—too much silence, quiet.

Take part. Take control.

He began running toward the nearest battle noise: mortar fire, eastward, High School Hill.

He saw where at least some of the assault choppers were: blasted on the ground. Their buried fuel tanks had been hit too; no one was fighting the fire. He passed on, crossed what had been Union Street, caught a glimpse of something big moving, and dove behind a toppled wall, peering out. Two tanks rumbled into view, two of the U.S. Army's wonderful new supertanks. Sixty-ton XM5 Creightons with eighteen-hundred HP jet engines, the most powerful and lethal tanks ever made. All nine had been sent south at dawn to meet the Red attack force coming up the river valley. These two seemed undamaged. They halted in the mud a hundred yards away, cut power, popped their hatches; they seemed to sag, dead, cannons drooping. Men in leather, the crews, climbed out and jumped to the ground, walked quickly away. Shaman sprang to his feet dismayed and ran to catch them. "Wait! Wait!" But they were already gone, vanished in the smoke.

We need those tanks!

Laser-sighted 105 millimeter cannons, rockets, twin fifties.

We could use those guns to stop—

We have to hold out, because—because . . .

He ran after the vanished tankers and bumped into a man, a curiously vague, shambling figure, like a wraith.

It said: "Oh-oh, hey, man, easy, daddy."

Shaman stopped, in shock. The figure was gone, but there were more men moving past him. They seemed to be stragglers, drifting, dozens of soldiers without helmets or weapons. He thought at first they might be walking wounded, but there was no blood and they were giggling and bopping. They were all around him. All were high.

Little round eye pupils gazed at him. He gazed back blankly. They passed and went on. Last came a man in a helmet, with a carbine on his shoulder, a sergeant wearing the brassard of the battle police.

Shaman raged at him: "You're supposed to make them fight!"

The sergeant stopped and stood silent.

Shaman roared: "Shoot them down if they retreat!"

The sergeant had hollow eye holes, like a horse's skull. "What the fuck? Back to barracks. The Reds took all our positions. We had to pull out."

"On whose orders?"

"There's nobody left."

"Drive them back! We have to hold out! Because—because . . . Drive them back!"

"What for? So more men can be killed? Ours and theirs? Guys like us? On both sides?"

"Yes!" Shaman said. He jerked the revolver from his hip, jammed it in the sergeant's stomach, and pulled the trigger. The hammer fell.

The hammer rose and fell five more times.

The sergeant's hollow eyes looked at him. "You can't kill everybody."

He wasn't there. Where he had been was a distant scene of the high school burning against the glassy sky. Shaman sat down suddenly on the ground.

"That wasn't real."

Revolvers don't misfire. Cartridges can fail, but not all six, not all at once, not ever, not possible.

What is it?

I don't know what it is.

He sat staring at the revolver dangling in his right hand. Blue is supposed to lose, yes, but it's supposed to fight first. It's supposed to hold out till Hardcore and Gralloch arrive. Blue has to hold out because—because that's the plan! That was always the plan, all there to read, ever since the beginning. Advantage here, advantage there, turnabout, balanced, forever, Blue versus Red in merciless and endless war!

To the last man.

But something happened to the plan. Face it.

Face what?

Noise still came from the river, from the north, from the south valley, but not much of it, not enough. He rose and stood looking at the fire on High School Hill—if the Reds were up there, they were lying low, not doing anything, not even firing into the Enclave. He began to walk. He crossed more mud flats, climbed more rubble, and the ground began to slope up beneath his feet. Halfway up the hill was the shattered luncheonette, and to the right of that was the lumberyard, and farther across the slope was a field of weeds, tin cans, garbage bags, rotten crates.

He took cover behind a large, old, rusty boiler tank. Panorama. Vantage point. From here he could look up and see the high school or down and see the smashed town and the river valley and the hills all around.

Fighting was still going on here and there on the perimeter, though on a small scale. Thousands of Reds out there somewhere, but not a one of them visible. The smoke was thin against the hard sky, and he could see movement inside the Enclave.

The movement was insectlike, antlike, beetlelike, a sort of slow scurry. All over the mud flats small figures were moving apparently at random, in no particular direction, with no sense of place or purpose.

In the town itself Vols were rising up out of the ground, gathering in little groups that joined other groups, which then broke apart, forming and reforming. Farther out, on the perimeter, was the same aimless stir, as men appeared, wandering from one place to another, as if questing, trying to capture signals from the air with waving antennae. Some desultory small-arms fire sounded— little last-ditch battles—across the river and in the hills to the north.

The general aim began to be discernible; the center of the

town was destination. More and more men, singly, by squads, by platoons and companies, were facing inward, gathering toward the intersection of Bridge and Main streets. From a point somewhere near the battered ruin of the First People's National Bank of Bugleburgh, a flare went up.

Shaman watched in bewildered fury. What was that for?

What the hell is going on now?

He found out what the hell was going on now.

A sound began nowhere and spread everywhere, faint and remote, then louder and closer. From one end to another of the Enclave Vols were beginning to talk, laugh, shout—and cheer. The cheering grew louder; it became a roar; it echoed back from the bowl of hills.

The surviving PA speakers on poles were squawking.

Single men were forming into squads, squads ino platoons, platoons into companies. All across the Enclave the defenders were shuffling into ranks and columns and files.

The hospital orderlies were handing out white sheets to all comers—to spread out on the ground.

The platoons and companies were displaying white flags—undershirts, handkerchiefs, miscellaneous scraps of rags.

Within minutes—like a magic trick—almost half the soldiers in the camp had discarded their helmets and put on red Day-Glo hats.

So that's it.

This time when the thing in the sky struck at him he saw it for what it was: a yellow fork of lightning out of a night of black thunder. And that couldn't be. The morning was clear as glass. *Who made that happen?*

But it brought the answer.

Now he knew what was going on—from the first unbelievable shelling and the surprise and the fear, to his hurt arm and the failed cartridges and the white flags and the red hats and the spoiled plan.

Now he knew it all.

He screamed harshly:

"*Kudelak!*"

He staggered in a little circle, screaming at the green steep hills all around:

"*I know you're out there!*"

CHAPTER EIGHT

Solus Ipse

Barraka

Gunfire still sounded from the cemetery where Kyte's battalion
was dug in; small battles were still going on in the hills to the
north and on the west shore of the river. But the town was
quiet. White flags hung drooping from utility poles and wires,
from tent peaks and the masts of radio-equipped vehicles—the
two XM5 tanks now flew emblems of surrender. Limp, motionless
rags in the still air. Nothing moved.

Timestop. He could see men and trucks and towers of smoke,
but nothing seemed to move. Or it was his own furious urgency
making everything slow down, halt, freeze. When he ran, it was
as though on a treadmill, through a shambles where flames stirred
as slowly as flower petals unfolding. When he stopped dead and
watched, he saw the figures of men changing positions as imper-
ceptibly as clockhands move. A burning wall tilted and toppled
in slow motion. An ambulance went by like a glacier. Watching,
even standing still, his eyesight joggled and jolted as though he
were running energetically in place.

Shock. It'll pass.

A figure rose up out of nowhere and droned at him, staying him with a raised hand: Danger.

"Can't. Go. Through."

It was an engineer captain. Shaman stopped.

He saw the wires and the plunger and the bent-over Vol sagging as slow as syrup over the handle. The wires led to Divisional Artillery's main ammunition supply point, an underground hall. Sparks jumped. He heard the subterranean thump and earsplitting crack.

Immediately time leaped into forward speed, as half an acre of mud quaked and bulged and split, vomiting fire. The engineer captain's nose was bleeding; he was yelling cheerfully: "There's *one* batch they'll never use against us!"

Clods and fragments whizzed; smoke boiled up; men scampered in all directions like mice. A tracked personnel carrier raced past, spurting dirt, men leaning out, hammering its side: *Faster!* Spun and dizzied, Shaman laughed out loud.

"I'll get it right yet."

Now he seemed hurried on across town by violent activity going on all around him. From behind came a yelling, gesticulating mob of men with hammers and wrecking bars—he sprang out of their way—they went on, halting at abandoned vehicles wherever they found them, smashing blocks, destroying carburators. A platoon of Vols under a major was collecting infantry weapons, assault rifles, and submachine guns, throwing away the bolts, bending the barrels. He saw company NCO's smashing radios, clerks burning maps and papers. Short, sharp explosions came from command posts and commo bunkers.

There was no sign yet, but the air prickled with a kind of panicky tension; everyone knew—the enemy was coming. He was almost there. It was like a countdown, seconds ticking away.

Shaman labored on, rushing without progress, trampling heavily in soft mud, among changing scenes. Near the demolished airstrip he saw men ripping wiring out of helicopters, pounding radios and navigational equipment to junk. Farther on, motorpool personnel were burning oil in drums, dropping engine parts into the crimson flames. The main gasoline dump was already ablaze, had been burning for the past half hour. Everywhere work parties were destroying electric generators. Artillery officers were crippling their guns.

Doubletoe stood hands on hips, presiding over the inciner-ation of Bugleburgh House. The hotel was a vast heap, like a trash fire, snapping and crackling. Men moving in files like bucket brigades were pouring baskets and baskets of papers onto the flames—codes, manuals, reports, evaluations, printouts, records. Intelligence HQ, down underneath, had been stripped of docu-ments, collapsed by a satchel charge.

Doubletoe looked at Shaman without recognizing him for a moment; then he said: "If you're reporting for duty, it's a little late."

He spoke in a voice clogged with resentment and disappoint-ment.

"It's a little late for everything, but then, you were on duty all the time, weren't you? You were on duty, all right. But not on our side. Kaul sent a message. He sent a message back to the kid that sent him a message. What are you going to do?"

"Do . . ."

Shaman sat down on the ground, cradling his left hand. Doubletoe sat down too, then got up on his knees quickly and sagged gently back, heels to buttocks. He watched the burning.

"Surrender . . ."

Voice thick with tears.

Shaman said: "Too soon—too fast." He explained it briefly as he could, hurrying and slurring; Doubletoe seemed to take forever to understand. The enemy was coming. "Blue was sup-posed to hold out until the entire Red force was concentrated around Bugleburgh. Hardcore, Gralloch—they were supposed to reinforce, to encircle—*then* there would be a battle. *Then* I was supposed to act—to offset Blue's power, help Red—make it an even fight."

Doubletoe gulped and quavered. He said:

"So it would go on forever. So nobody would win and the fight would go on forever. And the war."

Shaman looked at the sky. His head floated. "There's only one winning side."

"Yes, death. Kaul told us. That's what side. The side where

nobody can win, everybody loses. The side that takes even defeat and victory out of war. Till nothing is left but the killing."

Shaman looked high up. Lightning and thunder out of the clear, hard sky.

Kudelak's voice spoke. *The projection of a mind suicidal with hatred of itself and of life itself.*

"Something happened."

Doubletoe was staring emptily at him. He said:

"Are you going to kill me too?"

Shaman shook his head. "What's the point? It was in the plan. No point now—I might as well have left Kyte. Something happened."

He was struggling to his feet, using his right arm. Doubletoe looked up at him, like a child.

"Stavros happened," he said resentfully. "Stavros is what happened, and Kyte wouldn't have made any difference. Nothing would have made any difference because Stavros knew he was going to surrender. He already knew he was going to surrender before he ever sent the code word—before the Reds even attacked. He surrendered at dawn, but it takes time to get the order out. There are still line companies that didn't get the order yet. They're still killing each other out there. The Reds will come in shooting if they don't cut it out."

Shaman stood shakily, staring away downtown. He muttered: "Stavros—"

"They're all over in Hermit, waiting. Waiting until it's safe to come out. The Reds are coming in with General Markhausen, General Curcio, General Soga, and a bunch of high muckymucks from Red Central Committee. They're coming in to take the official surrender, but they're waiting until it's safe too."

Shaman lifted his injured arm and looked for his watch; it was gone. He felt confused. He said:

"It won't be safe for long, will it? Flight Hardcore and Task Force Gralloch are still on their way, aren't they?"

Doubletoe jumped up and waved his arms all around. "How the hell would I know? I'm only a poor, ignorant intelligence officer."

Then he backed away suddenly, as though alarmed. "But I know one thing—"

A thought struck him, and he patted himself all over, belt and breasts and pockets, searching himself for a weapon, finding none. Nevertheless, he stood his ground, facing Shaman valiantly.

"Kaul was right. What he said about you. Not about you being a Red infiltrator. The rest he told us—what you really are. Oh, I know what's behind that cold white calm of yours. You're mad!"

Shaman was inspecting his revolver. "Mad at what?"

"No, I mean *mad* mad," Doubletoe said. He sprang from frightened alertness into full motion, flight, like a child who had stood the dare, touched the hornet's nest once with his bare hand. Shaman watched him run away, capering painfully through the wreckage, yelling excitedly:

"Arrest that man! Arrest that man!"

Shaman sat down again. His feeling of haste was gone. Plenty of time. Hardcore and Gralloch would arrive on schedule but were not here yet, as was only to be expected because the surrender had come too soon, too fast. Stavros with his staff, Markhausen with his staff, were ready to meet and perform the official cere- monies on what was left of the parade ground, but not till the last fighting was over and it was safe to come out.

"Mad, am I?"

Kudelak's voice said drunkenly:

There is still my fourth possibility.

"I can't talk about that."

Back to business.

The revolver was clean and undamaged; he examined the misfired cartridges; all had deep indentations in their primers, sign of a perfectly functioning trigger mechanism and firing pin; the cylinder turned easily, the hammer rose and fell, clicking. Why, then?

Kudelak. That proves nothing.

He did some work in the haversack, awkwardly, sparing his left hand—it was considerably swollen. Then he got a fresh cartridge from the pouch on his belt and used his teeth to wiggle the lead slug out; it took time, and hurt him. The case seemed to contain the full charge of powder, the primer looked perfect. Instead of replacing the slug, he pinched off a bit of the plastic

explosive and puttied the casemouth shut. It made a cartridge
that was like a cross between a blank and an explosive bullet—
more than likely it would blow the revolver up, peel the barrel
back like a banana skin. He loaded it into the cylinder.

He put the gun into the haversack with the explosive, hung
the haversack around his neck, on his chest, under the zipped-
up flak vest. It bulged noticeably.

He preserved his cold white calm.

"Surrender—" he said.

"The major battle will go on as planned," Adjutant Frank
said.

"Defeat."

"Would you mind voicing your objection to *General* Stavros's
command decision into the voice-stress analyzer—*Colonel?* I believe you are hysterical. Perhaps it will be taken into account."

He was still feeding papers into a shredder. Noncoms were
hammering decoders with rifle butts. Officers were sending last-
minute messages to CIC. Operators were bellowing into radios,
trying to get the order out to last-ditch units on the perimeter:

"*Cease fire! Cease fire!*"

The victors were coming in.

Stavros was across the room, surrounded by staff officers,
talking to the correspondents. He was grinning the loose, easy
grin of a happy dog. "I've just received word that the first enemy
are approaching our MLR to the north, they are observing our
white flags, our troops have received their orders, there is a slight
communications problem about certain pockets of resistance, we
will quickly have that cleared up."

Shaman said: "What do you mean, the major battle?"

Frank said: "Whether we surrender or not, Hardcore and
Gralloch will arrive shortly and catch the enemy in our trap, as
originally planned."

"You just lost the major battle."

"Wrong. Quite wrong. General Cob at CIC was kind
enough to order a computer model of the total battle punched
up, at U.S. General Staff Computer Center. Full details of both
the enemy battle array and our own—including Hardcore and
Gralloch—were input and the prediction is indisputable. Whether

Bugleburgh resists or not, the outcome is the same. The same pitched battle between our paratroops and task force, and the hordes of the enemy. We are out of it. In fact, we were hardly ever in it, except as bait. Actually, the occupation of Bugleburgh has come to be considered an impractical proposition. A tactical and political blunder from the first."

"Considered by whom?"

"By those in command—*Colonel*."

"Do you know what you've done?"

"What we have done is save the lives of hundreds, perhaps thousands of men, the whole Bugleburgh force. Instead of being dead to the last man, we will be prisoners when help arrives. It may even be possible, as liberated prisoners, to join in the major battle."

"You've just lost the major battle," Shaman said again. "Bugleburgh was the major battle. Don't you see it? The Reds know your counter-offensive is coming. They don't mind being chased away into the hills again. They've made their point. Don't you see what a victory you've given them? They took Bugleburgh from the United States Army, that's all that matters. The turning point. They've won. And they'll win again. Not every time— but again. And then again. And again. You've lost the war."

"Ridiculous."

But Shaman was thinking.

"Unless something happens to them too. To offset their victory. Help Blue. Make it an even—"

"That could go on forever," Frank said.

"Till nothing is left but the killing."

Across the room General Stavros was speaking to the correspondents. Flashbulbs popped. "I've just been told that all our men have got the cease fire order by now, and the shooting's finished, and we're on open line to enemy field headquarters, and their party is on its way in, so I guess pretty soon we'll be getting this here show on the road."

He came lightly across the floor, bull-barreled and bandy-legged.

"How's it going, Frank?"

"Pretty good, Dom."

Stavros's eyes drifted.

"Well, I guess it's all over but the shouting."

Shaman said: "I can't believe Cob, CIC, or the General Staff know anything about this."

Stavros said saucily: "So, maybe they'll stop giving me combat commands."

"It's too late now anyway," Frank said, "and the General Staff has other fish to fry lately. Have you heard about the U.S. Armament and Military Preparedness Command at Fort Franklin, down the river? It's a SCAMP facility, with modern, automated, modular ammunition production lines, which turns out a thousand components per minute, six million bullets every month."

"That's marvelous!" Stavros said.

"The Reds blew it up," Frank said. "Day before yesterday, and over by Hazleton they ambushed a truck convoy and captured dozens of trucks, and their urban guerrilla units in Philadelphia, Pittsburgh, and Harrisburg are raising hob. And that's only in our sector. Not to mention the rest of the East. Let alone the rest of the nation. Cob had a hard enough time getting the General Staff to let him scrape together Task Force Gralloch."

"That's marvelous," Stavros said. He wasn't listening, trying to place Shaman. Then he did. "Oh, hello, there. Hey, I wasn't expecting to see *you* again. Are you waiting for the enemy delegation?" He turned to Frank. "What are you talking to *him* for?"

"Why not, Dom?"

"Didn't you see Doubletoe?"

"Not today."

"He got a PCM from NatPol, this man's a Red. Oh well, I guess it doesn't matter much now."

"*Like hell!*" Frank roared. He went for his pistol. A peevish-looking little twenty-five automatic.

Shaman couldn't take a chance. Even such a small bullet might penetrate his flak vest at so short range—worse, it might strike the haversack on his chest. He punched the forked fingers of his right hand into Adjutant Frank's eyes. Then he ran.

Looking back from the nearest exit he saw Frank with his hands to his face, explaining to an MP major, and Stavros spreading his arms out wide, palms up, then letting them slap resignedly to

his sides. Both men were wearing full-dress Class A uniforms
for the official ceremony.

"Crush his skull! Kill him dead!"

The major ran past, yelling orders; he and his men were
wearing Class A's too, and had white hats and white belts and
MP armbands, but carried no sidearms.

They turned them in!

Shaman hid, watching them run by; all they had was white
billy clubs on thongs, and at least one young man skipped past,
absorbedly singing to himself:

"Dooby-dooby."

However, even without guns, and some of them high, there
were a lot of them, and they were spreading the alarm as they
went. The center of town was becoming crowded with Vols
gathering gradually in from everywhere, collecting in little groups,
wandering slowly toward the parade ground. The major ran yelling
among them; most looked bored or stolid, but perked up on
joining the search.

"Red traitor! Red traitor!"

Shaman fled, crouching through an incredible clutter that
could only have been the remains of Woolworth's. Roof gone,
walls down, merchandise heaped and scattered and burned and
blasted—dishpans, pot holders, TV trays, can openers, doilies, doll
babies. Knee deep in an indescribable profusion of cheap junk,
he stopped and stood smiling.

The perfect war memorial.

"Here! Here!"

A voice cried out above him. Fifteen yards away on a
sawtoothed peak of broken wall a man stood, pointing at him,
screeching a warning like a hawk in a treetop:

"Here!"

Shaman ran the other way, kicking through plastic knick-
knacks. A wide sliding door fallen flat led him like a ramp to a
loading dock and out into what had been the alley behind the
store, now a tangle of fallen telephone poles and wires and
crumbled stone and wooden walls. Half-buried garbage cans
swarmed with rats. Along the way he heard a voice—in a ragged,
windowlike hole were the upside-down head and one arm and

shoulder of a man, pouring red like a butchered animal. Rats splashed in the puddle. The voice whispered: "Oh, my God, I am heartily sorry . . ."

At the end of the alley was a scattered heap of sandbags and a dugout with some boards across one end. He crawled under to hide for a moment and catch his breath—too much running, lungs aching, vision foggy—and sleep hit him like ether. He did not even know it. A warm gold glow changed suddenly to shock. Rapid footsteps overhead. Some thundered on the boards. It could only have been for a second or two.

Maybe a nice dream—

"Fool!"

Control!

When they were gone, he crept out, hurried on. Shouting around him; he thought he heard the major's voice, and hurried through a free-standing door, found himself in a roofless dead end. Two men sat by a small fire, Vol infantrymen, unarmed, both bandaged, one wearing a red Day-Glo hat. They were heating canned soup.

"Fuck 'em. I'm joining the Reds. Why the fuck not?"

Shaman took one long step and stood over them. They looked up with pink terrified eyes. Shaman said:

"Give me that hat with no argument and live to tell about it."

The one with the Day-Glo hat couldn't move; the other snatched it off his head and held it up in two shaking hands like an offering. Shaman put it on his head.

"Invisibility."

He turned away. Pink, terrified rabbit eyes watched him go.

Back the way he had come were two MP's and a dozen men, searching the rubble; they came toward him; he jerked his thumb, indicating the doorway. "Not in there. Couple of men cooking soup."

One MP said: "Yes, sir." The other said: "I didn't get no breakfast!" The men muttered: "*Nobody* got no breakfast today."

"Follow me." Shaman led the group past the scattered sandbags and into the street. Opposite the alley, more crumbled walls and broken doorways, MP's searching for the Red traitor. But by this time the street was full of Vols heading toward the parade ground. Some slunk, some sulked, some strode defiantly; a platoon marched by in good order under a sergeant; three officers stepped proudly along as though waiting to be jeered; a group of gigglers staggered down the middle of the street, shirts off, red Merthiolate letters daubed on their chests: POW.

Shaman walked toward the parade ground; his group followed; an unarmed, bandaged, pink-eyed figure came last.

The parade ground had been surrounded by the buildings of downtown Bugleburgh; most had now been burned or shelled flat, giving the field a vast appearance. The rubble and craters made it seem like a battlefield, though no battle had occurred there. The hundreds of disarmed men milling and muttering in place with nothing to do—more arriving each moment—looked like refugees, survivors, but something else too.

"Amnesiacs."

It was a prisoner camp already.

Far across the field a flagpole still stood, white flag flying. Some activity there, too far to see. Shaman halted in the middle of a crowd of miscellaneous troops, noncoms, and line-company officers. White MP hats were visible moving near him, but he was not worried. It wasn't going to happen that way.

A voice behind him whined: "He stole my fucking hat."

Shaman spun and saw the pink-eyed man and the MP major.

The major blew long shrieking blasts on a white whistle.

All around Shaman the crowd tightened like a fist.

MP's with white billy clubs worked their way through, coming to the force, surrounding him. Red traitor. The major shrieked like his whistle:

"*I want to see his brains on the ground!*"

"Hey, hey," a voice admonished. "Better not."

Little jolts like shocks of electricity ran through the crowd— a quiet came. Everybody was turning to see. The billy clubs sank down. Shaman lowered his good arm, raised defensively. At first he could see nothing over the heads except the distant pole. The white flag was gone. Another was being raised.

The green field symbolized the birth of the new freedom in forests and mountains; the red fist signified proletarian solidarity and blood sacrifice.

The crowd opened up, spread away a little distance. The

major and his MP's stood fast, looking uneasy. A skirmish for-
mation of heavily armed men was approaching. Most wore PFA
uniforms, but a few were dressed in denim and chambray or
hunting vests with shotgun-shell loops or the camouflage coats of
duck hunters. All had ragged beards and looked filthy and tired.
The point man reached Shaman; he wore a hunting knife and
smelled of wood smoke. In the center of the diamond with the
radioman was a young PFA officer.

Captain Posey Wells said: "Good morning, Colonel, sir. By
golly, I *knew* you'd make it!"

Weakness. Pain.
Hold out.
Posey Wells led him along.
"You did it! Operation Kalitan worked!"
"Not over yet."
"We *won!*"
Wells led him over what seemed rough ground but was not.
Flagpole.
"Why don't you unzip that vest halfway and put your arm
inside, like a sling?" Posey Wells said.
Shaman unzipped the vest halfway and put his arm inside
like a sling; it helped with the throbbing. It also made the bulge
less noticeable.
"Why didn't I think of that?"
Control.
At the base of the flagpole were vehicles; a small tent was
going up; a guard of PFA soldiers with assault rifles stood glaring
in all directions.
General Soga and a dozen field-grade officers were having a
conference; the officers were from NETC and various other East
Coast commands. One was saying:
"A blow from which the United States forces will never
recover. A loss of the last vestiges of public support, a loss of
manpower to our gain. But even more important, a loss of supplies,
weaponry, and matériel which a bankrupt capitalism will never
again have the tax revenues and other ill-gotten loot to replace.
We are on the road to final triumph!"

Captain Wells conferred deferentially with General Soga, chuckling in his ear.

General Soga raised a finger.

"Excuse, please," he said, "momentary but worthwhile digression. Contributory factor, at least, to successful realization of battle aims here this morning widely considered to be complex and curious scheme known as Operation Kalitan, of which you have heard."

"No, what's that?" a brigadier said.

General Soga turned to face Shaman. He drew himself to a pidgy, pudgy posture of attention. He executed a slow, stately salute.

"Architect of victory. We thank you."

Then he spoke to Wells. Wells led Shaman away, saying gaily:

"That's only the beginning! I'll get you medical attention and some clean clothes and chow and booze—but first there is somebody you have *got* to *see!*"

He led the way toward one of the vehicles, a type of van, guarded by dozens of soldiers and officers. Around to the rear stood a cluster of men, some in PFA uniform, some in civilian clothes with neckties. It was the official Red delegation, come to formally accept the official Blue surrender by Stavros and his staff. Among them:

Kudelak.

Time stopped again.

They looked into each other's faces.

Which of us is dreaming who?

There is no past, no future, only the eternal present eternally, instantaneously invented.

I can change it all!

Only the two of them moved among the frozen shapes. Kudelak approaching rapidly with welcoming arms out: "Here is the man!" Shaman removing his hurt hand from the vest and returning the embrace.

Chin over Shaman's shoulder and face exultantly to the sky, Kudelak cried in his joy:

"I win! I made it happen! My dream! Man's future! Millennium!"

Holding the embrace as best he could, Shaman put his right hand inside the flak vest, into the haversack.

"It hasn't been proved yet."

The bullet split the revolver barrel like a banana skin, and the three kilos of plastic explosive flashed.

The destruction spread outward from the two dismembered bodies: to the van, knocking it over on its side and setting off its gasoline tank; to the waiting officers—Markhausen and two more generals were killed instantly, six were wounded; to the guards—several were hurt, all were thrown flat by the concussion; to the tent, no sooner raised than knocked down, smoking; even to the flagpole some yards away—it cracked in the shock wave and toppled to the ground, flapping the newly flown flag.

There was no chance to examine the bodies. One of the other vehicles, a communications van, was disgorging numbers of waving and shouting men, and a siren on its roof was wailing.

A shadow passed over the ground.

General Curcio took command.

"Plan *Leaf*! Plan *Leaf*! Plan *Leaf*!"

Vipers from Steelton were overhead—they screamed and dived and strafed and bombed.

Four hundred yards in the air over the south valley droned half a dozen Buzzards, hatches gaping, paratroopers tumbling out.

Flight Hardcore had arrived.

The communications officer hurried up with a message: The spearhead of Task Force Gralloch was in sight five miles down the river.

As the first shells from Gralloch's mobile long-range artillery began thumping into the Enclave, Plan Leaf went into effect.

The main PFA force was waiting in the hills, having had no part to play in the official ceremony. It began withdrawing in various directions, following prearranged routes, breaking away in platoon- and company-sized units as it moved. The units became smaller and smaller, beginning to disappear, like leaves in the forest.

General Curcio led the relatively small number of PFA personnel who had come into the Enclave out of the Enclave. A tunnel in the quarry led them outside the perimeter to a system

of trenches; the trenches led them to the nearest wooded hill;
the hill was full of little hidden paths that wandered away to the
north.

Four hours later Task Force Gralloch entered the Enclave,
found it empty of enemy, and occupied it.

Two days later the first PFA attacks came from the hills to
the north: sneak raids and harassing fire.

Meantime in Philadelphia, Pittsburgh, and Harrisburg—not
to mention in the rest of the East, let alone in the rest of the
nation—guerrilla units were raising hob.

The war went on.

Atman

Shell!
    Tongue-puff interdom gun-puff pause: wooowowowhooo-
hooom, chant, chant, chant, rattle-clatter spaced chatter glass
casquette curve in on nip an out, teee down and dowahoom;
press moss to your nose bleed ant sharp shuck risking life and
limb: OOOUM!
    Pit pat patter tatter clod a clump clump clit clit-patter, pat
pit. Close. Shell! Foot foot foot. Next one I will not see, I
will not see. Get up, rise. I have risen. I remember. Who not
survive remember nothing. He sought cover. Ha ha ha ha ho
ho ho. Where soft moss banks slip down to rust-flecked mud.
Where was I gone? Parasitic vines crept up the tree, throttling
the trunk in masses of metal shivering green. Look out there in
the wide open plains. A burning thing. A spout of milk. They
will not see me if I hide. There they all are marching on metal
legs. No, no, over there is the landship big as a house, all afire.
Storm winds blow in the heavens.
    Twigs cracked with iron cold. Dancy needles of snow were
falling. They would not cover the ground. I thought I was alone.
I am supposed to tell these men something. What to do. Where.

He saw a hieroglyph of soldiers dancing on the wild air above a spewing, glaring crater, their guns-belts-hats-bags-sleeves-arms-feet-tripes flickering in the sky and falling back. Hallucination: in black and white the earth and these men, the sounds and my weight on the moss, in a roaring red spiral; black and white. The gongs. From their split skull cases splattered thick cream of cells, syrup, and paste of brains, dottering on his face and shoulders. Carefully he inched his weapon forward. The muzzle leaped alive and seared a hollow spot. Rarakickitat, tossing him over his heels.

They rose and ran for the shack. Someone was behind him. His feet sank in the muck of the fields—murderers' dead hands clutched from the frozen rows and gripped his boots—he fell and sprawled, and struggled up slithering. Eleven dogs, tin-can-tailed dogs, howled at his back. The rattle of forks and spoons and scabbards and bones rattled at his back. Widening his eyes and opening his arms, he fled toward the house.

Strangling, the soldiers fell down within the enclosure. They were on an island of fences of bamboo and burned grass in the middle of a sea of fields and winding paths. They were in a tumbled wooden hut with gaping walls. Rats ran away. A man lay doubled on the ground, back broken, legs smoking in a pit of coals. From the corners the rats peered back, with red eyes. Little tufts of rice-straw roof slipped into the room. In a pit dug in the earth floor sat tall urns of liquid, on skewers over the fire spun fine-haired hands.

The soldiers crouched with their weapons at the rough holes in the walls. In the distance the peaks loomed red and white, putty and crystal, in the last of the light. On the broad, dark plateau were smoke and fire, landships, mounds of sparks and brief flowering white conflagrations. The men crouched at the holes, red nervous tissue frozen in serum. Rest here. They shed their packs.

Like giant pile drivers, explosions drummed in the distance. Beyond the plain the last sun glared on high peaks and white frozen palisades. With pinched lips and stiffened skin the men gathered around the pit, clearing away the filth, piling lengths of bamboo on the smoking coals. Some drank water from furry green bladders. Far off he heard the noise of firing, he felt the black oh-screaming muzzles aim in his direction. As he listened, the gongs began to sound again, brass spirals radiating from a cave in his breast. He saw figures in the waist-high rows of stubble.

Roll out watch out the windows one hundred yards get them away go away rang rang rang! Muttering: There they go retreating back now claw them down their backs eat kill them the last of them. I can't I can't I can't. He knelt by a hole in the wall in shivers of straw and splinters and flying clods of dirt, automatic pistol jolting in his hands. Cursing them the enemy that in their caves and dungeons, heating metal instruments in the fires, they deftly inserted electrodes in his ears, the fine needlepoint wires curved and met, dug in his nerves, delicate sparks snapped in his vertebrae, thin brittle bones popped and split. He worried the fine wires in his ears with bony shoulders, wincing. He began to howl and plunge down a shaft, by bleeding soldiers hanging in chains.

A canteen cup clattered against his teeth, the sharp sour wine hurt his mouth. The men were drinking from two stone jugs. They were methodically demolishing the hut, refuge. All the straw and bamboo had been burned. They were tearing down the roof poles to burn in their fire. Through the roof he saw patches of stars and thin blowing clouds. When they jerked at the roof poles, crystals of rime drifted down and blew into the fire. Good-bye, he said to the crystals, which were vapor before they reached the flames. A wind was blowing, it whistled. The night air was made sharper by the ammoniac odor of the fields. I need to pay attention, to see things clearly, he thought.

Someone fitted a mask to his eyes—he wrenched it off and saw flights of meteors streaking up, and green and red and unnameable colors of the borealis, spires and crags of color frozen into the sky, the palisades like stairs. Would have to climb. If he need not climb them, it was not so cold. He felt the ice melt and drip in his bones. The lights flared once and faded, and he slept and dreamed of warm rain and yellow water roiling and children wading to their knees, and of the rain he thought: In it grow melons and cucumbers and rice. On the flooded fields children in black hats and yellow straw capes waded, picking fine fat gourds from the wet vines and calling to each other across the rows: Hi ho! But when he woke, it was a cold winter night rain becoming sleet, and there were ragged, unfamiliar figures moving around him in the darkness—headless behemoths, blazing gaudy masks, and sharp knives walking, and the skin drum outside banging. The plateau slanted up toward the palisades, and far away he saw flickering fires and heard gigantic bellows of sound that shook the earth. Someone looked into his open eyes.

A broken pole had been thrust down the pig's mouth through its body, out the bloody hole beneath its tail, its shrieks whistling in the mud-walled space and rising through the ruined roof. They hoisted the pig over the fire and roasted it, hunkering like jackals in a circle. With bayonets they impatiently hacked off slabs and layers of fat as it cooked, and when they cut too deeply into the blackened hide, seething raw blood ran on the coals. He watched the agony and death of the pig, then turned aside—and saw the nameless doubled dead man lying—and looked away, to the farthest corner of the room—and saw there the fine-haired skewered hands.

Betrayed! Betrayed! He leaped to his feet and seized his pistol and sprang betrayed to a gap in the wall to peer out—the soldiers laughing at him hoarsely, but pointing their weapons at his back, watchful in case he should turn to face them, become dangerous to them—but he was quiet, and gazed out at the shimmer of the fields in the starlight, stared across the plateau at the flickering lights, the solemn boom of guns, beneath the palisades.

How endlessly, how endlessly the naked plains stretched behind them to the sea—and now at last, the wall ahead, the fierce humped back of the continent, glacial in the northern lights. And it was there for them to climb, high off the face of the earth, into the absolute zero of the end.

Yesterday I stepped to my knees in water, knowing it was water, sure of water, its filth and animalcula, but seeing blood, splashing to my knees in this land's blood, in the rain walking, knowing it was only rain and staring with horror at shining crimson on my hands, the leaves and helmets and hills and skies pouring bright blood, which I knew was rain.

It's cold. There are people moving in the fields.

Corporal, who are the people moving in the fields? Far as the eye can see. Sergeant, who are those marching lights, far as the eye can see?

And he stepped through the wall, before the soldiers took

hold of him, before they could stop him, and they did not follow. And he ran and scrambled in the dim light of a flare that hung in the sky over the battleground, many miles away—then stood still and fired one long unaimed burst in a wide sweep at the black stubble.

"Show yourselves!"

I see you, dodging and whispering! Cradling his automatic pistol he staggered on, cold and fearful and suddenly panting. With shrapnel sounds a billion pods burst all around him, powdering the winter air with silvery, feathery seedlets that stuck in his brows and beard, clung to his lips and eyelids. Beyond the snow of pollen were human shapes, far as the eye could see: gray shapes from end to end of the plateau, hominidae, they swarmed in mock masks, with blind eyeholes, black, white, yellow foreheads, in smells of sweat and ginger and smoke and excrement, on a prairie of gesticulating sinuous arms, in a massy roar of sermons, orations, conversations, soliloquies, cries of pain, puzzlement, command, rapture; loud, unintelligible, hysterical, exultant, expostulatory. A man banged an iron-shod foot rhythmically, others followed; some blew horns, some whistled, some shrieked, all clapped hands rhythmically, shouting, whistling, shrieking, and a naked woman rose on her toes in a diva's posture, singing a high sharp note forever, the fog of her breath pouring on the cold air, the sound quivering in the flesh of her throat, holding-holding-holding a difficult note forever, neck, chest, and plexus muscles frozen. The air was awhirl with streaks of blood and tongues of live fire and the pollen and the pale snow. In the swarmed dark were vague, vast shark-shadows overhead. He closed his eyes. Behind closed lids a blazing, vivid light of magnesium flares exploded, blinding him to all sights, all images of memory and imagination, and somber gongs of veined brass in his breast deafened him to all sounds of past and present, and a padded wrapping enveloped his entire body, protecting him from the cold and the fire—until his complete isolation was accomplished and he stood in darkness hearing nothing, seeing nothing, sensing nothing—thinking about death in the cold in the ground.

But still thinking. Then he was running, plunging through potholes of filth, thinking: *It is not over yet, soon but not yet for a while*—and colliding with soldiers and limping beggars and

advocates and maharajahs like smoke. Out of the corner of his
eye he saw two men fighting, saw one thrust his jaws forward
and swallow the other's head—screamed, and fled again, his eyes
fixed on the ground, and crashed into a statue of someone: Eve
suckling an ape. From crevices in the soggy fields near the statue
rose an odor of the underground. He vaulted a low stone fence
and was surrounded. Crowds of amputees in white smocks and
dark goggles pressed close to him, jingling coins in cups and
threateningly offering him gray worn stream pebbles and souvenir
teeth—their hands ice cold and scratchy. *I have fallen down in
the burned stubble.* Bullets began to carom from the shoulders
and breast of the statue, spinning splinters of marble in all directions. Through the snowfall of seedlings he could see no
enemy. *I would kill anyone tangible enough. Or was the gun
gone? No. Wait.*

He felt in the mud by his boots for the shape of the automatic
pistol. It was there, fouled and slippery. Touching it, he felt
cold and alone. The lights beneath the palisades pulsed and
racketed and there were shouts all around him. In a puddle a
man lay prostrate, in danger of drowning. *Look, look—the mountains! Get up! We have crossed the desert, we have reached the
mountains. . . .* With his uninjured hand he caught the man's
coat and heaved, then slipped and fell back in the filth. From
the bridge of the nose to the larynx was an oval hole from which
stiff blood seeped. He felt ripped out of sleep into nightmare.
With a shrunken forefinger he absorbedly reamed a plug of mud
from the barrel of his pistol. The lubricant was congealing, the
mechanism moved reluctantly, spilling bright finger-length cartridges onto the thin skin of ice over the fields. He went forward,
crouched and silent in the monstrous noise. He began to pass
by the stumps of blasted trees. He passed the steaming ruin of
a tank. In one place the legs and hips of a man were standing
incredibly upright in the mud. Every so often he detoured around
a cadaver slowly sinking. Finally he came to a line of wire—it
was the point-of-departure for the new assault. Now he realized
that there were soldiers all around him, creeping and crawling.
One by one as they passed the barbed wire, they rose and walked
forward.

Unexplainably, in the windless night of soaked, freezing fields and distant noise, tidal clouds of dust rose and flapped like living black wings above. The starlight limned the far peaks and escarpments and shone on towering slopes of snow. He imagined blue light neither of the moon nor sun nor stars shining on the spires and crags that touched the sky, illuminating the bony walls of lost monasteries of Nestorian monks, discovering in a pale secret glow stone idols buried a million years in crevasses packed with clear glacial ice. The gongs clamored in him. He watched his feet and trudged upward. In stone keeps above were cups made of yellow ancient skulls, brimming with barley liquors; tallow candles burned; forgotten winds rammed against bronze doors. Within, the patient lamas waited through the centuries, silent, faceless, and wise; in stone vaults they stilled and froze to silver sculptures, secret, secret, where no one would ever come.

Up. Climb up.

In the roaring razor wind he crept higher and his flesh curled and shriveled and stiffened and the air was thin. For a time men climbed with him. He saw them and tried to warn them. He peered back, downward, to the beginning, where there were fire and smoke on the curve of the earth. The long climb behind them was littered with the bodies of the dead; the rest, in canvas hoods, stumbled upward with him, the sunless glare blinding them to him, to everything but the progress of their black, hobnailed boots on the ice and the vapor of their labored breathing. He had thought to warn them—now he saw that they could go no farther. As long as earth was round and circled the frigid sun, and the smoke on the horizon towered up from calculable depths of curvature, they might continue. But now the ramp had lifted up, leaned out from the curve of earth, planing away tangentially into infinity from the depths below in a sheet of polar frost.

He climbed alone, and it became unspeakably colder as the vast steely ramp climbed away from the world, ascending higher and ever higher and steeper toward the galactic end and out and out to the stiff absolute where the molecules gelled in their dance in gelid endless night. Intermittent streaks of meteors darting among the crags and peaks, and the glassy sheen of the ice caps, shone blindingly in his eyes, and seared his brain. He saw rapid flights of stars like driven sparks. The nails in his boots screamed on the ice. He crawled upward—with the motion of metal contracting with cold, he slid upward. In sawtoothed peaks ahead he heard the echo of trumpets and the ringing of gongs. He gripped the hard, frozen ledges like risers, felt his fingers snap like rods of glass. An ice-smooth-sharp gorge painted mural-like with glacial forms leaned over him, terrible in white silence. With glittering, ponderous, mile-long-wide slowness, sliding tons of hoarfrost, rime, snow, and storm groaned beneath the zodiacal and septentrional lights, in enormous incalefacient loom. Then, careening in one huge nightward plunge, sprawling over the lip of the precipice, darkening in the sourceless glare, crashed down.

Fallen now, his ashen face buried in the stiff snow, the luminous drifts, his legs trailing into the chasm, claw fingers of his uninjured hand dug in deep, the raw black stump of the other—now hard with frozen blood—jammed like a stake into the ice, he held himself hanging, and waited. Far below, the roar receded into silence, its echoes reverberating from crest to crest across the endless pinnacle distances of ribbed, rigid crystal and rock, and resounding in the packed storm-filled clouds racing white with speed above him. And the pale strange lights flared, illumining the desolate mile-high drifts, and black winds mourned; his flesh recoiled, flaked black, from bare white bones. Said the weather: *HeehihohohohahahaHIHIHIHEHEHEhihohooooo!*

Between blue-lit fissured blocks, profound wedges of ice expanded with earsplitting shrieks; coalesced gases of oxygen and ozone powdered the rocks; bottomless clefts cracked open hungrily under his feet; his gun barrel rang sharply on unscalable slopes, rang with a cry of metal from frozen cliffs. Stumbling on and bending protectively over the bitten hand, he peered with blanched eyes upward, measuring the distance—all the long canyons ascended blankly into nothingness and all the stairs and corridors led him irrevocably to its brink. He continued up, ascending toward the end. In a defile long ranks of giants horned and armed and awful stood beneath the stars in coruscant armor splattered with the blood of the birth of the world, unsheathed swords in their fists glinting with violet lights—and opposing them sat carven blocks of basalt, sober and brooding, with sunken eyes and massive brows, long cold cheeks encrusted with stone tears. Shimmering brass gongs clamored, the shawms of the wind sang, the gaze of the frozen faces followed him; silver and steel thin figures of the winter of the end leaned from their ramparts to watch, and mummies of monks in cold cells, cheeks cracked to the bone, watched, hands frozen in heaps of copper shavings, in the shivering light of gongs struck by the wind—watched as he climbed the defile to the cliff edge of emptiness, and fell down on the brink.

There formed on his shriveled tongue silver spangles of frost— he spoke not. Over his temples his hair stiffened and congealed; mercurial needles ran in his blood, fluids caked; his eyes froze; afferent fibers in his skin wrinkled and split; in the hollows of his skull clear liquids glazed and expanded, in paroxysms of pain. He struggled weakly. To the core, the coelom, the cold advanced— jagged fissures covered his vesicles; a bleeding rime encased his lungs; his stomach burst; skin of his chest cracked in red graphs, the red coagulated; his nostrils closed; thin secretions hardened to knots of pain in his groin and armpits. In sequence, with dry reports, ribs parted; fragile sheaths of myelin broke; his nerves died one by one; spine broke, corneas cracked, liver burst, heart withered, ice saltwater froze in his throat.

At last was the abyss, the endless absolute emptiness in infinite wheel, the void, on which was written in the macrographics of his disorder the conundrum syllables of his name.

Dakma

Professor Friedkin was a prisoner again. He was also in the disturbed ward again, but this time as an attendant; that was his official job, at any rate, since a prisoner of war couldn't be a member of the staff. Unofficially, as a qualified psychiatrist, he helped out. The regular doctors told him that this was the greatest, most advanced modern hospital in the world—it was, in fact, the size of a little city, with more buildings, more staff, more machines, more everything than any similar facility in history. Furthermore, they told him, this particular annex, a skyscraper in itself, was manned and equipped to handle every conceivable psychiatric problem. Then they asked if he'd mind helping out, because of his extensive experience with battle psychoses.

Friedkin didn't mind. But today's shift had been very long.

He had spent the whole of it with a catatonic who had been lying inert for the past two weeks and who had suddenly turned face down on his cot and clawed his way to the floor right through both mattress and spring. Now it was three o'clock in the morning and Friedkin was tired—when all at once he was wanted for something else.

"You're to come with me," the Nazi said.

He led the way down the bright, glossy halls between closed doors to the bank of elevators; they descended with sickening speed, went out the main entrance, and crossed the park, implausibly green under the arc lights. Friedkin caught only a glimpse of the dark sky and remote stars. They passed between tall walls of lighted windows to another open space, crossed it on a path between crisp wet lawns to the permanent-care building. Friedkin stopped for a moment to draw a long breath and locate the north star—Polaris—and the Nazi gave him a shove from behind. The Nazi was a powerful-looking young man with a snub-nosed pistol in a holster under his coat.

"Where are we going?" Friedkin said.

"Prisoner will speak when spoken to."

In the permanent-care building a guard at a desk checked them in and pointed wordlessly to a door; it concealed a closetlike secret elevator. They went up, bypassing floors two through eleven: wards and rooms and cells where untreatable cases lived and died. On the top floor they walked down a gloomy hall between small, cluttered offices with cheap desks, duplicating machines, and pasteboard file boxes. At the end, between the fire door and the water cooler, two more Nazis stood guarding a door marked: ELECTRICAL EQUIPMENT, KEEP OUT.

They went in. Kaul was sitting on a tool chest. The escort Nazi said: "This's him."

"Get out," Kaul said.

Kaul had a black briefcase on his lap. When the door had closed, he opened the briefcase and took out a sheaf of papers. "Sit."

The only seat available was a greasy-looking metal locker; Friedkin sat on it, but rucked up his white smock first. Kaul consulted his papers.

"Friedkin. Captured when we overran Northeast Tactical Headquarters two months ago. POW Camp Four. Reassigned to POW annex this hospital. Reassigned psychiatric annex, due to professional qualifications. Attendant. But acting as alienist. Got your own cases. Smart fellow. Better than running bedpans."

(*Nonths, TOW,* and *trofessional* were clear enough, but *dedtans* was incomprehensible.)

"That's a definite speech defect," Friedkin said.

"It is not a speech defect," Kaul said. "You know me?"

"Oh, yes, certainly. You were always a very prominent lesson at our Know Your Enemy lectures. We had to study your faces and biographies and modi operandi, so to speak. Aren't you quite powerful in the National Police now? Perhaps the director?"

"Who can send you back to the bedpans," Kaul said.

"I beg your pardon?"

"Make you an attendant again. Send you back to Camp Four."

"I see," Friedkin said. "What do you want?"

"Answer some questions."

He put his papers away. He slid his hand into a side opening of his briefcase. A strange expression seemed to expose a few more of his clenched teeth. It could hardly have been called a smile. But it suggested pleasure.

"You were not at Bugleburgh."

"No."

"But know what happened."

"I believe we won the day."

"Call that winning," Kaul said. "We killed Chairman Nicolai Kudelak, half your generals, took victory out of your mouths."

"If that's the way you see it, of course."

Kaul suddenly hissed like a snake: *"You know what really happened!"*

Friedkin was badly startled. "I don't—"

"You knew Shaman!"

"No, I don't think I—"

"He blew the both of them up!"

"Oh," Friedkin said.

"Hah!" Kaul said.

"Well, I thought you said Shannon," Friedkin said. "As a matter of fact, you *did* say Shannon. You mean Shaman. Sham'- man. Certainly I knew him."

"Treated him. He was a patient."

"No, not exactly. We had a few discussions, but I wouldn't call them treatments. Exploratory sessions, at most, and hardly that."

"Detail."

"I met him once in Northstate, where he was an inmate, it seemed at the time—although in the light of later events, apparently that was part of an escape plan. Then he was brought to me by General Soga after one of the earlier Bugleburgh battles. The general wanted a psychological profile done on him. Meanwhile I was to be bugged with microphones, so the general and Mr. Kudelak could listen to our sessions."

"I know all that."

"Then why—"

"What did you find *out?*"

"You know, it's a curious thing," Friedkin said musingly. "Somehow all through it all, I never felt we were really making progress. As though he weren't really there, if you see what I mean. It made me wonder. Was he talking to me?"

On anybody else's face, Kaul's expression would have suggested gloating.

"Which side was he on?"

"Oh, well, *that* has been established, at least. On neither side. Neither Red nor Blue, in the end. Or perhaps I should say from the beginning. Obviously he was playing us one against the other. Fixing the game from both ends, one might say. Tilting the odds in favor of the maximum death and destruction. A careful study of Operation Kalitan bears this out, in the light of events. We would have to assume that, consciously or unconsciously, he wished everyone to be dead. This was his monomania, if you will."

"Insane?"

"I don't know what *insane* means," Friedkin said. "We leave that to laymen."

"Don't get lofty," Kaul said. "He was a cold-blooded murderer."

Friedkin observed him curiously. Both dogteeth were clearly visible now. Not a grin, certainly—a grimace, rictus—but it suggested glee.

"That was a behavioral pattern. The question is why."

"Doesn't matter," Kaul said, and unexpectedly changed the subject. "Maybe I'll let you go."

"What?" Friedkin said. "Why would you do that?"

"Go back and tell them. What you're going to see."

Friedkin shrugged. He did not know what Kaul was driving at and did not take it seriously. For one thing, it wasn't all that earthshaking a possibility; prisoner exchanges occurred frequently. For another, his thoughts were elsewhere; he was interestedly reviewing his own mental case records.

"Shaman," he said. "My opportunity to study him in a professional way was strictly limited, as I explained, but I was not the only one on whom he made a striking impression, you know. Rather fascinating. He leaves behind an enigma."

"More like a trail of blood," Kaul said.

"Perhaps you remember a man he met in Northstate, a therapist by the name of Fosbert, who was also a psychologist."

"Killed him," Kaul said. "Shot him up the ass."

"Awful! But was it to preserve his secret, do you suppose? The intriguing thing was in some notes of Fosbert's—he believed Shaman was a judgment on us. Our own creation, evolved out of our history of violence and bloodletting into the form of a man—the man of our times, the final step in the long, slow suicide of the human race."

"He was crazy," Kaul said.

"Who?" Friedkin said, not listening. "There's more. I told you Mr. Kudelak listened to our sessions. He also had his own interview with Shaman; they were closeted together for hours at NETC, and General Soga was monitoring them. I heard those tapes too. Fascinating. Utterly fascinating."

"Get on," Kaul said. He was growing restless.

"Kudelak accused him of solipsism, and he fairly admitted it!"

"What's that?"

"Yes, well—" Friedkin stopped. He scratched his chin with one finger. "It's either a philosophical position or a psychosis."

"You're the expert."

"It isn't that simple. First you must understand what solipsism is."

"I know what solipsism is," Kaul said.

"Then why . . . ?"

"You tell me. For instance, what if it's a psychosis?"

"Then it wouldn't be all that uncommon. It's an extreme form of alienation, of course, gradually leading to a complete dissociation with reality and finally a total inability to function."

"For instance, what if it's a philosophical position?"

"That's not uncommon either; Kudelak covered that ground briefly. Kant and Fichte and so on—Bishop Berkeley, perhaps—Russell in modern times. Although it's an old enough idea. Democritus once said: 'Nothing exists except atoms and empty space; everything else is an opinion.' Presumably Shaman agreed with that."

"For instance, what if it's true?" Kaul said.

Friedkin laughed. "That's exactly what *he* said to Kudelak, as I recall. But that would be the absolute ultimate in meaninglessness, wouldn't it? If he were right?"

"What would?" Kaul said.

"I mean, I mean . . ." Friedkin chuckled, "if we and all had gone *pft* the moment he died?"

"Not dead," Kaul said.

Friedkin was tired; it had been a long shift, from six till three, and an edgy, uneasy time since, and now it was past five o'clock in the morning, and he didn't know what Kaul was driving at.

"I'm sorry, I don't get the point."

"What point?"

"What you said."

"What point? Fact. You said dead. I said not. Not dead."

It was a grin now. Pleased. Gloating. Gleeful.

Friedkin wobbled his head in wonder. "Not dead . . ."

"Come with me," Kaul said.

"Was wearing a flak vest. Protected his vitals. Explosive was plastic—no fragments, no shrapnel. Just blast," Kaul said, positively loquacious with satisfaction. "Couldn't hardly even find a chunk of Kudelak. Reds might have tried. Our paratroops ran them out too fast. Found what was left of Shaman in the vest. Thought he was dead. Surprise, surprise. Man of mine was present, called me. I was there in ten minutes, with the best medical team in the whole U.S. Army."

Friedkin murmured: "Freak . . ."

"Oh, yeah?" Kaul said.

It was more like the inside of some complex machine than a room. Friedkin only vaguely remembered being brought there; Kaul and the escort Nazi had led him down a flight of steel stairs, through massive steel doors, along white corridors. Doctors, nurses, winking lights, patients in chairs, beds, tanks, baths. Then nothing. No one to be seen, no sound but their steps, down another corridor to more doors, locked and barred, then a lightless empty hall, then a frosted square of light, then the room—not like a room.

Like the inside of a fantastic machine. Stainless steel, glass, chrome, screens, blips, cylinders, piles, coils, bellows, conduits, siphons, tubes, wires. Movement like pumps and rocker arms and centrifuges. And at the focal point of it all, the survival.

It was not immediately recognizable. Friedkin stared. Soon he began to shake. The more he looked, the worse it got. At first it was only a thing on a pole, flapped and wrapped in white and green rags and bandages. Then it seemed to be a headless man, then more exactly a faceless man, with a stump of a head, if that were possible. Armless also, he saw. Legless too. It was a trunk, a torso.

He heard Kaul's voice: "Not dead."

He heard his own: "That's a man!"

"Demon, you mean. Won't do any more harm, hung up on a pole."

Rubber gloves held a scalpel, and a mask spoke to him: "Hi, Professor, come to see our patient? Oh, gee, sorry I can't introduce you. No communication either way. Total isolation."

No eyes, no ears, no voice. Alone.

Friedkin shook deep inside. "Shaman . . ."

"What's left of him," the mask said.

Friedkin spoke his last intelligible words in that place: "The quick."

Tubes, rubber hoses, clamps, pressure gauges, skin thermometers, rectal thermometers—needles injecting food, drink, drugs to inhibit moving, coughing, screaming—taps to siphon bile, titrators adding a puff of gas, a milligram of dope, a squirt of fluid, a quart of blood, a breath of oxygen.

Friedkin swallowed, swallowed, swallowed.

He was being given a briefing, tour: points of interest.

". . . rather than a bed with all the attendant problems, supported and bone-wired in upright position, easier care, access to the various electrodes, intravenous and intramuscular insertions, the monitoring and telemetering connections, et cetera."

The survival was being unwrapped, unflapped.

"Just in time for routine debridement and wound care."

Scissors snipping, scalpels slicing.

"Doppler ultrasound," the mask said, working.

EKG, blood pressure, respiration, temperature, electroencephalograph.

"Microminiaturized sensors for telemetered monitoring—oh, he's a pincushion!"

CAT brain scan.

"Catheter from groin up and into aortal arch over the heart, inject X-ray-opaque dye into all three large arteries leading to the brain, watch fluoroscope movies of mental activity—lots of it!"

Working. Black scabs, dead glazed fat, chips of bone—skinless, red atrocious wounds trimmed and snipped and sliced and cauterized with silver nitrate and neatly wound and bound—till next time.

Total isolation.

All Friedkin could think was: *Pain!*

He heard Kaul's voice:

"How long can you keep him alive?"

"Oh, gee, literally forever," the mask said.

Kaul's tight clenched grin was a gargoyle's grimace of victory.

"Life imprisonment!"

(Life intrisonnent.)

*   *   *

Friedkin was sick. The escort Nazi rushed him across the lightless empty hall, through the doors, into some kind of lab, and let him puke in a sink. Then he took him away along white corridors.

"Back to barracks."

Two doctors and some nurses were chatting by the main elevators. Their shift was over. It had been a long, hard night. The car arrived, ding-donging. All rode down together. The doctors glanced interestedly at Friedkin, the nurses at the powerful-looking young Nazi. The doors whispered open. The doctors and nurses turned to go check out, while Friedkin and the Nazi crossed the deserted lobby and exited by the main door.

It was almost dawn. The crisp lawns were wet with dew. Shivering, Friedkin stopped for a moment to draw a long breath and look up at the sky, thinking. Soon a blue-white morning sun would rise on the horizon. The sun would rise and shine down on a world like nothing so much as . . . what? A madman's hallucination? Friedkin began to laugh. Nervously, the Nazi gave him a shove from behind.

"Prisoner will quit making noises like that."

Friedkin was shivering and sweating all over. "If he isn't dead, then it isn't disproven yet."

"Prisoner will speak when spoken to."

"What if it rises in the west?" Friedkin said.